The
Nightmare
Before *Kissmas*

The Nightmare Before *Kissmas*

Sara Raasch

BRAMBLE

tor publishing group
new york

This is a work of fiction. All of the characters, organizations, and events portrayed in this novel are either products of the author's imagination or are used fictitiously.

THE NIGHTMARE BEFORE KISSMAS

A Bramble Book
Published by Tom Doherty Associates / Tor Publishing Group
120 Broadway
New York, NY 10271

www.torpublishinggroup.com

Bramble™ is a trademark of Macmillan Publishing Group, LLC.

The Library of Congress Cataloging-in-Publication Data is available upon request.

ISBN 978-1-250-33319-3 (trade paperback)
ISBN 978-1-250-33320-9 (ebook)

Our books may be purchased in bulk for promotional, educational, or business use. Please contact your local bookseller or the Macmillan Corporate and Premium Sales Department at 1-800-221-7945, extension 5442, or by email at MacmillanSpecialMarkets@macmillan.com.

First Edition: 2024

Printed in the United States of America

0 9 8 7 6 5 4

I always joke that I'm going to dedicate my books to you, the reader.
But this one? I mean it. This book is for you.
I just want it to make you smile.
We all deserve that.

The
Nightmare
Before *Kissmas*

Chapter One

Summer Break After University Sophomore Year

I don't know why I thought I could pull it off.

This salmon-colored button-down, I mean. I'm too pale; it washes me out in every shot—or, no, wait, that one's not too bad. I'm standing on the steps of Lily and Iris's estate, right before shit hit the fan, so I'm still giving that masking cocky smile. Throw it in black-and-white, and it'd be a respectable picture of me.

Ha. Respectable.

After tonight, I'm surprised I can think that word without part of my brain spontaneously combusting.

So I think it again. *Respectable.*

No flames. It's like a magic trick.

And because I've had about four dirty vodka martinis where I order it by asking for "*vodka that at one point in time aspired to be in a martini before striking out on a solo career,*" I rock my head and go "Rrrrrespectable" to my phone, which leads to me humming, then softly singing, "R-E-S-P-E—"

"Don't drag Aretha Franklin into your bullshit."

The stool next to me groans as my brother heaves himself onto it. I glance around, but Iris isn't here—yet. She can't be far behind.

If she wants to see me anymore. How pissed will she be that I ruined her sister's birthday? Or will she be more pissed by the *way* I ruined her sister's birthday?

I lift the sweating glass of my fourth—fifth? Fourth. Fifth?—vodka martini and gulp half of my dry, bitter vice and go back to scrolling through the paparazzi site. Headlines fly past—*Prince Nicholas's Latest*

Disaster this and *Prince Nicholas: Finally Too Far?* that. The television above the bar is playing a basketball game, but there's a scrolling news alert at the bottom with headlines like NATION GRANTED MILLIONS OF GIFTS FROM "SANTA" OVERNIGHT; SUSPECTED SHIPPING ERROR TO BLAME; STORY DEVELOPING—

"Oh, now *that* picture's a winner," I tell Kris, because he followed me here, so he knows very well that that means he'll be the recipient of my . . . *me*-ness.

Me-ness rhymes a bit with another word.

I sit up straight on the barstool and look at the ceiling because *this* is where my limit is, apparently. Drunkenly laughing at self-inflicted dick jokes.

. . . it would not be out of line for self-inflicted dick jokes to be called masturbation jokes.

I bury my face in my hands. "Shit fucking fuck."

"Yep," Kris agrees. To the bartender, he says, "Two waters. He's cut off."

"Fuck you."

"On second thought, give me the soda gun so I can blast him in the face."

I drop my hands, only there's two of him, so I squint, and ah, there he is.

Kris looks like me, but if I were sober and not a disheveled mess. Brown curls, blue eyes, pale skin that I should tell him does *not* mesh well with pink tones, a friendly brotherly FYI. He has his long hair thrown into a topknot and he took off his suit jacket and button-down so he's in an undershirt—

It's not an undershirt. It's bright green and says *Sleigh My Name, Sleigh My Name* across the chest, some of his ink peeking out beneath the sleeves. He absolutely buys these shirts too tight on purpose.

"Did you have that under your suit the whole night?" I ask.

"Yeah, that's what we should talk about right now. Fashion."

I turn back to my phone. "That's what I was doing before you rudely stalked me."

"To the same bar you always run away to."

I like this bar because it's walkable from campus and has the benefit of never being too overcrowded. Even right now, at seven on a Friday night, it's half full, the booths and tables clustered with chattering students in the occasional Yale T-shirt, the jukebox playing some pulsing country song low enough for audible conversation.

Kris shrugs. "New Haven has other bars, you know, if you wanted to *actually* hide. The fact that you came here tells me you wanted me to find you."

"As my tiny baby brother, you are legally not allowed to psychoanalyze me."

His nose scrunches. "I'm barely fourteen months younger than you."

"Tiny. Baby." I poke his bicep. Then sneer in jealousy at the size of it. The younger sibling should also not be legally allowed to get more jacked than the older sibling. But that would probably require said older sibling setting foot in a gym on more than a rare occasion, so screw that, I'll let him have this.

When he inhales, clearly about to change the subject, I show him the first photo on the paparazzi site, of me in my salmon shirt.

"Why the *fuck* did you let me go out in public with—"

"Coal."

I drop my phone and reach for my glass, but Kris puts his hand over it.

"Do you realize how much you fucked up?" His voice is low.

"Yeah."

"All your bullshit, and I never thought you'd—wait, you do?"

I don't look up at him. Just stare at the condensation beading down the side of my glass, still trapped under his hand. "I do. I didn't—I just—fuck."

"You gotta give me more than that, dude."

My mouth hangs open like a gaping drunk fish. I have nothing, though. Nothing I can say to fix anything.

It's why I fled the party like a coward. Because I am. A coward and a screwup and tonight I bested my records in both of those areas.

Kris yanks his hand away from my glass to scrub it across his face. This energy out of my brother, pity and exhaustion and the slightest tinge of fed up, damn near burns the alcohol right out of my veins.

I always know Kris and Iris are borderline annoyed by my antics, but they usually end up laughing with me, and that laughter is more infusing than any consequence is punishing. If I can get a smile out of them, I know I not only haven't fucked up too badly, but I've hit the perfect note of endearingly goofy.

Like the time I arranged for our prep school building to go up for sale. Got a realtor involved and everything. Classes had to be canceled for a full week to hash out the confusion.

Or the time I filled a cathedral with chickens right before an Easter service.

Or the time during our annual Christmas Eve Ball where I rigged the sound system to play, on loop, "I Am Santa Claus," a parody set to the *Iron Man* song, and it took *seventeen rounds* before the staff could figure out how to shut it off. People were crying.

But that was harmless. Everything I've done has been harmless. That's what I have to offer: harmless, meaningless bullshit.

Until now.

"I didn't mean for anything bad to happen," I try. The air is stale and smells like something burned in the kitchen's fryer. "It wasn't supposed to be a prank."

"Then what the fuck was it supposed to be?" Kris is fighting not to be overtly pissed, I can tell, but it's warring hard with pity, and I can't decide which is worse. But then his face goes cold. "Wait. If you weren't doing it for shits and giggles, were you trying to make it an incident? Like sabotage to expose us to the real world?"

I blanch. "No. Kris. You really think I'd do that?"

His pause is louder than anything else he's said. If I were more sober, I'd be able to react better. Dive in with an explanation that would make all this okay. But as it is, I'm hit with a barrage of all my fuckups, my reputation for never taking things seriously and dicking around, and I can't get any explanation out, the words all dammed up against my tongue. I suck down the remnants of my drink but there my excuses stay, glued in my mouth.

Would anyone believe me if I said I'd been trying to make things better? Prince Nicholas, headline darling, was trying to do something *good* for once, and in truly poetic fashion managed to fuck up worse than usual?

The press wouldn't believe me. Would Kris?

"So what were you trying to do, then?" Kris asks slowly. "Get back at Dad for dragging you into training?"

I watch the side of his face and take a quaking breath. I will get these words out, because if I can't say them to *my brother,* explain what I'd meant to do and why I'd done it, then—

My phone buzzes next to my now empty glass.

I'm shocked it's taken him this long to call me.

Kris grabs it and holds it up. "Answer."

Normally, I'd argue, because he knows what he's asking of me, and I know he knows what he's asking of me. But his tone is still hanging in the air and all the vodka in my bloodstream is doing nothing to counteract the dread cracking apart my chest.

I answer and shove the phone between my shoulder and ear. "Hey, Dad."

"Nicholas. You will come home and assist in correcting this situation. *Now.*"

I scratch at a stain on the bar top. "I'm not sure my presence would help."

"You are in no position to decide what would or would not help," Dad says, voice immutable. "I have the staff already at work unpicking what you did, and you will be here to show that this *shipping error* is of utmost concern to you, and that you understand the gravity of such a mistake. This behavior is disgraceful in any respectable circles—"

My brain starts in on *R-E-S-P-E-C-T* again. One glance at Kris and I refocus on the call.

"—but it is *certainly* disgraceful for a Prince of Christmas."

Ah, there it is. The singular point to which every conversation with my father returns.

But the rest of what he said sinks into my brain like liquid trying to absorb into an oversaturated sponge.

He doesn't want me to fix what I did. He doesn't want me to take the blame. He wants me there for pictures. To pose and smile and reinforce whatever story is being spun for the Holiday press, a surface-level façade to salvage our reputation among the other Holidays and their people.

Fury sparks sudden and bright. I shouldn't be surprised that he's doing this again, but I am, and I'm pissed.

"Oh, yeah, I'll get right there," I snap. "Can't have the paparazzi thinking I'm anything less than adequately remorseful. Just like this whole training sham—had to start convincing them I'm not a total screwup, no matter how much of a lie that is."

"The training was not a *sham*," Dad says. He breezes right past me being a total screwup, and that avoidance is a confirmation I fight, hard, not to feel in the pit of my stomach. "It was far past time for you to take on a leadership role in Christmas. That you chose to get nothing out of the opportunity I gave you only solidifies that I was right in my reservations over trusting you."

"Again," I add without thinking.

"What?"

"Over trusting me *again*." I'm just woozy enough that I think it's a good idea to bring this up. "This wasn't my first training session, remember?"

He's quiet for a beat. *Does* he remember? He has to. I was really young, but so was he. He'd showed me the globe where we track joy and magic and gifts and *everything*, and he'd waved his hand over it like he was literally giving me the world.

"These are the people who need us," he'd told me. *"And I do mean us, Nicholas—you and me. One day, it will be your job to make the world happy."*

Even years later, the memory is so fucking potent for a number of reasons I refuse to acknowledge. And thinking of it all now just makes me hate myself for holding on to it.

"I remember," Dad says. Is that . . . fondness in his voice?

Oh look, I can be both annoyed and hopeful at the same time.

It crashes like a five-car pileup when he clears his throat and continues with, "You were a child. It's in the past. The only thing that matters is *now,* and *right now,* you have disappointed me."

It shouldn't hurt. I've made being a disappointment like 80 percent of my personality.

But I can't breathe for a second.

Dad's held me at arm's length for years since that childhood introduction that never went very far, because of his own shit and then later thanks to my *damaging reputation.* But something about me being halfway through my college career spurred him to action: it was time I begin *taking things seriously* this summer.

He'd had me start training under various North Pole department heads, which had sounded . . . great, to be honest. To be *involved* in shit, to see what was happening behind all the PR fog that Dad usually pumps out. That hope collapsed real quick under Dad's warning that I wasn't to touch anything. Just do exactly what the department heads tell you, Nicholas, listen to the pretty explanations of what each group does and smile for the photos so some of the headlines could be respectable for once. *King Claus trying to make something of Prince Nicholas: oh god, should he be allowed near heavy machinery?*

Training had been a lie, just like everything else. He didn't want me to *do* anything. It was a setup for the betterment of our reputation as the biggest, the best, blah blah *bullshit* and I'm tired and drunk and I fucking regret what I did more than I can put words to and the fact that I *can't* put words to it has me spewing the only words that come.

"You're right. You shouldn't have trusted me. Because I was trying to *help* people, not do whatever the fuck it is you normally do. Do you care what I'd tried to—"

"I do not care what you had intended, Nicholas, because the result was an *economic collapse.*"

A weight plummets down into my gut, snuffing out my anger so abruptly I wheeze at its absence. Dad is talking loudly enough that

Kris can hear both sides of the conversation and he sips at his water, looking less pissed at me, more sympathetic.

"I—" I pinch the skin between my eyes, fighting to breathe. "I don't—"

"The only way you can and *will* contribute to undoing this mess is by *being here* to offer your support. Never, in the history of our family, has a Christmas Prince so grossly misused our magic. Never—"

"I didn't *grossly* misuse it. I was—"

"You accessed the database of unfulfilled Christmas letters and gave every single child in the capital of New Koah all of their outstanding wishes. You may have made them happy *in the moment,* but you didn't think beyond that. You never think about the long-term consequences of your actions."

I see the glow of the computer screen I'd sat down at after a full day of being shuttled around by various department heads, trailed by Holiday journalists, every action masked and every emotion capped and it was all so *fake*.

So I'd gone back to Letters because that was real. That was the one connection to *real* kids, the outside world who believes in our magic.

I hadn't intended to do anything. I'd just wanted . . . *something*.

I'd wanted, and I still want, and it's an aching, empty hole in my chest.

Dear Santa, one letter had said. *My mom lost her job this year . . .*

Dear Santa. Grandma says we can't afford new shoes, so maybe you could help . . .

Dear Santa. Daddy left and I don't think he's coming back this time . . .

The department head had talked to the press vis-à-vis me about how they keep the letters filed to compare how the things kids ask for evolve, and extrapolate the best single gift for them each year, and so on, I'd stopped paying attention, because really? All these heartbreaking stories, and at the end, most kids ask for things like a PlayStation or a stuffed animal, and it won't bring back their parent, but fuck, we can give them all the material things they ask for, can't we?

Apparently, we can't.

Apparently, when you access the North Pole database, and pick a random small country—thank fuck I'd limited it to one city in one little place, not gone global—and channel Christmas's magic to grant every outstanding letter from every kid in that city, it causes . . . issues.

"*Millions* of gifts," Dad is shouting. "Many of which just *showed up* labeled as from Santa in people's houses in *June*. And aside from the gifts themselves, thousands of people were given exorbitant amounts of money directly into their accounts. You flooded their economy and instigated hyper-inflation and—"

"Dad—"

"—*riots*, Nicholas. The Prince of Christmas caused *riots*."

I glue my eyes to the bar top and will myself not to think about the ramifications of what I've done. The pain I've caused. *Riots*.

News of what I'd done just so happened to pop up right in the middle of Lily's birthday party, so my authentic horrified reaction got immortalized by the press as I'd managed to make it clear that I'd somehow caused this. And then Lily had started screaming at me, also immortalized, along with my very public running the fuck away because I *broke an entire country*.

My focus pops back up to the TV. One of the headlines scrolling above me now is *PRESUMED BANK AND SHIPPING ERRORS LEAD TO RIOTING AS CITIZENS BUY OUT STORES, ROBBERIES INCREASE.*

Whatever story the Holiday press are running with, it'll stay within our magically bubbled circles. The real world will continue to think this influx of cash and gifts was due to tech glitches from various shipping companies and banks.

Dear Santa.

Daddy left.

I don't think he's coming back this time.

I really want my mom to have some money for Christmas so she doesn't have to worry about him helping us, okay?

I'd been trying to help people. I'd *known* I was helping people.

But I made their lives so, so much worse.

"How—" I clear my throat, willing my vodka daze to evaporate, but it only seems to double down. "How are you fixing—"

Dad ignores me, barreling right on with his ranting, and I only let myself get pissed for half a beat. I have no leg to stand on right now, not a single one.

"Maybe you have not paid attention to our reality," Dad says, "and the fact that our Holiday is positioned to become more renowned worldwide than ever before in history. Spreading our reach will require things like magic and *reputation*."

"Is that really what's important right—"

"Christmas dominates the stories spun within Holiday presses. It is a responsibility and a *gift* you have for too long scorned. Do you see the way other Holidays are talked about? Valentine's Day, St. Patrick's Day, even Easter to some extent—they are barely taken seriously. *We* are the epitome of wholesomeness and joy—"

"Dad—"

"—and that means we *do not* initiate the economic collapse of a small Pacific Islands nation!"

"*STOP!*"

I don't mean to shout. Only I do mean it, a little, and Kris frowns at me, all understanding, and fuck if I deserve that from him. The people nearest me look over too and I curve down, pulling the phone to my chest to grimace before raising it back up to my other ear.

I slam my eyes shut. "I'll come home. I swear. Just . . . let me sober up."

"You're *drunk?*" Dad shrieks in my ear. "You left this disaster you created to get *drunk?*"

"I'm here." Kris leans over and speaks into my shoulder. "I won't let Coal do—"

"*Nicholas,*" Dad counters, and Kris flinches back.

Kris chose irreverent Christmas clothing and a myriad of tattoos he keeps hidden under said clothing as his hipster-like acts of rebellion; I chose, among other things, that nickname. It'd been too perfect to resist, right there in the name I inherited from dad. *Nick-coal-us.* My father has never appreciated the delicious irony.

Seems like a pretty fucking tame thing to do now, doesn't it.

Dad's silence is pointed. So pointed I can imagine exactly how he'd be glaring at me if he were here, eyes dark, using some kind of magic as an intimidation tactic—dimming the lights, plummeting the temperature. Kris and I may be able to tap into Christmas's magic in small ways, parlor tricks, but Dad's connection to it is a thing beyond.

"The things you do matter, Nicholas," Dad says. "The image you present to our people and other Holidays *matters*. Everyone involved in bringing Christmas to the normal world looks to our family. That's *thousands* of people, you realize, in North Pole City. What if they stopped taking their duties seriously because of the example you set? In the past few decades alone, Christmas has extended to countries we once could never have reached. Every Holiday looks to *us*."

"Looks to us for *what*?" My insides have been battered up and down this evening, and what is usually a background pain rages front and center where I'd naively woken it up by thinking I could effect any real change. "We plaster on a picture-perfect image for the Holiday press, the Claus name is blemish-free, we keep raking in joy for one single fucking day that's forgotten as soon as it happens, and *what*? That's really it?"

"Is that all you truly think we do?"

Yes. No. Fuck, I shouldn't have answered his call in this state.

Another well-earned sigh vibrates in my ear. "You see firsthand now why we do not use our magic more extensively. We do spread joy. Even if all we do is as frivolous as you make it seem, what more do you want? Isn't that enough?"

I'm so drunk. I'm so fucking drunk. And that's why my response is, "It wasn't enough to keep Mom from leaving."

All my muscles seize.

The line goes so quiet I think he hung up.

When he starts again, his tone is wholly emotionless. "This is the final warning I will give you. No more disasters, no more embarrassments. You will be the embodiment of the heir of Christmas.

Luckily, I will be able to fix your mess this time. *Come home.* This is not only your future at stake, Nicholas. This is Christmas's future. Your brother's future, even. It is high time you started thinking of more than yourself."

There's a click, and the call goes dead.

I gasp in the vacuum of silence.

Stiff, I lower my phone and swing back around the barstool, fighting for an expression that plays it all off. It's what I do. This was all another funny shenanigan from Coal, haha, more memories in the long line of my usual careless chicanery.

Kris is—blushing? So I know Iris is here, and the tunnel vision of vodka has my reaction processing beat by beat that that's her standing behind him.

I should warn him off Lentora women. Don't get involved, man, they'll—do what? *I* fucked up my relationship with Lily. She should be warning Iris off Claus men.

Iris has her arms folded, looking like she wants to be pissed but is waffling now with pity.

She went to her sister's birthday in full glory, and she's still done up from it, not a hair out of place. Her box braids are twisted into what she called fun buns, and they're set with purple gemstones that match her glittery purple dress. I don't think I've seen her in any other color, which is part of her own sculpted image as the perfect Easter Princess, even in this grungy college bar.

My throat grates as I force a swallow. I should explain to Kris and Iris why I did what I did. I should beg their forgiveness. I should do *something* to make up for being *me* but my phone is lead in my hand and the bar is suddenly so fucking hot, I can't get a full breath.

"What'd he say?" Kris asks like he's trying to calm a spooked animal.

"Are you all right?" Iris adds.

Great. Pity and caution.

"Nothing. It's fine," I lie and wedge my phone in my pocket. "I'm going home as soon as I sober up. I need some air."

"Coal." Kris starts to stand when I do, but I wave my hand at him and do fuck all to hide my panic.

"Just give me a second, all right? I'll be back."

"You *are* coming back," Kris tells me. "Don't make me chase you again. We'll go home together."

"Yeah, sure. I promise." And I head for the bar's front door.

But I take one glance at the window that looks out on the sidewalk, and I freeze.

The normal world hasn't figured out how my dad gets to "every house" in one night. It isn't that exciting: magic. The staff of hundreds doesn't hurt, of course, but it's mostly magic. One way is we take a sprig of mistletoe, jam it at the top of a doorframe, and: voilà! Instant portal anywhere we envision.

Which is how Holiday press have gotten here as fast as I did, once they figured out where I went; most Holidays have some form of transportation magic. And I realize I am rather predictable, like Kris said, because there are at least three Holiday reporters here, and when they see me heading out, they swing to attention, ready to photograph whatever I do or don't do and spread it across our tabloids. I recognize their badges and I *hate* that I see them enough to clock them by a glance through a grimy window: one is from *Christmas Inquirer,* an outlet that only features Christmas, while the other two are from *Holiday Herald* and *24-Hour Fête,* broader publications that harass—I mean, *feature*—the antics of a myriad of Holiday reigning families.

No small amount of our magic goes towards keeping us separate from the ordinary world, and that extends to the internet—so while normal people might see our pictures, all they'd be able to find out is that they're of foreign royals. They wouldn't see the captions, wouldn't see our names or who we are.

Doesn't stop it all from sucking the life out of me.

Headline: *Prince Nicholas drinks away sorrows in lieu of anything productive, but what did we really expect.*

I turn past Iris and Kris. "I'll be out back." And I'm gone before they respond.

I duck down a hall that leads to the bathrooms, bypass a door marked STORAGE, and shove into one labeled EMPLOYEES ONLY. How do I know this door leads to the back alley? Thanks to my first week of freshman year, a fake ID, and one too many tequila shots.

The alley is empty, thank god, a dead end capping off to my left and an opening to the road farther down on the right. The night air is no less muggy than it was inside, summer heat trapping the moisture from a recent rain, but I slam my back to the brick wall and breathe like it'll help balance the ever-wobbling scale lurching between *Everything is fine* and *Hahahahahahaha fuck*.

Usually, my only intention is ever *Oh, this will be funny*, and then I'm off and running with no other rationale able to beat through the concrete casing around my brain.

But this time?

I'd wanted to do something real. And it'd been easy. Easy to access the database, easy to set up the off-season gift deliveries. Easy to carry on like normal and go to Lily's party, and I'd been *happy*, because I'd done something good for once, and fuck, if that wasn't a sobering feeling.

I'd been so arrogant. So *certain* that I'd finally done something to spread joy.

And then the news reports of the New Koah collapse had started rolling in with dead-perfect timing.

I cannot believe I brought up my mother.

The door bangs open next to me and I jump about a foot in the air.

There's still enough vodka swirling through my system that I have trouble focusing on who it is—the alley has one light flickering a few yards down, and it backlights the guy, his frame thin and slight.

My first thought is *paparazzi*, but he has no camera or badge. He's in a black T-shirt and distressingly tight black skinny jeans, and my confusion clears because isn't that what the bartender was wearing? Then I remember the EMPLOYEES ONLY sign I barreled past, and I roll my eyes into my skull.

"Shit. I'm sorry."

The guy makes a startled noise, almost a laugh. "You're—what?"

For being shorter and smaller than me, his voice is gravelly deep, and him saying these two words sets off a roll of percussion that shakes down to the pit of my gut, a reverberation that could make a fortune doing ASMR.

I break through the hypnosis that causes and drop my shoulder against the alley wall. "Sorry. Which I should get used to saying, because I owe that word to a lot of people. Actually, if you wouldn't mind getting in line, that'd be great."

He blinks at me, still a bit alarmed. "I—"

"It's not a very long line." I press the heel of my hand to my temple. It doesn't stop the alley from gyrating like the inside of a zoetrope. "That's a lie. It is a long line. You'll be squashed in behind my ever-disappointed father, my girl—*ex*-girlfriend, whose birthday party I ruined, and the people who—uh—"

I cut myself off.

He's most likely a normal guy, and I can't admit to him what I did. It was bad enough spewing it all out at Lily's party in a way that just painted me as floundering and irresponsible—and Dad's made it clear whatever story is being spun now, it's more about saving face than owning up to what I did.

Which is fucked up. I should take the blame for it.

I will, though, by showing up at home and standing there as better people fix it.

God, that's pathetic.

I shut my eyes, swaying a little, and disjointedly, I chuckle. "You ever have one of those moments"—my lips are numb—"where you think you're doing a good thing, like you're fucking certain you're doing a *really good thing,* only it blows up so marvelously that you should offer your scorched-earth services to—to the um—fuck. The assholes. The people who follow wars around and siphon off money by selling weapons and shit."

The guy doesn't answer.

I look down. He should be fleeing back inside at the very least, reprimanding me for barging out the employee entrance at the most. But he stands there, cast into shadow. His stick-straight, glossy black hair is shorter on the sides but long enough on top that a few strands brush his forehead, and he's staring up at me with raised brows and the roundest, most focused eyes I've ever seen. I suddenly feel like being the object of his attention is a stroke of luck.

It makes my slack muscles go tense. My spinning, drunken mind latches on, an anchor, and I frown at him for lack of being able to make any other facial expression at the moment.

"You're drunk," he notes with a cast of those eyes up and down my body.

"Astute."

He meets my gaze again. "Please don't sell yourself to arms dealers."

"That's it! Arms dealers. Ow—shit." I snap my fingers. Or try to. My hand isn't working well and I end up scraping my thumbnail along my finger.

Is that . . .

It is. There's a hint of a smile on his lips. It drags—demands—*wrenches* my focus to those lips. And they are, suddenly, *those lips,* in *that way,* and I think, in some corner of my mind, that I should not be looking at this errant bar employee like that, but I can't remember why.

Oh. Because I just got dumped. Is there some kind of moratorium on flirting post-breakup? There should *definitely* be a moratorium on flirting post-collapsing-an-entire-economy.

So I say "It's not funny" to those lips, frowning harder, like it's their fault.

His ghost of a smile doesn't abate. "Of course not."

"No—no, it isn't. I know funny. I *am* funny. This? This wasn't funny."

One eyebrow lifts. Waiting. For me to keep talking?

Sure. Why the hell not. Because I suddenly need to talk about it, need to get it off my chest, and he's here, and maybe *he's* the crazy one, because he could leave but isn't.

Shit. *Is* he Holiday press? No. He's too hot to be paparazzi.

But here comes the whole sad damn story, like I've been shunted out of my body and I'm watching myself spill my guts to a perfect stranger.

This is officially the big red bulb ornament on the Charlie Brown Christmas tree that is my life.

"It would've been a doomed night from the start anyway, because Lily and I were going to break up after the party regardless—just had to hang on for one last night of press shots. Right? But last week, I'd— I'd *tried,* that was the dumbest thing. This was me *trying.* And I—my family has resources. Right?" Why do I keep asking him that? I think I'm pacing too. "And we never use them for anything that would actually help people. So I did. And it only made things *exponentially* worse, but of course it all came out during this party, so add a very public breakup on top of me realizing how badly I'd screwed up people's lives, and no, nothing is funny. At all. Shit."

I collapse against the alley wall and scrub my face, trying to get feeling back into my cheeks.

And I'm only now realizing I'm still wearing this *fucking salmon-colored shirt.*

The guy's brows are bent in an analytic squint, like he can't figure out how he got here, listening to a stranger divulge his disastrous evening, but he's not jotting down notes, so it's unlikely he's press after all. And he looks . . . sad, almost? Mournful. Like he understands.

Which is crazy. I'm drunk.

I wave my arms pathetically. "I shouldn't be saying this to you."

"No. I get it."

My face screws up in question.

He looks away, the absence of his gaze a visceral pull, and I stagger a step closer, one hand bracing on the wall because the alley is still undulating at the edges of my vision. He doesn't react to my movement, seemingly lost in thought.

Then he lifts his chin and looks up at me. "We can feel like we have the best of intentions," he whispers, "and still cause disaster."

His rawness beckons to me, bait on a line, and before I can stop it, I'm saying, "I just want to feel good. To feel *real*." I sound as fragile as his voice was, void of any of my previous self-deprecation, stripped down to the core of me, and I go immobile.

His gaze pins me in place, keeping me from shoving back inside to avoid the burn of reality.

"I don't know if feeling good should be the goal," he says, still in that brittle, aching tone. "It's more realistic to center on little things. One thing, each day, that isn't sullied by grief. One by one by one until you've started to rebuild the foundation that got obliterated. Because that's what happiness is, at the root. A foundation. And foundations aren't ever one thing, they're many little things interlocked together."

It's a pretty concept. But. "That's never been my experience, that little things have a long-term impact. They shatter the moment weight is put on them."

"Maybe you've been putting your weight on the wrong things."

"What are the right things?"

His smile changes. It's the contained kind where it doesn't reach any other part of his face, a kick of response more than an emotion.

"My," he says. "This is awfully philosophical for a bar alley chat."

"Wait." I put my hand up. Only he turns for the door, into my hand, and my fingers curve of their own accord around his arm.

He stops. Half turned away, my arm across his chest.

"What are the right things?" I ask again.

He's staring up at me, pupils shifting back and forth through mine. Then he licks his lips, and I'm dazed by the sheen of wetness on his lower lip, the quick flash of his pink tongue.

I should let go of his arm. I'm spellbound by the words out of him, *happiness* and *foundation,* and that's all I see, my disaster fading to the edges of my mind so everything is whittled to this moment. No, to *him,* and I can't tell if he's at all feeling this too or if I'm blowing it out of proportion in a combination of my regret and drunkenness.

The air is charged and drowsy and I don't think it's me at first. But suddenly there's a mouth, a mouth and a tongue and those lips against mine, and it had to have been me, and I collapse. My fingers dive into his hair and that is my anchor now, his face beneath mine, the taste of soda in his mouth but something else, something dazzlingly *male* and my pulse is driving hard against every vein in my neck and fingertips.

His hand clenches into a fist against my hip and his tongue darts out to lick at mine. I snatch it up, sucking on it, and am rewarded with a palpitation resonating from his throat—he's moaning. *Moaning,* and my god, I feel those vibrations in the arches of my feet.

There's a metallic squeal next to us, and reality knocks politely on the wall of my drunkenness and murmurs *the door to the bar is opening,* and I'm plunged back into this world like I got dunked in an ice bath.

The bar. The paparazzi. The breakup. The disaster I created. And here I am, kissing a stranger instead of doing the barest minimum.

I launch back from the guy, but he's already flying away too, and I spin, hands out, to see Iris pushing the door the rest of the way open.

"Shit," I say, because it was her sister I only recently got dumped by, and she's the one who catches me doing *this*?

She blinks, eyes adjusting to the shadows, and when she frowns, it's concerned, not accusing. "You've been out here awhile. You okay?"

"I'm—"

I turn. The alley is empty, and I spin again, which reawakens the heaving whirl of the bricks, and I grab the sides of my head. My headache is toppling down the back of my neck and my lips are all soft and warm and—

What the fuck just happened?

I turn again. No way he got out of the alley that fast, unless he seriously booked it to the open end. God, did I scare him off that badly?

"A guy," I say. "He was—he was *here*."

Iris gives me an unimpressed stare. "A guy."

"I swear! Iris—he was here. Where'd he go?"

"And you want to go off in search of a mystery guy instead of facing your own music, is that it?"

"No! No. That's not what—"

Did I hallucinate him? Fuck no, *his taste is still in my mouth.*

Was this interaction something else I screwed up tonight? I didn't even ask his *name.*

Wherever he is, *whoever* he is, it's just Iris in this alley now, but it *could have* been press opening that door, and I have to be smarter, I have to *change.* Shape up. Be a fucking adult.

"I'm sorry," I mumble at Iris.

Right before I bend double and vomit all over her shoes.

Iris and the Claus Boys

IRIS
did you find your mystery guy coal?

> no. bartender said no one by that
> description works there and he
> didn't see anyone like that even
> come in

IRIS
well that's not surprising. most
people can't see ghosts.

> HE WAS A REAL PERSON IRIS

KRIS
Honestly, you'd better hope he
was a ghost, because there's a
very good chance you spilled
your guts to and then slobbered
on a member of the Holiday
press.

> eloquently put, thank you

> we'll know if the details of the story
> come out won't we

> fuuuuuuuck

IRIS
allow me to distract you

> please

IRIS
i've decided it's up to us kris to think
of a suitable punishment for coal

KRIS
I'm always good with torturing my
brother. What'd you have in mind?

the staff reined in the effects of the gift situation before it caused any real damage

no one was hurt by the riots and the robberies were sorted out

i scared people but

god no "but"

there's no way you can punish me more than i'm punishing myself

IRIS
i'm not talking about punishment
for that

you puked on my favorite louboutin
heels you son of a bitch

okay no i literally JUST sent you the confirmation number for the new ones you had me buy

IRIS
yeah i decided that isn't good
enough

oh so you're an extortionist now

beneath that glitzy purple springtime exterior beats the heart of a cold blooded mob boss

KRIS
I could've told you that.

fine, whatever, i shall nobly take whatever punishment you idiots throw my way because i am the biggest person in this fucked up trio

IRIS
you say that now

will you keep saying that when i
have kris pick out an ugly christmas
sweater for you to wear every day of
your first month as a junior at yale

like not even a different sweater
every day, just the same nasty ass
sweater over and over

KRIS
OH I AM ALL OVER THIS

wait

KRIS
Okay, I have one that lights up, one
that has about a pound of tinsel
garland sewn into it, and one that's
neon yellow with two reindeer
fucking on it.

But like, in a classy way.

IRIS
oh yellow classy reindeer fucking
obviously

i have to give credit to the hilarity
of christmas embarrassment in
what will be august but why the
christmas motif exactly

IRIS
cuz we know it irritates you and
punishments should hurt

okay ouch christmas doesn't
irritate me that much

but just you wait, you both will
be back at university by then too,

which is plenty of time for me to
concoct payback

IRIS
payback for the consequences of
your own actions??

you're the one who chose to throw
the unstoppable force of practical
jokes up against the immovable
object of my personality

i will respond in kind

especially because i just spent
almost a grand on shoes for you

KRIS
A GRAND???

yeah that was ONE PAIR

really put into perspective how i
normally would've just sent you a
new pair with christmas's magic
and not thought twice about it,
so thanks for the second helping
of guilt-riddled self-awareness
iris

again, not sure why you're doling
out even MORE punishment

IRIS
because i bought that first pair
myself from working my shitty
uni job

do you know how many hours
i had to spend making deli
sandwiches to save up for those
shoes

KRIS
Yeah, fuck, you're right, this
punishment still isn't enough.

.... that is not the point i was
trying to make

MY ORIGINAL POINT is that you
two had better think long and hard
about what hell you inflict on me

it will come back upon you tenfold

IRIS
that, my darling, is what is
known as an empty threat given
that you promised to be a good
boy now and stop enacting
shenanigans

KRIS
Iris, I heard that mic drop.

HA. Coal's gone silent.

IRIS
did we really succeed in shutting
him up??

KRIS
Coal, don't pout.

Wait, sorry, I mean:

You'd better not pout.

IRIS
you'd better not cry

KRIS
The lyrics are off.

Shit, how does it go?

You'd better not—something
something, I'm telling you
why.

IRIS
oh is that what we were doing,
i was just telling him not to be a
baby

> i accept the terms of your
> punishment and do so solemnly
> swear not to carry out any
> payback, no matter how deserved
> it may be

KRIS
This text thread is legally binding.

> fuck you guys

> from here on out it's gonna be me
> and my ugly christmas sweater
> against the world

Chapter Two

One and a Half Years Later
Christmas Break, University Senior Year

I'm the last person in the dorm suite. None of my three roommates stays year-round, so there's no one left to see me sprawled across the couch in our shared living room, trying to mentally transport myself to a beach in the Caribbean like one of the guys said he'll be doing over break.

I could do it if I conjure up some mistletoe, shove it in a doorway. But all the Caribbean really makes me think about is the half-hearted Merry Christmas text Kris and I got from our mom last week—on American Thanksgiving, great timing—and the corresponding photo of her waist-deep in the ocean, not even *smiling*, one of those staged influencer bikini pics. What made her think her sons would want *that* picture of her? But the memory of it totally ruins any relaxing beach daydream.

I could always show up there. Every invitation from her has been hung with enough passive-aggressive guilt that I know she'd love holding any visit over our heads for the rest of my and Kris's lives. *"Your brother finally came to see me. Why haven't you, Kristopher? And Nicholas, you only stayed for a week. Children who love their mothers would visit for much longer."*

I could stay at school. Pretend the rec center where I work had an influx of students skipping their winter break trips and needed me to pick up extra shifts.

My phone buzzes on the coffee table. I dig the heels of my palms into my eyes.

Yes. I could definitely get away with prioritizing minimum wage at the student rec center over my duties as Santa's heir.

Dad said he has an *announcement* this year.

Something *big*.

Best case, he's only decided what role I'll be taking on under his guidance after I graduate in the spring. But a decision like that wouldn't warrant the maddening secrecy of a *big announcement,* would it? He'd have his assistant text me the details, especially with my track record of fucking up any actual involvement in Christmas's operation—Dad would avoid the tabloid fodder of letting anyone know I'm back under his training wing until I've proven myself.

So what's the worst case? My mind has been chewing on the possibilities for weeks. And I don't like any of the stuff I come up with. Which is why I'm lying on this musty couch that smells like beer—I mean, no, we definitely did not spill beer on it because this is campus housing and alcohol is strictly prohibited—and screwing my hands into my eyes until light spots dance.

"DON'T SCREAM."

I flail off the couch with a startled cry and slam my knee into the coffee table. Pain shoots up my leg and my phone skids across the room; my suitcase, open on the table, teeters and spills my stuff all over the floor.

And my brother *howls* with laughter.

"You suck," I moan from the floor.

He ignores my writhing to head into the kitchen. "I got tired of waiting for you to come home yourself. We're going to be late as it is." He pops open the fridge. "It's empty."

"Of course it's empty. No one will be here for a month and a half. And I was getting ready to leave."

"Clearly. Horizontal packing, wildly productive. Do you even *want* to come home?"

I climb to my feet, pocket my phone from where it spun across the carpet, and start balling up sweaters to shove back into my suitcase. "That is a complex question and I swore off answering complex questions after I very nearly failed Applied Quantitative Analysis this semester."

"Is that the class you had me write that paper for?" he asks, head submerged in a cupboard that still has a few half-eaten bags of chips. He pulls back, pokes through them, makes a face, and shuts the door.

I glare at him. "I asked you to *edit* that paper—*you* chose to rewrite the last two pages because 'my conclusion was wrong.' On an *opinion* piece."

"And it got what grade?" He pulses his eyebrows expectantly.

It passed with flying colors but he can bite me. "You don't get enough of your own dry classes at Cambridge? You gotta come across the ocean to steal mine?"

Kris opens another cupboard.

He goes quiet.

I can never get him to talk about how his school is going beyond the fact that what should be a three-year program will, for him, be stretching into four years. Dad may have pulled all kinds of strings to force me into Yale to *uphold the Claus legacy,* but he left Kris to apply to a predetermined list of schools on his own.

He didn't get into Yale.

"If you're done being a coward." Kris shuts the next cupboard. "We really will be late."

I hurl a wadded-up pair of socks at him. He turns from the kitchen and it hits him square in the nose.

But he's right.

I'm a full-on coward now. Despite my conviction about turning over a new leaf after the New Koah incident, I've avoided as many responsibilities back home as possible. School and my shitty jobs here have gotten the bulk of my focus, which you think would mean my grades are doing better. They aren't. And you'd think I'd be mastering my part-time work and at least have made manager at one of those jobs. I haven't.

But Dad also hasn't stepped in and forced me to reassert myself with Christmas.

Until this year. With my graduation one short semester away, all the looming responsibilities of my birthright will no longer be something I can skirt around or Dad can make excuses for.

I heave all my weight on my suitcase and manage to get it zipped shut. "You deleted that text from Mom?"

Kris tosses the socks back at me and I stick them in the front pocket. "Yeah, I swear. I really don't care that she's dating some guy who's a beach detector."

"No, the Merry Christmas—" I frown up at him. "Kris."

He looks away.

I straighten, vertebra by vertebra. "You've been talking with her? We promised neither of us would respond to her manipulation anymore. It was nearly a blood oath."

He crosses his arms and rocks back on his heels, suddenly finding the ceiling very, very interesting. "I didn't talk to her a lot. I wished her a Merry Christmas back. She told me some shit about her dating life. It was fine."

"Talking with our mother is never *fine*, Kris. What'd she say to you exactly?"

He gives me an offended look, redness creeping across his face. "Nothing. It really wasn't bad. Don't worry about it."

"Don't tell me not to worry about you." It comes out harsher than I'd intended.

His eyes droop, defeated and apologetic, because he knows exactly what I'm remembering: how the last time she unloaded the full force of her guilt trip on him, I couldn't get ahold of him for two days, and when I'd shown up in Cambridge, it was to find that he hadn't left his room or eaten in all that time.

Kris winces like I projected the memory on the wall. "I had the flu. That doesn't count."

"The flu, my ass. She fucked with your head about you not being able to convince me to answer her calls, and you got so stressed out you *stopped eating*. So I will fucking worry." Protectiveness rises up the back of my neck, but I keep my voice somewhat steady and ask again, "What did she say to you?"

Kris rolls his eyes. "*Nothing*. I promise, I won't talk to her again without checking with my real mother first." He waves at me, apparently christening me his *real mother,* and I hold out my hand.

"Give me your phone."

"What? Why?"

"I'm blocking her number."

"Fuck off. I don't need you to block her number for me."

"So you'll do it on your own?"

He runs his tongue across his teeth.

I grab for his arm. "Give me your phone."

He recoils, hip slamming into the kitchen counter. "Shit, ow—no! Get off me."

"Give it." I reach around him, knowing he has it lodged in his back pocket. "I'll kick your ass, Kris, I swear to god."

"I'm not giving you my phone, dipshit."

"Yes, you are. Drop it. Sit. Stay. Roll over."

"No! Jesus Christ—*I am not giving you my phone.* It's full of porn—"

He may have more muscle on me, but I have more height, and I try to use that advantage, cocooning him like a spider, all limbs and angles. My elbow jabs near his kidney—accidentally, sort of—and he plummets to one knee. I follow.

"Ow—*fuck*. This stalling tactic is pathetic, even for you," he grumbles from underneath me.

I peel myself off, and when he looks up, I point at him.

"Don't talk to her. I'm serious. If you need to say something to her, tell me, and I'll do it."

"When was the last time you even talked to her?"

"I . . . responded to her text."

"Liking her pic isn't responding."

"It's enough. I'm serious, Kris. If you need to talk to her, I'll do it for you. I don't give a shit."

Kris stands with a cautious stare. "If I agree, can I keep my phone?"

"Depends what kind of porn you have on it."

"Classy."

I go back and grab my suitcase. But I pause, staring at the wall, that protective anger still hot on the back of my neck.

Kris is quiet long enough that I look at him. He's toeing a spot on the carpet.

I wheel my suitcase over. "All right. Fine. Let's get this over with."

He cocks an eyebrow, relief showing, that we're done talking about her. For now. "Sound more miserable. Iris is already there."

"She texted me. Mostly to tell me that Lily wouldn't be there."

"She isn't," Kris assures me. "Just Iris and her dad."

"And I'll say the same thing to you that I told Iris—*I do not care where Lily is.* She's engaged now, yeah?" Newly sold off, I mean betrothed, to a Valentine Prince.

Kris gives the same look Iris gives me no matter how many times I swear I'm fine: pity.

"It's been almost two years!" I throw my head back. "The breakup was *mutual.*"

"You had one serious relationship, got dumped publicly, then never dated again. It's not healthy. Besides"—he drags in a quick breath—"we know Lily brings up . . . that night."

I make a cracking shriek noise, half laugh, half deranged feral panther. "Back up—you wanna come at me about *healthy relationships*? How many people have *you* dated, like *ever*?"

Kris focuses on pulling mistletoe out of his pocket, fascinated by the sprig of greenery. "I date. I date plenty."

"Sitting next to someone in the campus library doesn't count."

"I didn't *sit next to them*—it was an arranged date."

"You took a person to a library, Kris, a library on the campus where they also go to school."

"We went there for an exhibit to see the—"

"Between you with your lifelong devotion to pining after Iris and Dad with whatever the hell he's been doing since Mom left, I'm the only one in this family who even plays chicken with healthy relationships."

Kris snorts. "Being fuck buddies with your roommate isn't a *healthy relationship.*"

"You said you liked Steven!"

"I did. But you weren't *dating* him. *Hey, I failed my midterm, give me a blowjob* isn't a relationship. You're stalling. *Again.*"

I *am* stalling, so I groan and kick the floor. "It's weird that she's there early, right?"

The first event of the season is usually just Christmas upper crust.

Kris sticks the mistletoe in the front door of the dorm suite. "Maybe she needs a change of pace. Our classes are ramping up."

Iris swears she's happy in the UK alongside Kris, in the same course as him, even, but I know it was her father's influence that pushed her to also go to Cambridge instead of a fancy art school she once waxed on about. She's at least graduating on time, right as I will from Yale—and don't get me *started* on the fact that I got stuck in a four-year program while she's out after only three. I'd berate Kris for dragging his program out an extra year, but I know he isn't doing it on purpose.

"Yeah. Maybe." A weird feeling itches, something out of place I can't make sense of.

Kris finishes with the mistletoe. He steps back, and I give a confused hum.

"What the fuck is a beach detector?"

He shrugs. "One of those people who scours beaches with metal detectors."

"That's—*that's the guy's whole identifier*? Like that's all he does? Just—no. Never mind."

The pulse of magic from the mistletoe washes over both of us, and when Kris opens the door of my dorm suite, instead of the hallway, it shows Claus Palace in the northernmost part of frozen, tundra-coated Greenland.

If the palace's normal state is festive, this time of year, it's the Sugar Plum Fairy's wet dream.

The foyer is an explosion of green trimmings with clusters of vibrant red berries. Shining ornaments in a rainbow of colors hang from every free surface, including a massive chandelier done to look like a sleigh in flight, diamond reindeer at the helm. Lit candles flicker along the brown banisters that wrap up the two identical stair-cases and tables hold decorative scenes of Santas and reindeer and snowmen. A miniature train belches smoke as it laps the ceiling on a meandering track, and even its *chug-chugs* sound jovial.

People bustle all around, staff rushing to this or that preparation—not elves, much to the chagrin of the common myth, but they're decked out in holiday finery. And the *smells*—I linger behind Kris in the doorway and breathe for a beat, soaking in that scent, god I wish I could bottle it. Suddenly coming home doesn't seem so bad, not when the air is sugar-dusted from the kitchens, and the decorations add scents of evergreen sap. Beyond it all, there's the stinging crys-talline scent of bone-shaking cold: snow.

Kris nudges me. "Careful, Coal. Someone might think you like this stuff."

My chest kicks.

I don't *dislike* it. Quite the opposite, honestly. And that's sort of my problem.

"Oh, the horror." I drag my suitcase through and shut the door behind us.

We're set upon by Dad's head assistant, Wren, tablet in hand. Her white hair is pulled into a tight bun with a candy cane shoved through it and I can't decide whether that's a fashion choice or if she stuck it there and forgot about it.

"The trimming started ten minutes ago." She checks a watch, scowls, then snaps for one of the other staff. "We'll take your bag to your room. Change, please, and *quickly*—everyone else is waiting."

"Ah, jumping right into tree trimming." I give my most charming smile. "Why the rush? Let's catch up, Wren. How are you? How are things in North Pole City?"

She doesn't flinch, of course. One of Dad's right hands for years, she's an unflappable fixture who's morphed into an extension of his severity. "Go, please. Your outfit is laid out for you."

Something sours on my tongue and it's no one's fault but my own that Wren doesn't take my question seriously. The people who live in the city around our palace could be plotting a murderous coup and I'd be none the wiser. Dad probably knows how they're doing, right? He keeps up on things like that?

"Stylists are waiting in the hall," Wren continues. "You as well, Kristopher—be ready in five minutes. *Five*, please."

"You know, saying *please* doesn't add anything to the—hey!"

Kris hauls me towards the stairs. "Don't antagonize her. She oversees our stylists."

"Very wise, Kristopher," Wren calls. "Upset me and you'll be wearing neon corduroy for the rest of your lives."

"Is *that* why you occasionally still put me in salmon—*shit!*" I've somehow found myself in a headlock. "God, Kris, I'm coming, uncle, uncle."

Soon we're up the stairs and down the halls and he shoves me into my suite on the way to his own.

My suite is as decked out as the rest of the palace. A Christmas tree a little taller than I am set with ornaments and lights stands guard over a desk and sitting area near the lit fireplace, and the room through a side door shows a canopied bed with a scarlet velvet comforter and perfectly fluffed pillows.

Briefly, I consider dragging out the time to be an ass. But I have tried turning over a new leaf these past years, or at least picking my battles. And fighting this, the first of many photo ops of the Claus family partaking in Christmas revelry, has no benefit beyond pissing off my dad.

So I change quickly into a relaxed blue suit with a white button-down and polished black shoes. I'll have to thank Wren—Kris was right. Keep the woman in charge of making us look good on our side. Got it.

I open the door and stylists flurry in. They quickly fix my hair—my auburn curls are still short, and they set them from unruly and mildly frizzy to controlled and sleek. I've never been a big makeup guy, and they respect that with only minor touch-ups "*for photos.*"

Then I'm shuttled out the door to where Kris is already being similarly shuttled down the hall in a complementary blue suit a shade lighter, his with pinstripes.

I jut my chin at his topknot as we walk—briskly—down the halls. Magic pulses, and a candy cane appears skewered right through his hair.

He reaches up to thumb it. "Hysterical."

"They're all the rage this year."

A cavalcade of staff corrals us through the palace, back across the foyer, and down another hall until we get to our destination, the epicenter of not only the cheer and decorations, but the North Pole.

The Merry Measure.

Gold striates the wide ivory marble floor, leading up to a massive brass and gold behemoth that looks like a steampunk Christmas contraption designed by H.G. Wells. Pipes lead in and out of the room, syphoning down to a switchboard with gauges keeping track of the amounts.

The only other joy meter I've seen is in Easter, but I know every Holiday has something similar to collect the joy they generate, log the amounts, and feed it out to their cities. Each tube that stretches over our meter is labeled in a massive gilded plate: TOY ROOM, STABLES, KITCHENS, LETTERS, LIST ROOM, and more. Some magic funnels out to Dad, Kris, and I directly, a lifeline we can tap to spread good cheer to the world—or, more often, play dumb pranks on each other. Not the best use of magic, but it's not like it takes much to conjure a candy cane. Dad can siphon out magic to other people too, members of the noble houses or anyone in the North Pole who needs magic to do their jobs—but he's the dam on it, the bottleneck of power that decides who gets what and what goes where.

Normally, the Merry Measure is kept under careful lock and guard, but for the first official night of the season, Dad opens it to our court—and ample press shots. This time of year, our joy gauge is off the charts, the toggle dancing at the edge of *max*. Carefully placing that in the background of any pictures is just one of many intentional—and not exactly subtle—flexes.

Between the door and that towering machine stand about thirty people, all as Christmas-fancy as we are, as well as a half dozen staff who circulate with refreshments. Christmas press photographers wreath the crowd, from *Christmas Inquirer, Morning Yuletide Sun,* and several other outlets. Music plays, an instrumental version of "It's Beginning to Look a Lot Like Christmas," while everyone mills around a comically large tree in the center of the room, its boughs twined with strands of beads and popcorn. At its trunk wait boxes of ornaments.

As Kris and I stop just outside the threshold, the crowd takes note of us, and their energy shifts from blithe chatter to an arching of intent like several dozen hawks sighting the same two mice on a field.

Kris nudges me. "Once more," he whispers.

"Unto the breach," I finish, and we step inside.

I spot Dad across the room, closest to the Merry Measure with Iris and her father. Iris grins and waves—but getting to her means navigating a minefield of Christmas aristocracy, so I pull up my best smile as Kris and I *schmooze.*

People are here from all the main houses that oversee various parts of Christmas. Jacobs, with toys and engineering; Caroler, with treats and song; Luminaria, with creatures and decorations; and Frost, winter and all the frozen shit. We may be celebrated in the southern hemisphere too, but being located where Christmas equals winter means we dip into that association more often than not. The Frosts are also Mom's original house, and that small talk sucks the most, chatting aimlessly with a cousin about how yes I'm excited to be home and no I don't have a favorite event I'm looking forward to, all while emphatically not mentioning Mom.

I guide Kris away after two minutes with the Frosts.

"We'll catch up more at the next event, yes? All right. All right, yes—we'll—yes, we'll talk then—okay." I spin around Kris and blow out a long exhale. He's a little pale, and I hook my arm around his neck as photographers catch our angles at the edges of the room, and through my charming grin, I mutter, "Kill me."

He doesn't laugh. He takes a flute of champagne from a passing waiter and kicks it back as we finally, *finally* make it across the room.

"Since when do you drink champa—" I start, but I get my answer when Kris realizes you can't shoot a whole glass of *champagne,* and he sputters a cough as the carbonation fizzes up his nose, cheeks billowing to keep from spluttering the whole mess down his suit.

I crowd in front of him, blocking him from any pics. "That was refined as hell."

"Shut up." He wipes the back of his hand against his lips. But it breaks the tension and he shakes his head with a self-deprecating smirk.

"Coal!"

I turn as Iris darts for us, and she somehow does so elegantly and in heels, her shimmery purple dress catching the light of the massive chandelier.

She throws herself at me and I catch her, grinning as much as she is. I haven't seen her since October, when she and Kris last visited me in New Haven, and I give her a tight squeeze before setting her down.

She twists to Kris, who has recovered, and hugs him too. I'm very aware of our dads watching us, and of the snap of pictures being taken, so I behave and do not make any suggestive bedroom eyes at him over her shoulder.

Kris, though, must be able to tell I'm at least *thinking* of doing that, because the moment Iris steps away, he closes in on me and punches me in the thigh. A zap of cold comes with it.

He froze my pants to my leg.

I bat at the ice, breaking it apart so the cold shivers down my leg. "Dick."

"Idiot."

"Boys!" Dad spreads his arms like we'll rush to him. He's playing the Santa part with his styled white beard and scarlet suit.

I manage what hopefully passes as a cordial grin, and with Kris and Iris at my side, we join the group in front of the Merry Measure.

Dad sweeps both Kris and me into a pose for the photographers.

"Best behavior," he says to me through his smile.

"Wouldn't dream of anything else," I say. "The people of Christmas will surely Marie Antoinette us if they don't get their yearly photos of us hanging ornaments."

His grip on my shoulder tightens. That itch of something being out of place scratches me again, and my lips flatten, but the photo is over, and Dad spins me to Iris's father.

Who has never liked me. And the whole "dating his daughter then ruining her birthday by almost destroying a small country" thing did not help.

So when his expression of greeting is a poorly capped glower that tells me he still daydreams about popping my head off my shoulders like a dandelion, I keep my back straight and do not do anything to make the situation worse.

"Nicholas," King Neo says. "Are you enjoying school?"

Ah, pleasantries. "Very much." It was nicer last year when one of my roommates would fool around with me, but Steven transferred this year. Somehow I don't think Iris's dad would care about that tidbit.

"Your father tells me you have yet to decide on plans post-graduation."

I haven't? I rather thought my post-graduation plans were destined from birth. "I—"

Dad dives in. "Hardly! Nicholas will be getting his master's in Global Affairs, just as I did."

"I *will*?" I gag.

He doesn't look at me, but his hand pinches on my shoulder. "He's already been accepted to the program at Yale. I'm very proud."

Holy shit.

I stare at his profile.

This is how he tells me he's made that choice for me? *This* is how he tells me he *enrolled me in grad school?* Shit fuck, the doors money can open are truly grotesque, because honestly, with my grades, there's no way in hell I have any business going near a grad school, let alone one at *Yale,* that I *did not apply to myself.*

Not to mention *I do not want to get a master's, what the fuck.* I've taken great pains towards not being a disappointment to him and Christmas, and I think I've done a pretty damn good job of it—there have been almost no headlines caused by me since the gifts fiasco. So what did I do to deserve this manipulation?

He knows this is messed up. But he smiles at Neo and asks what Lily's plans are and thorny vines grow in my stomach.

Staff begin opening the boxes of ornaments, and our court shuffles around, lifting those ornaments, hanging them, posing just so. But I can't move as my father slaps my shoulder in faux camaraderie and I feel that plan sink in.

This has nothing to do with my behavior or a punishment. He's trying to turn me into him. And I get an image of what that will be like as I watch my father smile too broadly, laugh too loudly, every movement honed to paint a flawless portrait of our ruling family that will be displayed to our people and other Holidays, look how mighty Christmas is, look how *jolly* and *joyful*.

When was the last time anyone in this family felt actual joy?

An echo of a conversation scurries across my brain.

Maybe you've been putting your weight on the wrong things.

That's what happiness is, at the root. A foundation.

I shrug it off like I usually do. A drunken night, too fogged to really remember, I don't *actually* know what happened—but I'm only lying to myself, and doing a piss poor job of it, considering I think about that conversation a lot. And that guy. And that kiss.

How he felt. How he tasted. The way he'd moaned.

But I can't admit all that to myself so I'm going to keep living in my delusions about not *really* remembering where those nuggets of wisdom came from.

They don't matter, anyway. Because I'm going to grad school, then eventually taking over the family business of bringing quote-unquote joy to the world, behold my future.

It's suddenly very, very hot in here. This suit is too tight. The collar is too high—

Someone hands me an ornament. I go into the motion, step across to hang it on the tree; a photo snaps.

Okay, duty done, right? I can leave—

Iris eases up next to me. "Are you all right?"

"Yeah," I lie. "Great. Going to grad school, apparently."

She scoffs. "With your grades?"

"Thank you, I know, right?"

She looks back at our fathers, talking, sipping their drinks. "For what?"

"Global Affairs, because it isn't enough to have an undergrad degree I don't understand, let's add a master's too." I tip my head back, looking up at the massive tree. "God fucking damn it. *Grad school.* Why didn't I see it coming? I always underestimate him."

"I've stopped trying to estimate my father at all," Iris says. She hangs a red bulb on a branch that bends, too thin. "It's made everything way easier."

"Easier?" I frown at her. "Did something happen?"

"I've switched to taking mostly online courses. I didn't tell you?"

"You definitely did *not.* Why? You're still on campus, right?"

She shakes her head. "Dad's pulled me into day-to-day tasks since Lily—" She stops.

"It was years ago. I'm fine. Your sister's engaged. Continue."

Iris looks at Kris, who comes up alongside me and hooks a gingerbread ornament onto a branch. "I see Coal's still master of being *super fine, nothing is wrong.*"

"I don't know what you mean," Kris says. "Nothing is wrong. Coal said so."

"Anyway." Iris taps an ornament, a sleigh filled with gifts. "My father's been keeping me busy getting more into the coordinating of tasks with Easter since Lily will be split between us and Valentine's Day, and I'll be taking over some of her duties after I graduate."

I gape at her. Gape at Kris, who shrugs, but they're in the same course, taking mostly the same classes, so he had to have known, right?

"You haven't told me any of this," I hiss at her. "Since when do you keep things from me?"

Iris gives a rather fake yet bright smile, more for the cameras than my benefit. "I don't tell you everything."

"I tell *you* everything."

"To which I again have to remind you that you *do not need to tell me everything.* I don't give a shit about the gross things your roommates do. Stop texting me pictures of them."

"I mean everything *important,* Iris. You should tell me these things." My face falls, but when I open my mouth to push her more, she sighs.

"I don't need rescuing, Prince in Shining Armor."

I squint when her eyes don't meet mine, but then she remembers the cameras and crowd and pulls up an empty smile.

"Liar," I hiss at her.

"It isn't so bad, you know. Our jobs. Our—gasp—*duties.* We help make the world *happy.*"

No, we create a single day of one-off smiles that does nothing to stop bad shit from happening.

"Sure," I say. "But we don't get to be happy too?"

"I'm happy to see you and Kris," she says. She grabs another orna-ment, a stuffed teddy bear, and tosses it to me. "I'm happy to spend this month with the two of you."

Kris leans around me. "And I'll *happily* beat you at sleigh racing this year."

Iris blanches. "Oh *no.* Nope. Not doing that. I'll be a spectator."

My grin goes demonic. "Aw, why?" I look at Kris, all innocent wide eyes. "Did something happen?"

He puts his finger on his chin in exaggerated thinking. "Huh. I recall something . . . about sap, maybe?"

She'd gotten tossed from her sleigh and landed quite safely. In a pine tree.

Iris bats his arm. His cheeks go scarlet but he's grinning like mad.

"You have no idea how long it takes to wash off sap," she says.

"No, we know." I pop a pine needle off the Christmas tree. "You told us. Repeatedly. '*Oh, Coal, Christmas sucks*—'"

"You're a jerk." Iris hangs another ornament, her smile sickly sweet for the cameras.

"I wasn't even in the sleigh with you!"

"But you're mocking me, ergo, *jerk.*" She flips her braids over her shoulder with an overembellished flair, and I bark a laugh, and Kris smiles.

The cameras snap, getting photos of us legitimately happy. I want to ask for copies, but though I swore off reading any of the paparazzi crap that comes out since the New Koah incident, I could find them online easily enough. Maybe it's not always so bad to have reporters everywhere.

A presence looms behind us, and what happiness we'd managed to conjure evaporates. The joy we feel still goes towards Christmas's magic like the joy from normal people, but it's never felt particularly magical or lasting or like it has any real *purpose* at all.

My dad surveys the part of the tree that Iris has decorated. "Lovely, dear."

She smiles at him, amiable as ever, but I haven't forgiven him for dumping the grad school thing on me in the past five minutes, so I go stiff.

"Nicholas, Iris, if you would join us by the Merry Measure," he says and starts to steer me around.

I eye her. She's just as confused. We haven't finished trimming the tree yet, and that's the whole point of this evening, isn't it?

Kris gets left behind, his brow bending as he watches the three of us gather with Iris's dad.

The music stops, which draws a hush over the crowd, and everyone twists to us.

Iris pushes next to me. "What's this about?"

"No clue. Probably another photo op to—"

My words fall off as the chatter of voices crashes into the room, and staff lead in a whole gaggle of reporters, way more than are usually present—and we typically have a *lot* of reporters present. These are from outlets beyond just our internal Christmas ones: *Holiday Herald, Joy Gazette, 24-Hour Fête, Tradition Times;* there's a few specific to Easter too. They slip inside, skirting the edges to gather as close to us as possible, until we're front and center at an impromptu press conference.

I frown at the side of my dad's head.

Whatever he's announcing, he wants all the other Holidays to know about it.

Staff position us quickly. Iris in front of her father. Me next to her by my dad.

Those itchy feelings of something being *off* coalesce.

The room silences, cameras rolling, recorders outstretched, our court whispering softly to one another, and I hate that the reporters know more about what's happening than I do. They were summoned here for the promise of *something*, whereas Iris and I are being blindsided.

"The Claus family is thrilled to have the Lentora family with us as we participate in the usual festive calendar of activities that highlights the best of Christmas, culminating in our annual Christmas Eve Ball," Dad starts, one hand on my shoulder. It's weighing me down, making it so I can't move. "In the spirit of unity, we have come together not only in celebration, but to make an announcement."

Iris looks at me questioningly. I can only frown.

"Easter has begun the search for a marriage partner for Princess Iris," my father says so easily that his tone numbs his meaning until I see horror on Iris's face, and before I can form a reaction, Dad presses on: "I am happy to announce that Prince Nicholas has begun courting Princess Iris, and we expect an engagement by the end of the season."

Chapter Three

My dad's words send me buckling back a step like he hit me.

I'm stopped from moving at all by his hand, and I reel more, because he's gripping down, hard enough his knuckles grind against my bones. Again, *he knows how messed up this is,* but he's not doing a single thing to *not* do it, and so I stand there, stricken, as journalists call out questions and cameras flash and our court gasps and murmurs and then *applauds,* and I can feel every ounce of blood in my body drain away.

Iris is just as horrified, eyes wide and lips in a thin line, and her dad has a hand on her back, holding her up the same way.

"The union between Christmas and Easter will strengthen what has long been at the crux of both our enterprises: joy," my father says to the reporters. "Christmas in particular will continue our goals of not only bringing toys to the world's children"—he pauses with a glint of a smile as the crowd expectedly coos and awws—"but ensuring that the cheer we spread is capable of reaching every corner of the world. Our outreach will only grow, thanks to the magic and resources that Easter will now contribute. This union is a long time coming, and will be a boon to both our peoples, and to the world."

Out of the corner of my eye, I see Iris start to shake. She clasps her arms around herself; her dad whispers to her, and she straightens, dragging on her perfect façade, but it's tissue thin.

I've known her all my life. But I didn't *really* know her until her mom's funeral when I was eleven and she was ten, when Kris, Dad, and I went to honor the passing of the Easter Queen. She hadn't been the official queen, because Iris's mom hadn't been from any royal family, not a Holidayer at all—she'd been from France, and Iris's dad had met her during his treks there during the Easter season. It'd been quite the scandal when they'd gotten together, enough that Dad had told us about it years after the fact, only to warn Kris and I off *ever trying to bring a normal person home like that.* I'd made a point to try to date as many *normal people* as possible afterwards. None stuck like Iris's parents did, nothing like what made him, an Easter King, bring someone from the real world into our hidden universe.

Her funeral was horrific. Neo had sat next to her casket, stone-faced and bloodshot eyes and a slumped, grieving posture like he'd been crying but wasn't done yet and was holding it all in because *crowd* and *cameras* and *duty.* I remembered thinking how it'd been three years since my own mom had left—not died, just *left,* willingly—and I knew what that restraint felt like, the not falling apart; but that was a lie, the falling apart happened internally, wreaking havoc on organs and muscles and sinew because it was more proper to choke down the nuke of grief than to hurt anyone else with your pain.

Then Iris had come up to her father. He'd taken her hand, taken Lily's, and they'd walked to the casket.

Iris had peered in at her mom and screamed.

A member of their staff swooped in and ushered her away. Her dad didn't stop it, just took Lily and sat down like he wasn't aware Iris was gone or that she was *feeling* anything at all. The service continued, but I could hear Iris's muffled sobbing from the hallway of the massive cathedral we were in, noise ricocheting off the soulless stone.

Then she went silent.

So I slipped out of the pew. Ducked down the hall. And saw her on a bench under a wide, bright window, sniffling quietly into her lap, that staff member on a phone a few paces away.

I'd held out my hand. "Come with me."

Iris looked up at me.

"Come with me," I'd whispered again.

She took my hand and I raced us out of the cathedral, to the graveyard out back. No one else was there yet except for the rounded stones of other people who'd been wept over, and there was the empty, waiting hole in the ground ready to consume Iris's mother.

She fell to her knees next to it. But she didn't cry.

So I did. I knelt next to her and dropped my head into my hands and let go of that tight decorum, because my mom had left me. She'd been gone for *three years.* We only heard from her a few weeks after she left, when she texted Dad to tell us we should come visit her on the beach, and I hadn't *cried* and maybe if I did, it would stop hurting and I'd be able to, I don't know, not move on, but stop thinking about it for one full hour.

I felt Iris watch me sob, and she told me later that she had no idea why I was so upset over the loss of *her* mother, but it was the permission she needed—she fell apart over the empty grave, and we sat there in the churned dirt, making noises we weren't allowed to make in front of the cameras, feeling all the things that existed beyond the frames and the captions and the poses.

Now, as we stand in front of my court and my father manipulates our lives, I do what I did back then. She may have told me she doesn't need to be rescued, but I'm not going to let them treat my friend this way.

I take Iris's arm and thread it in mine. "Come with me."

We get two steps to the side.

Dad doesn't let go of my shoulder. "Nicholas," he says through his teeth.

I whip a glare to him, my back to the room. I could so easily mess this up for him.

The headline: *Christmas conniption: Prince Nicholas throws a fit during tree trimming.*

That would do nothing for me, nothing for this situation, and Iris is shaking against me.

But I grimace at him, and I let every bit of my anger show. "Let. Me. Go."

Dad hesitates. Disappointment flashes in him, but he relents and faces the crowd with a smile. "King Neo and I will answer any questions you may have," he says, and I waste no time ushering Iris the hell out of there.

We pass by Kris, who steps in with us, and I can't look at him— get out of this room. That's all I can do. Just *get out of here.*

Our court parts for us, and I wonder if I look panicked, I wonder if they can tell Iris is shaking, I wonder if Kris is fuming. The three of us bolt out, down the hallway, and I yank us into a sitting room, overstuffed armchairs bathed in soft orange light from a crackling fire.

I kick the door shut and twist to Iris. Who has gone gray. "Sit down. Here—sit."

I guide her to one of the chairs and she sinks into it. I won't make it to one myself—I drop to the floor, on my knees before her, propping my palms on my thighs and rocking in place.

Kris takes a step in front of us. Keeping distance. I can feel the wash of emotions palpitating off him—dread, shock—and god my heart aches more.

"Why would they do that?" Iris breathes, half a question, half a gust of air.

"So we couldn't make a scene," I say.

"I wouldn't have—"

"So *I* couldn't make a scene," I amend.

Iris's dark eyes brim with tears but she fights for a soft, forced smile. "Is it such a terrible fate to be engaged to me?"

I echo her grin. It hurts. "Do you want to be engaged to *me*?"

Another thing that bonded us over the years: the absolute bi confusion induced by movies like *Pirates of the Caribbean* or *The Mummy*. Kris got in on that confusion too, but the only thing stopping me from calling us *NSYNC* (ya know, Bi Bi Bi) was him cringing at any kind of label, and when I told Iris, "*I guess that forces you and me to be Bi Bi Buddies, but the first Bi is for two,*" she'd smacked the back of my head. Which was just proof that I am way too much of a loud-mouthed asshole to be her type, and she has her shit together too much to be mine. What can I say, I get off on a mess. Like calls to like.

She falls back against the chair with an involuntary nose-curl.

"Then yeah," I say to her silence. "It is terrible. Because this isn't the goddamn Middle Ages."

"But it's still happening."

"Like hell it will."

She drops forward, head in her hands. "What do you propose we do?"

"Ugh, don't use the word *propose*."

"Stop it, Coal. What are our options, really? We fight this and refuse—and our fathers retract the joint announcement they're making? You may be okay being labeled unreliable, but I work hard to be trustworthy."

She throws that out so quickly, I have to stop myself from asking if *she* thinks I'm unreliable.

So it makes me feel abnormally sleazy when I offer, "I could lean into my reputation, then. Refuse this engagement scheme. That way you don't get blamed at all."

She pulls back to look at me. "But what would that do to whatever alliance exists between Christmas and Easter?"

"You think we'd stop being friends if we can't get married?"

"I'm not talking about *us*. I think our *Holidays* would struggle."

"Well, *I'm* talking about us. Because that's what matters here. *Us*. Lily and I broke up, and it didn't shatter any political alliances or whatever you're worried about. So we'll refuse this, and it'll be fine too."

Her face looks suddenly pitying. "You have no idea what your breakup with Lily did or didn't shatter."

My mind reels and I know it shows in the way I gape at her. I glance at Kris, but he shrugs.

"What are you—"

Iris cuts me off with a flick of her wrist and sinks into the chair, her head lolling on the back so she stares up at the ceiling. "I didn't mean it like that. I just—" She sighs, muscles going slack. "Nothing *happened*. Not really. It made some people in our court start up that conversation again about my family's ability to lead Easter forward, that's all."

Her mom's been dead for more than ten years, and there are still people in Easter who like to poke at the fact that Neo *destabilized* our whole Holiday world by marrying a normal person. Which is bullshit and just an excuse for assholes to wrestle power away from

Iris's dad. I know other factions within Easter have been circling her family her whole life, but I had no idea they'd used my rather short relationship with Lily to feed into that.

Violation churns in my stomach. "You never told me that. Iris—"

She shrugs. "Nothing actually happened, like I said. It started a few arguments in some meetings. I would've told you if it caused any real problems."

Normally, I wouldn't hesitate to believe her. But I frown.

What else is she not telling me?

She's still looking up at the ceiling, and the emotions I catch flashing over her face are all so saturated in exhaustion that my heart breaks even more. "Your relationship with Lily was never announced like this. It was never presented as a clear sign of merging our two Holidays, but it was still interpreted that way. This is different. Our fathers put bigger things into play with this announcement, and if we walk back on it . . ."

Her voice fades and she shrugs again, a few tears gathering in little pools at the edges of her eyes.

First, my relationship with Lily fell apart. Now, Iris and I immediately split up before we've even really been in a relationship.

The people within Easter set against Iris's family would have a field day.

"Would they force your dad to abdicate?" I manage.

Iris finally looks at me, her brows popping in surprise. "No. Not over this. But they'd get responsibilities reassigned to other houses under the guise of him being *clearly overworked*. They've done shit like that before."

I shove to my feet and drag my hand across my jaw. My eyes flash to Kris, silent and severe, backlit by the fire.

Why couldn't it have been Kris with Iris? It would've been some romantic fairy tale if it'd been those two in an arranged marriage. Not that I want my brother being used as a pawn any more than I want Iris or me wrapped up in this.

But honestly, it isn't hard to guess why Dad used me. Kris isn't the one who needs to be tied down out of fear of public embarrassment; he's always been the mellow one. I'm still the risk, even after years of my best attempts at fixing my behavior. And half the time, I think Dad forgets Kris is an option. I'm pretty sure that's part of why Kris is the way he is, steady and straitlaced and well-behaved—that's his way of trying to get Dad's attention. I've got manic acts of negligence covered.

And look how that's turned out.

"So you're okay with this?" My voice catches. I hate it.

Iris nods. Shrugs. "It could be worse."

"Gee, thanks."

"Coal—"

"Fine."

The skin between her eyebrows bends in a question.

"Fine," I say again. "We'll do it. But I don't love you."

Iris flinches. "I don't love you either, asshole."

"No. Not like that. I mean I'm not *in love* with—"

But she stands, smiling that small, brittle smile again. "I'm messing with you."

"It's hard to tell right now."

"I know."

"None of this is funny."

"You must be in hell."

God, she knows me.

She's right—this could be worse. But it could be better. A lot better.

Kris turns away, hand on the back of his neck, but I have no idea what to say to him.

The door opens.

Dad walks in, trailed by Neo, and we all stand there for a second, making passive-aggressive eye contact.

I can't handle talking to my dad yet, so I whirl on Neo. "You're allowing your daughter to be sold off like some—some—goddamn it, I'm so worked up I can't even think of something people sell. But how are you allowing this to happen?"

Neo doesn't look at me as he scratches a hand through his short blond hair. "My feelings regarding you are of no consequence to this transaction," he says like some goddamn automaton.

"That isn't what I meant. I meant you're okay with forcing your daughter into an arranged marriage—yeah, to a guy you hate—when your own marriage was for love? What hypocritical bull—"

Iris takes my hand. "Coal. Stop."

Neo turns away, pale skin reddening, looking so eerily similar to the capped grief he'd held at his wife's funeral that I draw back.

"This decision is for the betterment of Easter," he says to the floor. "My wife would understand. Iris, too, understands. Don't you?"

He looks at her, and he's so damn . . . *delicate*.

And it's worse because Iris *does* understand. She immediately understood the gravity of what they did, and even now, she's standing here wilted under duty instead of being livid like I am.

"You know what you did was wrong," I say to Neo when Iris is quiet. "We're not pawns."

"No, you aren't," Dad speaks up.

I finally look at him. I *know* him, I know what he prioritizes and how he operates now, but there's still a small part of me that pulses with hope that maybe this time, he'll go back to the guy I remember as a child. The one who showed me around the different departments himself rather than shunting off the task on others while journalists recorded it. Who stood in front of that globe with me and made me believe that bringing happiness to the world was our purpose.

I don't know what it'll take for this spark of hope to extinguish.

Sometimes I wonder if my mom realizes how extensively she fucked things up when she left. Because the Christmas King Dad is now? Not even recognizable as the same man.

"You are duty-bound servants of Easter and Christmas," Dad continues, "and this is the way you can fulfill that. It is a business transaction. Nothing more. I did allow you space in the hope that your relationship with Lily would rekindle, but enough time has passed. We are moving forward through other means."

I laugh so hard it's a gag. "My relationship with Lily was a disaster, and it wasn't even *staged* like this—how on earth do you expect this to turn out better?"

"Hm. That is a fair point." Dad looks at Neo, and I'm dumb-struck, thinking he might have *heard* me, when he goes, "We should consider the benefits against the ramifications of Lily's presence at the wedding. She may stir up too many prior negative associations."

I flinch. "The wedding?" I pause, gut seizing. "You already started planning it?"

Dad eyes me like I asked why doors have knobs. "Of course. You will court Iris throughout our Christmas activities these next weeks, then propose before the end of the month. You will be married at the Christmas Eve Ball."

Holy fucking shit.

Married at the Christmas Eve Ball? Not just *engaged* by then, but fully *married*—

"You—" I can't get a full sentence to settle. "I—"

Neo scratches his chin and continues, like I didn't speak at all, "Lily is busy planning her own wedding. I am sure she would accept whatever we decide."

"How about we ask *Iris* if she wants her sister at her wedding?" I cut in, then groan at myself. "Except there shouldn't even *be* a wed-ding—in less than a *month*? This is—"

"You do not understand the scope of what it means to bring a Holiday to an area where it was not previously"—Dad turns on me—"or to restrengthen places where it waned. There is a finite amount of joy in this world. Easter will be contributing a portion of their joy to Christmas's efforts at extending our reach across the world—and, through that, Easter's reach as well. It takes magic to deliver toys to children, and there are, as you well know, many, *many* children in need across the world."

I wince. Dad lingers on that for a beat, and I half expect him to pull out a receipt of all the magic I wasted in New Koah, and all the magic it took to *fix* what I wasted.

"Do they get what they need, though?" I ask. "All this magic use—is it *doing* anything? Is it really helping anyone?"

"It is one of our greatest hopes that *every* child receives a piece of Christmas magic," Dad continues.

"Cheap plastic trinkets, you mean." My neck is hot. "Gotta make sure the world has full access to *stuff*, both for Christmas and Easter." I look at Neo, Iris. "That's what selling off your daughter has bought. That's all we're capable of putting into the world. Cheap plastic shit—"

Iris's grip on my hand is viselike. "Please," she whispers, and I hear the pinch in her throat, the way she's barely holding herself together.

My mouth snaps shut. I'm making this worse.

I slide my arm around her waist and we start to leave again.

"Iris," her father calls.

She stops. I stop with her.

"Are you sure?" I ask.

A beat. Then she nods. "I want to hear what he has to say."

I land a kiss on her head. "You know where to find me."

She walks away, arms going to her sides, shoulders leveling in that perfect posture, that learned bearing. It stokes my rage again, that she has to cap herself with him.

Dad shakes his head. "I must return to the tree trimming. I suggest you do as well—the evening is far from over."

Before I can refuse, he leaves in a huff like he has any reason to be upset.

I stomp towards Kris. "My suite. Now."

His jaw sets. But he nods and follows me out of the room.

Staff are rattling around the halls as I lead us up through the palace. Everywhere are people dedicated to making sure Christmas goes off without a hitch—toys being made, routes being organized, treats being prepped, lists being checked, decorations being hung. Meanwhile, Dad, Kris, and I lead the upper crust in events meant to celebrate our season, display its best qualities, put on the pageantry. And fake an engagement and wedding to my best friend, apparently.

It seemed so magical when I was younger. Before my grandfather died and Dad became Santa; before Mom decided she couldn't handle being Mrs. Claus and bolted; before I woke up to the reality that this isn't *about* making the world happy, it's a *job,* a *business.* Joy is revenue, and revenue doesn't do a damn thing to actually help anyone.

Toys left under trees or cocoa steaming in mugs or snowball fights or—or—*any* of it, it doesn't matter how much joy is brought in the moment, every single thing that comes out of our Holiday is only important as long as it brings more joy back *into* our Holiday. It isn't meant to last; it's meant to turn a profit.

I shove into my room and Kris shuts the door behind him with a quiet click.

"Yell at me," I tell him as I rip off my suit coat.

"What?"

"Yell at me."

"This isn't your fault."

"But you're pissed at me."

He considers. He looks exhausted. And he's still got that candy cane in his hair.

"Why would I be pissed at you?" he asks.

"Because I'm now courting—fuck, I sound like I tumbled out of *Bridgerton.* I'm now forced to pretend to date the girl you've been in love with for more than half your life."

He buckles against the door. "Honestly, I thought she was in love with *you* until about ten minutes ago."

"I'm glad that at least got cleared up for you. *Yell at me.*"

"I'm not helping your weird flagellation tendencies. Yell at yourself."

I drop to sit on my bed. "God, you and Iris know me too well. I need new friends."

Kris laughs, but it's empty. We go silent.

"I hate that he did this," I whisper. "To Iris. To you."

"Not to *you?*"

"I expect him to manipulate my life. He doesn't have any idea he hurt you." *And I can't do a damn thing to help you.*

With Dad. With Mom.

Kris straightens, a resolve similar to Iris's settling over him. "Well, he did. And we have to live with it like everything else they fucking do."

I stand. "Kris—"

"I'm going to bed."

He leaves before I can find anything to say. There is nothing *to* say. As always. Just me and him and the broken pieces of this messed-up family-slash-duty we share.

I stay up for a while, door cracked, hoping Iris will come and talk. About what, I don't know.

My phone's white screen is the only source of light in my room as I pull up her text thread.

IRIS

> you okay?
>
> of course you're not okay.
>
> iris.
>
> iris come talk to me.

IRIS
just got done talking with my dad.

i'm exhausted.

don't want to talk more. get some sleep.

> yeah sleep isn't gonna happen tonight.
>
> what'd your dad say? anything that even remotely made you feel better?

An ellipsis pops up in her text box, then vanishes. She doesn't respond.

Fuck.

i'm sorry. sweet dreams peep

I haven't called her that in years. Since she made the brilliant or maybe terrible decision to wear a flower crown set with faux Peeps and it was one of the best gifts my sense of humor has ever been given. I only bring it up now as a Hail Mary.

I watch the ellipsis pop up again. This time:

IRIS
go to bed, grinch.

and i'm sorry too.

The room goes dark when I click off my phone. It's a small consolation that she at least responded with the stupid nickname she came up with for me. So there's levity there.

It doesn't feel like it'll do anything to help. It never does.

I toss my phone onto the table and stare up at my ceiling in the dark and eventually I fall asleep in my dress shirt and pants, sinking into a dreamless void that doesn't give me any answers or even restfulness.

"Coal! *Coal!* Wake the hell up!"

I bolt upright and narrowly avoid smashing my forehead into my brother's nose.

A tension headache careens over me and I double forward, fingers digging into my temples. "What time is it?"

"Nearly eight. Get up. Now."

Kris is halfway to the door. He's still in his clothes from last night too, and good lord, the sight the two of us make, like we crashed a wedding and passed out in our groomsmen outfits.

Wedding.

Marriage.

Oh, god.

"*What?*" I groan, head thundering.

Kris doubles back and grabs my arm and *rips* me out of bed. He throws my shoes at me. "Get. Up."

I finally catch the severity in his voice.

"What's wrong?" I tug into my shoes. "What happened?"

"Halloween is here."

I go rigid, one leg up, one shoe on.

"Say that again?"

"An envoy from Halloween is here. They heard about you and Iris. And they're *furious*."

We stumble out of my room, me leaning on Kris, or him leaning on me; together, we make about one functional person, what with how much sleep I think the two of us got.

"How—*what*? They sent someone here? Holy shit."

"Exactly."

"Holy *shit*. When was the last time Halloween was in the North Pole?"

Kris's look says, *Never, duh.*

There are certain Holidays that Christmas is known for interacting with. The cheerier, brighter Holidays. Everything for reputation.

Halloween is, shockingly, neither cheery nor bright.

They're a major player in our world in their own right, but they keep to themselves, we stick with Easter and Valentine's Day and a few others, and everything's good, and no one encroaches on each other's seasons or shit. Everyone wins.

As far as I know, Halloween is based out of—New England, I think? Hell, that might be wrong. I know next to nothing about them. Never particularly had to.

Kris and I come to the landing at the top of the foyer, and there, down in the middle of a room flooded with Christmas decorations, stand two people who clearly do not belong here.

They're dressed all in black, sleek suits with a pop of orange in their pocket squares. In spite of the reason for their presence, they're oddly calm, expressions cool as they face off with Wren.

"Where's Dad?" I whisper to Kris.

He shrugs.

We stay at the top of the staircase. No one's noticed us yet.

"—alliance goes through," one of the Halloween delegates is saying. "The reigning Santa must understand how this comes across."

"We assure you," Wren says, "this is not meant to be perceived as a threat. We hardly see how this matter involves you at all."

"We disagree," the man says. All this *royal we* speak and forced civility tinges the air with electric strain. "The unionization of two of the most powerful Holidays very much involves us. Christmas has toyed with such unions for far too long—to act on what has previously only been threats has taken your ploy for control too far."

"There is no ploy at work."

The voice booms through the foyer. The candles surge brighter, the scent on the air deepens in sugary richness, and snowflakes fall, indoors, drifting down from unseen clouds in a gentle peppering of white.

Below us, Dad saunters into the foyer.

He, at least, has changed from last night, wearing a bright red sweater, a reminiscent nod to his famous uniform. It gives him an immediate presence and I can't help but wonder if he took the time to change into that once he heard Halloween had sent people. He's certainly using enough magic to give himself clout.

The Halloween delegate bats a snowflake from the air. "Ah, King Claus. A pleasure for you to join us."

"A pity Halloween could not coordinate a more official meeting," my dad cuts back. "But since you are here, I would like to personally assure you that the arrangement between my son and Princess Iris is not as severe as you claim. Nothing has been finalized."

Oh, that's a *bold-faced lie*. They're planning our wedding already, for fuck's sake.

The delegate huffs. "Is that so? We interpreted your announcement to be quite resolute."

"If anything, I am glad it brought you to my doorstep."

Dad pauses, and I note the reporters clustering at the edges of the

foyer. Not just our Christmas ones; some of the broader Holiday publications too, and I'm shocked Dad let them follow him in here—

Disquiet eats at me.

He *wants* them in here.

The delegate clocks the reporters too, or maybe he did already;
now, he openly looks at them, and eyes my father. "Are you?"

"Yes." Dad steps forward. "I am the first to admit that Christmas
has for too long been a source of contention for Halloween."

We have? When have we ever interacted with Halloween? But
the envoys share a look that confirms whatever Dad implied, and my
confusion manifests in a scowl.

"We have more in common than we have differences that divide
us," Dad continues. "But I know well how distrusting Halloween is
of us, and I do not expect such distrust to be easily bridged. We all
have the same goal: to be the mightiest sources of joy possible. I am
not wrong in assuming that both Easter and Halloween, two equally
substantial Holidays, would benefit from a union."

Both of the delegates seem at a loss. "What are you suggesting?"
one asks.

"Return to Halloween with this message from Christmas: that
we are apologetic for the perceived threats and do not wish to in-
cite further discord among autumn Holidays." He pauses to smile.
"My offer is that I would serve as an intermediary, if your superiors
agree, to oversee a union—between Easter and Halloween."

"*What is he doing?*" I hiss at Kris, but my brother is stuck in shocked
silence.

The delegate's eyes widen, the first sign of true surprise, and he
cocks his head. "You are honestly proposing a marriage between the
Easter Princess, your son's betrothed, and—"

"The betrothal is not finalized, I told you. My announcement was
that Easter had begun searching for a partner for Princess Iris, and
Prince Nicholas has long been one of her close friends. But I have spoken with King Neo at length, and his goal for Easter is whatever will
be best all around, which could, if you choose, be Halloween. Your
objection to the arrangement between Christmas and Easter is being

taken quite seriously." Another pause. There's something he's communicating in those pauses, because the envoys share another look.

I also note that Dad still isn't putting Kris up for sale in this fucked-up arrangement rather than dissolving the Easter engagement—why isn't he? He'd get everything then, tie everyone up together. Why is he sacrificing Iris?

"If Halloween is so concerned about the power Christmas would amass in joining with Easter," Dad says, "then you are welcome to come and vie for Princess Iris's hand. My palace is open to Halloween."

One delegate twists to whisper to his companion. With a tight smile, he faces my Dad again. "We will take this offer to our monarchs." He bows, but it feels like a mockery. "Santa."

My dad doesn't react. Not as the delegates turn, facing the door they came through—still open, rimmed in palpitating shadows, a dark-cloaked hall beyond.

One of the Halloween delegate's eyes snaps to the top of the staircase. "Princes," he calls with a smaller bow.

They leave, the door shuts, and I bolt down the stairs.

"Nicholas—" My dad tries to intercept my outburst, but I'm *done*.

"Now you're giving Iris to Halloween?" I demand. "She isn't even *yours*—"

He clamps his hand on my arm bruisingly tight. "Contain yourself. Come."

The reporters are still there. Watching. Recording devices at the ready.

Dad drags me out of the foyer, ducking into a side sitting room. The curtains are pulled wide, showing the front of the palace, snow-coated landscape stretching out in rippling hills that settle around the bulk of North Pole City in the distance.

As he turns to shut the door, Kris slips in. Usually, my brother concedes to me as the one who yells at our father—but his whole face is red, his fists clenched.

"You can't do this," Kris says. "You can't treat her like this!"

Dad seems momentarily stunned that *Kris* is the one talking back to him. His eyes dart between the two of us, noting our rumpled outfits from last night, and he sighs heavily.

"It's business, boys," he tells us. "It's a ploy to appease them until we can finalize the marriage between Nicholas and Iris."

I jerk back. "Wait—what?"

"Why do you think we are pressing so quickly for your marriage and kept our plans silent until last night? Because we suspected it would be met with this reaction. Halloween was merely the first to come forward with objections. This is to mollify them until we can proceed. Nothing they do would actually stop us, but the hassle of being delayed by any acts of drama from them is easily sidestepped by a few weeks of half-truths. We allow them to feel as though they are making their own play; meanwhile, our plans carry on, unmolested."

Kris shakes his head, and I watch his brief spurt of fight ebb away.

My turn.

"This is wrong," I say. "All this manipulation—it's *wrong*. And you know it."

Dad's face drops, showing a flicker of something like sorrow, but it's gone in a flash. "What I know is that the type of joy that Christmas brings—tradition, camaraderie, and family—is capable of global transformation. The more we can strengthen our holdings, the more we will be able to bring that sort of joy to the world."

"Do we?" I ask. "Bring that sort of joy now? Because from what I see, Christmas is—well, it's what I was railing about before. Cheap plastic shit and gifts and nothing *meaningful*—"

"For now." Dad's lips are in a thin line. "We must make concessions for what can be easily reproduced with the least amount of magic in favor of extending Christmas's reach."

I shake my head. "So you *are* focusing on Christmas being cheap and commodified?"

"Temporarily. For this initial goal, to spread our influence beyond that of any other Holiday, we must make adjustments."

I'd been half joking before when I'd snapped at Neo about trading Iris for cheap plastic trinkets. But—I wasn't wrong. Dad is letting Christmas be known for *stuff* and ineffectual nonsense so he can stretch our control, sacrificing any true, lasting goodness we might create.

Has Christmas *ever* been capable of true, lasting goodness, though? If it was, wouldn't things be . . . *different?*

He believed we were capable of bringing happiness to the world. The look on his face when I was younger and he'd talked about *our*—his and mine—duties. He'd *believed* in Christmas, more than *this.*

Hadn't he?

"So Iris and I get married after you *lie* to Halloween," I say. "Which gives them double the incentive to carry through on any retaliation afterwards. They could turn opinion against us, at the very least. I know you hate that."

"Christmas and Easter will be united. Halloween will realize they won't win."

I grab my head, my headache doubling, tripling, until streaks of light pulse across my eyelids.

"And what if I just don't want to marry her?" I ask. Because it's all I have left. "What if I just hate seeing you treat my best friend like this?"

I feel his presence move.

I feel him stand in front of me.

"You will trust, then, that the decisions I make are the best things for you and our Holiday," he tells me.

No magic threat needed. His tone is enough. Confident, calm. He honestly believes this is right.

I want to scream at him that he's wrong, but he wasn't *always* wrong, and I don't know how to get back to the way things used to be because I don't really *remember* the way things used to be, I'm just holding on to this little ember of hope based around flashes of childhood memories.

Maybe this is who Dad has always really been. I was just too young and idealistic to realize it.

He turns away. "It goes without saying, but this discussion is not to leave this room. Now get dressed—I expect better from you both."

He leaves.

Kris shakes his head in the proceeding silence. "We should, um—we should go see Iris."

"Her father will probably tell her."

"Maybe." I hear the dip in Kris's voice. Yeah, *maybe*. Or she'll find out about it when Halloween comes back and agrees and all this shit hits the fan.

The worst part is watching my brother try to pull himself together. And imagining Iris's face when she finds out she's been used, *again*.

One of the first ways I tried to harness magic was to guarantee that my brother had a merry Christmas. But I'd created a self-fulfilling prophecy, because I made sure he had all his favorite foods—waffles and roast turkey and gingerbread cookies—and the best gifts—a bunch of video games and some really nice leather-bound notebooks because he's always writing about something, even when we were kids—and we did all the activities he loved most—sleigh racing, snowball fights, ice skating. So he did have a merry Christmas, but it wasn't made because of magic. It's not that easy.

I almost do it now, reach down into the part of me that's twelve and wants to make sure my brother is *happy*.

I hook my arm around Kris and steer him for the door. "The most wonderful time of the year, huh?"

Iris and the Claus Boys

IRIS
maybe we all get food poisoning
to avoid this halloween welcome
party. or what's that thing about
poinsettias being poisonous?
they're everywhere, so they
infected us

KRIS
I think that's only for cats who eat
them.

                    but i like where your head's at. i'll
                    boycott if you will

IRIS
ughhhhh. no. i'll go. i just need to
be dramatic about it first.

        **Coal named the conversation "Two Bros and a
        Ho Ho Ho"**

IRIS
nicholas claus if you value our
friendship you will delete that
group name right now

        **Coal named the conversation "50 Shades of
        Sleighs"**

IRIS
i'm having a full crisis over here
and you're googling christmas
puns aren't you

                    excuse you i have these locked
                    and loaded at all times baby

but what do you want me to do

seriously, name it. because all i got is to try to make you laugh

hey watch this

theirs nothing wrong with trying to make someone laugh

KRIS
Coal, I hate you.

Fucking delete it.

My eyes are bleeding.

IRIS
what? is this another stupid inside joke i don't get

KRIS
You really don't see it? Why do I talk to either of you.

He used the wrong "there" to piss me off.

And it's working.

i don't know what your talking about

your
your your your

KRIS
COAL. NOT FUNNY.

IRIS
a little funny

YOURRRRR

KRIS
Oh my god, I'm getting hives.

For each time you make a mockery
of the English language, I'm going
to hide one Elf on the Shelf somewhere in your room.

CROSSING THE LINE KRIS

KRIS
You're up to two. Two elves. With
those beady soulless eyes. Just
watching you from the shadows.
You won't know where. But you'll
feel them.

Studying.

Learning.

Waiting.

your not funny

your a dick

i can do this all day

KRIS
Four.

Are you really going to keep testing
me, Nicholas?

I don't fuck around with grammar.

iris are you laughing

i'm doing this for you

you'd better be laughing because
i'm now risking my very life for a bit

you know those elves have killed
before and they'll kill again

IRIS
yeah i'm laughing

against my will you punk ass nerd.

nerds.

both of you. huge punk ass nerds.

                                    but you love us

IRIS
also against my will.

**Iris named the conversation "Iris and the Punk-
Ass Claus Boys"**

Chapter Four

"I *hate* him."

"Pretty sure I initiated you into that club years ago."

Iris leans on me to adjust her shoe. "I didn't sign up for that. You and Kris complain—well, *you* complain—but I always tried to give him the benefit of the doubt. I never wanted to hate *Santa*."

I throw a glance over the crowd. This part of Claus Palace is packed with the same group from the Merry Measure tree trimming, all decked out as befitting Christmas at, well, *Christmas,* only the background is now our massive ballroom. Heavy, deep brown wood adorns the walls, giving the feel of a ski lodge with greenery strung through the rafters and two enormous fireplaces on either end of the room gilding everything and making the air smell woodsy and cozy.

The only imperfection in the scene is the reporters still lurking at the edges of the ballroom.

I willfully put my back to them. Iris and I are off to the side on a stage where a full orchestra usually sits, and it's easy enough to make it so I only see her and the rear wall of windows that caps off the ballroom.

"He isn't Santa," I say.

Her look of disbelief is puckered, like I'm stretching to make a point. "So he has the white beard and dresses in red because . . ."

"It's my dad. It's a publicity stunt. But he's *not* Santa. He's the King of Christmas. The ideal of *Santa* exists beyond all of us." My tone dips, and that makes her frown at me in mild confusion. I know I don't often get serious, but it shouldn't be *that* surprising. "He's Santa the way you're the Easter Bunny."

Iris cracks a smile. "Don't blow my cover, Claus. I work hard to hide my werebunny transformations from you."

She makes claws with her fingers and hisses at me.

"We are, need I remind you"—I'm grinning—"currently at a party to welcome a suitor for *you,* costumed up into believable facsimiles of functioning adults. Don't blow *our* cover, Lentora."

She drops her hands with an eyeroll. "You used to be fun."

"You're upset that I won't hiss at you in public?"

"Yes."

"Sorry, I was too distracted picturing a feral fanged rabbit breaking into little kids' bedrooms and pilfering their carefully situated pastel baskets."

She straightens, playing for righteous, but her eyes sparkle. "Well, maybe the next time you try to start something silly and fun, I'll be too distracted imagining you as Santa, which is honestly a far more horrifying mental picture."

My head jerks back on an instinctive recoil.

I've never really imagined myself as *Santa* either despite knowing I was born into the role, but for some reason Iris's easy dismissal of me in that position . . . hurts. More than it should. I'm sure as hell nothing like my dad, but I'm nothing like the jolly, loving, boundlessly joyful visage of the mythical Santa figure either.

So her flippancy isn't misplaced.

And it shouldn't be unsettling.

Iris closes her eyes and scrunches her face. "Like right now. I'm trying to picture it and—oh my god. You look terrible in red."

"Hilarious." And honestly, well documented; we've established that ruddy hues are not my color.

"No, seriously." She holds a hand to her mouth. "It's *grotesque*—"

Kris bounds up onto the stage. "What's grotesque?"

Iris opens her eyes and bats her hand at me. "Your brother as Santa."

"Well, yeah." Kris sizes me up. "He's too skinny."

Now *this* time I let my offense show. "I've been doing those weight training videos you sent me!"

He squints. Sizes me up again. "You have?"

"Fuck you."

Kris grins and looks back at Iris. "They'll be here in ten minutes."

She spins on me. "How do I look?"

She's in a lavender dress that's all descending layers of tulle with clusters of flowers stitched at random intervals. Half of her box braids are looped through a flower crown of tulips and daisies, and in this very Christmas room full of very Christmas people, she's a riot of springtime and renewal and freshness.

But I don't tell her any of that and squint at her. "You care?"

"Of course I care, I *always* care. When this whole thing blows up in our faces, it will *not* be because of anything I did. I will be *perfect*. Now, *Kris*"—she twists her question to him, probably realizing I won't give her a straight answer and rightly so because it is super messed up that she would equate her physical appearance to being perfect—"how do I look?"

Kris goes as red as the checkerboard print blankets draped over the chairs in the ballroom's alcoves. But before I can decide whether to intervene, he looks up and down her body.

"Perfect," he says softly.

Iris must miss his tone, because she says only "Thank you" pointedly, then looks at me. "*That's* how you respond when a woman asks how she looks."

Kris gets an odd expression, eyes still on her profile where she's looking at me, but he doesn't seem hurt or rebuffed—it's more of a *well huh. That didn't work.* He's always handled her obliviousness rather gallantly for someone who proclaims to be in love with her.

"Next time," I say to Iris, "I will release a sonnet to your beauty."

She nods, satisfied. "About damn time, Claus."

"With all the pomp and extravagance of a Taylor Swift midnight single drop."

"You know, when you say things like that, it's hard to take your adoration seriously."

Dad comes up onto the stage, trailed by Neo, as Easter-y as his daughter in pastels and flowers. He ushers Iris away—since his announcement three days ago followed sharply by another announcement of *Oh, and now Halloween is vying for Iris's hand too, isn't that quaint,* he and my dad have kept the two of us out of as many photos together as possible to avoid, quote unquote, "playing favorites." Even though one of the contenders is also the host of this little competition and has already basically won. Yeah, it's definitely going to be fair.

Iris wasn't concerned about how that change of plans looked to Easter. She said her father was certain it would only make their family look *desirable*. Which made my nose curl, but Iris had shrugged and changed the subject, and I can't shake the persistent itch that there's shit she's not sharing with me. Important shit, important to *her*.

My eyes dart over the ballroom again, at the individual chatting groups as they munch on hors d'oeuvres. I think back on what Iris said, about losing the trust of our people by backing out on our announced relationship. But none of *these* people would be concerned about shifting alliances, would they? It wouldn't negatively affect their lives. They'll carry on being the noble houses of Christmas no matter what happens.

What do the thousands of people out in North Pole City think? What story is Dad feeding them? I should find it within myself to start reading the tabloids again.

Now *that's* a horrifying image.

I tug on the sleeves of my suit jacket. I sent Wren a thank-you gift for the nice blue suit at the tree trimming, and she responded with *this* number, an azure blazer done with baroque filigree in gold and green. I look fine as hell in it—Christmas Prince, I see no Christmas Prince, just a runway model.

Iris is center stage with our fathers. Dad is in a vibrant red suit, Santa but make it Versace, and the three of them turn forward.

One of our staff pounds on the floor at the rear of the ballroom, yanking all attention to the doors as they open.

The energy of the ballroom shifts. That hunter-level intent I usually feel directed at me and Kris is now pinned on a trio of people, trailed by half a dozen of their staff.

An enormous cloud of smoke pours in behind them, a shifting gray-black whorl that dissolves them into nothing more than silhouettes. There are no cries of alarm, so I'm guessing this is all part of their entrance and what I can only hope is passive-aggressive retaliation for the way Dad displayed our magic when just the Halloween envoys were here.

My eyes cut to Dad's profile, and at the sight of his barely suppressed scowl, I don't even try to hide my smirk.

The smoke undulates and shapeless shadows begin darting in and out of the silhouettes, the barest suggestion of something *other* lurking in the mist. It would be sufficiently "This Is Halloween," but then a crackle of lightning skitters through the smoke, flashing sickly yellow light on a face here, a disembodied smile there.

The Christmas crowd jumps, a few people letting loose startled laughter.

Kris is one of the people who jumps, but he doesn't laugh. "Fucking hell," he mutters.

I spider-walk my fingers up the back of his arm.

He jumps again before cursing and batting me away.

The smoke fades in graceful corkscrews to reveal the people behind the silhouettes, now halfway into the ballroom.

If we're clinging to the whole Christmas theme, then they're clinging to a gothic Halloween vibe. No one in their group has a pop of color among their form-fitting black gowns, their sleek onyx suits.

Except for—

I'd thought about researching the Halloween royal family out of a morbid curiosity to see who my Dad is trying to fake-matchmake Iris with. She said she knew who the prince was, or had seen pictures of him at least, and refused to delve any deeper—but I'd never needed to care about anyone outside of Christmas and the Holidays Dad interacts most with, like Easter and Valentine's Day. Halloween doesn't allow paparazzi to the extent we do, lucky bastards, so any research would've required a dive into specialized Holiday sites, but every time I sat down to do it, I got super paranoid that Dad would check my browser history. And then I realized that yeah, he definitely has people tracking our browser history when we're staying at the palace, and that idea was mind-numbingly nauseating because I am, in some iterations of myself, a twenty-two-year-old guy with twenty-two-year-old guy hobbies.

But I really, really should've risked it and fucking done even a single fucking minute of fucking research because now I'm standing on this stage and half of my mind is screaming at me to inhale but I legitimately cannot remember what muscles that act uses, and the other half of my mind is ravenously consumed with staring at the Halloween Prince.

The last time I saw him, I had his tongue in my mouth outside a bar in New Haven.

He'd just simplified one of my biggest unanswerable questions and then I kissed him and he vanished and I really had started to think I'd made him up, a fever dream brought on by vodka and regret.

But he's here, he's *real,* and he's disastrously hot, wearing a goddamn *corset vest.*

The satiny black vest has vertical ribs that taper his chest into his waist in the very definition of a perfect V. I want nothing more than to drop to my knees and *weep,* good lord how I have never seen a corset vest before—I mean, I've seen one, but I've never *seen one,* not on someone whose body looks physically sculpted to fill out this apex of human fashion.

He's got the only pop of color in the entire group, a scarlet silk button-up under the vest, the color such a deep red that there's no question it's meant to symbolize gore and darkness rather than Christmas's cherry brightness. Tight black pants taper into calf-high combat boots and the tips of his black hair now brush his shoulders, half the strands pulled behind his head, showing—*displaying*—the blade-edge sharpness of his jaw and cheekbones and the array of piercings up the shell of his left ear. Wide, observant dark eyes rimmed with black liner go from the floor up to my dad and Iris, no emotion at all on his face, but that lack of emotion is reaction enough—I get the distinct feeling he's pissed to be here. His hands hang at his sides, loosely clenched in fists, most of his fingers set with thick silver rings.

"The royal house of Halloween," an announcer bellows. "King Ichabod Hallow. Queen Carina Hallow. And their son Prince Hex Hallow."

His name rebounds in my head, cracking into the parts of my body that have gone immobile, and against every rational thought—I have no rational thoughts, none, not in this moment—I remember how to inhale and I gasp.

Loudly.

Attention swings to me. Dad, glaring; Iris, confused; Kris, like I've lost my mind, and I have, because Hex is looking at me now. And he doesn't seem at all surprised that I'm here, even if there is a beat of recognition; he just emits that same capped fury.

He's here to fake-compete with me over Iris. And will be staying in Claus Palace until Christmas Eve to keep Halloween appeased until Iris and I can get married. And is at this moment cocking one slender eyebrow and just the contact of his eyes on me yanks forward the memory of his lips beneath mine and fire crawls across my body.

Oh, no.

Oh no no *noooo*—

Dad turns back to the Halloween contingent. "Welcome to Christmas," he booms.

Chapter Five

Headline: *Christmas Prince falls into minor coma at sight of guy he kissed one and a half years ago who had the audacity to get even hotter in the interim.*

Too wordy. Not sure I care. There's nothing but a rolling air-raid siren in my head as Dad goes through all the pomp of having a royal family visiting. So glad you're here, yadda yadda. The Halloween family comes up on stage and they pose with Dad, Iris, and her father, and I think Kris and I should join in, but no one pushes us to, so we step down into the shadows beside the stage and I have a silent panic attack.

Kris chuckles. "You're pale. And sweating. You feel like an ass for mocking my jumpiness over their Halloween woo-woo spooky shit now, don't you?"

"I—what? No, I'm not—that's him."

He gives me a puzzled look. "Him? The Halloween Prince? You—"

"No. No." I pinch the skin over my nose. "That's *him*. The guy I kissed in the alley. At the bar. After the New Koah screwup. *That* guy."

Kris swings in front of me, trying to block me from any stray pictures. "Woah, woah—wait, really?"

"Yes. *Yes*. Holy shit—"

"Look, I love you, Coal, don't take this the wrong way—but I was on Iris's side in the whole *is this guy real* camp. It was dark, you were hammered and stressed. Maybe the Halloween prince sort of *looks* like the guy you thought—"

"*That's the guy!*" I hiss, thank god, but I want to shout. "The guy I thought was someone normal and he's—he's *the fucking Prince of Halloween*."

Kris lifts his hands like he can contain my freak-out. "Breathe. You're hyperventilating."

"How is this possible? Why was he even *at* that bar? Christmas and Halloween don't interact."

"Clearly."

"Shut up. This is serious. Did he target me? No. No, that's insane, right?"

Did Hex know who I was? I couldn't pick him or his family out of a lineup, so why would he have recognized me? What would have been the *point*? Nothing negative came of it, no leaked stories to the press or repercussions at all, so much so that Iris and Kris don't believe it happened.

But it did. Fuck, did it, because I've thought about that guy and that kiss way more than I'd ever admit to anyone. Even myself.

. . . foundations aren't ever one thing, they're many little things interlocked together.

In all the moments since then when I've asked myself what I should do instead of acting on impulse, that conversation would flash through my mind. The stranger—Hex—had known so easily what I don't let myself admit I want. Foundation, solidity, happiness. And he *was* a stranger, the longer time went on and nothing popped up and I couldn't find him afterwards, so I let the fantasy of him roil to embarrassing proportions because what did it matter, I'd never see him again.

Until now, apparently, because *fuck my life.*

"It was like years ago," Kris says. "Nothing bad came of it, not from Halloween, at least. I'll give you that it's weird, but I think you might be overreacting. Just a tad."

Oh great. "Cover for me."

I ease away and race to the bathroom where I consider dunking my head under the faucet but decide against it and pat my cheeks with cold water. The iciness washes a spurt of calm through me, and I rock forward, forehead hitting the mirror.

Kris is right. I am overreacting. It was a weird coincidence almost two years ago that didn't result in any fallout so I have no reason to be *losing my ever-loving mind.*

I will *not* mess this up. My dad has done a fine enough job of that himself, and I'm firmly on Iris's side—*when* this blows up, it will not be because of anything I do. Not again. I am a changed person, god-damn it, no matter what wayward fantasies I've been reliving like some lovestruck schoolboy.

Fantasies that have been, apparently, about the heir of Hallow-een.

I shove back and glare at my reflection.

"You will go back out there and be a perfect Christmas Prince," I hiss at myself. "You will *pull yourself together, you pathetic asshole.* He's just a guy." My intensity wanes. "Just a guy in a corset vest." I deflate more. "Why did it have to be a *corset vest.*"

By the time I get back into the ballroom, everyone is mingling. I spot Iris and Hex across the room, Iris talking politely with some-one from House Caroler while Hex stares down into a mug like he's trying to will it to transform into something less Christmassy. Maybe he's using Halloween's magic to do that; cocoa into . . . what's a Halloween drink? Apple cider? Goat blood?

Kris sidles up next to me. "You all right now? Freak-out over?"

I take a glass of eggnog from a passing server. "Of course. What could I possibly have to freak out about?"

"Oh, let me count the reasons." Kris's gaze trails to Iris and his levity dips.

"Are *you* all right?" I push back at him.

For a second, he shows me how not all right he is, but then a cam-era flashes, and he forces a smile.

"Shit." I take a gulp of the eggnog. It's not spiked. I can't win tonight.

Kris and I rotate around the room, expertly ducking any attempts at small talk until we haul up at a high-top table that gives a perfect view of where Iris and Hex hold court with rotating members of the Christmas noble houses. Dad, Neo, and the Halloween King and Queen stay with them for a bit, eventually getting pulled into other groups and conversations, but it gives me a chance to study Hex's parents. He definitely takes after his dad, a taller, older, and some-how paler and leaner version of Hex, with less adornments and a sullen expression befitting someone who might've just levitated out of a coffin. His mom is a little taller than Hex is, with intense dark eyes that mirror his initial stifled anger. She's got a wide necklace of small pearly skulls across her collarbone, and they catch the light in sharp flashes.

Kris grabs a handful of appetizers from a passing waiter and dumps them between us. Bacon-wrapped dates. Score.

I pop one into my mouth and definitely do not stare at the side of Hex's face. The way his jaw is bundled in tension.

It's not a big deal that he's here. That he's *that* guy. It's totally normal to know what your best friend's fake new potential fiancé tastes like.

See? I'm fine.

"We'll do this all one day," I say. Desperately needing to talk about literally anything the fuck else.

"Do what?" Kris asks.

"*This.*" I wave at the room. "The parties. The food. *Christmas.* It'll be ours."

"Yours, you mean."

"Like I'd leave you out in the cold."

What I want to say is, *Don't let me do this alone, for fuck's sake.*

Kris seizes a stack of crackers. "Do you even want to be Santa?"

"What kind of question is that?"

There's something on his face I'm not reading correctly. Something he hides behind a dismissive shrug.

"Exactly as it is," he says. "What do you want to do?"

"What do *you* want to do?"

"International Relations. Obviously. Boyhood dream of mine, really."

"Oh yeah, of course. But that's not what you *want* to do. You want to be a writer, right? God, not a journalist, I beg of you."

His lips slant in amusement. "No. Not a journalist. But I asked you that question first."

I prop my chin in my hands and bat my eyes at him and mimic intense listening.

He shakes his head, exasperated, but he's grinning. "You're such an ass."

I hold. Listening. Very, very intent listening.

Kris sighs. "I don't know. I try not to think about it. I have another year and a half left"—he winces, but recovers with a head shake—"and I'm the spare."

My instinct is to slap anyone who calls my brother that, but *he's* the one who said it. I punch his shoulder anyway. "No, you're not."

"Yes, I am. Dad's never had me involved in any kind of training. I expect he'll slot me in somewhere once I've graduated to keep me in reserve."

"*Slot you in? Keep you in reserve?* That shouldn't be the attitude you have for not only what you'll be doing with the rest of your life, but for something that's supposed to bring joy to the world."

His eyebrow cocks as he takes a sip of cocoa. "And your attitude is different how?"

"I—" Well, shit. "You have a choice."

He sputters. "Yeah. Sure. I could choose to run off to become a reclusive author in a cabin somewhere, and Dad would be a-okay with that."

"An author?" I home in on that word. "Is that really what you'd choose to do?"

Kris stiffens, watching me, before he shakes his head and decides against something. "Eat the fucking crackers. I think they have bits of dried apricot in them."

The appetizers are suddenly sitting like rocks in my stomach. Not because Kris has that option, to leave—but because he might take it. He had that bit about being a reclusive author a little too at the ready. And not only would that mean he'd be *somewhere else,* but that'd also mean he'd leave me alone, with all of this, the head of an empire that has a death grip on one of the biggest Holidays in the world, with no real ability to do anything other than keep chunking out plastic baubles.

If that's what he wants to do, though, of course I'd help him make it happen.

But him leaving would break my fucking heart.

So I do what I usually do when my emotions skew too dark: I torment my brother.

"Tell me what you wanna be when you grow up. Kris. Kris." I poke his cheek. "*Kriiiiiis. Kristopher Kringleeeee.*"

He *hates* when I use his middle name.

So he snaps right back with, "Shut up, *Niiiiick,* Nicholas *Noëlllll.*"

I laugh. I laugh and eat the stupid crackers and Kris smiles at me.

"You're not the spare to me," I tell him. My smile slips. "You know that, right?"

"Yeah, Coal," Kris says. "I know that."

"And when we—*we*—inherit this grand realm"—I wave my hand around again in mockery, but honestly, it *is* pretty grand—"I still want you to do what you want to do. Even if that isn't being part of this."

Kris stares at me for a long moment. His lips quirk slightly. "I'll stick around if you will."

The tension in my chest releases. A little.

"Safety in numbers, right?" I pop another cracker and go, "Buddy system," only, with my full mouth, it comes out "Buddy fyst'm," and crumbs spray everywhere.

Kris's stare is deadpan as he flicks a crumb off his sleeve. "Can I choose a different buddy?"

"Nope. You're stuck with me."

"Damn."

"Blame genetics, bitch."

Dad catches my eye as he makes his way towards us, his brows raised in intent before he even gets to the table.

I paste a pleasant smile on my face when he approaches. "Father."

"Why aren't you over there?" Dad nods at where it's now just Hex and Iris against a seemingly endless parade of Christmas nobles.

"Over—?"

"The Halloween Prince has had ample time alone with her," Dad hisses, angling close. "You must play into this competition. Go over there. Stake your claim."

"*Stake my claim?* What, should I stick a flag in her?"

Kris snorts next to me.

"Nicholas." Dad's look goes from a glare to a performative smile as someone passes by our table. They leave, and he bends back in. "Make it look like you are trying to win her. That is, after all, the story we are promoting. *Go.*"

An argument winds up in me. How I never agreed to any of this—

But my eyes dip behind Dad, to a clock across the room. It's past I A.M.

Fuck. I let this whole event go long enough without doing something unforgivably unsettling, but I've been too busy wallowing.

"Fine," I say between clenched teeth, giving a sweet smile. "Consider my stake claimed."

I grab Kris and haul him away with me before Dad can protest.

Kris frowns. "Are you really going to—"

"God no. It's just time to save Iris."

"Ah. You escort her away, I'll cover for you both?"

Our usual play. But—

"Nah," I hear myself say. "You take her. Tell her how *perfect* she looks."

"Bite me."

"I think you mean bite *her.*"

"I—what?"

I rub the skin over my nose. "Halloween. Vampires. Werebunnies. It's where my head went. Let's go."

Kris laughs, confused, as I drag us across the room.

A member of House Luminaria is fawning over Iris while giving furtive, distrustful glances at the Halloween prince.

I lurch between the Luminaria duke and Hex.

"We have bacon-wrapped dates," I say to the duke, and I *hear* the hardness in my voice, but I can't figure how to stop it, and it sounds mildly hilarious to say *bacon-wrapped dates* with the same inflection that someone might say *go screw yourself.*

I point across the room.

The duke gives me a strange frown. "Uh—thank you, Prince Nicholas. Princess." He bows his head at Iris.

There's a pause.

Then he looks at Hex. "Prince Hex."

But he doesn't bow, and it's a good thing he leaves. My hand is in a fist.

There's a general sense of distrust in Christmas regarding Holidays we don't often interact with—Dad's whole philosophy of Christmas being *better* means most other Holidays are *lesser*. And putting me in direct competition with the Halloween Prince just reinforces all of that, so the duke's reaction isn't unusual. But why is it pissing me off so much? I have no reason to feel protective over Hex.

Oh god. Is that what this is? Feeling *protective* of him?

Kris sweeps past me. "Princess—you're needed straightaway."

She physically wilts, but turns to Hex and gives him a smile that surprisingly isn't fake. "Prince Hex," she says with a curtsy.

He bows at the waist—that waist, god, *stop staring at his waist*—and straightens. "Princess."

Oh, save me from his voice. Why would it have changed? It hasn't, still rich and heavy and doing completely furious things to my stomach.

Iris lets Kris guide her away, but not before I catch her hiss at him, "Took you long enough."

"Sorry—ow!" Kris rubs his side. "Did you pinch me?"

Hex and I are on the side of the room. And I must be giving off some serious *back the fuck up* vibes, because no more Christmas aristocracy come forward for pleasantries, so we are, effectively, alone.

I go stock-still. Hex stands there too, being this insanely attractive mash-up of a pirate and a vampire and Loki from that one scene in *Thor: Ragnarok* when he's in New York and first had me realizing that I was, in fact, deeply attracted to dudes in addition to girls. Both Iris and Kris thought I was nuts when, according to them, "*Chris Hemsworth is right there.*" We mended this falling-out in our friendship by bonding over the great sexuality equalizer: Cate Blanchett in leather.

Never let it be said that I have no self-control, because even as the silence stretches between me and Hex, I do *not* talk about any of these internal pirate/vampire/Loki/leather thoughts.

It's Hex who breaks the never-ending nothingness when his face goes from patiently studying me to tight in exasperation.

"We are rivals, it seems." He pockets his hands.

It drags a laugh out of me. *Rivals.* That's how Dad wants me to react to Hex. But I can't summon up any scrap of fake offense, can't get myself to stop following the rim of his eyeliner around his still very attractive eyes.

Eyes that are crooked in annoyance.

Not in surprise.

"You're not surprised to see me." It pops out before I can stop it.

"The Christmas Prince, at the Christmas palace?" His voice is steel. "Hardly."

"No, I mean—*me.*"

Glasses clink around us. Someone laughs across the room. And Hex keeps giving me that unimpressed stare.

He probably wasn't an absolute idiot and researched Christmas before coming here, so he knew we'd see each other again—

But then he says, "I was wondering if the infamous Prince Nicholas would remember."

And something in his tone makes my whole brain overturn.

"You—you knew, back then, who I was." I say each word purposefully, making sure I'm getting this because *what the fuck.* "You *knew.*"

"Of course." A pause, and his eyes narrow. "Are you saying you did not know who *I* was?"

"No! I mean, yes, I didn't know who you were. How—how were you *there*?" I angle closer, whisper-hissing my shock down at him. "You just—you *happened* to be at *my bar,* and you *happened* to come out into *that alley,* and—"

His face contorts like he's seeing that night through a new lens, but a foggy lens, one that doesn't make anything clearer. "You expect me to believe you did not have the slightest idea who I was?" He blinks and points to the stage. "And you did not realize it until *that moment*?"

His tone of *are you a moron* is deserved, but still stings.

"I thought you were like a bartender or something." Heat wells in my chest, making my ribs feel brittle and unable to expand enough. "I've spent a year and a half thinking you were either some normal guy that I'd never be able to find again or a very vivid figment of my imagination."

He arches one brow. "You've spent the past year and a half thinking about me?"

Well fuck. "I—" Nope, let's just lean into it. "You thought I'd forget you?"

"I thought Prince Nicholas had enough dalliances that one kiss would be quickly overlooked."

It wasn't just a kiss. I mean, the kiss was great, but it was everything else too, how he'd let me dump all my shit out and he'd listened and said exactly what I needed to hear.

I almost tell him all of that. How much that single interaction meant to me. But I'm already way too close to humiliating myself.

"I don't have *dalliances*," I hook on instead.

It's not a far jump from stupid pranks and irresponsibility to sleeping around, and the tabloids have warped every person I've dated the past few years into some kind of scandalous relationship or one-night stand. Some of them were. But still. I'm a hellion, but I'm not heartless.

Hex's stare is full of incredulity. "Ah. My apologies. You are, of course, madly in love with Princess Iris."

There's something baited in his voice, but I don't want to talk about Iris, can't, not with all the unanswered questions welling up in me and the still-potent fact that he's *here.* He's *that* guy, and he's here, in front of me, and instead of flirting my ass off to make up for being a drunk idiot last time, I'm scrambling to find sense in the senseless.

"Wait." I flare my hands. "You thought I knew who you were at the bar and that I was trying to, what, make you a feather in my cap?" Which probably got cemented when I never contacted him or reached out afterwards.

He shrugs, and I'm temporarily derailed by what should be a small, mundane movement. His shoulders are thin, bony, as sharp as his eyebrows and that cutting look in his gaze, everything about him is filed to a knifepoint and I suddenly want nothing more than for him to make me bleed.

I shake my head. Squish my eyes closed. Maybe if I talk to him with my eyes shut, it'll make this easier? Creepier, but easier.

"How else was I meant to interpret your intentions?" he asks.

My eyes open reluctantly and I grunt. "What the fuck part of our conversation came across as me *picking you up*? Is that how mating dances normally go in Halloween—one person is blackout drunk and word-vomits nonsensically over the other?"

Hex's unamused stare flickers ever so slightly. I think he'd chuckle if he wasn't so set on being offended by my continued existence.

I press on anyway. "And that doesn't explain why you were at that bar or what you got out of that interaction, because—" All my racing thoughts crash to a halt and I almost bounce up and down at a realization. "Because *you* came after *me* out into that alley. *I* didn't pursue *you*."

For a beat, Hex's façade cracks, and I see all the emotions he's been suppressing this evening—uncertainty, wariness, a caravan of things that slams the brakes on any desire of mine to come out of this conversation with some kind of moral victory. This isn't a game, and whatever we had wasn't some frivolous bar hookup because neither of our positions allows for any of this to be simple.

His attention slips past me and catches on his parents, across the room in the crowd. They hit him with a very obvious look of *Need us to intervene?*

I don't relax until he shakes his head at them.

Okay. He's not trying to escape. That's good, right?

"I did follow you into that alley." He shrugs again, arms folding over his chest. "The tabloids made no secret of your preference for that bar, and I was in the area. I was . . . let's say *curious* to see what kind of person you were."

"What?" I shake my head again, hoping it'll jostle sense into everything. "Why?"

Hex's face falls in the smallest, the *barest* flicker of something directed inward—shame, maybe? He runs his thumb across his bottom lip, wiping it away.

My focus whittles to that contact. His thumb on his lip. He has a ring on that finger, a silver skull, and before I can realize what a presumptuous thing it is to do, my gaze stays on his mouth.

It is utterly selfish, the relief I feel at knowing I didn't imagine how full his lips are. But the dark light of the alley hid the color, a roseate flush I see clearly now, and I'm overwhelmed by the taste-memory of him, the feel of those soft lips moving under mine.

My mouth waters, stomach tightening.

What am I doing.

I pop my gaze back up, braced for his offended fury.

But Hex's eyes snag on mine, widen slightly, and he doesn't call me on very obviously ogling him. He doesn't scoff or put space between us or do anything at all to imply that my attention was unwanted.

The faintest hue of pink blooms on his cheeks. Two perfect circles against his pale skin.

It could be from the heat in here, from the exertion of the night.

My swallow abrades my throat, sand and beaten stones.

"Why what?" he asks, a quick feather of breath across my face.

"Why were you curious about what kind of person I was?" I repeat the question.

A question he'd forgotten.

While blushing.

I grip my hands into fists so hard one of my thumbs cracks.

Hex looks away, gathers himself, and when he meets my eyes again, he holds, waiting. When I nod, prodding him along, he cocks his head.

He'd thought I would say something. Something I *didn't* say, and the way he's looking at me now is all shock. "Why wouldn't I be interested in what the Christmas Prince is like?" is all he finally says, a bit mockingly.

"What is going on?" My voice is only low because I can't get in a full breath. "How are you so calm about this?"

The answer comes in a blow of clarity: because that night didn't matter as much to him. Because he knew who I was before we kissed, and me being here isn't shocking to him, and he probably hasn't thought about that night until now, and he's got way bigger things to worry about than a one-off bar alley kiss.

I vehemently ignore the ache in my chest. Everything I've been feeling in regard to that night was a fantasy. I know that. It's dumb to feel rejected over shit I built up in my head. His blush could have been uneasiness because he's here to romance *someone else,* someone who I also am supposed to be romancing.

"It was a long time ago," he says stiffly. Like he's upset, maybe disgusted, and I pull back and wipe a hand over my mouth and I've never felt so slimy in my life.

"This is overdue, then," I say.

Hex frowns. "What is overdue?"

"Apologizing. I told you I owed you one that night, but I never actually did it. So—I'm sorry I made you feel that you were some conquest. I shouldn't have kissed you without at least asking your name first. I can assure you, nothing like that will happen again."

Hex watches me stumble through the apology. I can feel every sweep of his eyes on my face, like he's reading my thoughts beyond my words.

Nothing in his posture changes, but I'm hit with the feeling that I need to go quiet, to let him work out whatever he wants to say.

"You don't need to . . ." He fingers the sleeve of his scarlet shirt, the only outward hint at his discomfort, and it forces all the blood out of my limbs when he doesn't look back up at me. "You don't need to apologize for that kiss. You weren't the one who initiated it."

I wouldn't be able to move if the whole room started to shake. "Excuse me?"

But he walks away.

He walks away and leaves me there, running those words through my head until their edges soften and bend.

You weren't the one who initiated it.

WHAT

THE

FUCK?

Baby It's Coal-d Outside

IRIS
coal—kris told me our Halloween
prince was that guy from the bar??

HE'S REAL?? holy shit!!

what did you guys talk about? you
looked petrified when you left the
ballroom.

also stop renaming the group chat

**Iris named the conversation "Iris and the Claus
Boys"**

nothing.

and he's not OUR halloween
prince. he's just YOURS.

and i wasn't petrified

**Coal named the conversation "When I Think
About You I Touch My Elf"**

IRIS
nothing? liar.

and i meant the Royal We, like all
of ours, not just yours and mine, so
it's really telling that that's where
your mind went.

oh god coal

**Iris named the conversation "Iris and the Claus
Boys, Coal Don't Change It"**

KRIS
All of ours? I don't remember
ordering a goth prince.

But, Coal, you were for sure petrified.

What'd he say to you?

Did you try to kiss him again?

> yep right in the middle of the ballroom
>
> cuz you know me, raging pervert can't keep it in my pants
>
> i mean mouth. tongue in mouth.
>
> nothing came out of my pants or mouth
>
> i'm going to bed

KRIS
Dude, you're a trainwreck.

Coal named the conversation "Not Just the Stockings are Hung"

IRIS
coal!! gross

Iris named the conversation "Coal Is Overcompensating for His Tiny Candy Cane"

> i beg your fucking pardon peep
>
> did you just dick joke me
>
> iris
>
> iris just dick joked me kris

IRIS
you started it

KRIS
I know, I witnessed the whole thing.

As a completely innocent third party bystander, I'm declaring her the winner.

Kris named the conversation "Peep, Mini Candy Cane, and the Best Claus"

Conversation Name Locked

YOU CAN LOCK IT??

KRIS

OPEN IT BACK UP

KRIS
Tell us what you and Hex talked about.

IRIS
ooooo i see how you brought it back around like that kris, bravo, bravo, he only responds to black-mail

you guys suck

me and my perfectly adequate candy cane are going to bed

Chapter Six

You weren't the one who initiated it.

I fall out of bed at dawn the next morning, barely having slept, and yank on a hoodie Kris gave me last year—it has two Christmas bulbs on it and the words *I've Got Balls*. But it's a damn comfortable hoodie and I have a deep-seated need to be as cozy as possible right now.

You weren't the one who initiated it.

I traipse out of my bedroom, hood up, hands in the pockets, barefoot and still in my red flannel pajama pants.

He'd kissed me.

He'd kissed *me*. In my drunken, messy state.

You weren't the one who initiated it.

I slump down to the kitchen. Grab a tray. Load it up with two massive stacks of cinnamon roll pancakes—nothing beats our kitchen this time of year, *nothing*—and a giant carafe of fresh pour-over coffee and a pitcher of oat milk.

"Renee," I call across the kitchen to the head chef, who is over-seeing meal prep for lunch already. "I love you and your staff more than I love Kris."

She pops her head up with a bright smile. The people around her look my way too, pausing their chopping and writing notes, a few waving, all of them with amused smirks that match hers.

"Thank you, Prince Nicholas," Renee says. She glances at my tray and sighs. "Why am I not surprised that you have two servings of carbs and sugar, but no fruits or vegetables?"

"This isn't all for me—"

She points to the breakfast spread I've turned away from. "At least get fruit. Or I will be forced to resume pureeing spinach into the pancakes."

I pivot and grab a bowl of sliced melon, but my shoulders go stiff.

"I'm sorry." I twist back around to her. "Did you say *resume* puree-ing spinach into the pancakes?"

Renee shakes her head at how one of her staff is slicing carrots, only half paying attention to me. "Yes, of course."

"*Of course?*"

"It was the only way to get either of you boys to eat vegetables when you were younger." She looks at me again, head cocking. "Did you never wonder why your pancakes were green?"

"They were—it was—they were *Christmassy!*"

"Yes. Thanks to the spinach."

"You have *children!* Do you treat them with as much subterfuge as you treat me and Kris?"

"Unapologetically."

Her sous chef is failing to hide a smirk as she reads a production sheet.

"Lacie! You knew about this?" I demand.

Lacie's eyebrows go up and she shakes her head. "I'm not getting involved."

"Oh, silence is incriminating." My attention zips over the rest of them, half a dozen people laughing into their meal preps. "How, from the bottom of my heart, dare you. All of you. You've shattered my trust. I should go on a hunger strike to spite you."

"Mhmm." Renee cuts me a smile as I leave.

"Tell your children I said hello and I'm sorry on their behalf, you traitor."

"I will. Enjoy your breakfast, Prince Nicholas."

The kitchen staff's laughter follows me as I balance the tray and head back up the stairs, the safe bubble of humor deflating when I snake around to avoid any of the main areas—just in case. I know where Hex is being put up, in a wing on the opposite side of the palace. But still.

You weren't the one who initiated it.

Goddamn it.

A rolling mantra of curses barrels through my mind as I stumble to a halt outside Iris's door. I kick it and rest my forehead against the doorframe.

Within, I hear shuffling, the pad of footsteps, then she unlocks and opens the door.

I moan pathetically. "I'm sorry we didn't rescue you sooner last night."

"I don't need saving, I told you." A pause. "But next time, do it before midnight."

I cut her a smile and hold up the tray. "I promise, Cinderella."

She surveys my offering and deems it acceptable with a satisfied hum. "Oooh, cinnamon. But I'm not getting Kris to unlock the group chat name."

My gasp is more than a touch overdramatic. "I am hurt, *hurt,* that you think breakfast comes with asterisks."

"Oh, so this isn't also your way of trying to *woo* me as one of my adoring suitors?"

She's joking, I know she is; she's batting her fucking eyelashes at me.

But it shuts me up, because that didn't even occur to me. I do stuff like this all the time. But it's *different* now, isn't it? If someone sees—

Iris rolls her eyes with a grin. "Get in here, you idiot."

I hesitate. Then hate myself for hesitating because this is all *fake,* Dad's lies cocooning around me, so I shake it off and head inside as she closes the door behind me.

She's dressed already, courtesy of the earlier start time for reindeer racing, in a warm wool gown, still purple, her braids tucked into a long side knot.

"Did you sleep at all last night?" I set the tray on the table in her suite's front room. It's a guest room in the Christmas palace, but there are touches of Easter everywhere—magically budding tulips, baskets of pastel eggs. Her father's room, two halls over, is decked out the same.

"A few hours." She goes right for the coffee as we sit. "Did you?"

I crack a laugh. It breaks apart into another pathetic moan.

She sets down her mug with a sigh and digs into a bag next to the table. Art supplies topple out, the odd ball of yarn and brush—she's tried to get me to *"channel stress into crafting"* like she does, to laughable results every time—until she comes up with a thing of nail polish. I don't ask the color; I splay my hand on the table for her, eating with my other one.

"Your nails are a disgrace," she says.

"All right, *Wren.* I'm a guy."

"Sexist."

"I mean—"

"I know what you mean. Hold still." She sets to work, and I eat, eyes drifting to where she has her flower crown on a pedestal under a grow light. She can keep them alive with Easter's magic, but she's always done that, gone the extra step with plants and Easter creatures to make sure they don't *have* to depend on her magic, that she *isn't* a frivolous Easter Princess.

"So," she says softly after a beat, dragging the polish brush across my thumb. "Want to talk about Hex?"

"Nope. I'm sorry I used your mom to argue with your dad about our sham of an engagement. I should've apologized sooner. It was out of line."

She blinks up at me. Her surprise morphs into a shrug and she refocuses on painting. "You didn't say anything that wasn't true."

"Still. It was disrespectful."

"No, what was disrespectful was what *he* said, that she would've understood this arrangement. He knows damn well that she'd have been livid with him."

"Are things really that precarious in Easter? I mean, Lily's marrying into Valentine's Day, which has gotta be fostering some confidence. Why do you need Christmas too?"

Iris dips the brush into the paint bottle, lifts it back out, dunks it again, does this a few times before she shakes her head. "He's been like this since Mom died. Not power-hungry, but more . . . susceptible to suggestions. From our court, telling him he needs to do more; from your dad. He's hurting. He misses her. I get it. But—I don't know. I've tried to help him ever since she died. It never felt like enough, and lately, it *really* doesn't feel like enough, like no matter what I do, he'll have that blank look, and mutter something about Easter needing me. As if I don't know. I *know* Easter needs me. I know *he* needs me. I'm well-aware."

My brow furrows, and I watch the way she scrambles too forcefully in her bag for another bottle of polish.

"What do you want to do after you graduate?" I ask. "Just like—for real. Do you know?"

Iris squints. "I'm pretty sure I'm doing it, Coal."

"Not your duties. I mean what do you *really* want to do. There has to be something? You wanted to go to art school once." It's bothering me that Kris didn't answer that question.

It's bothering me more that *I* don't have an answer to that question.

Iris sets down the nail polish and takes a bite of her pancakes. Her eyes drift out, and a spark of a smile flashes.

"What?" I echo her grin.

"Okay." She dusts her hands off and flares her palms together, parting them back to show me an egg. Not just any egg—it's an Easter decoration, a delicate sculpture with a surface coated in painstakingly perfect geometric designs, the colors all rich, intense jewel tones.

"It's pretty," I say, eyeing her.

Iris pinches it between her thumb and forefinger. "It's called a kraslice. A type of egg painting they do in Eastern Europe. They layer wax and paint and then peel it off to reveal this level of detail—you see the shading? The blue beneath the green? It takes *hours*. It takes *skill*."

"So . . . you want to make kraslice?"

Iris flips her hand and the egg vanishes. "Yes. No. I want—" She sighs and stuffs in another bite. As she chews, she shakes her head. "All the stuff we put out of Easter now is getting more and more . . . cheap. Ease and speed prioritized over stuff like a kraslice. We do some things that are beautiful, and it's important that the things we offer are accessible. But . . . I don't know." She sinks back in her chair. "I wish we could prioritize more stuff like that. More stuff that's true tradition, not for the sake of convenience."

"I get it."

She flattens her lips at me.

"What? I do."

"Oh, really? *Coal* cares about Christmas traditions?"

That's the second time something she's said has dug into me, and I let it show now.

"I do care." I set down my fork. "I just don't see how caring will change things. And I used to be okay with it, because maybe I didn't understand the full breadth of responsibilities of Christmas, maybe there was more at work than what I was seeing—but god, anymore, that's not true."

Iris watches me carefully. "How so?"

"Okay." I guess I'm doing this. "You mentioned old traditions, right? I remember when I was younger, and Kris and I studied Christmas's history—which we haven't in years, and it was disappointing to stop, because I did used to love it—"

"You did?"

"Yeah. That was before you." Before Mom left. Before everything changed.

God, I haven't thought about this old version of me in . . . years. Even starting to now has a piece of me lighting up helplessly, a spirited levity in my chest.

"We learned about stuff like our noble houses. The Luminarias and the Jacobs, the Frosts, the Carolers—how they developed from different pockets of joy created by Christmas in different communities across the world. There are hundreds more different cultural touches that combine or can combine to create a celebration that's encompassing, not just *easy*. But no one ever talks about it? All the shit we put out is the same old regurgitated stuff that only fits one set type of person."

"Yeah, exactly." Iris screws the lid back onto one of the polishes. "We could be doing so much more. But we *aren't*. My dad and yours keep saying how this merger of our Holidays will change things, but my dad has never taken any other steps to improve things beyond a generic ploy for *expansion*. His complacency grows each year and I don't know how to break out of it."

"It isn't just your dad."

Iris's face squishes. "Speak for your own Holiday."

"I mean—it isn't just at the top. You know how most of my friends back at school see Christmas? The same way I do—not wanting to go home, not wanting to deal with their families, hoping maybe they'll get a cool gift to soften the stress of whatever arguments they get into. And here I find out that that attitude is exactly what my dad's been letting fester, because he'd rather focus on the commodification of Christmas so he can stretch our resources than narrow in on making our Holiday resonate with anything meaningful. But would it *be* meaningful? Would anything we provide really resonate, really be able to make anything in this world *better*?"

Iris frowns. "We do. We make people—"

"Happy. I know. But what good is one day of happiness when it's proven over and over again that it does jack all to stop anything bad from happening? Would we be better to siphon off all the money and assets we have to charities? Wouldn't *that* do more?"

"Christmas is involved with charities. I know you are."

"Yeah, we are. But it's a negligible amount, in the big scheme of things. And the sad thing is, the small percent we kick off to charities probably does more good than all of the other shit we peddle combined. Because at the end of the day, what would people rather have: a white Christmas and a single day of magical feelings, or a roof over their head?"

Iris rocks to the side. "I've never heard you talk like this."

I sit back in the chair—I'd leaned forward, shoulders caved in—and have to take a breath to fight the tightness welling in my lungs. "Yeah. Well. I guess I don't tell you everything either."

She exhales. "I'm sorry I didn't tell you about switching my class load. It isn't a big deal."

That isn't exactly what I was referring to, but I'll take it. "Would you stop saying that? It is. It's allowed to be. You're allowed to be pissed about your dad forcing your life to go a certain way."

"I'm *not* though." She waves the polish bottle around to encompass something intangible. "I don't hate my classes. Some of them are interesting. And *applicable*. Did I tell you I was at the top of my statistics class?"

I yank my head back, face fully wide in revulsion. "Oh, god, Iris, this is so much worse than I thought. I might stage an intervention for you."

"And"—she inches closer, all conspicuous—"I *liked* it."

"No one *likes* statistics. It's philosophy but with numbers."

Her face screws up. "What? No, it isn't."

"Yeah—it's all theoretical shit. If you can argue well, you can get any answer you want."

That confused look breaks on a chuckle. "If that's what you think statistics is, it's really no wonder you bombed it."

"I eventually passed." Barely. "My point is that liking statistics is a cry for help."

"Well, I must be screaming for help, because I liked my philosophy classes too."

I mimic throwing up. Violently. "I have failed you, utterly, to let your mind become so corrupted by the educational enticements of—" My eyes finally land on my right hand. "You painted my nails black and orange."

She smirks. "Figured you should pay homage to a certain Halloween guest."

I try to decide whether I should be horrified, but I clench my hand into a fist—the paint's dry—and stuff it into my hoodie's pocket.

Iris makes a high-pitched chirp. "Oh my *god*! You *like* him."

I have my hood up, but it isn't hiding me enough. "I do not—"

"Coal, you didn't fight me on the nail colors. You *like* him. Oh my god!" She tucks her legs up into the chair, beset by manic giggles. "Kris told me you were unhinged last night because of Hex, but I thought it was everything else, not—"

"Okay, okay, *stop,* because yes, it *is* everything else. This whole fake vying for your hand bullshit. That isn't enough? Let's not make up other stressors."

But her grin is downright *feral.* "Uh-huh. Sure. I definitely believe you."

"The way you believed me about him existing?"

"Exactly."

"No. Iris." Kris and Iris are the only two people who ever see this side of me, and even they see it so rarely that it takes Iris a beat to realize I'm not dicking around, that the severity on my face is real—real and pleading.

She drops her legs back to the floor and matches my stance, arched towards me. "Coal?"

"I do not like him," I tell her, stating each word in a level, calm voice that I hope to god sounds convincing. "I cannot like him. You have to help me not like him."

She shakes her head. "Why?" Then winces. "I know you and I will be . . . together, but we won't be *together* together, so we're free to be with other people. In secret, I guess." She scowls. "Fuck. That's pathetic, isn't it?"

"No. Well, yes, but we really don't need to discuss covert bedroom schedules right now." *Because part of me is still hoping we'll get out of this somehow,* I don't add. "But why are *you* going along with this fake shit? Why aren't you fighting your dad more? Because I will not mess this up. Because I'm pissed off about what Christmas has become but—but I still fucking *care,* and I will not endanger my Holiday over some guy. Plus, I know what ramifications this could have for you and Easter if I fuck it up, and I won't be the cause of any more shit for you."

Iris gapes at me, and I wonder for a second if I have pancake on my face.

But she takes my hand. "All right. All right, Coal. I hear you."

I wilt over our clasped hands.

"Something's changed in you," she says softly.

I groan. "Don't say that. Makes me want to go streaking through the Toy Factory to prove you wrong."

"Oh, I think those days might be past you, Nicholas Claus." She smiles. "You're almost acting *responsible*."

"Ugh, and to think, you're someone who claims to love me." I drop her hands and slouch in the chair. "And why did we get talking about *me* again? When I haven't heard your opinion on your fabulous and completely drama-free suitor party. Did Hex sufficiently sweep you off your feet? Do I have competition?"

The questions make my stomach cramp and I'm regretting the few bites of food I've had. That's an outcome I hadn't considered: I don't know what Hex's deal is, but what if he and Iris legitimately fall for each other?

I rub my chest absently, pretty sure the pancakes are giving me heartburn.

Iris spears a slice of melon with her fork, eyes on the table. Her mood dips so abruptly that all my senses go on alert.

"Can we not talk about that?" she asks.

"Oka-ay," I drag out. "Why? I came fully prepared to mock each and every aspect of that faux-event."

"That's exactly it." Iris uses her fork to cut the melon slice into smaller and smaller pieces. "I'm sure I'll want to joke about it someday. But I'm not in the mood for it right now. It's shitty and I—I don't really want to talk about it with you yet."

I frown, watching her cut the melon, no, *pulverize* it.

"We don't have to joke about it," I say.

Iris throws me the very definition of a disbelieving look. "Oh really? So you *didn't* bring up last night's party so you *could* start making jokes and steer the conversation away from all the serious bits we'd been discussing?"

My jaw drops open.

Part of me wants to be offended. The rest of me feels like Iris just forehead-smacked my psyche.

"Are you sure you haven't been taking psychology classes too?" I mutter.

She huffs. "You're not that difficult to figure out, Coal. I'm not saying we can't joke around now. I know how uncomfortable talking about anything real makes you, and I don't think we've ever had a conversation that stayed serious for as long as the one we just had. I'm saying I don't want to joke around about this fake relationship shit. Not yet. Let's talk about something else—you look like you're going to vomit."

That's why she's been keeping stuff from me?

I pull one leg up onto the chair beneath me, unable to stop shifting awkwardly. "If you need to talk about it, or anything else, I'll listen. I won't mock it. I swear. And if you think I can't do that for you, then I've been an epically shitty friend, and I'm sorry."

Iris eats some of her melon mush and smiles. "I know you would if I really needed you to. But I don't need that." She pauses. "Not yet."

"Okay." But something still feels off. Unbalanced. Like Iris *does* need to talk about how all this competing for her hand nonsense is affecting her, but she's holding back, not because she's not ready, but because she knows, on some level, that I won't help her or be able to listen.

Fuck. Have I always been a shitty friend?

I know she doesn't want to marry me, even if she was the one who convinced me to go along with this because *duty* and *what will it do to our people,* but is it getting too much for her? Is she having second thoughts?

Could I actually do anything to get us out of it if I tried, or would I just mess things up way worse?

I take a breath and blow it out, but Iris waves at my plate before I can try to begin piecing together an apology or an escape plan or anything beneficial.

"*Eat.* You only have an hour or so until reindeer racing."

I smirk half-heartedly. "I think you mean *we* only have an hour until reindeer racing."

She sips her coffee, nonplussed. "I shall happily cheer on you and Kris from the heated spectators' tent."

"Coward."

"What's that?" She cups her hand around her ear. "It's the sound of someone who had one mildly serious conversation yet is now so stricken with responsibility by it that he will *sedately* drive his sleigh instead of whipping carelessly around the track, which means he will—gasp—lose to his brother."

"Don't put your money on Kris. You know his competitiveness feeds my competitiveness until we're a perpetual motion machine of egging each other on, and I really doubt one serious moment will break that grand tradition."

Iris laughs, but the sound of it, the feel of it, rings hollow, tapping on the insecurity that's always camped deep inside of me: that nothing I do has any real impact. That everything I'm capable of is so far short of *enough* that I'll never be able to help when it's most needed, never be able to support those I love in any way that matters.

But Iris dives into talking about last year's race and how both Kris and I lost, so I let her carry me on to that topic, cracking jokes, trying to pretend this isn't the pinnacle of what I have to offer her or anyone else.

Reindeer racing is one time-honored Christmas tradition I have no problem with.

The track starts at the stables and meanders through the pine forest that beards the palace grounds, going up and down over hills and crossing natural ice bridges before ending right back at the stables. Every few years, someone gets the bright idea to make it an airborne race, but Dad usually decides it's a waste of magic—so we're grounded, which is all the better, because few people are skilled enough to drive flying sleighs.

The winner gets gloating rights. And a trophy, but mostly the gloating rights.

Last year, one of our cousins from House Frost won, so as Kris and I head down for the start of the event, our game faces are on.

But this is more about photos and press than any actual competition, so Wren and her stylists dolled us up in swanky yet surprisingly functional snow gear, not like we're going full-on skiing, but more like we're doing a shoot for a magazine advertising skiing—sleek fleece and polar thermals. My blue jacket is thin enough to move in yet comfortably warm, and I tug down the knit white-and-blue hat that presses my curls to my forehead.

We duck out of a side door in the palace to Wren already waiting for us in her own functional outerwear, tablet in hand. Along with space heaters, energy-saving lighting has been set up everywhere, giant bright beaming contraptions to combat the fact that we're in the top of the northern hemisphere and daylight is in short supply this time of year. But we've rather perfected mimicking the sun, and the lights make it look midmorning enough.

"Everyone else is in place," she says. "Why are you two always the last ones?"

"Kris has a crush on you. You set him all aflutter," I say, and Wren sighs heavily, the awkwardness of my snark too much of a burden.

Kris tugs on his gloves as we round the side of the palace, snow crunching under our boots. The air is so cold it *tastes* like winter, that chilly, bitter trace that sinks in with each breath. But the sky is clear over the lights, no fresh snow today, and all around is the same buzzing, busy energy of Christmas prep alongside the chaos of event prep. There's a whole layer of the North Pole that runs parallel to ours—we're swept up in staged events while everyone else is working to bring Christmas to the world.

I watch a team of people oversee a delivery as Kris leans into me. "Once more," he starts.

I spin to the setup by the stables. "Unto the breach."

A wide, festive tent fills half of the stable yard, closed off on three sides to keep the warmth from more space heaters clustered around lush seating areas. Members of the court are already there, cozied up under thick blankets, staff overseeing a buffet made by Renee and her team.

My focus zips around. I can't help it.

Iris is off to the side with Dad, her father, and Hex, all talking with reporters.

He's not wearing a corset vest this time. That I can tell. Because he's in a form-fitting black peacoat with a white button-up giving a pop of contrast beneath. Collar pins glint on his lapels, each one linked by two staggered chains draped over the knot of his black tie.

If my mind flashes with the image of grabbing those silver chains and wrenching his face up to mine, I willfully ignore it.

I will not make a fool of myself. I said what I needed to say to Hex. There's no further reason to interact with him. Ever.

Even if he was the one who kissed me.

God, shut up, self.

All my flustered internal chaos goes to frozen silence when Hex holds out something he'd had by his side: a bouquet of flowers. They're jet-black, and might actually be dead, because a petal crumbles off and drifts down to the snow at his feet.

He extends them to Iris with an uncomfortable smile, forced and pinched, and his movements are stiff.

The reporters *eat it up* though, people from *Christmas Inquirer* and *Joy Gazette* and others snapping pics and cooing, and it only intensifies Hex's look of extreme discomfort.

I take a step forward, not sure what I can do, when Iris takes the bouquet with her signature easy grace. Her smile is genuine and kind, and it seems to set Hex a bit at ease, but I suddenly find myself not sure whether that's a good thing.

She'd teased me about liking him, so I doubt she'd actually make a move on him, but—but I *don't* like him, because that would be ridiculous. So if they make each other happy, then . . .

Then that's great.

Fantastic.

Definitely completely fine.

The bouquet in her hands transforms. What had for sure been dead flowers blossom in a gentle unfurling of buttercup yellow and sunset orange and stalks of healthy, vibrant green, Easter's magic breathing life back into the darkness.

That sets the reporters off cooing again, and Iris smiles wider at Hex.

"Easter is a bit the antithesis of Halloween, isn't it?" she says.

He grins, more real than any emotion he's shown yet, and the fact that it's aimed at Iris has me all knotted up in an insane barrage of conflicting feelings. The most virulent of which, I'm loathe to admit, is jealousy, which is *so fucking dumb*. Because I'm supposed to be interested in *Iris,* or pretending to be, but all I want to do is drop-kick my best friend away from Hex even though she's as trapped as we are.

I am going to need so much therapy after this.

I shoot a glance at Kris, who is watching this unfold with the same complicated expression I can feel on my own face.

Dad finally notes us and waves us over. "Boys! Come here for a picture."

Kris wordlessly tells me to keep it together—right back at ya, bro—and we trudge over.

Dad slaps his arm around me and pulls us into a staged stance.

Headline: *Claus Family all smiles with Halloween Prince, who is definitely not here against his will.*

The reporters get their shots and our group starts to disperse. Kris and Iris beeline into the tent. Iris's fast retreat has my shoulders unwinding—she doesn't like Hex. This is all an act.

Fuck, she *is* having second thoughts about going along with this, isn't she?

"What do you think of your time in Christmas so far, Prince Hex?" asks a reporter from—I check his badge—*Morning Yuletide Sun,* a Christmas-only tabloid. The press from the wider audience outlets listen in, ready to make sure every Holiday keeps abreast of just what a *big deal* this whole engagement thing is.

Dad lingers, likely wanting to know whatever Hex says to the reporter, so I linger too. From this angle, I can see around the tent to where the sleighs are lined up, stable hands fixing the reindeer in place and double-checking the harnesses.

Hex's jaw works. His hair is pulled back fully, showing how his ears are already red with cold, his cheeks similarly rosy in the downright frigid air.

So when he deadpans, "It's cold," I snort.

He casts a look at me.

I spin away, fascinated by the edge of my glove.

"Halloween can be a chilly time of year as well," the reporter presses.

I feel Hex's eyes on me for one more beat before he shifts to the reporter. "I spend most of my time in Mexico," he says.

"Mexico?" Paper flips as the reporter checks something. "Halloween's presence was strongest in the US, I thought?"

"My mother helps her older brother oversee Día de Muertos," he says. "So I stay down there sometimes to balance her responsibilities. And I—"

Dad swoops in. He lands a hand on Hex's shoulder, rocking him, and my teeth clamp in a punch of protectiveness.

I take a step forward. Iris, with Kris by a space heater in the tent, watches me, but I purposefully don't meet her eyes, fixed intently on Hex and my dad.

"We are eager to show the Halloween Prince all that Christmas has to offer," he says. "Such as this tradition. We'll see how Halloween fares against Christmas!"

I take another step.

Hex's face is mild—except for the sharp pulse of his eyebrows. "I'm not made for cold."

"Will you not be racing, then?" There's all kinds of intention in the reporter's tone.

Hex starts to say *No,* and I watch my dad's grip tighten on his shoulder.

I'm next to them in a heartbeat. "Dad. Wren needs you." Which is probably not a lie, but it's the first thing I can think of and I honestly don't care.

Dad looks down at me.

I'm so aware of his fingers gripping Hex's shoulder that my vision starts to go red.

Dad gives Hex a friendly pat and nods at the reporter. "Of course. Excuse me."

He walks away, snow crunching in his wake, and my eyes are on Hex's coat, the part of it now wrinkled from my father.

My gaze scrambles over the crowd, finds Iris, locks on, and she immediately crosses back over to us. That split second of me wordlessly needing her and her instantly coming is familiar, but guilt sours my stomach. In a situation where she is arguably more victimized than I am, I'm still needing her to step in? God, I'm pathetic.

"Are you not participating in the race, then, Prince Hex?" The reporter is standing next to us. Camera at the ready.

Hex is staring at me. Curious. Wondering, probably, why I'm gasping, why I keep staring at his shoulder, why I haven't said anything to him.

"I was not aware that it was expected of me," Hex finally says.

Iris slides up between us. "Participating in the race isn't *expected,* but think of the scandal if Halloween wins." She links her arm through his, smooths the wrinkled spot on his coat, and I release a shuddering exhale.

Hex considers. His eyes don't leave mine. Is it weird that the reporter is here, that Iris is here, but we're only looking at each other? God, I still haven't *said anything.*

"Are you racing, Princess?" Hex asks her. Again, watching me. "I'll ride with you."

She laughs, that perfected trill. "Not this year, unfortunately."

The air shifts a breath before I can find the sense to look at her.

I see her wide, not-at-all-cordial grin. It's a downright demented *smirk.*

"But you can ride with Prince Nicholas," she announces.

Somewhere deep beneath my self-pity, I know I deserved that.

"Brilliant!" the reporter coos. "The two heirs, racing together!"

A flash of a picture being taken. There's no hiding the stunned shock on my face, so *that* will make for an interesting photo.

I find my voice and moan out what might be a refusal as Hex goes, "All right."

All . . .

. . . right?

Iris beams. "Come. Let's get some cocoa before the race."

Hex blanches. "If you insist."

The shock of his disgust against his fixed docile expression makes the faintest blip of a laugh bubble in me. It's enough that it sends sensation back into my body, freeing me from the single-minded focus that dragged me over here.

As Iris leads him into the tent, she flips a too-pleased-with-herself leer at me.

Oh, the Princess of Easter is *evil*.

Chapter Seven

A few minutes later, an announcer calls for all racers to mount their sleighs, and there's a brief moment of chaos in the tent as a dozen or so people shuffle out into the cold.

Kris tosses the rest of an iced cookie into his mouth and straightens his hat. "See you at the finish line."

"I'll make sure they keep it up for you," I say.

He grabs his stomach and pantomimes laughter. "This guy. *So funny*. Try not to fall off the sleigh laughing."

He says it to Hex. Who has been standing with us as we picked at the buffet, those intense eyes taking in everything around us with silent, patient care.

At Kris's words, Hex sets down his untouched plate of food. "Fall off the sleigh? Is that a true possibility?"

"Coal will not let you fall off," says Iris, punctuating the words at me, and I throw up my hands.

"I make no such promises."

"Is this race . . . safe?" It's a simple enough question, but asked with reservation, it rings with concern that he must not have intended to let slip. He quickly clears his throat.

I don't want to lie to him, but Iris says, "Yes" at the same time Kris goes, "Meh."

She glares at him. "It's *safe*. The whole track is well-lit, and even if you fall, it's in snow."

"Or a tree," Kris mumbles.

Iris swats his arm.

Hex makes a low hum. "I see."

"Racers, to your marks!" the announcer calls a final time.

I draw on every ounce of my seemingly limitless cocky confidence to face Hex and crook my arm for him. "Shall we?"

He studies Iris. The crowd in the tent. The reporters stationed around the stable yard.

"You don't have to," I add, arm dropping, voice coming in a tight gush. "I'm good at getting out of responsibilities. My services are at your disposal."

But Hex shakes his head. "No. I won't back down."

That's . . . loaded. I almost push him, but he waves for me to lead the way.

I trail Kris out of the tent, Hex behind me, and we part ways at the sleighs.

"Remember," I call after my brother. "There's no need to throw a tantrum when you lose. Everyone gets a participation trophy."

Kris smiles sweetly at me in a way that's more unnerving than if he'd snapped back with something cutting.

"The fuck?" I frown at him.

"Oh, I just don't need to exert energy on any more trash-talking. My skills will speak for themselves."

"Yeah—well—damn it. You took the fun out of it."

He laughs and jumps up into his sleigh with a parting middle finger.

I take a second to pat the reindeer attached to mine. Being away at school so much means the actual care and training of our reindeer is left to staff, but when we are here, Kris and I both try to stay involved. And even though this guy didn't lead me to victory last year—or the year before—when he paws at the ground and pushes his nose into my shoulder in recognition, I scratch behind his ears.

"Don't try to butter me up," I mutter, but he nudges me again, and I smirk.

"Which one is this?" Hex is next to me. A respectful distance between us.

"Which one what?"

"The song? Dasher, Dancer—"

I laugh. A fog of steam hits the cold air. "They're not all named after that. We'd have like a dozen reindeer named Blitzen."

"Ah." The redness on Hex's cheeks deepens. Is he . . . embarrassed?

Holy hell, that's cute.

God, I'm in trouble.

I vault up into the sleigh and flip on the space heater that'll make it bearable to be out in the arctic weather.

Hex stays below me for a beat. "They don't . . . this is a race on the *ground*, yes?"

"Oh—god, you thought we were flying?" His reservations make more sense now. "No, I swear. We're forbidden from using magic during the race—ask me how I know."

My cheesy grin does nothing to soothe him, his neutral expression taking on an unamused twist.

I sober. "All four hooves stay on the ground. I promise."

He considers. His lips tighten, the color draining slightly under the way he bites them into his mouth.

"What?" I ask, making a concerted effort to not let my gaze linger on his lips again.

"I'm trying to decide if a promise from you has merit."

"You think I'd lie about the sleigh flying?"

"Yes." No pause. "Are we or are we not contenders in an alliance with Easter?"

My chin jerks back. "And that means I have it out for you during a sleigh race?"

He gives a stiff shrug, and something tugs in my chest.

"You don't think very highly of me, do you? Or is it my Holiday in general?" *Please be my Holiday in general, not just me.*

That would explain why he's acting like being around me is morally offensive, though—he kissed me, realized I'm a disaster of a human being, and passionately regrets it. Awesome. But why did he admit to initiating the kiss at all, then? He didn't have to say anything about it.

What is the point of having a Yale education if I can't figure out shit like this?

Hex's shoulders droop. His eyes cut around again, at the other racers mounted and ready, at the photographers off to the side.

"Your parents went back to—Mexico, was it?" I ask.

Hex nods.

"And they left you here?"

"I can handle Christmas. They're needed back home."

"Is everything okay?"

He looks up at me for another of those long, searching moments. There's a pucker on his face, distaste maybe? But when I give no change in expression, he frowns.

It hits me in a lightning bolt. *Of course* everything *isn't* okay—he was forced here into a possible arranged marriage. But . . . Halloween should be happy about this? God, I don't know how Dad keeps all these lies straight and I go stiff with not being sure what to do with my body.

"It's our yearly summit," he says like he's testing the water for my reaction. "They're more useful there than posing for photos and participating in . . . death races."

"It isn't a death race. But—summit? Shouldn't you be there for that?"

"Not necessarily. There will be dozens of people in attendance from Halloween, and all the autumn Holidays, like my mother's— but the look on your face tells me you have no idea what I'm speaking of. Does Christmas never strategize with the other winter Holidays?"

"We have our noble houses. And Easter, I guess. But we've never really had any other Holidays we'd consider equals."

Hex looks mildly annoyed. "And equality is only measured in joy and assets?"

"That's not what I said."

"But it's what you meant. Christmas has never seen anyone else as an equal, because anyone close to being your equal is deemed a threat first."

"No—that's not—I mean, that's why you're here, isn't it? A *partnership*." But as soon as I say it, my gut sinks. No, he's *not* here because Christmas sees any kindred spirit in his Holiday—it's exactly what

Hex said. Dad views them as a threat, so we're lying to them until we can outmaneuver them.

He sucks in a breath. "Well. The point is, I am here because I can handle this month on my own."

I steady on the edge of the sleigh and bend down. Hex flinches at the sudden close proximity.

But he doesn't move away.

I stretch out my hand. "You aren't here alone. Or at least, you don't have to be."

"You're offering me support?" His tone is flat with skepticism.

I shrug, hand still out towards him. "Why not?"

"We are set up in direct opposition. At the first sign of divided loyalties, you would immediately side with Christmas, and I with Halloween."

I could be imagining things, but I'm starting to realize that he's never actually said he *wants* to win over Iris. He phrases it purely from the angle of the competition itself, with an irritated tone, and I don't know why that seems important, but I cling to it.

"Is that your way of saying, *I'm not here to make friends?*" I ask, cranking up the sarcasm.

That eyebrow of his could cut through solid rock. "You joke, but this situation is complicated, and no, I did not come here to make friends. Thank you, Prince Nicholas, but we both well know where our allegiances stand."

"Fair. You don't trust me, and you don't have to. I get that you're here for shitty reasons and this whole situation is fucked up." I try another smile. "I'm not asking for us to swear fealty to one another above king and country, Prince Hex."

There's a spark in his eyes, a burning ember of amusement he can't fully smother under his annoyance.

My grin widens. "I'm saying we can take it one moment at a time." *One by one by one,* I almost add, almost repeat what he said to me all those months ago, but I can't, *can't* let him know I think about that conversation as much as I do. "Start by letting me help you into the sleigh."

Hex's gaze goes to my gloved hand. "And then?"

I wait until he looks back up at me. The impact of his eyes is quickly becoming a necessity, a tangible, violent connection that feels predatory and consuming, sends a shiver walking dazedly down my spine. Does he look at everyone with this level of intensity? How does he not have trailing worshippers foaming at the mouth for him to glance at them?

There's a moment where I think maybe he realizes the effect his attention has on me. The power he wields, unintentionally or not.

He watches me, a muscle jumping on his cheekbone.

"And then," I echo, "we take off on a merry little death race."

He rolls his eyes.

"I'm kidding. *And then* we take a lovely, brisk sleigh ride that might go fast at points. We don't have to think too far beyond that. Just right now."

My voice lowers, the pressure of his eyes pushing down on my volume until I'm trapped under that destructive intensity. Hex sways closer to hear me, so I hear when he swallows, a sharp click in his throat.

He sniffs. Straightens. "Fine."

He takes my offering. He's wearing black fingerless gloves, totally inappropriate for being in the snow, and I grip his hand and haul him up next to me. He lands in the sleigh and sways as it rocks and I don't get a chance to move, worried he'll topple back over the edge—so he's close, as close as he was in the alley outside the bar.

His body presses the full length of mine, warm and solid in the chill air. He's shorter than me, my chin at his temple, and it puts me at the perfect angle to see the palpitation of a vein that runs down the side of his neck.

I linger. Just enough to *feel* that I linger, and awareness rips through me in a serrated torrent.

My hand spasms around his fingers and I release him with a lurch backwards, putting space between us so abruptly Hex's eyes burst wide in alarm. He doesn't say anything, though, just jerks his hand to his side.

He's made it clear; he doesn't trust me. Doesn't even *like* me.

I will not make his time here harder than it has to be. That includes but is not limited to *drooling on him.* Obviously.

The other sleighs are rolling towards the starting line and I grab the reins and snap to follow.

Hex comes up alongside me. There's a bench seat, but he stands like I do, balancing against our sleigh's curved front with a good foot of distance between us.

Fucking hell, I don't think I've ever been more aware of the space between me and another person in my life. For something that is technically *nothing,* it sure is taking up a lot of room in my thoughts.

Hex breaks the silence first. "So what's the reindeer's name?"

"Oh. Yeah. Sven," I say.

There's a pause.

Then he *laughs.*

I've always been hypnotized by seeing joy on people, and I thought it was because of who I am, a Holiday prince and all, and so I don't usually question it, and just revel in it. When Kris laughs. When Iris laughs. When I crack a joke and they roll their eyes but I know they're grinning.

But the shattering crash of Hex's laugh demands every ounce of my attention so urgently, so *aggressively,* that I have a full-on crisis. It's as deep as his voice, husky and warm, but there's an added layer of roughness to it like he doesn't do it enough and his throat is unfamiliar with the motions.

Every single one of those instances when I thought I was hypnotized by seeing joy on other people, I'd been *searching,* searching specifically for *his* joy. Because now that I've experienced it, it renders all past joy obsolete.

Hex wipes a hand down his face and settles, but a smirk remains on his lips, a slight curl, just there.

"What's so funny?" I ask, winded.

"Really? Sven?" He points across my body, at my brother in the sleigh next to us. "Kristoff?"

"Kristopher."

"No. That's what's funny. Sven. Kristoff. *Frozen?*"

I grin. "Really? *That's* your sense of humor? Disney jokes?"

"You can't deny the coincidence is amusing."

"Yeah, I can, because I'm not eleven."

Hex smiles at me, those full lips slightly crooked. "So the Christmas Prince has no opinion on whether he'd be Elsa or Anna?"

Is he bantering with me? My god, I think this guy is *bantering with me.*

"On your marks," the announcer starts. "Ready—"

I rip off one of my gloves and let a pulse of magic flood my hand with snow. "Let it go, baby," I say, and because I can, I wink, what the hell.

His smirk widens.

Then he sights something on my hand, and that smile freezes.

My nails. My black and orange nails, courtesy of Iris.

"Set—" the announcer bellows.

Reindeer stomp the ground up and down the row, the air misting with their anxious exhales. A few other racers whoop, but most are fixed in the concentration of the race.

I'm fixed on Hex.

On the way those eyes hit me when they rise back up.

"Not exactly Christmas colors," he says. And he sounds winded now too, the same gust of missing air I'd felt when he'd laughed.

But I can't read any emotion on him. Can't discern any teasing or flirting or disdain. He's in such delirious control of himself and it's downright *infuriating.*

"GO!" A starter gun pops, and a dozen sleighs bolt into action.

"Shit." I dust the snow off my palm and slam my glove back on to grab the reins and jolt Sven into action. He darts onto the track, second from last—Kris will never let me hear the end of this if I lose.

Hex grips the edge of the sleigh with both hands, but there's tension in the air now. Again. Did it ever really leave? *Were* we flirting, or am I completely unable to read him?

But there'd been a moment.

A beat where he'd been smiling at me.

"Watch out!" Hex recoils as the sleigh in front of us veers towards an ice patch, and I narrowly avoid it by pulling Sven to the left.

"I got it!" I call back, the wind pelting us with icy cold.

"Are you sure?"

"I've been driving sleighs since I could walk."

We lurch around a turn, taking it maybe a *bit* too fast.

"Since you could walk?" Hex clarifies.

"Don't worry; I've only flipped a sleigh once—"

"*Once?*" Hex shrieks. His attention swings to me, back to the track, and he points frantically. "Branch! *Branch!*"

"I see it!"

"Do you? *Turn—*"

I obey, but I would have turned anyway, throwing us down the next arc of the track. We blow past two more sleighs, finally gaining ground, and I can see my brother up ahead.

I urge Sven faster, and he launches over the packed trail, the sleigh whooshing past evergreens that loom tall against the spotlights illuminating the track. *This* is racing; this is the reprieve, the true prize, this moment of pause, and I steal a glance at Hex.

He's holding on to the edge, one elbow up to shield his face from the bite of the wind, but he—he's smiling.

Oh, it's on now.

I crack the reins. Sven ducks his head and pushes faster, leaving Kris in our snow-dust. My brother shouts something that gets lost in the speed, and I cackle as we pass him.

Up ahead, the track curves to the left, and I know there's a bridge coming up—but I've taken that turn at faster speeds than this.

"Nicholas!" Hex shouts, and it's the first time he's said my name without any loaded title attached to it.

Something like that shouldn't rattle me—but he grabs my arm. He grabs my arm, and he clamps down, and I forget where we are, what we're doing, because he's actively touching me. Through the layers of my sweater and coat, but it's intentional, and my sight temporarily goes blank.

Sven turns, our sleigh careening on the track, and the whole thing dips too far left even for my liking. I yank the reins and at the last second, it rights itself, settling back onto the slick path.

The weight lifts from my arm.

Hex.

I twist to him—

But he's gone.

He fell off the sleigh.

I yank the reins, *hard*. Sven rears up before slowing into a stilted canter but I leap off, the sleigh fishtailing. Horror drives my limbs faster than my brain can make a plan as I slide on the icy track, heart thrashing against my ribs like it's trying to crack one of them.

"Hex!" I scramble back up the path. We have a few seconds, half a minute at most, until my brother catches up to us—if Hex landed on the track, there's no way Kris will be able to stop in time without plowing over him.

Shit, shit, *shit*—

"HEX!" I'm running, eyes scrambling over the road, but there's nothing, no prone body, no swath of black wool.

I spin, and—there. In a bank off the path that leads to one of the massive lights, a shadow has sunk down into the snow.

"*Hex!*" I launch up the hill, tearing through snow like a madman, chest pinching tighter with each passing second of echoing, empty silence.

I drop to my knees in the snow and grasp into the sunken depression. An arm—that's an arm. I pull, pull with everything in me.

And Hex bolts upright and slams a fistful of snow into my face.

My body goes stationary, stuck in the transition from being downright terrified to pummeled by a snowball.

I scrape the snow off and see Hex, red and wind-bitten and *coated* in snow, glaring at me, but it's a light glare, a laughing glare.

"You lied," he says simply, teeth clacking with cold.

"I—" My brain stutters. "I said it wouldn't *fly*—"

"You threw me off the sleigh."

"I did not! That's the risk of sleigh racing!"

"You promised you wouldn't do that."

"I distinctly did *not* make that promise—*Iris* made that promise, and I agreed with Kris, that there's a chance of it happening!" All the adrenaline crashes over me, breaks apart in a listing wave of relief. I can't stop myself—I pat up his arm. "You're all right?"

Hex heaves a sigh. "Pride, wounded. *Freezing.* But fine." He bats snow off his sleeve. "If this is how you treat people to whom you offer support, remind me not to become your enemy."

My hand gets to his shoulder. "But—you're okay?"

Hex tips his head. His hair has broken out of its tie, falling around him in tangles of inky black. "I told you."

"Say it." I don't mean to be demanding, I really don't. I don't mean to feel this way, this uncappable welling of protection, realizing how alone he is in the North Pole, how all the strain and stress in his life right now is totally out of my control to fix. All this magic, and I can't stop what's happening to him.

Hex leans forward, and the angle puts him so close that I can feel the heat of his exhale on my lips, a violent contrast to the cold air. It curls over my tongue, a diaphanous cloud, and even this subtle there-then-gone sizzle of his taste makes my eyelashes flutter.

"I'm all right," he whispers. His gaze shifts through mine, rapid, rattled flickers of those black-lined depths, like he's trying to read me but can't, can't make sense of something.

His eyes. Those eyes. They drop to my lips.

A lightning-fast bounce, then they're up again, and I hadn't known the limits of my own restraint until this moment.

A clatter of hooves breaks us apart. It breaks *him* apart—Hex shoves back and spins a flustered glance at the track.

I'm in a fog. My hand is on his shoulder. We're in a snowbank but my body is all liquid fire. And it's Kris approaching—just Kris, just my brother—but if it'd been anyone else, this position, the energy coming off us in waves, would have been hard to ignore.

Stumbling in the snow, I wobble to my feet and put a full yard between me and Hex.

Kris reins his sleigh up sharp, coasting down the turn before he looks back. "You all right?" he shouts.

I wave him off. "Yeah. Tumbled out. We're good."

Hex digs himself out of the snowbank. I should help him. I can't bring myself to touch him. My hands clench and unclench uselessly at my sides, but Hex doesn't make eye contact, and that drop of awareness feels like a reprimand.

I shouldn't have let it go so far. *I* did that, touched him, hovered, breathing him in—

But he looked at my lips.

You weren't the one who initiated it.

Hex and I claw our way down the snowbank as Kris smacks his reins and bolts off, dipping around our discarded sleigh. Two other riders fly past us before Hex and I are back in, kicking snow off our boots, but I feel the chill of it deep in my bones now.

Neither of us says anything the rest of the ride, and Iris is right; I do drive sedately.

Kris takes the win. I come in second to last. We all clap for Kris and I smile as he gets his photos, and then Dad gets into the pics too, and I can't be the only one who notices that Kris's whole demeanor changes.

Cameras flash.

Iris and Hex are next. A reporter calls for me too. "The two heirs! Photo, photo!"

My body moves, on autopilot since that moment in the snowdrift.

It's all so fake. All of this, every second, it aches with how much of a mockery this is of anything real. But I find myself standing with my front against Hex's back, him positioned towards Iris so I see him in profile, the harsh angle of his jaw, the dusting of snow still on the collar of his coat.

Everything around me reeks of fakeness. Except for him. And it's crushing me, because he's not real either, is he?

He deserves real. He deserves more than what we're doing to him.

Chapter Eight

The library of the Claus Palace is a work of art, it really is. Towering mahogany shelves of books with glinting gold spines are accessible by sliding ladders that rim the dark, cozy walls, with more reasonable-height shelves segregating the room throughout. One end is a massive gray stone fireplace, the mantel decked out with a tiny porcelain Christmas village, and cushioned chairs and a table are set in front of it, loaded with a relaxed dinner spread of all the Christmas trimmings.

Roast beef and juicy ham and candied sweet potatoes and cranberries broiled over triple cream brie all combine to assault me with a sweet, savory barrage of dinners of Christmas past. Like that smell alone could cocoon me up and transport me to this exact dinner when I was a kid, when I hadn't seen beyond the magic yet and could still be consumed by it.

We had a break between the end of the race and dinner. I showered and changed into a Christmas sweater that looks like it's stripes of holly and candy canes, but on closer inspection it's rows of red and green robots blasting each other to bits—I don't know where Kris finds these things. I'd hoped freshening up would cleanse what happened, but I'm stuck in some kind of *Groundhog Day,* which is borderline treasonous, given that that's not even sort of a Holiday I have any dominion over. But here I am again, feeling like I messed up things with Hex; here I am again, not knowing how to apologize, knowing I need to.

Kris drops into a chair next to me and takes a gulp from his drink. Beer in a wine glass. We're chic. "So. That sleigh ride was. Something."

I pick at the plate of food I'd grabbed before giving up and shoving it onto a nearby end table. Shit, I must really be morose if Renee's cooking is losing its appeal.

This isn't a formal dinner. Dad even opted out—something about overseeing a new reserve tank for the Merry Measure; it's *overflowing* with joy, he'd been sure to say, loudly, as we left the stable yard. So the people milling around now—some of our court, not everyone; more intimate—eat as they like, chat idly.

Hex might not come.

Iris joins us, licking brown sugar sauce from a spoon. "I'm going to poach Renee from you one day."

I don't react to that. Not to what Kris said either. Kris and Iris share a look and pivot to me more purposefully and shit, I do need new friends.

"What'd you do?" Iris asks.

"Nothing." I swing on her. "I thought you were on my side, Iris. I *told you* what I needed from you."

I hear my words as I say them, and my eyes roll shut on a pained wince. I shouldn't be asking anything of her. I should be trying to win her trust—did I ever really have it?—to get her to tell me what she's thinking now and if she wants out of this whole arrangement. Because if she does want out, I—

—don't actually know what I'd do. Throw some kind of gigantic hissy fit at the next event? Set up a stupid prank where I figure out a way to melt the ice skating rink or put permanent dye in cookie frosting so everyone's mouths are green for a month? Yeah, that'll help.

She bats the spoon at me. "I changed my mind once I saw the way he looked at you."

That's more distracting than if she'd socked me in the throat. "He looked at me? How did he look at me? Wait, no, god—*Iris.*"

I sink back into the overstuffed armchair, shaking my head, wanting so badly to make a joke out of this. But it's not funny. At all.

She balks. "You're actually angry."

I bolt forward, so aware of the people nearby—there's only one reporter, this one from *Christmas Inquirer.* He snaps a few not-exactly-covert photos of me and Iris, and even though the conversation we're having is basically an argument, the headlines will be shit like *Prince Nicholas and Princess Iris cozy up over a quiet firelit dinner; will she choose him over Prince Hex?*

I glare at the reporter long enough that he shifts uncomfortably and swivels his attention to a member of the Christmas court.

"Yeah, I'm mad," I say to Iris. "This is already a shitty situation for all of us and I cannot mess it up more. He doesn't deserve this, *you* don't deserve this, and I won't—"

Iris's eyes snap over my shoulder. "Prince Hex."

I lurch to my feet, startling her backwards, and spin to see Hex, far enough away that I know he didn't hear anything, but close enough that my body shakes with him being in the same room as me.

The gold firelight pulses across him. He's in a black button-up and black pants with his black boots, a short black tie hanging around his neck, a simple yet effective display of his Holiday in one color. His hair is pulled back again, showing the strain in his jaw when his eyes meet mine.

But he looks down at Iris. "Princess."

"Help yourself." She waves at the table by the fire.

He crosses the room to the food. Taking a longer route, circling around, to avoid coming too close to me, moving with such graceful intent that the air around him barely rustles.

Iris tugs on my hand. "What did you *do*?"

"One of them fell off the sleigh," Kris whispers at her.

"*What?*" She yanks on my arm and I drop back into the seat. "Coal! You let him fall off?"

"I didn't . . . no, I did, I definitely did."

"Is that all? He feels angrier than that."

I cut a glare at Kris before he can say anything. My brother lifts his hands. "I saw nothing."

Iris pokes my chest. "What. Did you. *Do?*"

"*Nothing.*" I grab her wrist and drop my voice so low I'm not sure she'll hear me. "I did *absolutely nothing,* and that feels like *everything,* and I don't know what to *do*, Iris. I needed you to keep me away from him, goddamn it—"

Her eyebrows bend. "Oh my god, Coal. You've got it *bad*."

"You need to talk to him," Kris says. "Clear this up."

"Talking to him doesn't tend to go well."

"Figure it out." Kris bumps my shoulder. "It's a long month. You can't avoid him. The palace isn't *that* big, and this tension is gonna get old fast."

The strain on my face is a full-on conversation with no words spoken.

Oh, THIS tension is gonna get old? What about the tension between you and Iris, HMMMM? What about THAT tension, that we've been living with for YEARS, brother of mine?

Kris ducks his head, swirling the beer around his wine glass in silent surrender.

But honestly. He's right. This month will be hard enough on all of us without me making every interaction worse.

I drop my head into my hands. Then quickly realize how that looks to everyone else around and sit up, but I hate that too, I can't properly freak out in my own *home* because lord forbid someone might *see*.

Hex is at the table, eyeing the food, an empty plate in his hands.

I surge to my feet.

Pause.

Then lean over Kris like I'm going to whisper something to him, and at the last second, I go, "Ball tag," and hit him in the groin.

"*Shit*—" He rocks forward with a suppressed groan.

I walk away, my steps a little lighter, as Iris sighs defeatedly and mutters something about not knowing why she's even friends with two idiot white boys.

I refocus on Hex, and I know he feels my gaze on him because he turns to me seconds before I stop next to him.

"Prince Nicholas," he says.

"Coal," I correct.

His lips twitch. "Coal."

"Can we talk?"

"Aren't we?"

"Not here."

"In . . . private?" Hex pushes his chin over my shoulder, at the guy from *Christmas Inquirer*.

Ah. Yeah. Iris's two supposed suitors sneaking off to talk? It was headline-grabbing enough that we were in a sleigh together; this is downright *scandalous*.

I look around. "Four rows back. By the window. In five minutes? We can stagger."

As soon as I say that, I hear how *much* it sounds. Like I'm planning some secret tryst. *Which I definitely am not.* But talking candidly in Claus Palace requires feats of insanity.

And this guy makes me want to be insane.

But Hex sets down his plate. "Five minutes."

My gut twists, pulse detonating like fireworks, *this is not a tryst.* "Good."

I spin on my heels and duck across the room before I can think better of all this.

I could try to avoid him for the next few weeks. It'd been my original plan—to not get anywhere near him so I didn't make a fool of myself. But apparently I'm destined for that fate no matter what I do, so might as well be up-front about it.

The bulk of the library is silent and dim, the light from the fireplace in the sitting area creating a cozy atmosphere. I weave through shelves, deeper into the narrowing embrace of books on Christmas's past and traditions and lore, and I realize this was a huge mistake, because the flickering, distant firelight is romantic. By the time I reach the far wall, looming windowpanes showing the arctic scene swathed in starlight and navy blue–black sky, I've talked myself out of all this.

I'll go to my room. He'll know I chickened out but I'll save us both the embarrassment of whatever dumb thing I'll do next.

But I don't go.

I stay, because the books in this row are judging me.

Kris and I had private tutors up until we hit our teenage years. And these books are well worn with our fingerprints—the history of Christmas. Our family. Past Santas, dozens of them, all leading back, back, back to the origin of the Clauses. How all this started because one guy wanted to spread cheer among his village during the deepest, darkest part of winter, so he became famous for leaving secret gifts and mysterious acts of charity to crack joy into a time of year that used to be deadly and miserable.

I'd *loved* that story.

Another memory comes charging out in full Technicolor— shortly after Dad had taken me on that brief training introduction where he'd showed me the globe, he'd asked me what we were learning about in our studies.

I'd exploded all over him about our origins. *"Isn't it awesome? We're destined to do that too! We bring joy to the whole WORLD!"*

I'd been, maybe, seven? Seven and bright-eyed and Mom hadn't left yet, and so Dad was bright-eyed too. I remember him bending down to me and *smiling*—I haven't seen that smile in years, maybe since then.

He'd put his hand on my head. *"I'm proud of you. You're taking all this to heart."*

My throat gets tight and I shake it off with a sniff.

Shit, I'm melancholy tonight. It's the damn dinner smells—leave it to the olfactory sense to conjure up the worst nostalgia. That part of my brain is aching with how all these triggered memories— childhood dinners and unadulterated excitement and learning about Christmas—are a lost golden age I'll never reclaim. But the rest of me *knows,* fucking *knows,* I'm romanticizing it. These memories only feel idyllic because I hadn't been able to comprehend reality at the time.

That's really the golden age, isn't it? That's what my brain is longing for, a time when I only saw the sparkle. A time when I loved this unabashedly because I hadn't realized that the sparkle was a distraction layered over a complex concept full of cracks and mold, and the day you see beyond the glitter for the first time is the day you officially grow up, no going back.

I feel a presence to my right, at the end of this aisle, and I turn to Hex.

We're in beams of muted firelight that cut through the shelves, the hazy ivory hue of stars from the windows behind me. The crowd is a muffled background noise, giving further gravity to how alone we are now, and I groan.

"I keep doing this," I admit.

He glances over his shoulder, and with a flick of his hand, rings glinting, he lets a burst of magic fly. Holiday magic takes on the traits associated with the joy that produces it; some of Christmas's manifests in snow and lights and creating silly little gifts or candy. So it makes sense that Halloween is *this* but intensified, shadows and mystery with an edge of spookiness. Hex uses it to coat the end of this row in a heavier sheet of darkness, giving us privacy should anyone come near where we are.

"Doing what, exactly?" he asks.

Is he going to make me say it? Well, that's why I asked to talk with him, isn't it? To *say* all this, to get on the same page, once and for all, and *stick to that page even if it kills me.*

I hang my head into my hands and rip my fingers back through my curls, sending them springing around my face. "Okay. Look. I'm sorry. Again. I have a problem, it seems, and even though I promised I wouldn't put you in that situation again, I did."

Hex sips in a breath. It's so faint I barely hear the scratch of it on his throat.

"I don't want to make things awkward for you," I say. "I keep— *ugh,* god, I can't even *say* what I keep doing because I feel like that will make things awkward for you more, and I'm misreading all these things from you and building them up in my head to mean something they *don't.* You're having a hard enough time being . . . being used as a marriage pawn. I don't want to make it harder on you."

I barely say the last few words. My lungs are swelling shut. Closing, closing, because he *isn't a marriage pawn,* he's a straight-up *pawn,* and Hex stands there, thumbs in his pockets, eyes narrow in silent consideration, totally unaware of how much we're screwing over him and his Holiday.

His brows pulse together. The only change on his impossibly pulled-together front.

"You aren't making it harder on me," he says.

I rock forward. "Ha. Sure. I threw you from a sleigh. I almost let my brother see us . . . close. And now! All I wanted was to talk to you, and *look where I had us go*." I point at the starlit sky and the rolling hills of ivory and the cozy bookshelves and the pulsing light of a crackling fire like all of it is solely responsible for being so picturesque that we might as well be standing in a romance novel.

One edge of Hex's lips lifts. Is he smiling?

I will not survive you smiling, so help me—

"Your palace lends itself to a certain atmosphere," he says. "That's hardly your fault."

I point at him. "No. No. Don't make light of this—you should be mad at me."

"I should?"

"Yes!"

"Why?"

"*Why?*"

He frowns. "That tone *will* serve to get me angry with you. I'm not an idiot. Don't speak to me as such."

And he talks like a poet, a cadence in his words that's half song.

It cracks my chest apart. Decides something for me that I hadn't known was an option.

"It's a lie," I say.

Hex's frown deepens. "That I'm not an idiot? Excuse me?"

"No! No." I step closer. Too close for how I know I have to cap myself, but my hands are shaking and if I don't say this now, I'll combust. "Your presence here, this competition over Iris. It's a lie. I'm set up to marry her regardless of what happens, which is a whole other story because neither of us wants it at *all*—that doesn't matter, what matters is we're moving forward with that alliance. You're just here to appease Halloween—"

"I know."

I go stiff. Bend towards him. "You . . . know? Know what, exactly?"

Hex steps around me, moving to the window, as far from the fire and other guests as he can get. He stops at the cold glass and folds his arms, gazing out at the tundra.

He looks back at me.

I stumble after him and steady against the window, facing him, but he stares out at the ice and snow and stars.

"I know this competition is fake," he says to the glass. It fogs with his breath. "I am, as I said, not an idiot."

"How—how? When?"

"All my life. My parents knew from an early age that I wouldn't be an idiot—"

"Not that." My voice drops. Normally, I would be losing my mind that he's teasing me—but I need him to explain, now, I'm on the edge of one of those hills out there, seconds away from toppling end over end into a dark, icy expanse.

Hex's jaw swells below his ear, and I'm caught on the knot of tension as he stays pointedly looking outside.

"After the Halloween envoys returned," he says.

"*That long?* You've known for that long, and you still came here? Why?"

"A few hours after the conversation they had with your father, another message was sent over—a *stronger ultimatum,* your father called it. He would push through the marriage between his son and the Easter Princess"—he doesn't look at me, every word laid out carefully, every movement composed—"and Halloween would be *kept in line* while it happens."

"What?" An electric current of shock zaps through me. "He—he threatened you?"

He gives another easy shrug, but I'm starting to see that these acts of supposed dismissal are deeply meaningful for him—whereas I flail around at the slightest spurt of emotion, he keeps such a tight lid on his reactions that even a shift of his head, a pulse of his eyebrows, is a sign that he's restraining himself with everything he has.

"Not directly," he says.

"How? Why? He doesn't—we don't—" I cut myself off, too many words trying to get out. I palm my face and breathe before looking at Hex's profile. "Tell me. Please."

But he responds with a question. "How much of the world's joy does Christmas monopolize?"

The pivot has me shaking my head. "Um—fifty-seven percent, last I checked." And by *checked* I mean heard my father raving about it.

Hex's eyes, finally, slide to mine. "More than half. In a single Holiday. And with Easter now too, stretching out from just one segment of the year? Christmas has almost endless resources. A relentless grasp on the world. And there are things, even in our society of joy and goodness, that can become threats. This competition is a cover to make my presence here acceptable."

There is no air in this room, in the space between our bodies, and I steady myself on the window ledge, bearing down on it for dear life.

"You're our prisoner," I state.

Hex convulses. "That's a bit overstating things—"

His eyes dip to the side. Surprise breaks his severity.

I follow his gaze.

To see that I've blasted ice across the glass, down the wall, a sheet of sparkling, geometric frost spreading out beneath the tense fingers with black and orange nails.

I yank away, staring at my hand in disbelief.

Hex is studying me. Again, still, maybe he's always studying me, always watching my reaction and assessing options and planning, analyzing. He has to be, doesn't he? If all this is a bigger scheme than I knew.

He must be exhausted.

"What is he threatening you with if Halloween doesn't go along with this?" I ask.

Hex's surprise shifts into . . . awe. "You honestly don't know."

He should be furious, hurt, raging at me, but he's looking at me in this stunned wonder and I can't make it fit with anything we've said. He has no reason to look at me like that.

"Of course I don't know," I snap, but not at him, not at *him,* and he seems to understand, because he lets me fall apart and doesn't flinch. "I don't know anything, apparently. I didn't know that Christmas was in the business of making threats so potent that other Holidays would willingly concede to any demand and send us a *prisoner* as *collateral*—"

"I'm not a prisoner, Coal. It isn't as—"

"Can you go back home of your own free will without something awful happening?"

His lips stiffen.

"So you are." I'm shaking. "A prisoner. We have *a prisoner.* And it's *you*—and I was—*oh my god*—"

Feeding into the tension between us was bad enough when I thought we were lying to him about competing for Iris.

But now that I know he's trapped here—and I was *coming on to him*—

"Oh my god," I can't say anything else, hands going into my hair, "oh my god, I'm so sorry—I'm—"

I drop to my knees.

I can't hold myself up anymore.

And I don't deserve to, I don't deserve to stand there and have him watching me with *empathy,* like he should in any way feel bad for me, not after everything we've put him and his Holiday through.

"You deserve so much more than *this,*" I say to his legs. "You and Halloween both. And Iris too, because *fuck.* We should not be treating any of you this way; my father was . . . he's insane. I'll fix this. I'll—"

"I did not tell you to get you to fix this," Hex says. Is it a whisper? I barely hear him speak, and I sit on my heels to look up at him.

His profile is washed gray-white in starlight, the other side sheathed in darkness, his lips softly parted. His arms are still crossed, but his fingers are arched and tense against his elbows, the lines of his body taken from lax resignation to something razor-edged and alert. It makes me so aware of the fact that I'm on my knees before him that a bolt of effervescent lightning spiderwebs from my head down to my gut and pins me in place.

"The deal Halloween has with your father is under control," he says, his usual detached tone marred by hesitation. "If you are unaware of the details, all the better, honestly. You don't need to be involved. You don't need to fix anything."

"But we're better than this," I tell him. "Christmas is better than this. And I will not let my father ruin Halloween. I won't let him *touch* you, ever again. I promise."

I make jokes. I'm a smartass. I don't talk like this, with weight, but every second of a life spent being the comedic relief has been saving up sincerity for him.

Hex's arms drop from around his chest, rip down like some invisible force jerked him open.

He's quiet for a long, agonizing moment, his face unreadable.

"Trying to decide if a promise from the disreputable Christmas Prince has merit?" I ask, and I smile, but this has smothered any joy I could have clung to—

Hex falls to the ground in front of me.

Something deep beneath my belly button wrenches, hard.

I surge up to match him, balancing on my knees. There's maybe two inches of space between us, and my breath comes in a pinched gasp, disbelief and apology and unworthiness all lassoing around my neck so I hold there, strung in place.

He smells like sweet oranges with a hit of something spicy, a living version of this cocktail Renee made one year, a cinnamon bourbon old-fashioned with brûléed oranges. Burnt sugar and heat from the spice and sunshine brightness in the citrus, it makes my mouth water, but I am stationary. I exist in this moment to be at his will, the spark of his exhale on my tongue.

"I do not expect you to fix this," he tells me again.

I almost promise I will. I almost promise him everything. I'm jerked back and forth between reality and wishes and I'm getting intoxicated on the way the air tastes like him.

"It is *my* job to protect my Holiday and the people who depend on it"—he's talking faster; he's unhinging, and I feel like I'm privy to something holy in watching him lose control—"and it is *your* job to protect yours. I can take care of myself. Do not risk your responsibilities for me."

I can't promise that.

But he doesn't make me.

"I can take care of myself," he repeats, and I finally clock what that softness in his tone is: he's nervous.

The reverberations of a moan rattle in my chest moments before it splinters the air. It silences him.

A sway forward, a plunge, and he kisses me—again.

All it takes is him closing that distance and the lightest swell of his mouth against mine, and I grab the back of his neck and devour him. I've been starving, for a year and a half, I've been living in a suspended state of hunger, all normal appetite wrecked by one single drunken kiss. And it was so *dumb,* wasn't it? To be obsessed with *one kiss*; so I'd ignored it and carried on because he was gone, he was basically a figment of a drunken dream, and I'd never get that kiss again. I'd have to learn to live without it. Without him. To be okay going back to grays and beiges when I now knew that the world could exist in magenta and aquamarine and violent auburn.

But he's *here.* His lips are on mine again, no alcohol fog, no uncertainty about who initiated it or who wants it. I'm ravenous and he is my only satisfaction, his lips separating for my tongue, the taste of him minty and hemmed in that spicy-orange smell and it is vital, *vital* that I re-memorize every divot of his lips. And I'm absolutely shredded in two, half curling with desire; half knowing I'm well and truly fucked.

One kiss from him damn near shattered me, and that was when I was able to play it off as something I'd built up in my head. But now that I know his lips feel as perfect as I'd been imagining, that all of this is as effortlessly cataclysmic as I'd hoped and feared?

Scalded. Ruined. Eviscerated.

I make a completely unselfconscious whine of greed and with it almost comes a tidal wave of stuff that's theatrically poetic but batshit to say to someone I hardly know. Things like, *I've missed you, I know that's insane, we're barely friends* and *Tell me you've thought about me a fraction as often as I've thought about you, even just once* and *Please, please,* begging for way more than I have any right to.

I get some grip on myself and peel back enough to fill his mouth with, "You taste as good as I remember."

A little gasp escapes him, but in the second where his shock might give way to discomfort—was that still too forward? Probably, fuck—he echoes that greedy whine, *echoes* it, a resonant warble high in his throat.

He pushes into me and bites at my tongue and I mewl in his mouth, hand clenching at the base of his hair, riding the motion of his chest forming against mine. I grab onto the ridges of his spine, arching over him, feeling the bow of his ribs as I bend him backwards, and I think I could lay us out on the floor, I think he'd let me. But the mere thought of that has me so painfully aware of the way our hip bones align, the hard connection where each inch of our bodies touches, that I have to break the kiss and gasp for air.

I rock my forehead to his, noting his fingers twisted in the front of my sweater, knuckles white in the low light, pale, pale skin against the silvery black of his rings.

He didn't tell me what it is my dad has over him and his Holiday. I start to ask him again, but I don't want it here, in the air with us both on our knees, so I nip at his mouth and feel, see, taste the way he smiles. He runs one hand up my arm, across my shoulder, and touches my neck. That millimeter of skin on skin makes me forget my damn name.

"Coal!"

I tense. Hex shoves back, but my arms stay around him, one of his hands stays knotted up in my sweater.

"Coaaaal," Iris singsongs, her heels clacking on the library's polished wood floor. "They want pictures before the night ends. Are you back here . . . reading? You should *read* later."

She's walking slowly, talking *loudly*. Giving us warning.

Hex climbs to his feet, grabbing onto the window ledge, leaving a handprint in the melting frost I made. My own hands fall limp in my lap, and I hold there for one long, rattling breath before I can stand.

He bats his fingers and the shadow wall falls. No word, nothing at all, and he walks away, angling for another row of shelves.

"Wait—" I shoot after him but he twists a look back that holds me in place.

His cheeks are flushed and his hair is ruffled—I did that, *I did that*—and he's *smiling* at me, and I want to grin back. The urge rises.

But all I can see are the shackles we have on him. Those words dragging him down, *threat* and *kept in line*.

"Good night, Coal," he says, and he darts off into the shadows as Iris slides to the entrance of this row.

I run my hand across my open mouth, but there is no schooling my expression now, no restraining the way the past few minutes have unmade me.

When I show Iris my face, she goes from coy to shocked in two seconds.

"What happened?" she asks, eyes launching around, but he's gone, and I'm fuming.

"Tell the reporter to shove his camera up his ass," I say as I move around her. "I need to talk to my father."

Chapter Nine

I head back through the library. Kris sees me, bolts up from his chair, but I give one solid shake of my head.

This is between me and Dad.

I rush through the palace to his office, knowing he'll be there. Hoping he'll be there. I don't know how long this anger hurricane will carry me before I hit a wall of exhaustion.

It was bad enough that I didn't know who Hex was at the bar. That I didn't recognize him, because why would Prince Coal, irresponsible wild child, need to worry about shit like the monarchs of a Holiday he'd never interact with? I left all that stuff to Dad.

Because the one time I tried to do anything real, I messed up to epic proportions.

But now. Not knowing the real reason Hex is here because I left all this stuff to Dad, *again*—

When I do get involved, shit blows up. When I don't get involved, shit *blows up.* So what the fuck is the solution? I don't know. I don't know, but I'm going, and that's the only choice I can see right now.

My heart is bruised from rocking against my ribs, each breath feeling like knives in my chest. I reach Dad's office, a few doors down from the Merry Measure, which is locked up tight now behind thick doors and a wall of protective magic. Dad's office, on the other hand, has the door cracked open, a light on within, and I shove inside without pretense.

It's a nice office. Homey and cozy, woodsy and warm, hung with holly and ivy and the same façade of Christmas cheer that makes me woozy now. Especially when I see him at his huge mahogany desk, bent over a stack of papers, glasses on the tip of his nose like he's the embodiment of the visage we're both supposed to live up to.

"He's our *prisoner*?" My voice cuts through the crackling of the fire in the far wall.

Dad lifts his head, peeking at me over the rim of his glasses. "Nicholas?"

I slam the door behind me and stomp into the middle of the room, pulse flurrying in my wrists, my neck.

I can still taste Hex.

Still feel his spine under my fingers.

"Our Halloween guest," I say. "You're not keeping him here on the promise of an alliance with Easter; you're keeping him here under threat of hurting his Holiday. We—"

"Who told you that?" Dad's eyes narrow.

Oh.

Oh, that was *dumb*.

Hex told me that in confidence, and what do I do? Immediately run to my dad and shatter that confidence with a sledgehammer.

"I—" *Lie, fucking lie, through my teeth, through my ears, through every fucking orifice.* "I overheard him talking on the phone. To his parents, I think. Did I hear wrong? Because it sure as hell sounded like we have a *prisoner*." *Don't just lie; deflect. Put this all on Dad, where it should be.* "How many other prisoners do we have? Is there a dungeon somewhere I should know about?"

Dad rolls his eyes, like *that's* crossing the line, but he buys my explanation and I stifle relief as he tosses his glasses onto his desk. "The Halloween Prince will be sent home after you and Iris are finalized. I am surprised by your reaction—his presence here is largely unchanged from the story you know. This is the reality of our position. Of *your* position, someday. We have to keep certain people in line."

I'm coming to really, really hate that phrase.

But then my gut bottoms out. "Certain people? Who else?"

The question feels like a door opening. All of this evening has been a door opening, honestly, a door that opened and I stepped through and there's no going back now.

Dad considers for a moment. Then he stands.

"Are you ready to ask that question? I'm not sure you are."

A well of resolve gushes through me, and I draw on the pieces of me still reeling over what happened in the library.

I've been passive for way too long. But my version of stepping up is disastrous—*this* is disastrous, though, too. So maybe that's exactly what we need, my version of disastrous to break whatever is happening.

I look at the floor. The red-patterned rug.

When I face my father again, my gaze is level, echoing his calm.

"I messed up," I start. "With New Koah. With so many other things. I know I messed up, but if I'm going to do this someday, then I should know *how* to, more than staged training for press shots. I should know what you're doing there"—I point at whatever papers he's going over—"and I should know how Christmas's inner workings operate and what you're planning so I can help it move forward rather than hinder it. I want to be a part of it."

It isn't a lie. It's so very much *not* a lie that I have to grit my teeth, hard, to keep from gasping, these words like a cork zooming off a bottle and here come all the desires I've been suppressing. How I want to be worthy of this legacy, the *original* legacy, an overexcited seven-year-old boy who thought his father wanted him to help bring joy to the world. How I want to *improve* this legacy, for what we do to *mean something* more than small fleeting moments, something lasting and real and—

Dad gives me a look of honest surprise. For once, I don't try to hide the truth, don't make a joke before someone else can.

Holding back makes my chest ache; I'm stripped raw.

Silently, Dad moves to a filing cabinet next to his desk. He shuffles through it for a second and pulls out a manila folder before he faces me, one more cursory stare.

"This is a test."

"Yes."

"You have failed far too many tests. The trainings I have arranged for you. Every opportunity to step up during events. Everything I've given you."

"I know."

"Do not abuse the knowledge I share with you. Hopefully, through seeing this, you will come to understand the full breadth of what Christmas can be."

That small part of me springs up with hope again. That stupid, childish hope that he'll prove himself better. That he'll reveal some master plan that makes everything he's done okay, and he'll be *Santa,* like he should be, like I thought he was once.

He extends the folder to me. I take it, flip it open, and start scanning through the handful of pages within. There are entries dated in the past decade or so, percentages, and the word *Tithe,* over and over, next to repeating names. The list of those names grows, until I shift to the latest entries.

Yule.

Thanksgiving.

New Year.

And more, more Holidays I recognize as happening in and around Christmas. All next to the word *Tithe,* and percentages, and those percentages fluctuate sometimes, larger some years, growing—10 percent, to 15, to 30 and 40.

"What is this?" I ask, tongue dry.

"Joy tithes. These Holidays send a percentage of their accumulated joy to Christmas in exchange for being under Christmas's umbrella."

Our umbrella? But—"These are massive percentages. What kind of *umbrella* would be worth this? Why would they agree to these amounts?"

Dad gives a smile that doesn't reach his eyes. "It is a sad reality of any successful enterprise to have to, as I said, keep certain people in line so events unfold to the betterment of all. These Holidays were . . . persuaded to sign contracts with us for their own best interests."

If all these Holidays—and there are more than a dozen—were brought on under whatever the fuck *persuasion* means. Then . . .

My mind scrambles, fighting through the math.

Christmas gets more than *three-quarters* of our joy from *other Holidays.*

All the joy we claim to have. All the happiness we claim to spread to the world—we're stealing it from other winter Holidays. And then using it to spread Christmas's influence further, so it touches more areas of the world than *any other Holiday.*

Well, no shit we can go further than any other Holiday.

"And after you marry Iris." Dad slides a paper onto the folder in my hands. It's a chart showing Easter's joy, how it will fit in with Christmas's.

My eyes climb to his.

He's smiling.

"Why?" I hear myself ask.

"Why? Why." Dad chuckles, but there's no humor in it. "You yourself pointed out the way Christmas is currently viewed—cheap trinkets, I believe you said? That is an unfortunate side effect of needing to ration our magic for expansion, but it was once our whole reputation. Gifts, nothing more. Greed. We *are* capable of more than that. Every Holiday is. Celebrations worldwide have become so commodified as to be degrading, and the joy we bring is *the* joy that the world needs. Christmas is, at its core, a Holiday of family and belonging, and that is the magic we will foster once we have solidified our global hold."

I stare at him, willing this to congeal. Because I *agree* with him, don't I? We want the same thing.

But not like this.

My shocked silence must come off as encouragement, because Dad carries on.

"All the Holidays who tithe to us are on their way out," he says, nodding at the file. "Their joy decreasing steadily, their offerings cheapened and broken down by capitalism. They are slipping into the obscurity that has come for far too many Holidays in the past. I saw the same happening to Christmas, and rather than let this shift whittle away at us, I took action. These other Holidays now contribute their fading joy to keep Christmas going rather than let their demise happen senselessly, and we will use their tithed joy to give the world a type of Holiday that has been missing for far too long."

Holidays come and go. That's a reality of our world. Traditions change, and what was once a celebration of a god becomes a celebration of a harvest, evolving with the ways people grow; or forcibly, with colonization. And while the Holidays listed in Dad's file *have* waned, they aren't in any way *slipping into obscurity,* and neither is Christmas, not by a long shot.

They're failing *now,* though, because of Dad's demanded tithes.

Holidays fade over time.

But they fade through natural human changes, not *another Holiday overtaking them.*

I wondered once what it would take for that little bit of childish hope inside of me, the belief that my dad once cared about Christmas bringing true happiness, to finally die.

I know now.

All my muscles lock up, thoughts scattered and slippery. "Why—" My voice croaks. "Why would any of these Holidays agree to this?"

"We may all be based in joy, but at the core, each Holiday is a business. And those businesses run, sometimes, on things like information. You know well how important Christmas's reputation is. We are not the only Holiday with something we are willing to go to great lengths to keep balanced."

"You've been blackmailing them," I say. It's a fist slamming into my gut, a burst of air popping between my lips. "You've got dirt on them, and you're demanding joy in exchange for keeping whatever it is under wraps."

"Hardly. These are business arrangements. Contracts. A trade in all of our best interests."

Except for the Holidays who will eventually be bled dry by Dad's *best interests.*

But there's something I'm not seeing. A piece not connecting, and I let myself frown, concern breaking through my unease. "How does Halloween factor into this?"

Oh no. He wants to branch out from manipulating only winter Holidays. He wants Halloween too.

"They had their chance to be a part of our progression," Dad says.

"They chose to step aside. To their detriment—they will see they chose wrong."

"Wait. You *had* considered merging—acquiring—whatever, with *Halloween?* When?"

Dad gives me an even look, analytic and calm, and after a minute of considering, he inhales with a decisive nod. "Years back. It was not made public as it barely made it past a preliminary inquiry from them, but they were also the ones who rapidly backed out once they learned that their autumn allies were vehemently opposed to a union with Christmas. They have been kept docile by the mere threat of news of that clandestine deal becoming public with their allies, and at the time, we had other Holiday arrangements to firm up"—he waves at the list—"so we did not pursue them in their indecisiveness, and they do not find themselves in quite the same boat of decreasing joy as these Holidays."

In other words, they were too big to take on, so Dad let them continue unmolested.

"But we have solidified our position among the winter Holidays now," he continues, "and it is time we begin branching out. We chose to focus on Easter, as—"

"Oh my god." A shudder runs up through my body. I manage to stop myself from exploding at the last moment, a tight, painful swallow, until all that comes out is, "You *persuaded* Easter too?"

Dad gets my meaning and gives my slip of emotion a tight look. "No, Nicholas. Easter did not need to be *persuaded;* they have always been among our friends. The arrangement with them is mutually agreed upon. They entered into it willingly. It was Halloween's vocal objection to that union that had to be met with action."

"With action. With a *threat,* you mean."

"Halloween is the one who moved first. Their autumn allies would see it as an immeasurable breach of trust that they had ever considered joining with us, and they would pull their support. You act as though this arrangement I have with the winter Holidays is unique and heartless; Holidays have been trading joy for centuries. Halloween is no different with their own allies."

I stare at him, recalling the conversation I had with Hex before the sleigh race, where he'd talked about Halloween meeting with other autumn Holidays. No part of what he said had sounded at all like Dad's single-minded rampage for joy, and I cannot get what I've seen of Hex so far to fit in with someone who'd be okay taking magic so backhandedly.

"That Halloween felt they could have any say in *Christmas's* business without repercussion could not go unaddressed," Dad says. "The situation as you know it is to remind Halloween that *they* chose to upset the balance. I could easily let news of our prior negotiations spread to their allies—but instead I made sure that the stories being printed paint Christmas as having conceded to Halloween in their objections, and playing host to their prince as he courts Princess Iris is a mark of our public apology. Even at the end, when we still win the Easter alliance, they will get to run back to their allies the victim, solidified in distrusting us, but heroes for attempting to swipe Easter out from under us. We will have the Christmas-Easter union, unopposed. Everyone will have what they want."

My head throbs with fighting to see through all Dad's political doublespeak to get to the root of what he actually *did*.

That was why he was so weird when the Halloween envoys arrived at the palace a while back. He was *intentionally* groveling to them—or as close to groveling as he ever gets—in front of the press in order to start laying the groundwork for this lie.

When he sent his real threat later, that Halloween would be *kept in line,* they had no choice, did they? They could have refused, but then it would have looked like they were the ones being assholes when Christmas had more or less bowed to what Halloween wanted; but refusing would also have given Dad permission to let slip this dirt he has on them.

It wasn't enough that he threaten them into silence again with his blackmail shit; he wanted to *punish* them. To make sure they know not to mess with Christmas.

My jaw cracks as I pry it open. "And the only way to do all this is to have a *live person* trapped in our palace?"

"He is not trapped, Nicholas. He is free to come and go as he wishes. But he came here willingly, and his court agreed to this knowing it was a faux-engagement from the start."

"Because the alternative was you leaking the previous Christmas-Halloween negotiations to their allies. That's *blackmail*."

I say the word like a plea. *Don't be like this. Please.*

Dad yanks the folder out of my hands. His face darkens, and the temperature of the room goes frigid, my breath suddenly a visible cloud on the air. I fight to keep from backing up a step.

"That is the reality of managing the largest Holiday in the world," he says. "You do not yet understand the things that must be done, the decisions that must be made. This may seem cruel, but the alternative is to allow us to fade away, and that I will not permit." He points at me, and I can't help it; I flinch. "Do not act on this information. Do not *speak* of this information. You will sit on it, absorb it, and process what it means before I give you any role in this. I am trusting you, Nicholas, trusting you when you have only ever proven that you are unworthy of that trust. What you do with the things I have told you will determine the kind of Santa you will be."

He's never said anything truer in my life.

In the place where that childish hope once lived is just emptiness now. It's empty and hollow but aching, and I didn't think this conversation would leave me feeling so alone.

Dad sits back down at his desk. "And clean that paint off your nails before the next event."

The black and orange nails. I'd forgotten about them. Hadn't tried to hide them.

Nausea squirms down my stomach. Hex and I . . . is that something Dad would use against Halloween too? But it would counteract the plot that makes Christmas look like they're bowing to Halloween.

Still. The fact that I have to ask myself that question—*would my dad resort to blackmailing the guy I was kissing?*—has my vision going spotty.

"I do want to be good at this," I hear myself say. It's the first time I've ever admitted that aloud, to myself, to *anyone*. I've bared my soul more in the past ten minutes than I have maybe ever, and to my father, of all people.

And the fact that he seems to *understand* has me on edge. He isn't rolling his eyes at me, isn't brushing off my attempts as hopeless. As if he thinks I could actually do this.

But his version of *this* is . . . intolerable.

"I want you to be good at this as well," Dad says. "And I want this to be good *for* you. For you and Kristopher both. For the thousands of employees who depend on Christmas's success. For the people who will benefit from the joy that we bring. We have such potential to do good in this world."

We *do* have potential. We do. That's what's *choking* me. I don't know how to harness it, and Dad sees it too, but this isn't the way to harness it either, so where does that put us?

"Sleep on it, Nicholas." He waves at the door. "We can speak more after you've had time to process what I've told you. At the next events, be attentive to Iris and play your part."

One last flip of his eyes up at me. One last, intense look.

"Do not disappoint our family," he says.

The words sink into the ache in my chest. They're the source of that ache, the ever-present knot fueling my rigidity these past years. *Don't be a disappointment. Don't hurt anyone.*

I nod, stiff, and leave the office.

Then take off sprinting through the palace.

I make it back to my suite, get the door shut, and collapse against it, sliding to the floor in a lead-like heap.

Here I've been worried about how we're not bringing real joy to the world, and my father's been plotting a global Christmas take-over and blackmailing other Holidays.

The room is dark and cool but it's suddenly closing in, crushing me, I'm sweating and shaking and can't catch my breath.

How am I supposed to fix any of this?

Chapter Ten

The next scheduled Christmas PR celebration event isn't for another day, so I take full advantage of that and stay in bed.

I need to process ... everything. I need to lie in silence and roll back through every memory of my father and every blip of knowledge I've been given on Christmas and our joy and try, *try*, to figure out how I missed this—and what I'm going to do about it.

But every time my brain slams up against that question, I only see scrolling headlines.

Riots. Robberies.

Dear Santa, Mommy left and I don't think she's—

No, shit, that wasn't it. The kid lost her *dad*, not her *mom*.

I roll over and bury my face in the pillows and will the bed to eat me whole.

I'm asking myself to undo the foundation of stolen joy and performative acts my father has built Christmas on. Not to just let Iris and me out of this marriage or maybe not be a jerk to Halloween— but to stop manipulating people I didn't know we were oppressing. And every time I start to think *maybe I can try this,* my whole body seizes up with dread, because the last and only time I ever tried to fix something, I broke an entire country. What if I collapse Christmas *and* these other Holidays?

Not to mention the fact that moving against my father at all isn't just a familial dispute; it'd be *treason*. I'd joked about us having a dungeon, but what would the consequence be for getting caught doing something like this?

Hex didn't expect me to fix anything. Maybe he was right— maybe I *can't* fix this. But what am I supposed to do? Show up at the next Christmas event all smiles and pose with Hex for more photos like everything's fine, like Christmas is holly and jolly and not actively ruining lives? Marry Iris on Christmas Eve then graduate next semester and flit off to grad school like any of this will help my Holiday?

My bedroom door opens. I groan into my pillow. "Wren, I told you, I'm taking a—"

"Not Wren," Kris says. The door clicks shut behind him.

I sigh, body wilting into the bedding.

He sets something on my bedside table. I turn and see a tray of food, a sandwich and a steaming mug and a salad.

"What happened with Hex?" He drops onto the bed next to me with a bounce. "Iris and I need to know whether we should ostracize him and you're not answering your texts."

I push up onto my elbows. That's the one good memory from last night. The one I've been dropping into when thinking about Dad gets overwhelming.

I sit up and face Kris, pajama pants tangling in the sheets. "Don't ostracize him. Actually . . . that went great." A totally involuntary smile creeps up on me. "Really great."

And then I disappeared for the full day after. For warranted reasons—well, *sulking*. Not exactly warranted, then.

I'm not usually this bad at relationships. Lily might disagree. And maybe my roommate. And, like, one or two other brief romantic encounters that didn't last longer than a month or two.

Shit. Maybe I am bad at relationships?

Kris pulls the tray onto the bed and pushes it towards me. "Good. Because we like him. He was at lunch and he's a creepy son of a bitch, but he's much, much funnier than you."

I pick up the mug—cocoa. "I do not fall for such easy baiting."

He grins.

"But I'm glad you like him." I take a sip, let the warmth wash through me. "I like him too."

"Understatement. Massive. Colossal. But why are you in bed?" He surveys me with more scrutiny. "Are you sick?"

"No. I'm fine."

"Then what happened? Iris said you went to see Dad last night." Kris's voice twists. Bracing himself. "Did he do something?"

The cocoa leaves a too-sweet film on my tongue.

I know Kris would be as pissed as I am about all this. What's stopping me from telling him?

Hex was so sure of our roles—he protects Halloween, I protect Christmas.

I've done a terrible job of protecting anything.

That awareness is a spotlight, swerving yellow and unavoidable onto the way Kris's shoulders are set, ready to spring to action if I ask. My focus pulls back to the tray of food, to the unspoken way he knew to bring it, and yeah, I'd do the same for him, but . . . I don't usually have to.

"You take care of me. A lot," I state.

There's a beat before Kris gives a dismissive shrug. The beat is long enough that I know he realized that well before I did.

"It's what we do," he says.

All the times he's taken care of me crash through my mind at once. How he's the one to come get me from school or trips or my wilder shenanigans. How he always comes to check on me like he has now, and leaps to do whatever he can to help.

"No," I say. "It's what *you* do."

He looks away.

I hit on something.

His neck bunches and his fingers start picking at the hem of his jeans and I feel like I ripped open a wound I was unaware he had.

"What happened with Dad?" he asks again.

I set down the mug. "Nothing. What's wrong? What did you—"

"It isn't *nothing*, Coal. It's never *nothing*." His eyes pin on me, an abrupt show of despair that has me rocking back. "If it was nothing, you wouldn't be in here hiding. He did something, *again*, like he always does, and he's getting closer and closer to that *something* being the thing to—"

His lips slam shut.

He twists away, sucking his teeth, self-deprecation blossoming red stains on his cheeks.

The air in the room is too heavy. "Closer to what?"

"I do take care of you," he whispers to the bed. He flicks the tray. "But I won't be able to stop it, will I?"

"Stop—?"

"You leaving."

My head dips to the side, mind working overtime to interpret what he said like he spoke to me in an entirely different language. But even *that* would be less difficult to figure out since our magic lets us understand *every* language—it does nothing to help me piece together what he means.

"Leaving? Why would I leave? Like to school again?"

His look cuts me off. "Not to school. Go to school—go to a hundred schools. I mean *leaving*. Because you don't want any of this. Because Dad is forcing you into something shitty and controlling and you've never been okay with it, and you're getting to the point where you're going to realize that the only way to *stop* it is to go."

I stare at my brother for what feels like hours. Days. So long that my eyes burn from being open, absolute, wrenching horror tearing long shreds into my soul.

"You think," I start, a whisper, "that I'd leave you like she did."

Kris doesn't look at me.

I push out of bed. I can't be still right now. My bare feet hit the floor and I shiver but I'm not at all cold, my skin is too tight, stifling, and I pace next to my bed before I cut around and stand over him.

"You honestly think I'd do what she did?" I gasp the question. I think I might splinter into pieces right over top of him.

Kris pushes a fist into the bed. "You fight him every chance you get. And you should—I don't blame you for that. He's *wrong*, about a lot of things, but I've been watching you all my life." Finally he looks at me. And I wish he hadn't—his eyes are glossy, and it kills me. "You've tried to buck these chains forever, Coal. Tell me you've never once dreamed about giving it all up."

"I've never once dreamed about giving it all up," I tell him immediately, I *promise* him.

Kris's brows pinch.

"I've *never* considered leaving." Even saying these words is unimaginable. I've never, not once, thought about running. The idea hasn't been in my brain until this moment. "Not just because all this shit would fall on you—and I *won't* put all this on you—but because she left me too. And what's worse, what makes it so I will never forgive her, is that I had to watch her leave *you*. And Dad, even. And I have to watch her keep digging that knife in deeper every time she texts us, every time she gets it in her head to torment us. To torment *you*. I failed you, unforgivably, if you think for a second that I'm capable of hurting you the way she did."

My whole face burns up with how much I'm trying to convince him of all this. Desperation builds in my body and I think it will fillet me right in half, but if that's what it takes, I'll let it.

The conversation I had with Iris comes roaring back on me. Where she hadn't wanted to talk about the marriage competition stuff because she knew I'd make jokes about it. That's what I do. I twist every conversation into either jokes or something light but whatever it is, it ends up being about *me,* about what makes *me* comfortable, about what *I* can offer, rather than what my friends need.

Kris has never talked to me about how Mom leaving affected him. I know he feels more deeply than I do, because I'm only ever furious with her; but he still *hopes.* He still reacts to her attempts to reach out as if her passive-aggressive narcissism could somehow hatch into maternal love. I *know* that about him, but I've only ever responded to his feelings from a place of my own rage, being pissed that she's hurting him. I've never stopped to *see* his hurt.

He presses the heel of his hand to his forehead and drags in a shuddering breath.

"What was it like for you? When she left," I ask. It's stilted.

Kris glances up. That glossiness to his eyes has intensified. "You were there. You know."

"I was. And I remember you crying. A lot. For weeks. I remember

Dad—shutting down. And no one could really tell us *why* she was gone. I remember being mad at her." I shake my head, restart. "I'm not talking about what *I* experienced. I asked what it was like for *you*."

Kris looks down at his hands in his lap. "We don't need to talk about this now. Dad did something to fuck with your head, and I came in here to help with—"

"Kris." I cut him off so forcefully that he whips his eyes back up to me. "Please."

It comes out of him in a jerky rush, "I don't think I've ever been mad at her."

He blinks, surprised by his own admission.

He looks down at his hands again.

A kernel of my own anger flares up, but I ignore it. "Why?"

He shrugs, picking at his thumb.

I sit next to him on the bed and pin my eyes to the far wall. His shoulders relax a little without my attention directly on him.

"I remember—" He stops, gripping his hands tight together.

I bump his shoulder but don't say anything.

After a moment, he makes an aggrieved noise. "Why are you asking me about this right now? Fuck."

I stay quiet. Just sitting next to him.

"I hate you sometimes," he mutters.

Then, finally, "She'd been reading me a book every night before bed," he says in a painfully delicate voice. "We'd only gotten a few chapters into it. I remember thinking, *She has to come back to finish it. She wouldn't just leave. The book isn't finished.*"

His words end in a topple. Like he's trying to get them out before he can feel their impact.

"What was the book?" I whisper.

He chuckles and scrubs his hand across his thigh. "*Bridge to Terabithia.*" Any humor gets strangled. "I finished reading it a few months after she left. When she was reading it to me, I thought it was a magical fantasy book. It never occurred to me that it wouldn't end *happily.* I—" He sucks in a breath, and it takes me a beat to realize it's a gasp of shock. "I don't think I knew books could *be* sad until I finished that one. I assumed every story ended in happy ever after until—*fuck*." Kris drops his head into his hands and hunches over. "Why are you making me drag all this up? You're an asshole."

I ignore that. Ignore his attempt to push the conversation back onto me because for the first time in a long, long time, maybe ever, I feel like I'm seeing my brother beyond his caretaker façade. Feel like I'm seeing *him*.

"*Bridge to Terabithia* is fucking sad," I agree.

He looks sidelong at me. "You read it?"

"Movie."

"Ah. That makes more sense."

So not only did Mom break Kris's childhood innocence when she left, she doubled down by introducing him to what is quite possibly the saddest kids' book ever written.

Whenever she texts us, I immediately get furious. I never respond, and I hound Kris not to respond either. All that anger feels productive, like I'm able to *do* something against how fucking helpless she makes me feel.

But Kris wants *her* to be the one to do something, to come back and apologize and be better. He wants those happy endings she stole from him.

Tears prick my eyes. I dig down for some of my usual anger at her, that protective shield of defense, but I find nothing, just sorrow, sorrow for how much this hurt my brother.

He's still picking at his thumb. I put my hand over his and squeeze, hard, until he looks up at me again, pensive and brittle.

"I'm not going to leave. Not you. Not Christmas. I hate what Dad's doing, but I'm not going to give up, because *I am not our mother.* This is my home. *You* are my home, Kris." My own words kick me mid-breath. "I don't know what to do, but I'm gonna *try,* and I'll be *here, trying,* even if I fuck it all up, because I was serious earlier—one day, I'm going to be Santa, and you're going to be right there with me, and it'll all be *ours.* Ours, Kris. *That's* your happy ever after."

He exhales, then he's twisting into me and I throw my arms around him. We're a tangled mess of a pain that's almost fourteen years old—god, has it been fourteen years since she left? Screw her—but certain pains don't age, they don't shrivel up, they go dormant like a volcano, never losing their ability to be apocalyptically devastating.

Dealing with that pain was part of the reason I was always so . . . *me.* But this was another way that the pain has lived on, because my irresponsibility was hurting Kris all this time.

We'll never be fully rid of it. Not of what she did, not of our duties to Christmas, not of my dad's manipulation and all the shit he's putting us through.

But I'm done letting my body play host to it. I'm done letting their choices be parasites on my future. I cling to my brother and make a promise to myself, to him, that this is the start of something new.

I have no idea what *new* is.

My eyes snag on a bundle tucked up behind my headboard and my mood immediately does a one-eighty.

"You," I start, "absolute fucker."

Kris yanks back.

I shove away from him, leap onto my bed, and grab the cursed object from behind my headboard. *"What the hell is this?"*

Kris is blotchy from holding back tears but he laughs so hard he chokes. "You haven't found any of them yet?"

The goddamn Elf on the Shelf goes limp in my hand. "You actually hid one in my room?"

"Four. Four of them."

"Kristopher."

"I told you I don't fuck around with grammar."

I throw it at him. It smacks off his chest but he's laughing again, eyes tearing for a way better reason now, and I can't help it. I laugh too.

Even with that fucking possessed Christmas doll staring up at us.

Emotional hangovers are definitely worse than alcohol hangovers.

Headache. Dry mouth. Slight nausea. Intense exhaustion. The next day, I let Wren and her stylists doll me up for the Christmas event while I sink into my stupor, mind blank like I'm in a meditative preparation state.

I truly have no idea what version of me will appear at this event.

I don't remember what the event *is*—something outside, because I pull on layers the staff left out for me, finishing the outfit with a double-breasted red wool coat and stylish black leather gloves.

Sure enough, I'm led out front, joining Kris and Iris where they already wait on the palace's front lawn with a few larger sleighs. Most are burdened with various members of our court under thick, cozy blankets; Dad's in the lead sleigh with Iris's father.

It's another perfect arctic day, the dark sky clear but the lights so bright I duck my head and wince.

"That's what you get for hiding in your room," Iris says.

I jostle her with my shoulder. She's in black tights and a long, chunky purple sweater, and I recognize the purpose of that outfit.

"Ice skating," I say.

"I will be expected to participate again, I assume?"

I spin around.

Hex is coming out of the palace, the doors closing behind him.

I have to ask Wren whether he has a stylist or makes his own fashion choices, because I need to know who to blame for how goddamn distracting every single piece of his clothing is. He's in a long leather jacket, black again, form-fitting and sleek and the collar is popped, which makes him look so much like a sexy goth vampire that I get hit with wicked visions of him biting my neck.

He slides his hands into his pockets, tugging the jacket down, showing a tie on his black button-up done with tiny jack-o'-lanterns. In Santa hats.

My lips pinch in a smile. "What—"

"Oh, it looks great!" Kris smirks at me. "Appropriate, right? I couldn't resist."

I start to laugh, then realize with a flash of concern that though *I* know the truth now, we're playing my dad's game with the press— and if anything, Hex should be wearing something that symbolizes Halloween and *Easter*. What if photos of him in that tie get back to his autumn allies? He's probably considered that risk. So this tie is an intentional choice?

But I can't scrounge up too much worry, because I like seeing him wearing something of Christmas.

I grin. "My brother gave you crazy Christmas clothes. You've officially been initiated. Congratulations."

Hex weighs my words. Thinks about our kiss? I can't figure out what's going on in his head, but he finally lets half his lips rise up.

"I've been marked by you, it seems," he says, and it sucks the air out of my body so fast that my ears pop. "By your Holiday," he amends, slowly, enough that I know he intended the insinuation.

Holy shit. Is *that* why he took the risk of wearing this tie? To flirt with me? Mr. *Don't Risk Your Responsibilities for Me?*

It could be a middle finger to this whole arrangement. A subtle way of saying, *I know what Christmas is doing with this blackmail shit.*

That's gotta be it.

Hex must be the last person we're waiting on, because from my unexpected trance, I hear the lead sleigh kick off. Others follow until only one remains, empty, and I thank whatever lucky stars I have that we won't be forced to ride with my father.

Iris and Kris start for the sleigh and I linger until Hex comes down the steps, the heat of his body pulling me around to walk alongside him.

"You're wrong. I didn't mark you," I echo his unfair, wildly innuendo-heavy words that I cannot let go unaddressed. "*That*"—I bend closer and swing my hand up to touch the knot of his tie, a quick tap—"is from my brother and entirely innocent. You'll know damn well when I mark you." The barest pause. "If you'll let me."

Hex's breath is a quaking white cloud in the air. His tongue dips out to lick his bottom lip before he rolls that lip in between his teeth, all so quick that it's innocuous, except for the not innocuous reaction my body is having.

Ah. So this is how it's going to be at every event between now and . . . my wedding.

Just like that, the fog is shattered.

Hex watches my expression change and his head cocks, but we reach the sleigh. Kris and Iris are sitting across from one another, and I pull back to let Hex climb up first and settle next to Iris.

Which pisses me off.

So *this* is how it's going to be at every event. Ping-ponging from flirtation so hot I'll need a steady stream of frost on my body to cool down, to roiling fury at the shitty game we're dancing around.

Our driver glances down at me, now the only one still standing in the yard. "Prince Nicholas?"

I break out of my thoughts. "Yeah, I'm ready," I say on reflex, then blink up at him. "Hey, Bart, your kid was trying to get into Yale? Dare I ask if my recommendation letter did a lick of good?"

Why on *earth* he asked *me* to write that letter instead of getting one from Dad, I'll never know.

Bart smiles down at me. "It helped very much. She starts next fall. Thank you again, Prince Nicholas."

I climb up into the sleigh with a headshake. "I had absolutely nothing to do with her success. Tell her congrats from me." And good fucking luck. But she seemed legitimately excited by the prospect of Yale, unlike me, who didn't get a choice; so maybe she will actually like it.

Bart's pleased hum is cut by him snapping the reins, and we lurch off down the path.

Hex is directly across from where I sit next to Kris, and I feel his attention on me. It holds, and when I meet his eyes, he tips his head in some unspoken question I can't read.

I smile at him. Because there are no photographers around—yet.

But the moment we get to the ice rink, in the center of North Pole City, we'll be bombarded not just with reporters and journalists, but with our people. This is one of the few events that takes us out of the palace grounds, which Dad has drilled into our heads means that it's more important we keep our public image pristine. Doctored palace photos are easy to control; but in-public events where some of the very people Dad hopes to manipulate are watching our every move?

It'd be the perfect place to do . . . something. If I had any idea what would help begin to fix things. But I highly doubt my usual manic acts of negligence will be of any use from now on. They were never beneficial, anyway.

"Do you skate?" Iris asks Hex as our sleigh bumps out of the palace grounds and swings onto a wide, snow-flattened road. Pine trees stand sentinel, each decorated in bulbs and strands of red ribbon garland, the path lit here by strands of lights instead of the massive floodlights.

Hex grimaces. His face sets quickly. "No. But I expect your father will insist I participate."

"You don't have to," I tell him. "I won't let him make you."

I will not let him touch you again.

Hex smiles. It's small and grateful. "Thank you. But I can, at least, try." He pauses. Winces. "How hard is it, truly?"

Iris makes a squeaky laugh. "Well . . ."

I nudge her with my foot at the concern on Hex's face.

"You two grew up doing it!" says Iris. "It's not as easy—"

"—as walking. It's walking. But on ice," says Kris with a wide grin because he knows that sets her off.

"*It is nothing like walking,*" Iris snaps.

"Don't worry," I tell Hex. "We'll help you."

"Or we can get him one of those training aids." Kris smirks. "The bar contraption that slides around. But he'll have to squat down to use it since they only come in children's—"

Kris's words end in a garbled cough as I pulse my hand at his mouth and fill it with holly.

He hacks and spits it into his lap. "This stuff is poisonous!"

"Well, don't eat it."

He tosses it at me and I flick it over the side of the sleigh.

Hex grins, a soft amusement, like he's shocked we're *this,* irreverent teasing morons.

"I'd love to say you'll eventually get used to their antics," Iris says to him, "but it's been more than a decade and I still find them both obnoxious."

"Hey." My eyes narrow in mock threat. "I'll holly you too, just try me."

"You have all known each other long?" Hex asks.

"Long enough that I'd *also* love to say that surely they'll grow out of this phase, but they've both had the combined maturity level of a thirteen-year-old for the past eleven years."

"So we're twenty-four, at least," Kris says.

Iris squints. "What?"

"Thirteen and eleven. Twenty-four. So we're *older* than either of us—"

"That is not what I said."

"Sure it was. A combined maturity level of thirteen for eleven years. Math."

Iris cocks her head towards Hex and says, exasperated, "That guy got himself into Cambridge."

"Cambridge?" Hex's brows go up. "Really?"

Kris sobers. "Is that surprising?"

Bart guides the sleigh through a covered bridge, the clop of the reindeer hooves echoing off the aged wood. If he can hear our conversation over the noise of the sleigh, he doesn't react.

"Not at all," Hex says. "I had wondered which colleges your Holidays tended to prefer. You mentioned Yale too?"

"I'm at Cambridge with Kris." Iris points at me. "Coal's the only one who had his path predestined."

Hex frowns.

I splay my hands. "My father shipped me off to his alma mater to *reshape my image* from the various humiliations in what I now refer to as my errant youth."

Kris snorts. "That would imply that that time of your life is done?"

"I have been scandal-free for quite a while, thank you. But that's not the point: the point is that I had it coming when Dad nixed my original college plans. But where do you go?"

Hex's eyes flit over me. I don't see any pity, more a considering, narrow concern, like he knows I'm downplaying it for his benefit.

But then his face relaxes. "There's a reformatory in northern Ohio where they filmed *The Shawshank Redemption*."

Iris, Kris, and I share a look. Then turn that look on Hex.

At our confusion, he says, like it should be obvious, "It's one of the most haunted buildings in America."

"And you—" I clear my throat. "Study there? Like, classes? At a . . . haunted reformatory?"

Hex holds my eyes for a beat too long, and just before I catch on, he cracks a smile.

"No. I'm messing with you. I go to UNAM in Mexico City."

Iris chirps first. "Holy shit, you were scary convincing. I'm never playing poker with you."

Hex nods sagely. "That's probably in your best interest."

"You shouldn't joke about ghosts." Kris shudders next to me. "Don't draw attention to that kind of shit."

Hex's grin collapses. "By the very nature of being a Halloween prince, I draw the attention of *that sort of stuff* whether I joke about it or not. For instance—are you aware of the ghosts that haunt your palace?"

Kris's gaze narrows in suspicion. Then widens again in concern. Narrow. Wide.

Is he being fucked with? He really can't seem to decide.

On a blink, Hex's already dark eyes go completely black in such a startling switch from normal to something demonic that even I jump.

Kris honest-to-god *squeaks.*

Iris seems more amused by Kris's reaction than by whatever Hex is doing.

"I can still hear them, even out here," Hex says, his voice a little echoey, a little ethereal, those black eyes unfocused. "They wail for you, Kristopher. The ghosts . . . of Christmas past, present, and future."

Another blink, and Hex's eyes go back to normal, matched by a toying smile.

Kris's discomfort vanishes with an immediate surge of red to his cheeks. "Oh, fuck off."

I bark a laugh and put a hand to Kris's chest. "Shit, dude, your heart is racing."

"His eyes went *black*." He smacks me away and frowns at Hex before pointing at his own eyes. "Halloween's magic?"

My brows shoot up. "And the other explanation would be . . . ?"

"I don't—it could've—oh, you fuck off too."

Hex looks like he's weighing prolonging this torture with Kris. Finally, he relents with a smile and a nod. "Yes, it was magic. I considered creating an apparition flying alongside our sleigh, but—"

"No," Kris says immediately, then clears his throat. "I mean, no, we don't need any more demonstrations of Halloween's magic. Thanks. Consider us sufficiently *oohed* and *ahhed*."

"If you do create an apparition"—Iris leans over to Hex and feigns a whisper behind her hand—"have it look like a clown."

Hex crooks one eyebrow, sizes up Kris, and makes a thoughtful, mildly devilish hum in his throat.

Fuck, why is that hot.

Kris sucks his teeth. "I hate everyone in this sleigh."

Taking pity on my brother—and suddenly desperate to change the topic away from anything that makes me have to adjust how I'm sitting—I grin at Hex. "So what do you study at UNAM? Other than the occult. Or—no, no, wait." I shift upright and hold my hands out like I'm keeping everyone from leaping out of the sleigh. "Everyone say their major on three."

Iris rolls her eyes.

"One, two, three—"

Iris and Kris simultaneously say, "International Relations."

I go, "Global Affairs," and mime gagging.

Hex pauses, so we're quiet when he says, "International Development and Management."

"Wow." I lean back on the seat. "We are a fun bunch. Look at us. So diverse. No one would ever be able to guess what family obligations we come from."

"It is hardly surprising that we all have similar avenues of study," Hex says. "What else would we do?"

"I tried to major in Theater at first."

Hex's face flies into such a look of charmed surprise that I want to keep talking and I've found that that's an incredibly dangerous state for me to be in.

"Theater?" he echoes. "At Yale? You want to be an actor?"

"Oh, no. I did it because it made my father threaten to disinherit me"—among other things—"but luckily for him, the Yale Theater Department is apparently rather *elite* and not prone to letting wayward obscure royals fuck around to piss off their dads."

"Then he majored in Classic Civilization," Kris says with a shitty grin.

Hex's surprise is shifting to all-out delight and I'm chasing it like a hunting dog. But like a new, untrained hunting dog that has no idea what he's going to do once he catches it.

"You majored in Classic Civilization?" Hex clarifies.

"And Humanities. Then Burmese with a Dutch minor, and that set me off on a language kick—Punjabi, Russian. Somewhere around me switching from Latin to Czech, Dad cut me off from everything. Phone, money, magic. I caved after two days, he told me I'd get a degree in Global Affairs, and here we are."

"Why did you do that?" Hex laughs, a too-quick burst of an airy chuckle.

"All the same reason: velociraptoring my dad's fences."

"*What?*" Hex rocks forward, his look saying he had to have misheard me.

Iris groans. "Oh, do not get him started. He's way too pleased with himself and this analogy."

I ignore her because yes, I am too pleased with myself and this analogy. "*Jurassic Park.* The velociraptors would hurl themselves into the electric fences to test them for weak spots. Thus, velociraptoring my dad's fences—testing him for weak spots. Where he'll cave, what he'll let slide. My life's goal, really."

"Imagine if you'd applied yourself to something useful," Kris mumbles, but he's smirking, and it's the same joke everyone's been making my whole life.

Only now, it yanks the smile off my face and I look up to see Hex's own smile dimming.

"So yeah." I force my grin back up. "I've trademarked that phrase and I will happily charge you a negligible fee if you want to use it."

His lips cock. Not that teetering amusement again, not the joy I'd almost drawn out in him, the sun that had started to peek above the horizon.

"I will refrain from using that term without prior arrangement with you," he says. His eyes stay on mine, studying my dip. Iris and Kris are oblivious to my shift, but he catches it, and I'm not sure what to do with that awareness.

The sleigh takes a turn, and North Pole City comes into view. We're getting closer to reporters.

Hex's eyes stay on me.

And I should look away.

But I don't.

Chapter Eleven

The North Pole ice rink sits in the center of a picture-perfect ski resort of a town, lit by more of those giant lights along with what have to be *miles* of twinkly strand lights. All the buildings are in storybook Tudor-style wood-and-plaster architecture, interspersed with garland-draped market booths selling fragrant roasted nuts and handmade gifts and, of course, cocoa. Dozens of people mill around, giggling and chatting and snapping pictures of the heater-warmed area where the sleighs deposited the palace group, a cluster of royals spread over benches, all tying on skates.

I can feel the sharpening of attention on Hex. This is the first time he's been out of the palace, and tons of people have their phones on him, pointing and whispering and it's the invasiveness of every journalist interaction but cranked to the max. All the images taken and shared are feeding the story that Halloween's allies believe, that Christmas bowed to them like a kicked puppy and they have a shot at linking with Easter now. Is anyone really buying that Halloween has an honest chance at getting that alliance? Maybe that's the point: they believe whatever story my dad is letting out because Christmas is so *wonderful* and *gracious* and why would Santa lie?

My arms itch to put myself between Hex and the onslaught, but there *is* no division—it's everywhere. Pummeling us in a 360-degree sweep, and here we are, supposed to have a *fun* and *candid* day of skating *among the people.*

I yank my laces too tight as a shadow falls over me.

Dad's in full Santa mode. Red coat and red hat trimmed in white fur.

"Photo before we take to the ice," he says and heads over to the gate.

Next to me, Iris finishes tying on her skates. Hex, on the other side of Iris, has his skates on, and analyzes the way Kris is standing by his bench before he pushes up.

He wobbles and immediately sits back down.

I hear the quickest gasp from him, a husky, "Oh, no."

Iris reaches for Kris. "Up." And she throws me a knowing bob of her eyebrows.

That leaves me to walk over in front of Hex.

He sighs to my legs. "Just like walking?"

"Sure." No, not at all.

"Gather," Dad calls from where he's standing near the opening to the rink. Photographers wait.

I suppose I could *tell them* what my father has done. Overtaking other winter Holidays. Blackmailing people, Halloween included. They'd report it, wouldn't they?

Even if I did, what would happen? All the thousands of people of Christmas would rise up against us in a furious tirade of revolution? Plus, I seriously doubt Halloween and the other Holidays would appreciate me hinting at something blackmail-worthy, because the first thing any reporter worth their salt would do is dig into that story.

Nothing good would come from involving the press in my dad's secrets.

Another sigh from Hex. He extends his hands like a man being led to the gallows.

"*Bum-bum.*" I make the noise deep in my chest. "*Bum-bum—*"

His eyes raise to mine and he squints. "Is that meant to be an execution dirge?"

I grin. "Just matching your *this is how I die* energy."

His annoyance is almost, *almost,* seething. But one side of his mouth pulses up and he noticeably has to bite his lips together.

I curl my fingers around his thin wrists. "Come on. It's bad form to murder guests via ice skating. I promise to keep you alive."

He lets me haul him to his feet. His ankles sway, but he braces on me, hands grasping tight to my forearms, and I'd stand here forever to feel him letting me take his weight as he orients himself.

I see the moment he realizes how close we're standing. *Feel* it, more like, a shuddering ripple that makes his fingers palpitate on my arms.

That grip tightens. Each fingertip through his gloves, through my sleeve, pushes down, ten pressure points that turn my entire body into a wound wall of muscle.

After a strung-out moment of him just making me feel this, he whispers, "What is your preferred form of murdering guests, then?"

Sexual tension, I want to say.

But I grin again, effusively charming. "I can't tell you that. Christmas has to have *some* element of mystery."

Hex shakes his head, a smile playing at his mouth, and glances back to his feet. "All right," he says, to himself, to me. "Walking."

I hook his arm through mine. It doesn't feel like enough, though, how he wavers with each step, but his face is pure determination as we make our way over to the gate.

Dad starts to reach for Hex. To pull him in front, because that's the best photo, the one everyone wants to see.

Headline: *Halloween Prince ~~forced~~ overjoyed to participate in Christmas traditions.*

But I don't surrender him. I twist my shoulder and pretend I didn't see Dad reach for him and my heart lodges itself in my throat.

I can feel my father's eyes on me. Considering. He won't make a scene here, though.

Cameras flash.

A crowd has gathered, more people now, phones taking pics. The rink has been emptied for us—how no one realizes that absurdity, that we came to skate with our people but not actually *with* any of our people, is beyond me—and music starts from speakers set around the square, an airy, festive rendition of "Carol of the Bells."

Dad is first out onto the ice. The rest of our court snakes in behind him, pushing through the gate.

Everyone from Christmas has some level of skill—it's in our ancestry—but I'm drawn to watching specifically the members of House Frost. This is one of their specialties, one of the things that they alone brought to Christmas, and I wonder now what else we're missing from them. What other things have we not embraced or lost in the name of cohesion?

I linger off to the side with Hex, letting the bulk of people funnel past us so we can take our time getting out.

"Are Christmas events always like this?" Hex asks, gripping my arm with one hand, white-knuckling the railing on the other side.

"Like what?"

He nods at the photos being taken. The press. The people with their phones.

"As long as I can remember. Well—" That's not true, is it? "It didn't used to be this bad. We've always had journalists recording our events and writing articles about us, but it used to be one or two, not half a dozen all the time. It's only been this overbearing for the past twelve, thirteen years."

Hex gawks at the side of my face. "You usually have *half a dozen* journalists documenting your Christmas seasons?"

"Ha. I wish. No, it's like this even outside of Christmas. We go visit Iris—press. I come home on a break from school—press. Dad likes to make sure our public has a specific image of their ruling family."

There's a rising sympathetic horror on Hex, so I shrug, like it's not a big deal. "You learn to live with it." No, you definitely don't; you learn to blatantly ignore it and stay off social media, which I've been told is way better for my mental health in the long run. "Why? What's Halloween like?"

They may read whatever articles get printed about us, but I know they don't have nearly as many active paparazzi invading their lives.

"More cobwebs," Hex says, not missing a beat. "Candy corn instead of candy canes. The occasional temporary possession. And our events are enjoyable."

His teasing washes a smile across my face. "The month is young—there may yet be a possession during Christmas too. But are you saying you didn't enjoy sleigh racing?"

"And I doubt very much that I will enjoy skidding around a pad of ice on razor blades."

"Blasphemer."

"Not my Holiday, so no, I'm not."

"*Bum-bum,*" I start the dirge again. "*Bum—*"

He shoulder-checks me, but it makes him wobble, and he scrambles to tighten his grip on me in a flustered panic. That panic only lasts about two seconds, and when he catches himself, he glares breathlessly at me.

"Do not. Let me. Fall," he punctuates.

"I won't. Let you. Fall." I hold his arm tight to my chest to emphasize the promise, but it pulls him to me. Reminds me of what it felt like to have his body pressed up against mine.

Yeah, maybe sexual tension really *will* be how I kill us.

All of my court has worked their way onto the ice. There's plenty of space for the two of us to ease out, but I only let us take another slow step, keeping him next to me, talking to me. I know photos are being taken, but I actively do not let myself consider what sorts of headlines will accompany Iris's two suitors talking together.

"What kinds of events do you do for Halloween, then?"

Hex turns away to watch the people around the edge of the rink, his cheeks brushed the faintest shade of pink.

He clears his throat. "Lots of things. We have many traditions from both Halloween and Día de Muertos. My brothers love—"

"You have brothers?"

"Three. Triplets. They're nine."

I crack a laugh. "That sounds—"

"Messy? Chaotic? Extraordinarily creepy when they all dress identically and hide around the house?"

"I was going to say fantastic, but honestly, that last bit sounds downright brilliant of them."

His smile is all fondness. "They are far too brilliant for their own good, that's true. They love hayrides, haunted houses; they love trick-or-treating, of course. My parents have a terrible time stopping them from using our magic to create candy whenever they please."

"Oh my god." A huge grin tugs up my lips. "I did the *exact* same thing when I was younger. Figured out how to use Christmas's magic to make this one type of ginger-flavored chocolate I really loved, and made *piles* of it. Just an insane amount of candy. I spent all night puking my guts up. Still can't eat that type of chocolate without gagging."

Hex's grin mirrors mine. "One of my brothers—Salem—did that. Only it was Skittles. Think about that for a moment."

Realization connects and I wince. "Oh no—"

"Oh yes. Rainbow vomit *everywhere*. This was only a few months ago."

"Mine was too."

Hex snorts.

"What about you?" I have us take another step towards the gate to make it look like we're trying to get out on the ice.

"Me?"

"Yeah. What tradition do you love most? Aside from the séances and possessions."

Hex braces himself on the railing and me, and his face takes on a look of pure joy, a memory blossoming—but it just as quickly dissolves into sorrow, a weird, contrasting mix of happiness and grief.

I push closer to him, feeling like I can soften wherever he's coming in to land.

"Our ofrendas," he whispers.

"The altars in memory of the dead. Right?"

He pulls back with an appraising look. "Correct."

"Hey, I know things. But why is that your favorite?"

Hex sucks in a breath. Holds. It's that studious, considering look again, like he's evaluating my merit, and I go perfectly still, letting him read me, hoping to god he finds me worthy.

"I wasn't the original heir of Halloween," he whispers. "I had an older sister. Raven."

His words are instantly sobering. "What?"

"She was . . . amazing. Big-hearted. Funny." He cracks a small smile. "A lot like you, honestly."

I don't dare speak. Couldn't, even if I'd wanted to.

"So I like ofrendas best," he continues, "because they let her know we miss her, and that she can celebrate with us. It's what I love most about Halloween too—we create joy in what is terrifying, and Día de Muertos creates joy with what is gone."

"And that's enough?"

The question is out of me before I can stop it. Dragged to the forefront by the certainty in his voice, the simplicity.

Hex frowns slightly. "Why wouldn't it be?"

I want to look away. Want to hide this cracking open, but I don't, because in some way, I owe him this. "Whatever we help people create with these Holidays—it doesn't stop terror. It doesn't stop things from being gone. Like with Christmas's joy—nothing we do prevents bad things from happening or fixes things that already happened."

His frown smooths, his head tips. "And that is the only purpose for what we do? If we don't prevent bad things, we shouldn't try?"

"I just—" I roll my lips into my mouth, breathing the bitter, iced air. "We're supposed to make people happy. But it doesn't *last*. So what's the point?"

Hex straightens, leaning on me a little less, but only so he can twist, facing me. "You said something like that once before. In the alley." He squints. "Do you remember?"

No point in lying to him, or myself, anymore. "I remember everything from that night."

He shows a little flash of surprise at the intensity in my eyes, the way I let him see that I mean it, that everything he said is and has been branded on my mind.

"I don't think our purpose is to prevent all the bad things in the world," he says. "I think our purpose is to help people endure those things."

"With that foundation you talked about? One by one by one, until they have something to stand on."

An unexpected, sensational grin brightens Hex's face.

We don't generally concern ourselves with the religious elements associated with our Holidays—they fluctuate as much as joy intake—but I understand now how people are driven to worship.

His smile makes me want to swear my soul to whatever god created him.

"You do remember," he says. "And yes. We give them the foundation to withstand whatever they may have to face."

I walk us forward another step. Dad glides past us on the ice and gives me an intense look that says, *Get out here.* Defense wells in me, my grip tightening on Hex's arm.

"Why does that not feel like enough?" I whisper.

Hex watches me still, and I can feel his exhale on the side of my face. "I think you're trying to make each little thing too big. I don't expect the ofrenda to bring Raven back. In that moment, when I set up the altar for her, I feel a little less alone. A little less broken by her loss. If I can have that, then I know other people are getting the same comfort out of this Holiday. And that's all I expect to get or create by any of the magic I'm destined to build—one small moment."

I wish I could have a flicker of his conviction. To believe in what we do, to know it resonates and people need it.

But I realize, in listening to him talk, at the bar and up to now—being with him is the only time in my life when I started to think that the joy we bring might be enough. Because *he* thinks it's enough.

"How did she die?" I ask. "Or you don't have to talk about her if—"

"It's fine. A car accident. Two and a half years ago. I—"

He stops. His eyebrows crease.

"What?" I ask.

He takes a fortifying breath, expression pleading and intense. "Actually. I'd rather you not ask me about her."

Instantly, I want to surrender, hold up my hands and back away, but I can't let him go, so I nod. "Okay. I'm sorry. I didn't mean to—"

"Don't apologize. Really. I don't—" Another deep breath, another shuddering exhale, and he looks out at the rink. "I don't do well talking about her. Even years later."

"No. I get it." I spend every anniversary of the day Mom left re-reading the handful of texts she's sent over the years, then hating myself for it. "I . . . thank you for telling me. I wish I could've met her."

Hex whips towards me so fast I jump. His brows bend in that pleading look again, his lashes pulse, and maybe it's the sting of the bitter winter air, but his eyes are glassy.

"I wish you could have met her too," he says like a promise, hanging such weight on each word that my knees go weak.

Then he smiles, straightens up. "Now. Show me this next Christmas death trap."

"It's hardly a *death trap*. You're so morbid."

"Halloween."

"If you adhere to Halloween's morbid stereotype, then that means I have to adhere to Christmas's jolliness, and I'm not sure I'm physically capable of shaking my belly like a bowl full of jelly."

Hex laughs.

Someone help me, please, because this guy makes me want to learn hymns but only recite them if I'm moaning and I think that might be sacrilege, but I'm okay with damnation if he's the reason, I just want to know for sure which way is up.

Hex's hold stiffens on my arm as we reach the gate. "All right. Don't let go."

"Never," I say instantly, maybe too forcefully.

Iris and Kris are out there, Kris staying within a few feet of Iris as she takes small strides, but even with her unsteadiness, it looks natural, and I can see Hex's brow set in study.

"You'll learn better trying it," I whisper. But I'm starting to understand him more. Why he's so controlled, so contained. He's living up to not only his position in Halloween, but his sister's memory.

His jaw sharpens. "You won't let me fall." It's not a question.

"I promise." I adjust my hold on him, because if I'm only grabbing onto his arm, then, yeah, he's going to go shooting out of my grip the moment we hit the ice. So I prop my arm around his hips, which pulls him into me, and I keep my other hand in a tight pinch on his upper arm.

This was a huge mistake.

What was the word Kris used? *Colossal.*

Because with Hex in my arms, and all these cameras going off, there is no way, no *way,* that anyone looking won't see how I feel about him.

Nothing about the way I'm holding him must be off-putting to him, because he nods. "Let's do this."

And I don't care at all what anyone else might think.

I'm going to skate with this guy, and in this moment, I'm going to pretend we're a normal couple doing a normal Christmas activity because I know that simplicity is something I will never get. This is as close as we'll ever be.

I work us to the gate and step out onto the ice first. Hex takes a breath and follows.

"Glide one foot forward," I say, demonstrating as much as I can without letting him go.

His cheeks are reddening, half cold, half concentration. He moves his legs, increment by increment, and I cling him to me so tightly that soon we're moving solely because of me, legs wound and arms like vises as I guide him around the rink. I'm going to be sore as hell tomorrow, but it's worth it, in the way I can feel him leaning into me, the startled huff of a laugh as he realizes we've completed one full lap.

The song changes.

To Michael Bublé's "All I Want for Christmas Is You."

I bring all this upon myself, I know I do, but Christmas must hate me, because I did not ask to have this perfect guy in my arms while what has to be the most romantic Christmas song of all time blares around us.

A squealing giggle blissfully drags my attention up, and I see Iris grinning wide as Kris spins her in a circle, like they're dancing on the ice. He's smiling too, and when she teeters, he catches her, but she's laughing, and my heart nearly bursts.

"They're cute," Hex says.

I look down at him. "I wish she'd—"

Holy hell, he's *so close* to me.

His face tips up, and there's a disassociating second where the whole breadth of our kiss in the library plays across the refracting light in his eyes to the point where the collision of his gaze on my skin feels tactile. He looks from my temple, to my cheek, to my lips, and each touch of that focus leaves a spark of fizzing awareness as Michael Bublé croons about wanting you here tonight, holding on to me so tight.

We coast to a stop.

"Coal," he says like he's begging for something. I think—hope— for one red-hot second that he'll ask me to kiss him, and I would, right here, in front of everyone, and take whatever damage comes from that impact.

But then the yearning in his eyes changes, tenses. "Stop looking at me like that."

"Stop—" I echo the first word, and it rips me out of the spell.

We've been standing here, staring at each other, for long enough that it's obvious what we're thinking.

Before any sense of flagellating horror can get a chance to stab into me, Dad skids to a stop in front of us.

"Prince Hex. With Princess Iris," he says. But his eyes are on me. Fuming. "I need a word with my son."

Hex goes as solid as the ice we're standing on. Iris isn't far—but too far for someone who can't skate to reach her. And are those tears in her eyes?

Kris is nowhere near her now.

My head snaps around, and I spot him behind me, furious glare on our father.

"All right," I force out. "I'll take him to—"

"Prince Hex," Dad says again. "Now. This is a perfect opportunity to continue getting to know her. As you should be focused on doing."

"He can't—"

"Nicholas."

I promised him I wouldn't let him fall. That I wouldn't let him *go*. Well, this is how it ends, then, on an ice skating rink, because I am outright *done* breaking promises to him.

So, when Hex pushes against me, I stare at him dumbly. What's he doing?

"It's all right," he tells me. "I can manage."

He nods at the railing. It's close enough that he can reach out and grab it.

But—

"Prince Nicholas," Hex says, "thank you for your help."

He doesn't look at my father, but he adds, "Sir," and pushes on me again.

I release him, only because he gives me one last entreating look. He eases away and I don't breathe until he grabs the wall and begins pulling himself down it.

Iris slides forward and takes his arm, her glance at me saying, *I got this. We're okay.*

Like hell.

Kris comes up next to me.

I cut my chin to the side. "What—"

"Iris," is all he says.

He was skating with Iris. Skating, and they were laughing.

And then Hex and I. Skating. Looking at each other like that.

"The two of you know how delicate these events are," Dad says. But his face has gone pleasant so the crowd won't see that anything's amiss. No wonder Kris and I have such issues. Dad's *smiling* as he berates us. "When we are in the public eye, the image of what alliances our family presents is paramount. You know that well."

"It's a *lie*," I hear myself say. Echoey and empty still, hollow and achy.

I'm too on edge, and so I say those three words and watch my dad's face go analytical, then ripe with distrust.

"Was I wrong to share that information with you, Nicholas?" He glances over his shoulder, to where Hex and Iris are working their

way around another lap of the rink. "The Halloween Prince is playing to your sympathies?"

I can't put a name to the feeling that comes to life in my body
when Dad talks about Hex. I feel my vision start to slip.

"He has nothing to do with that," I say through my teeth.

Kris presses closer. "What are you talking about? What information?"

Members of our court skate around us, smiling in the crisp air,
and the song is now something bright and tinkling and merry.

Dad shifts from performative calm to offense back to nothing-is-
wrong so skillfully that it makes me dizzy.

"Stay away from him," Dad tells me. He eyes Kris for the first
time. "And stay away from *her.* You will both do your part to make
this competition with the Halloween Prince authentic. If I catch
either of you doing anything to weaken that story, you will not like
the consequences."

He skates off, waving to the crowd that presses around the rink.

"What the hell was that about?" Kris gasps.

He doesn't know about Hex. Not the truth.

I twist, letting the skates glide me around—Hex and Iris are outside the rink, surrounded by members of our court, caught in more
idle talk.

"The marriage competition is a lie," I tell Kris. I keep my voice
low, not having to try; it comes out stunted and weak.

"I know—"

"No—the whole thing is a *lie.* Even the part where we're lying
to Halloween. Hex isn't here because he thinks he's going to win
Easter—he's here because Dad forced them to hand over something, some*one,* to keep them in check about voicing discontent until
Christmas Eve."

A puff of white bursts out of Kris's mouth. "What?"

Iris is sitting now, working off her skates, while Hex is talking
cordially with one of the journalists.

I have more questions than answers. More concerns than solu-
tions.

But I know how to resolve one of those questions right now.

"I'll be right back." I pat Kris's arm and push off him as he goes, "You can't drop that and run off on me!"

Shit. I'll tell him everything, I really will.

I cut across the rink, dodge people skating the opposite direction, and step out in front of Iris.

She glances around—no one else is close by. "Your dad's an ass."

"What'd he say to you?" I drop onto the bench next to her.

She rips off her last skate and tosses it to the ground. "Accused me of not only jeopardizing the story about you and Hex courting me, but being *loose* about my commitment to you."

My face scrunches. "What the—"

"Just for skating with Kris." She yanks on her boots and slams her feet down. Her shoulders deflate, anger venting. "But I shouldn't have let you skate with Hex. I lost focus. I'm sorry, Coal."

"Don't you dare apologize."

"You were pissed at me the other night for pushing you and Hex together."

"Yeah, well, I got over it."

There's no one around us close enough to listen; Hex is off to the side now, currently undoing his own skates.

Dad, though, glides past us on the ice and gives me a solemn nod of approval. Presumably for sitting next to Iris.

I look away, jaw tight.

"Does Easter want to be allied with Christmas?" I whisper.

Iris frowns. "Yeah. That's rather the point of this whole situation between us."

"No, I mean—I know you said your dad's doing it now to appease the people in Easter who think he isn't a good enough leader, but was it really something your father decided he wanted to do, or did my dad force his hand?"

Iris looks out at the ice. Her dad is skating. Smiling.

"Why are you asking?" The question is dense with reservation. Not wanting to talk about it? Or not wanting to talk with *me* about it?

"Dad told me some things that have started clarifying a lot," I say. "And I never stopped to wonder what you're actually getting out of this alliance. All the benefits my dad's talked about are purely for Christmas, with Easter as an afterthought."

"Well, I at least get your sparkling company." She tries for a smile.

I hold her gaze, eyebrows lifting, and she blinks in surprise.

"All right." She adjusts, shoulders leveling. "My father does want to appease our court. He wants the notoriety Christmas has. And more joy, of course. That's what it's all about, right?" But she sighs. "He doesn't talk about this union with Christmas like it's a partnership anymore. I think he likes that someone is telling him what to do and making decisions that at least *look* like they'll benefit us so he doesn't have to think about how he's ruling Easter by himself."

"He isn't ruling Easter by himself," I say with a pointed look at her.

She shrugs. "I do what I can. And Lily . . . well, you know what Lily's like."

Lily puts on a persona as flawless as Iris's, but she's five thousand times more controlling. She'd get fixated on the small details that only affected her—a boyfriend who ruined her birthday—rather than anything bigger—said boyfriend ruining her birthday because he *bankrupted a country.*

"She wants what's best," Iris continues, "but she doesn't have the resolve that your father does. So they agree with whatever he says, and so far, the decisions he's made soothe the naysayers in our court. It's not that your dad *forced* us into an alliance. It's just that it never occurred to my father that we could rule Easter on our own."

I arch forward, arms braced on the bench, one knee bouncing. "So we aren't . . . blackmailing you into this engagement?"

She tips her head, studying me. "You really think so little of yourself?"

I grin, because that isn't what I was getting at, and my genuine amusement smooths her concern. "I'm gonna keep it real with you, Lentora. I'm way out of your league."

She laughs, like a deep, full-belly seal-bark of a laugh.

I drop my mouth open. "Ouch, Peep. You could've laughed a little less demonically."

Dad isn't keeping her here with blackmail, then. It's only a little relieving, but I blow out a breath anyway.

She leans her head on my shoulder and tucks her arm through mine. We sit like that for a moment, watching skaters whirl by, listening to Christmas songs vibrate the cold air.

A few photographers catch pictures of us. The only satisfying thought I can drudge up is that it'll mollify Dad for a bit. *Princess Iris and Prince Nicholas cuddle at ice skating event.*

Ahead of us, Kris got dragged into a conversation with some courtiers on the ice.

Hex is at the railing of the rink a few yards down, back in his normal boots and studying the poses and methods of the people skating by him, still trying to work it out. But his fingers twitch absently at his side, and his gaze darts to the edge of the crowd and back twice as I watch.

A gaggle of kids is laughing and bouncing up and down, batting at what looks like three little birds that dart in and out of their group. I squint—not birds. Tiny reindeer. Tiny reindeer *ghosts,* but at first glance, they could almost be made of snow.

My eyes go back to Hex, a smile leaping across my lips.

He must feel me watching him, because he looks over. He notes Iris's head on my shoulder and his focus snaps away, redness forming a curl from his jaw up to his temple.

"I think we're making him jealous," Iris tells me.

I stiffen. I can't help it.

She peels away with a smile.

"I have no idea who you're talking about," I say defiantly.

My god, *is* he jealous?

"Uh-huh." She kicks the ground below the bench. "Thanks for being concerned about me. Thanks for just listening."

I swallow any immediate reaction and instead, I ask, "Are you still okay with all this? The fake-courting scam. Our . . . eventual marriage."

Iris bites the inside of her cheek. "I still worry what it would do to our people's trust if they found out this was all a lie," she whispers. "And now that this *competition* is underway, I worry that it would make me look flippant and selfish to *not* choose one of you at the end."

"Fuck what—" I bite my tongue to cut back my response of *Fuck what other people think*. Because she's always cared what people think of her, how she's perceived in her position, in Easter, in life; and it's all for a valid reason, what with some of her court questioning her family since before she was even born. I won't cheapen her concerns with my own reactions anymore.

I take her hand and squeeze her fingers. "I'm sorry. If I can figure out a way to stop this and have it be for a legitimate reason, I'll let you know."

She squeezes my hand back and releases it with a soft sigh. "In some ways, being forced into this is easier. I can see the appeal in just letting your father take the lead and make decisions the way my father does."

"You deserve better than this though. You deserve two people fighting over you because they're both madly in love with you, not because they got lassoed into it."

One corner of her mouth lifts, but the smile doesn't blossom, just stays wilted on her face. "I used to want a love story like my parents. To look up in a café and know—*it's you*."

"You could have one. A better one."

"No." She meets my eyes. "I *used to* want their love story. My dad always said he saw my mom at a café in Strasbourg and just *knew* that she'd be important to him. But I've seen what it can do now, when *happily ever after* ends. This isn't a fairy tale, Coal. We're a prince and a princess but it's our jobs, not some storybook title, and I know Easter has problems but I barely know how to keep it afloat as is, let alone fix the issues. What are we supposed to do?"

She's as stuck as I am. And she's been pushed to the point where she's starting to doubt that there will be a happy resolution, and *god*, how did I let things get this bad on so many fronts?

My eyes find Hex again.

"I don't know," I whisper to Iris. "But I know it isn't like this in all the Holidays, so maybe it doesn't have to be like this *here*."

Chapter Twelve

Dad makes Iris and Hex ride in his sleigh back to the palace. At dinner, another more relaxed event in the library, he never strays far from the two of them, surveying what they say and who they talk to. He eventually transfers Iris off to me, supposedly when he's decided she's had enough *Hex* time, and I bite back any retort at the look of exhaustion on her face and just go along with it.

It's only after Iris excuses herself for the evening that I make my way over to Kris, who is fuming as openly as I am. He's usually way better at capping himself—*was* he better, or did he spend more time worrying about how I'd react to what Dad does?

He isn't concerned about it now, though, and it almost makes me relax. At least he's put any notion of me abandoning him out of his head.

"So you think Halloween's setup is better than ours?" he whispers.

We'd had a sleigh to ourselves on the way back, and he'd taken the news about the blackmail and other Holidays as well as I had.

We're next to the fire, eyeing Dad, a few members of our court, and Hex, and every muscle in my body is aching with holding tense for so long. And from the skating. I'm going to need an ice bath at this rate.

"I don't know. It seemed like it, the way he mentioned it. And they have to be pretty intrinsically tied, if Halloween is so worried about losing their support."

"Dad worries about losing support too, though," Kris says. "All his shit about keeping our image clean for the press—"

"That's not about keeping allies appeased. It's about keeping people believing certain things to feed the Christmas-wholesome image. Because honestly, I've never heard Dad worry about losing an ally. What we have are . . . joy-victims, mostly."

"God, that's harrowing." Kris tugs at the collar of his shirt. Another festive sweater, this one bright red with white stripes that says *Is That a Candy Cane or Are You Just Happy to See Me?* across the chest.

The goofiness clashes so potently with his palpable rage that I can't help but grin, and I could hug him for that break in the seriousness.

"Do you remember much about the stuff we studied when we were kids?" I whisper. "About Christmas's history?"

"Some of it, yeah." Kris shrugs, dismissive at first, but he softens. "The origin stuff. And I remember one thing about a gift tradition—people started giving books during the Victorian era, elaborate illuminated things. I wrote a letter asking Dad for one, like kids are supposed to, because I wanted to be all formal about it. And there it was at Christmas. I still have it. He had no business giving an antique to a nine-year-old."

I smile. That happened after Mom left. So Dad was capable of not being cruel, even in the after.

We used to be happy, weren't we? At points.

Kris's eyes cut over my shoulder and he pushes off the fireplace. "Go time."

I swing around to see Hex walking for the door, nodding his good night to a few people.

He gets to the door of the library. His eyes swivel to mine.

But he ducks out into the hall.

Kris is already over with Dad, angling so Dad has to put his back to the door to talk to him.

I bolt.

But I don't want it to be creepy, so I hang around outside the library for a few minutes, beating my hands on my thighs.

He's probably in his suite now, right? Gonna risk it.

I take off, heading through the palace, but cut up short when

I hit the staircase that will angle me towards the wing with my suite. I veer left to a separate staircase, dipping through halls I rarely visit because they're for guests who aren't regulars like Iris.

It isn't hard to figure out which suite the staff put him in—all the doors have wreaths on them, but only one has a wreath that's set with glowing jack-o'-lanterns and arched black cats.

Up the hall, the way is empty; no staff or anyone wandering this late in the evening.

My heart ricochets against my ribs as I stop in front of that door. I tug at the hem of my blue button-up. Tug again. There's a wrinkle. Crap. I can go change?

My phone buzzes.

KRIS

KRIS
Don't chicken out.

how very dare you assume i would chicken out

KRIS
You're considering leaving right now, aren't you?

listen here you little shit

KRIS
Stop texting me and KNOCK ON HIS DOOR.

YOU TEXTED ME FIRST

I put my phone on mute and knock. Not because Kris told me to but because I am a fully grown adult capable of making my own choices.

And then I wince.

Because I know how this will look. Me, going to Hex's room, alone. But I *do* need to talk to him, privately, and this was the best thing Kris and I could come up with.

I'd originally thought that the two of us combined would make one serviceable leader. Maybe that's not necessarily the case.

After a few long seconds, the door opens.

Hex looks out at me. He hasn't changed yet, still in the black on black of his pants, button-up, and vest, and his jack-o'-lantern-in-Santa-hats tie. That's the only part of him that's disheveled; he'd loosened the tie, and that minor imperfection in his usual pristine appearance makes my mind go staticky.

"Coal," he says. He glances up the hallway. "Is something wrong?"

Yes. It has been forty-eight hours since I kissed you and that is *way too damn long.*

"No. I wanted to talk to you. In private."

He frowns uncertainly. "Your father—"

"I can take care of myself too." I give him a dashing smile.

But Hex doesn't smile back. "I told you—do not risk your responsibilities for me."

But you're worth it. "I'm here because I want to talk to you about Halloween. How it's set up. I have . . . suspicions. And I think you can help me work out some things."

Hex hesitates for one more beat. He eyes the empty hall again.

Then he sighs and steps aside, ushering me into his suite.

It's dim, one lamp on by the desk. His room is smaller than mine, with a canopied bed on one side and a small dividing wall creating a living room on the other. There's a couch and chair set before a fireplace, but no fire lit, and a small Christmas tree in the corner. Even in the low light, I can see the tree is black, strung with orange ribbon and witches and other Halloween trimmings.

Hex waves me to sit on the couch.

I obey.

He takes the chair.

All the better, honestly. Distance. Space. *Professionalism.*

I lean back and fold one leg over my knee, foot bouncing, needing to expel this nervous energy somehow. "My father told me certain things about Christmas, and I . . . I knew we had problems. But I didn't know, until two nights ago, how deep all this went with what we're doing to other Holidays. To Halloween."

Hex's brows go up. "He told you the details?"

"That Halloween and Christmas were almost in negotiations at one point. That you guys backed out rather than suffer the ramifications of your other allies turning on you for throwing your lot in with us. And this whole marriage competition came about as a way for Dad to reassert his dominance over you for objecting to the Christmas-Easter alliance." Anger heats my chest. "It wasn't enough for him to remind you of that dirt he has over you, how damaging it could be to your allegiances. He set up this thing as a *punishment*."

Hex studies me, his lips parted. Even in the dimness, I catch a flush to his cheeks, and it throws me into silence, long enough that he sits back in the chair and nods at me to continue.

Did I miss something?

My eyes go back to that stain on his cheeks.

"But," I clear my throat, and he's blushing stronger now, but his body language changes, blossoms and expands with my eyes on him. I smile, I can't help it; then I clear my throat *again*. Just talk fast, goddamn it. "It turns out my dad isn't doing the whole *It's not blackmail, it's an understanding* thing to only you; he's doing it to a bunch of winter Holidays, and—I think the way Halloween is set up with your autumn Holidays is different. Better."

Hex watches me for another silent moment, then his lips furl up. "Well, you're right. Halloween is better than Christmas."

"Okay," I smirk, "maybe *better* was a strong—"

"Ah-ah, no arguing, Christmas Prince. You are the one who sought me out for Halloween's undeniable better qualities. Do you want me to adopt you?"

"Oh yes, Daddyyy—" WHAT.

Oh my god, stop talking, *stop talking*—

I don't.

"—*yyyyyy*," is what keeps coming out of my mouth, followed by a strangled, "*Noooo.*"

And then, for no discernible reason, I make finger guns at him.

I fly to my feet and spin my back to him because I need to reset, like, *immediately,* and I refuse to see whatever reaction he's having because *I did not say that, it did not happen.*

Did I make finger guns at him?

What the fuuuuuuuuck.

"I mean—Halloween is *structured* better. With the other autumn Holidays. You made it sound like it's more collaborative. Less coercion. Like you guys support each other."

There's a long pause.

I turn around, hands bearing down into the back of the couch, and my eyes hit him as a grin is sliding off his face.

He shrugs. "It is more collaborative."

God, elaborate, please elaborate, save me from myself.

"My family represents Halloween," he continues, "but my mother is part of Día de Muertos, as I've said—and we come together with a dozen or so other autumn Holidays. We all work together throughout the year, and we all take equal shares of the joy we bring in. It is a collective, not a mere alliance."

"You pool your joy?"

"Yes."

"And you all get along? No one tries to usurp the others?"

"That would be counterproductive. We bring in joy from different sections of the world; taking over each other would risk that. We are stronger allowing ourselves to evolve as we are." He hesitates. "Which is what my family realized, once we were informed of what a Christmas alliance would require, demanding a percentage of our joy with little in return. There are faint rumors that Christmas is rather underhanded in their partnership tactics, as has been proven. But at the time, we were . . . hopeful that these fears were misplaced. That Christmas would be open to collaboration. Many of the other autumn Holidays distrust Christmas—they fear that if one of us gets pulled into Christmas's orbit, what would stop the rest from being dragged in as well?"

So Dad's let our reputation among other Holidays be less than perfect; is it only our people he cares about manipulating? Or does he not have as much control as he believes?

"The other autumn Holidays would force you out of the collective if they found out you tried to negotiate with Christmas?"

"They may, depending on how your father phrases whatever he lets slip. Even now, the way that my presence here is being spun, it is keeping our allies mollified—they happily believed that Christmas bowed to our request to forego an Easter alliance, which was rather clever of your father, to be honest. It gave the autumn allies exactly what they wanted, seeing Christmas recoil. But the fact that I am here, even under the guise of linking with Easter, is being met with . . . strain. They are questioning our commitment to a fair distribution of magic rather than Christmas's monopoly." Hex's lips tighten. "Which further solidifies that we are right to fear their reaction to any past Christmas-Halloween negotiations coming out."

A shiver walks up my spine. Is that part of why Dad orchestrated this whole thing too? To remind Halloween how detrimental his blackmail could be? Fuck.

"And you think your allies will forgive and forget when it comes out that we screwed you over in this engagement sham?"

Hex gives a careful smile. "I told you I don't need you to fix my Holiday. We have it under control."

"I'm not trying to fix it."

His look flattens.

"Fine, I'm not *only* trying to fix it. I want to understand as much as I can. I want to make sure I'm seeing everything for once in my fucking life so if—when, *when* I do something, I don't screw it up." *Again.*

I start pacing behind the couch, pivoting back and forth.

"And what are you trying to do?" Hex asks.

I stop, staring at the wall behind his head. "What if your autumn allies found out that the real reason you were in the North Pole is that you were helping the Christmas Prince put together his own collective?"

Hex pushes up from his chair. "What?"

A fire lights in me, a plan forming between each word. "A winter Holidays collective. It'd be easy to negotiate a pool like the one you mentioned with the Holidays Dad is taking advantage of so they're not just something we leech off—and maybe that way, we'll be able to focus on doing *actual good,* rather than worry so much about global reach. If all the Holidays Dad is bullying rally together, he'd have less leverage to screw them over."

Hex isn't picking up on my wonder. He looks worried, the same twist of hesitation that almost kept him from letting me into his suite. "Won't your father be opposed to this?"

"He won't have to know until I get something set up, see if the other Holidays are willing to discuss it. And if you're part of it, then your collective can't be upset with you for any association with Christmas, because you were really here to help me start this. Right? And we could spin that into the reason for Halloween's original negotiations with Christmas, so it'd take all the leverage out of Dad revealing that."

Plus, Iris couldn't be faulted for not choosing either of us at the end if Hex and I were working on this all along. Yeah, it was a lie, but it was to cover up something *good.* We could finagle Easter into the collective too so they get benefits that would shut up any of the people gunning for weaknesses around Iris's family—Easter isn't a winter Holiday, but what *is* winter, really? Christmas also happens during the summer in half the world. It snows on Easter. Somewhere. Whatever, this collective doesn't have to be bound by a season.

Could this be a solution Iris would approve of? Should I tell her about this? I don't even know if there is a *this,* not yet; all the winter Holidays could laugh at any attempt of mine to fix what my dad has done. Even telling Hex this much—

I rock backwards. "Oh my *god*. I did this to you again."

"Did what?"

"I put you in another awkward position." Panic drains all the warmth from my face. "Because if you *don't* want to be involved in this, then the *prince of a rival Holiday* now knows that I'm planning *a small coup against the reigning Santa*—oh my god. As if my dad needed more shit to blackmail you with. Holy *fuck,* why am I so *toxic*—"

I spin on my heels and am halfway to hurling myself out the door when Hex grabs my wrist.

I stop.

There's no other response than to go pliant when he's touching me.

"I'm glad you told me," he whispers.

I throw a disbelieving stare at him. In the low glow from the lamp, I can see the way his eyes are waiting to snag mine, his face falling open in a rare look of complete, utter vulnerability.

"I was going to keep my head down and get through this charade," he tells me. "Halloween wears a mask better than anyone, or so we like to believe. It was only a few weeks. I had all these *plans*. And then you storm upon me, and—and you've been nothing at all that I've expected. Not from the very start."

"You were expecting a hot mess, and I'm really a supernova mess?"

His smile is dazed. "In an endearing way. You've been . . . honorable."

"Honorable? Ha. Sure."

"You are. Like some kind of red and green Captain America."

That joke only lands because I am so obviously *not* anything remotely superhero worthy.

Breath returns to me. One sip, another, until a thought rattles free. "How are you *glad* I told you? I've put you in danger by letting you know this."

God, I'm so fucking terrified of messing anything up, it's a wonder I can walk a straight line.

"There's that honor," he says, taking in the change of my expression and so easily reading the thoughts that race through my head.

My brows go up in mixed surprise that I'm so transparent to him and panic about what else he might see. What unworthy, disastrous parts of me might creep across my face and make him withdraw instead of looking at me like he's in awe? Which that look just—just isn't possible to begin with. There's nothing at all in me deserving of that look, especially from him.

"I'm glad you told me," he continues, "because I do want to help you. However I can. I have prepared, Halloween has prepared, to endure backlash from your father already. I don't know that I should announce my involvement with any plans of yours to the world quite yet, but I'll be fine. You don't need to protect me."

"I can't help myself." Then, since I have no shame left, "There's a lot I can't help myself with around you."

It's another instance where something's changed in his posture but I can't figure out what, all I know is the energy plummets to an aching severity.

And he's still holding on to my arm.

"What else can you not help yourself with around me?" he asks.

I'm half certain it's a hallucination. No way in any reality would someone like him let me be here; fumbling, unsteady, desperate *me* next to confident, controlled, assured *him*.

"I can't help," I hardly hear myself, "this insufferable need to find out what it's like to witness every shade of joy on your face."

Right now, his face shows only shock. Breathless, disoriented shock identical to the emotion batting around in my head, and it's bewitching, because I feel like this is an expression he shows less willingly than awe.

"What about—" He stops himself. Bites his lips together and winces in self-deprecation.

"What?"

"I have no right to ask this of you. But I . . . I think I have to. You said neither of you wants your engagement, but I've come to like Iris, and I don't wish to hurt her with any of—" He stops again. His hand pulses on my wrist, filling in the unspoken words.

A smile sweeps across me. "You *were* jealous."

His wide eyes hold on mine, jaw bunching in refusal to show embarrassment, and he doesn't pick up on any of my teasing.

"Honestly," I whisper, smile dimming. "I was too. Watching you give her flowers. Every time my dad forces you two together. And Iris is fully aware that I feel this way—that I'm jealous of *her,* not of you. I'm jealous that she gets to be the object of your attention. This whole thing I have with her is unbearable, for both her and me, and it's something I'm still figuring out how to undo. But god no, there's nothing real between us. She relentlessly mocks me for the way I trip over myself around you."

Hex exhales, but something remains in his eyes, shifting back and forth as he studies me. "Perhaps it is a bit mockable. The allure is merely because I am still that mystery guy who threw himself at you in an alley."

"It started that way." I shift, closing a meager extra inch of space to chase off that look of doubt. "But it wouldn't be this consuming if that was all it still was. If you weren't also the guy who went to that bar in the first place, knowing you'd get exactly what you wanted. If you weren't also brave and caring and so fucking quick-witted you give me a run for my money. You're challenging and entrancing and yeah, you've got some issues, but god, don't we all. The fantasy of you was pretty great—but everything I've gotten to know about the real you is so much better."

I stop talking, because I can't breathe, hearing what I said—that was *a lot,* like all the crap rattling around in my head that I was trying really hard to *keep to myself.* But here it all is now, churning in the air between us, to whatever end, and my pulse is hammering in my wrists so hard that my arm twitches in Hex's grip.

He's barely moved. His eyes are fixed on me, and he whispers something I don't catch over the roaring of blood in my ears.

"What did you say?" It comes out as a rumble. Weird, feral anger that isn't anger but *is* because he's up against my body and not close enough.

We're alone in his room. Nothing I've ever done has felt as carnal as being this close to him with walls between us and anyone else.

He works the fingers of his other hand through the edge of my button-up, hooking his grip in and fisting it against my chest. "Kiss me," he tells me.

Yes, yes, *god yes.*

His eyes shut, his lips part, gasping, gasping, and I drink that breath, lap up this energy he lets me have, until I rest my lips on the corner of his mouth.

He smells like sweet citrus and spice again, and I chase that scent, tugging aside the collar of his shirt and his loosened tie to drop my mouth to his neck. I don't think he was expecting me to go straight for his neck and he croons, a syrupy warble of a moan that rockets up the list of my favorite noises. My knees go fully liquid, body assaulted on one side from that moan and another from the scent of him, this is the origin of that burnt-sugar cinnamon orange aphrodisiac, resting right over the rapid-fire beat of his pulse.

Fingers under his chin, I tilt his head, giving my lips more access. His reaction is far more controlled now, a discreet catch of breath that feels like a challenge. I work my lips up the side of his throat, slow open-mouthed kisses, and he shudders but stays quiet, and oh *fuck* no.

I know what he sounds like now. These discreet little breath-sips just won't do.

My lips climb higher, and I pull his hair out of its knot so it's messy and I can twine my fingers in it.

"How much?" I dip my tongue against the shell of his ear. Fuck, his taste will ruin me.

"How—how much what?" His throat bobs. I hear the rasp of his swallow.

"How much do you want me to kiss you?"

"Rather—" He stutters. "Rather badly, it would seem."

I smile, pressing that smile to the side of his face. "No, sweetheart—I mean how *much,* how far, because I'm hanging by a thread here and I need you to tell me where the finish line is before I shove us both out into the race."

"Race."

"Mm."

"Planning to throw me off a sleigh again?"

A low, predatory growl throbs in my chest, but I'm grinning, and I walk us backwards. Just one step. Almost to the wall, to something I can push him up against.

"You didn't answer my question."

"I—I don't know," he admits. "I don't know. I haven't . . . done this . . . much. In a while. I have done this. Not excessively. I—" He looks up at the ceiling. "I am done speaking now."

I pull back. "You not talking doesn't work for me. I need to know what you're thinking, and I'll ask, but the moment, *the moment,* it *borders* on uncomfortable for you, *you tell me.*"

He nods. Nods again.

"What I want is *you* wanting this," I say, low, I can't seem to speak any higher, not with the heat welling in my chest—if I talk too loud, we'll both combust. "That's my finish line. You."

"All right." His voice is hoarse. He nods again, more desperately.

"Where should I start?" I ask into his cheek.

He whimpers and grabs my lips with his. I cup his head in my hands and open his mouth with my tongue and goose bumps prickle up my arms, down across my back, thighs shaking, eyelids heavy with fervor.

Everything in my life is spinning out around me, but the most irreversible part of it all is what he's doing to me.

"Start here," he says into my mouth.

His back collides with the wall and I box my body around him.

"And then?"

He touches my neck. "Here."

"And then?"

His fingers walk to the edge of my shoulder. He hesitates.

"And then," he echoes, a quake in the hollow of his throat.

His hand slides down my arm, over my elbow, and he wraps his fingers around my forearm and holds on in a suddenly relentless grip, like he's bracing himself. My forehead touches his and we gasp into the concave space we create and I almost tell him, again, that he's in control of this, but those words well up and it wouldn't be him that I'm reassuring—it's me. Me and my anxiety and the fissure of desire cracking apart my body, this brief pause letting me feel that we're *here,* oh god I'm *here,* and I can't get a full breath.

Then Hex angles up and kisses me again and *oh god I'm here* becomes a long, drawn-out whimper against the feel of his rough tongue running along the seam of my lips. I open my mouth and kiss him with all the last fleeting remnants of disbelief and anxiety, hands bearing down on his hips, his fingers iron-gripped around my forearms.

The map he'd drawn, of his body by touching mine, replays through my head—lips, neck, shoulder, arms; lips, neck, shoulder—

I move, mouth working across his jaw, needing the taste of his neck again, that warm skin, the spiced citrus sweetness of him, and the moment my tongue collides with that space, I groan.

"Fuck, Hex, the way you taste." I suck on his skin and earn a shiver in response. "Even your shivers taste good."

"Coal," my name pops out of his mouth, a startled burst so swollen with need that my whole body whittles to the singular point of his desperation.

I nuzzle into his neck, thumbs dragging circles on his hips. "I want to make you feel good." Do I sound begging? God, I am, I am begging.

He whines. *Writhes,* his body arching up into mine, and he's biting my neck, the spot below my ear. The sensation of his teeth on me is transcendent, and I think I must black out, coming to when we're nothing but panting and the pop of lips on skin.

The top buttons of his shirt come apart under my fingers and I loop a hand around his neck, making a feast of his collarbone, teeth pushing lightly on skin, scraping. Finally, *finally,* he makes that noise again, that syrupy moan and his legs part so my thigh drags between his. He rocks, and I can feel him against me, a hard grind on my hip that sets off hemorrhagic fireworks in my veins.

I say it again. A prayer tumbling out of me into the hot, hot air as I push back against his movement. "I want to make you feel good, Hex."

"You are," he tells me, each word a little desperate huff. "All of this—feels—very, very good." A pause, a sudden tension, his eyes are shut but the skin tightens there. "Do—is this—for you, I mean—"

He's babbling. All his proprieties, all his rigid formality—I broke it down, brought him to single syllables and incomplete questions.

That's the remaining thread. I can feel it strung taut, one more shift of his hips against my leg and it'd snap, radiance and ether.

I kiss his cheekbone, that tension next to his eye, but I make it reverent, dragging a brake on the riot.

His eyes are shut still, lips parted, and I close around him, bracing one arm on the wall next to his head, my other hand molded to the curve of his hip, his fingers holding me there, viselike, and if I looked I know his knuckles would be white. But I can't look anywhere other than his face.

"God yes, it's good for me," I say, jaw thrust forward. "But I'm going to go back to my room."

His thumb hooks into my belt, and the way those eyes flare open and look up at me screams confusion.

"I'm going to go back to my room," I say again, "because I want to take my time with you. Because you deserve that."

I really don't mean it to come out all gritty. But I feel the reverberating tremor that shudders up through Hex's body in response.

And all he says is a strained, needy, "All right."

I am leaving. *I am leaving.*

Hands off the wall.

Feet taking a full step back.

One more, just to be safe.

The air is cold without his body up against mine. But he's there on the wall still, wilted and hands flat on either side of his hips as if he's staying upright only by that contact. The low light of his room throws him into shadows, and he is every bit a Halloween prince, an interplay of joy hidden in darkness, sparks in the night.

His hair is mussed, collar spread open and a spot on his shoulder is red.

He sees me looking at it. And reaches up, lays fingers on that spot.

His eyelashes flutter.

Oh fuck.

I dive back in, half rabid, half ecstatic, and he meets me there, driving up against me with his mouth open already and my lips meet his and I need to leave *right now* or else—

I lurch back, fingers splayed, and do not look at him. Cannot. I'm staring at the floor. The very, very interesting pattern of his rug.

Our hard breaths grate in the ensuing silence.

"I'm leaving now," I say. My lips feel bruised.

Why the fuck am I leaving now?

Because I'm a goddamn gentleman. I *am*. Leaving. And a gentleman.

"All right," he says again. He's ragged.

I walk. Determined, intensified steps. And it isn't until I get to the door that I trust myself enough to turn and look, but at the space by his feet.

"Good night," I say, stupidly, because what else do you say to someone who let you take the first layers off, see the flush and the pebbled skin?

At the edge of my vision, I note Hex's hand on his mouth, the barest touch of his fingertips to his lips.

"Good night," he echoes.

Peep, Mini Candy Cane, and the Best Claus

KRIS
Iris, Coal isn't answering his texts again. Have you seen him?

Coal?? The fuck dude, you said you'd let me know how it went last night.

IRIS
how what went?

KRIS
He went to talk to Hex about some things.

IRIS
. . . . . . you sent coal to talk to hex alone

KRIS
Yeah, that was the general plan.

IRIS
kristopher.

KRIS
Oh shit.

Coal.

COAL, DID YOU FUCK THE HALLOWEEN PRINCE

We were going to be PROFESSIONAL, seriously.

IRIS
KRIS!! you can't put that in a text thread!

omg delete it you idiot

i did not fuck him

[the longest pause in the history of group chats]

IRIS
coal. i say this with the greatest
amount of love for you.

bring me breakfast, i'm sore from
skating

> okay that pause took 10 years off
> my life and that's the only thing
> you have to say

IRIS
why would that pause have taken
years off your life? huh? HUHHH??

if you didn't do anything

KRIS
Yeah, Coal, I think you should
bring me breakfast too.

Considering I have been beside
myself with worry over my only
brother's fate.

While you've been boning.

Coal

Your silence is incriminating.

IRIS
yeah he definitely fucked my fake
suitor

KRIS
You're allowed to text that but I
can't??

IRIS
this whole thread is a PR disaster,
i'm deleting everything

Chapter Thirteen

The moment it gets to a reasonable hour, I *leave my fucking phone in my room,* Iris and Kris can get their own breakfasts, and fly out of bed. Quick minor styling, a hoodie, then I race down to the kitchen.

Renee and her staff already have a buffet spread across a side table. At—I check a clock in the corner—six thirty in the morning.

Reasonable-*ish* hour.

Shit. Will he even be awake yet?

I start loading up a tray, grabbing one of everything because I have no idea what he likes. Pancakes. Waffles. Bacon. Eggs. Fruit. Coffee. Sausages? No, my self-control can only go so far, I cannot sit there watching him eat sausages—

"Hungry this morning, Prince Nicholas?"

I jump and damn near knock over the tower of bacon I have mounded on my tray.

Next to me, Renee's sous chef Lacie is adding a platter of sliced melon to the buffet. She looks at my tray, then me, with a curious glint.

"Starving. It's not all for me. But yes, very hungry. It's for Iris too. And Kris."

Lacie's eyes narrow, that glint growing into a full-fledged spark. She glances over her shoulder at Renee, who is already crossing to us, extending a box and a little pot with steam creeping out the neck.

"Hot water and tea." Renee wedges both items onto the tray.

"Tea?"

She holds my gaze. "Trust me." Then she and Lacie go back to work.

All right. Sure. Can't hurt.

The early hour means the halls are mostly empty, a few staff up and heading off on errands. It makes it easy to avoid passing anyone who might ask questions, and then I'm back in front of Hex's door.

If a reporter had caught me outside Iris's door with breakfast, it would've at least played into Dad's lie, but this?

I knock quickly.

My heart is all hasty thundering and I survey the haul I grabbed. This is . . . a lot of food.

The door opens after a few seconds, which likely means I didn't wake him up.

I'd seen him disheveled last night. Because of me. But he's wearing a sleeveless gray robe now, hastily thrown on so the sash isn't knotted, the hood up, and it hangs open to show a V-cut white tank beneath, black pajama pants and his bare feet on the carpet.

It's more skin than he's shown yet.

So I stand there gawking and I don't care at all if a reporter might see us because *holy fuck he's stupid hot* and that is absolutely headline worthy.

"Coal." He tips his head, catching my eyes, because I was staring at his arms. The swell of his bicep.

"Sorry." No, I'm not; has he seen himself? I lift the tray. "Breakfast?"

He blushes and pulls open the door to usher me in, his eyes on mine the whole time I cross the threshold.

I set the tray on the nearest table, one next to the couch, and he shuts the door and we stand there like fools, grinning at each other.

"I, um," I twist to the tray, "I didn't know what you liked. So I got everything."

He moves. Closing the distance. Stepping up beside me.

And laughs. "You are not exaggerating."

"But no cocoa."

His eyes snap to the side of my face.

"You don't seem to like cocoa," I say.

"You noticed that?"

My gaze drifts to his, lazily. It feels like we have all the time in the world, like if we stay locked in this bubble of giddy happiness, we can be here as long as we want.

"Yeah," I say. "Plus, it's majorly offensive to diss on the cocoa.

Like, that's all anyone talks about, how unforgivable it is that Prince Hex cringes over *melted chocolate in a mug*. We're questioning if you're even human."

"Oh, I'm not, but—and I truly mean this with no offense to Christmas's sensitive disposition—whatever you're serving is *not* melted chocolate in a mug."

I pick up the coffee carafe, but Hex shakes his head and grabs for the tea. I nudge him away and make it for him, face heating, because . . . how did Renee and Lacie know? *Did* they know? They couldn't have known I was bringing this to *Hex*. Did they? No.

Did they?

Choosing to ignore this.

"What is it, then?" I hand the cup to him.

He takes it, fingers brushing mine. "Watery."

I gasp in mock horror. "Oh, Christmas will never forgive you. Our hot cocoa is not *watery*."

He sips the tea. I track the movement of his lips on the rim.

"Come to Mexico," he says, "and I'll give you *real* cacao. Frothy and thick and decadent. And *spicy* too. If you can handle heat."

My lips split in a wide smile. "Oh, I can handle it."

The grin he gives is all devilish, hypnotic.

He closes one hand, the other still holding his tea, and when he opens his fist, something small and black sits in his hand. A—tube? A plunger?

I give him a sultry look. "Kinky."

He rolls his eyes. "It's *candy*. You said you can handle heat—and this is the *extra* spicy version."

I take it and read the label. "'*Pelon Pelo Rico. Hot, Intenso.*' Lovely. Likely not something kinky after all, then."

He sips his tea again, his eyes going purposefully to the tube of candy. As if I need any further incentive to do whatever the fuck he asks of me.

I pull off the cap, and after some fiddling, figure out that it is a plunger of sorts, and when I push on it, orange goo shoots up in tendrils from the top.

"Cheers." I tip it at Hex and his watchful grin then squirt a mouthful across my tongue.

At first, it's only salty and sweet, more savory than the sugary treats I'm used to.

Then.

Spice hits me, a tingle at the back of my throat that rises. And rises. And ignites into a flame that makes every white person cell in my body scream out in terror.

I cough and sputter but swallow, obediently, scorching my throat all the way down.

Hex curls his lips into his mouth. "How's that heat handling for you?"

"What heat?" I grab for a cup of coffee and gulp it.

"My brothers constantly have their pockets stuffed with those. My *nine-year-old* brothers."

"Why wouldn't they love this stuff?" My tongue is numb. "This is obviously something for children."

"You're a terrible liar. I see why Christmas has to water down their hot cocoa."

I chug another cup of coffee. It only mildly helps, and I shove in a bite of pancake, which does, finally, cut the spice. Even so, I stretch my mouth, roll my tongue, and Hex laughs.

"You're amused by my pain," I say, but I overemphasize my numb tongue, mashing every word into a pathetic garble.

"Oh, I'm not trying to be subtle about that." His grin is turning my insides to mush.

I hold up a bite of pancake for him. He shakes his head, takes another sip of tea, and I grunt in objection.

"No. No. Absolutely not. You can't tell me you don't like *pancakes* either."

Hex smirks. "Breakfast in general, honestly. I don't usually eat in the morning."

"Oh god. Don't let Renee figure that out—she'll hog-tie and force-feed you."

"Renee?"

"Our head chef. So, I basically brought all this food for myself."

Hex shrugs. "I appreciate the tea."

I cock my hip on the back of the couch and fold my arms across my chest and shake my head, this smile will be the death of me, and I can think of no sweeter way to go.

"You're looking at me like that again," he says, cup to his lips.

"Like what?"

"Like—" He fumbles, and I rock towards him, the smallest crack in his façade lets pieces of him slip through and I want to catch every single one.

My nearness has his breath hitching and he sets down the tea, forcefully, a little sloshing over the side.

"Like what?" I ask again, and I drag my lips from his shoulder to his temple. There's still the burn of spice on my tongue, and I wonder if he can feel the heat of it, caressing his skin.

He hisses air out his nose. "You know like what."

"I want to hear you say it."

"You didn't hear me say enough last night?"

My hands clasp his upper arms. I thought taking it slow would help me develop a tolerance to him, build up my ability to not disintegrate at the feel of his skin or the little noises he makes. But if anything, all the sensation is even more intense; I'm cursed that every interaction with his body will forever shred my soul until the only thing that remains is the part of me hooked to his needy moan.

"No," I say into his temple. "I am an insatiable sap. A greedy romantic, and I will never get enough of hearing you talk about what I'm doing to you and the reaction your body is having."

He teeters, catches himself with his arms around my neck, and I do want to make him tell me, but I need to kiss him more. And so I drive against his sharp hip bones as he devours my lips in a heady, frantic rush. The fact that he's as starved for me as I am for him has me aiming us for the couch in a scramble—we're not going to make it, it's too far away and I need him against me *now*. My thigh slams into the table, rocks the tray, his cup tips over, so I lift him and there's a brief crash of shock when he's airborne.

His eyes widen. Then go intent as he dutifully hooks his legs around my hips and settles in my arms.

Everything else on earth vanishes because he strokes his nails across my scalp, tugs lightly on my curls, angling me back and up so he can arch down to suck on my lip. I directed us last night, he allowed me to, and I go malleable to his control now.

Someone knocks on his door.

He freezes, mouth on mine, hands in my hair. "Oh, no."

My brain is in a delicious fog and I rise up out of it like pushing through honey.

"Prince Hex?" comes Wren's voice from the hall. "I have your itinerary for the day."

Her presence crashes over me.

I'm in Hex's room.

At six-something in the morning.

And he's still playing the role of unwilling fake possible fiancé to Easter to stop Dad from screwing things up with their collective; and I'm doing that too, only now also trying to unravel my dad's whole blackmail scheme in what is effectively treason and—

And I'm holding the Halloween Prince while we're both in our pajamas.

"Put me down." He squirms against me and that does *nothing* to help break my fog, but I comply.

"Coming!" he shouts at the door. To me, he mouths, panicked, "Hide."

Hide?

Hide.

God, this fog won't lift—I whip around the room, settle on his bathroom, and bolt for it as Hex moves to the door.

"Wait!" he whisper-shouts. "The tray!"

The tray of an embarrassing amount of food, *way* too much for one person, and the cup that's on its side and currently dripping English Breakfast tea onto the carpet.

I wheel around. "Damn it."

"Yes. That." He's closest, grabs it, and I meet him to take it from his hands.

I cock my head. "I don't think I've ever heard you cuss."

"Halloween's magic doesn't like when I curse."

I'm halfway to throwing myself into the bathroom when I come to a full stop.

"What?" I had to have misheard him.

"Prince Hex?" Wren knocks again. "Is everything all right?"

"Everything is fine! Just a moment!" Hex growls out a frustrated breath and glares at me. "Go!"

"No—wait, hang on, you're saying your magic doesn't let you cuss?"

"It's not that it doesn't *let* me, it's that it—I cannot have this conversation with you right now!" He puts his hands on my shoulders and pushes, and I've got a good half a foot on him, but I take a few small steps backwards.

"Why? What happens if you do?"

"Coal—"

"If Halloween's magic is hurting you—"

"It isn't anything bad. It's . . . irritating."

"Irritating? How?"

"You are *impossible*." He shakes his head in a *I can't believe I'm doing this* way, which makes me grin. "Our magic evolves based on the beliefs and traditions that feed the joy we create, yes?" he whispers, and I nod. "Well. *Cursing* is a rather serious item for Halloween. In every classification of the word."

"Okay . . ."

Hex hangs his head. Takes a fortifying breath.

Then he deadpans, "Shit."

If the shock of hearing him cuss wasn't enough, a spark of magic sizzles in the air between us, and then a *full jack-o'-lantern* pops into existence.

He catches it as it falls.

And I *lose it*.

"*Oh my god.*"

I can't breathe. The laugh gets stuck against my need to stay quiet and I start wheeze-coughing, eyes tearing. *"What the—"*

"Now HIDE." Hex shoves me into the bathroom, the tray clattering in my fumbling grip, and I relent, fighting down a laugh so hard I'm practically sobbing.

I bend forward and kiss him again. I've completely fallen for this guy. Spontaneous pumpkin creation and all. "That was the single greatest thing I've ever seen."

He deposits the pumpkin onto a nearby table. "That a member of the Halloween aristocracy can conjure a jack-o'-lantern? You need to get out more."

"I really—wait!" I rear back. "Can you *actually* curse someone then?"

"Can *you* curse someone? Our magic comes from joy and mine does not allow me to inflict harm on people."

"That makes sense, I—"

Hex pushes the door closed, at the last second not letting it slam.

I live in this joy for about ten seconds, the time it takes him to cross the room and open the main door, and then I hear Wren. She asks him if everything is all right, again, then explains the schedule for the day—some concert—and asks if he needs anything.

I imagine what it'll be like at events now. Watching him get paraded around with Iris, with my dad, and not being able to touch him or *look* at him because apparently I *look at him like that* rather strongly.

But if I can get Christmas's control of other Holidays out from under my father's thumb. If I can wrest away the coercion and lies and divvy up a *fair* running of things, then there will be no need to manipulate anyone. There will be no need for me to marry Iris or solidify any alliances that way.

Wren leaves, the main door shuts, and I wait until Hex opens the bathroom door.

Whatever lightness I'd inspired in him is gone. His strain is back, and I can see him realizing what awaits us too, lies and distance and playing this stupid game.

I put the tray on the floor and take his face in my hands. His eyes slam shut, bracing himself.

"I can fix this," I say to him, but I'm saying it to myself too.

Hex's throat bobs against my fingers. "What can I do?"

I press my forehead to his. Breathing him in.

There's a lot I want to do. Contact the other rulers of the Holidays. Get them to agree to a collective and unite against my dad's threats. But I also want to know what the people of Christmas think of us—do they know what my father has done? Do they agree with the goals he perpetuates? Dad has worked so hard to paint a certain image of us, but what do people *think*?

And then there's the whole matter of understanding the inner workings of Christmas. I should know this stuff. How the Merry Measure works and how the routes are organized and what needs to happen for the Toy Factory to function. So I want to start doing *that* too, but how does that fit in with my other plans?

Will any of these things help? Or is this all another preamble to disaster?

I lean into Hex, letting him keep me steady. "You can—hell, you can keep being *you*, because I've kind of become infatuated with you, Hex Hallow."

A whimper resonates in the back of his throat. I wouldn't have heard it if I hadn't been so close to him.

"You are going to make it impossible," he starts, eyes shut, lips swollen from me, "to get through these events now. The pretense was already difficult before—but every time you look at me, it is progressively more excruciating how much I want you to kiss me."

My turn to whimper. My turn to dissolve.

"Here." I take his hand and work off one of his rings to slide it onto my thumb.

He stares down at his ring on my hand. "You're wearing a skull ring, Christmas Prince."

"Well, my nails aren't black and orange anymore, so this way, I'm always touching you. Sort of." I twist the ring so the skull bit faces my palm and from the side, it's a silver band. "Every time we're in public and I want to touch you but can't, I'll touch this ring instead."

"And then?" His eyes meet mine, wide and mischievous and *god* I love this side of him, so different from the façade he wears around everyone else.

"And then," I echo those words he whispered last night, the lights that lit the path he guided me on, "I'll sneak away to your suite and show you what every touch meant."

"But I don't have something of yours."

I don't wear jewelry. Or anything he could discreetly have.

"There's always plenty of Christmas stuff around." I nod at the décor in his room, the tree and statues of snow-covered houses on his fireplace mantel. "Just touch something, and I'll know."

"Are you saying that when I want to kiss you, I should fondle a Christmas tree?"

I cringe. "Oh, god, don't make it weird. I was trying to be cute!"

"I was thinking I could have your *phone number,* and simply text you. Something easily done. But I must say, this has been an educational diplomatic mission. I knew the symbolism of Christmas's decorations ran deep, but I never would have guessed they played roles in things of *that* nature—*Coal!*"

His words cut off in a startled cry as I squat down and heave him over my shoulder. By the time I toss him bodily onto the couch, his cheeks are beautifully pink and I dive down over top of him.

"When are they expecting you?" I ask against his mouth.

"An hour. You as well, I assume. A brunch before the concert."

"Mm." I bury my face in his neck, the hood of his sleeveless robe falling back, and I growl against the sweet, soft skin there. "An hour. It's mine."

"Yes," Hex agrees. "It is."

He pushes on me, and I buck back instantly, eyes narrowed in concern. But he doesn't say anything else, just pushes again until I'm sitting up on the couch.

Then he swings around, straddling my lap, and I'm very, very aware of the thinness of my pajama pants, and the thinness of *his* pajama pants, and the way his body moves as he arches over me, his hands grabbing the couch on either side of my head.

His face is right up against mine, so close he's all angles and tendons. I reach to trace the line of his jaw, that sharp edge, following it to the curve of his ear. Can he feel the way my hand is shaking? Fuck, probably, but I have to touch him, have to know the way the texture of his skin changes inch by inch.

Hex's eyes slip closed under my fingers stroking down the side of his throat. He leans into it with a feline curve, neck bending for my touch, and when he swallows, I watch the muscles work, contracting, goose bumps racing across his skin, down over his collarbone, his shoulder.

He has freckles on his shoulder.

That's going to be what does me in. Discovering these little spots on his body, layer by layer peeled back.

"What—" he starts, head lolled to the side, eyes still closed. "What do you want to do, exactly?"

I peel my hand off his shoulder. The retraction of contact and my lack of response has his eyes opening, finding mine, vulnerability in his wide gaze.

"Hex." I rest my hands on his thighs, fighting to find somewhere that isn't overtly sexual. "You're letting me touch you. I'm content."

"With that? That's it?"

"I'm content with whatever makes *you* content. I told you—my goal is you wanting this. I am remarkably easy to please."

He puts a hand on the center of my chest and gives an uncertain huff. "Really?"

Something snags between my ribs, below his palm. A jolt of regret.

"I'm really not as selfish as my reputation makes it seem," I manage.

He shrinks. "I meant—"

I catch his hand in mine, flip it so his wrist is exposed, and rest my lips there, on that thin layer of skin.

"Four," I say. "I've been with four people. A rather even split of committed relationships and casual arrangements, but I was never flippant with them. Most other areas of my life may be chaos embodied, but I was always rather confident in this one." I think for a beat. "That sounds cocky. Not confident in a gross way. Just sure that I know what I'm doing. The relationships I had were a bit . . . transactional? That sounds more heartless than it was, but it was about mutual satisfaction over anything else. None of the scandal or romance that the tabloids craved."

Hex lifts one brow, sardonic. "So is that what we're doing? Mutual satisfaction?"

"No," I say. Simple, self-contained.

I'm fully transfixed staring up at him. It's equal parts horrifying and tantalizing to watch in real time as he grasps the power he has over me.

There was a layer of separation with everyone else. A firm line drawn, like with my roommate, where it wasn't anything serious; or the stalking knowledge that it was doomed, like with Lily. But with Hex, any firm line feels like a path to follow, and any stalking knowledge feels like a whisper augmented with promise and I should be speaking in respectful murmurs and begging permission for every brush of contact. He strips me down to this squirming creature of awe and desire and uncertainty, like everything is new and permanent.

His shoulders bow a little. His hand slips down, rests on my forearm.

"Oh," he whispers.

"So I am perfectly happy," I say quickly, "with whatever you want. Kissing or lying together on the couch or nothing at all, and we could—"

"I don't want nothing."

My lips slam shut.

"I didn't mean to imply anything about your reputation," he says. "My incredulity was not because of you at all. I am—I don't—" He sighs, an abrupt, heavy exhale. "I'm not good at this. I don't have a large social circle. Honestly, this time here, around you and Iris and

Kris, has been more interaction than I've gotten in . . . years, outside of school."

"Years?" I try hard not to look too pitying, but my heart breaks. He seems to brace for some kind of pity too, so I force up a smile, rub a circle into his thigh. "Well. A few weeks with us, and you'll be begging to go back to solitude."

"Oh, never solitude. My brothers refuse to give me that. But—"

"Wait." My smile turns amused. "Are you saying your main source of socializing is with three nine-year-olds?"

Hex's lips thin as he fights his own smile. "And functions for Halloween and Día de Muertos. Don't make it sound so pathetic."

"It's not pathetic. It's adorable."

His blush is fast and scarlet. "I regret saying anything. I certainly do not wish to speak about my brothers right now anyway. I—" He seems to remember what it was we'd been talking about, and while I would have no problem spending the next hour before the concert listening to him tell me about his family, the intensity of his expression changes, grows richer, warmer.

Another pause, then Hex puts his thumb on my bottom lip and holds it there. I grind my teeth shut, aching against the heavy thud of my heartbeat, both of us still a bit sleep-soft and disheveled. He could say anything he wants with his thumb on my mouth like this.

"I've . . . been with one person." His eyes fix on the couch beside my head. "And it wasn't—we didn't—we didn't do much, but what we did was not preceded by nearly as much talking as you and I are doing."

I translate that and can't stop the flare of possessiveness that has my hands bearing down on his thighs again. "It should have been. You deserve to know exactly what we're doing and what we both want."

"You do love talking."

"And it makes you uncomfortable?" I'm trying to read his body language.

He drags his thumb over my chin, presses against the bob of my throat. It sends an electric current to the base of my spine. "No.

Confused, I think." He laughs soullessly. "Confused that"—a breath, a blush—"you are not having us rip each other's clothes off."

"Is that what you want?"

He hesitates.

I lean up, pressing to his chest, his lips a warm weight above me. I hold there until his eyes slip to mine, all wide and imploring and whoever he was with before, whoever filled him with this uncertainty about the way he should be treated, they'd better hope I never meet them.

"We're still learning each other," I tell him. "So yeah, I'm going to make you talk, because right now, I want to be sure I'm not misreading anything. But, fuck, sweetheart"—I drag my hand up his bare arm, watching goose bumps trail my fingers—"the moment I become fluent in your shivers, it's gonna be meteoric."

His breath quickens, serrated pulls against his tongue, and the color of his eyes deepens to a fixating blackness that searches my face.

He puts his thumb on my mouth again, tugging the skin of my bottom lip. Focused there, he says softly, "I want—"

He anchors his forehead to mine.

After a second, another, he tells me like each word is wrapped in velvet, "I want to touch you."

I used to be made of something other than nerve endings. But suddenly, that's all I am.

"And I want you to touch me," he says.

I note how tight my grip is on him and force my fingers to relax. "Okay." It squeezes out of me. "Okay. I—"

He kisses me again, and nothing much changes about his posture, but the way he's sitting on my lap is suddenly like it's a throne. And though we technically have the same title, no, in this moment I feel more than ever just how princely he is, the irresistible command he can emanate. Without words or a look or even a gesture of his hands, he is elegance and confidence, a spill of pure authority poured across my thighs, licking at my mouth.

He reaches down, working between his body and mine, and rests his palm on me through my pajama pants.

Holy fuck, holy shit, holy—

I jolt, rock-solid rigidity launching out to every muscle.

Hex echoes my abrupt rigidity. "Is this all right?"

I laugh, high and pealing, and cant my hips up into his touch, intending that to be my response—but it briefly makes everything so much more intense and I claw my way through a full breath.

"I think you have the answer to that question literally in the palm of your hand," I say.

Any concern eases away, a coy smile, a bite of his lip. Good god, his teeth on his lip, the puncture—I feel it echoed on my neck, electricity zapping off sensitive points in a wild winding-up.

His fingers climb. He exhales, and I taste it, tea and toothpaste, and the pad of his thumb slips beneath fabric, strokes along the skin at my waist.

In any other situation, with any other person, I'd be rattling off a stream of jokes to lighten the mood but there is nothing, nothing funny about this, any of this. He's all darkness arched over me, hair and eyes, a juxtaposition because he's shadows that emit light, golden, a candle glow on a clouded night. I want to burn up in him.

The elastic band of my sweatpants stretches, and there's something unabashedly graceful about the arch of his shoulder as his arm twists, a dancer-like move and lunge.

His long fingers close around me and my body shakes with another jolt of rigidity and I suck in a lungful of air and hold it, hold it.

Hex whimpers. It trills in his chest. *He's* the one who whimpers, his hand around me, and my brain whites out.

"Fuck, you're beautiful," I say too fast, too breathy, but I have to talk, have to get out all these words that keep building up around him. "It's destructive how much I want you. You're going to pull me apart."

"Maybe you could do with being pulled apart," he whispers.

I kiss him so fast I can feel the reverberations of those words on his lips, tremors that kick into my mouth.

His hand moves. One stroke, slow, teasing, and I fist his hair and he makes this *noise* when it snags in my fingers—goddamn it, his shivers and his *fucking noises*. I twist my grip and watch, enthralled, as his eyes roll shut, I'm not sure he knows he's doing it, but god I do. I do, and that ripple of pleasure is a new center, a new purpose. I want more. I want to know what makes him look like that, every single thing that causes his face to unravel with satisfaction.

I keep my grip tight in his hair as I crawl my other hand up his thigh, across his waist.

Another pull of his long fingers wrapped around me, and I lock my lips to his as I reach in for him. I want to taste the changes in him. I want, and want, just *want,* and I barely get oriented in touching him when his hips start pitching rhythmically, these hips that have completely destroyed me every second of every day since he got here, and this is their final judgment on me, the unendurable collision of shudders building up through his body as he thrusts into my hand.

Forehead to forehead, we fall into that movement, or maybe I don't move at all and let him take what he wants from me, give what he wants to me. I'm too consumed in memorizing the reactions he has—the hitch of his breath and the furrow between his closed eyes and the growing spots of pink on his cheeks. It's how I note the change, the push towards the edge, a deepening of that furrow, that pink darkening to crimson.

My grip tightens. On him. On his hair. I'm desperate and stripped, want and need.

"Coal—" His closed eyes pinch shut more and a rolling tremor forces his mouth open in a breathy cry, swollen lips and a sheen on his skin.

"Oh my god." I lap up the retreating quakes of that cry, pressing into him to soak up every last twitch. It's all I need—I get out a mumbled warning, but he makes that noise again, affirmation now, and I'm fucking lost.

Heat and a sparking cry and rupturing fireworks, a shuddering thrust and those eyes above me the whole time.

I devour his mouth between wet gasps, nails scraping his scalp. Vaguely, I think I try to put my thoughts into words, but maybe it's just his name, a moan.

"Hm."

I blink, eyesight a bit hazy. "What?" A burst of panic. "Are you all right? Was—"

But he's looking at the couch next to us, then the table on our other side. His face contorts, considering. "I expected ice," he says, a bit short of breath.

That derails my concern. "Ice?"

"I guess it's only when you're upset?"

He throws a smile.

"You—" I wheeze. "I do not *blast ice* when I orgasm!"

His smile dissolves into mock innocence. "I had no way of knowing for certain. Part of me thought I could have been taking my life into my hands just now."

"Oh, you're one to talk, Mr. Spontaneous Pumpkin." I pinch him above his hip.

His squirm is so destructively sexy that I forget what we're talking about. He's ticklish. I'm done for.

"Would *that* not have been a delightful situation to have to explain the next time Wren came knocking?" He smirks. "Why the Easter Princess's competing suitor is frozen to your lap."

I curl my thumb into my hand, the metal of his ring pressing against my palm.

Hex slides off me, stumbling a bit on no doubt unsteady legs, and he suddenly seems to realize the aftermath of what we did.

His face goes more red.

"You take the bathroom." I grab a box of tissues off the coffee table. "I'll be fine."

He nods, and after a few minutes of setting ourselves to rights, he comes back, the hood of his gray sleeveless robe thrown up over his head again. He folds his arms across his chest, standing awkwardly a few feet from the couch where I still sit, and silence spirals around us.

I should leave—we both need time to get ready for another day of fake-ass events. But the mood has shifted, and I'll be damned if I let it end this way.

I reach out to him.

His stiffness melts, a relieved droop, and he takes my hand and lets me tug him back down on my lap. He slips into place, and it disintegrates my worry because yeah, this *is* his place now, right here, on top of me.

"We should get ready," he says, echoing the responsibility itching at my mind.

Fuck responsibility, honestly, for a few more minutes.

I dump us to our sides on the couch.

"Just let me kiss you for a little while," I tell him, that low murmur like I'm worshipping at some altar.

His finger is on my cheek, and every one of my muscles softens into liquid sugar when he lays his lips across mine.

Somewhere in the last twenty minutes I'm pretty sure I died, or at least ascended, because I can't imagine anything but the afterlife encapsulating more of a fantasy than this.

Chapter Fourteen

"Read it back to me again."

Kris rattles off the Holidays that I told him were on Dad's list. "That all?"

"Yeah. I think so. I only got a glance, but—yeah." I kick in my desk chair so it spins, head thrown back, watching the ceiling heave over me. "What more info do you think we should have? Crap, like maybe the exact percentages they're giving? I don't remember—"

"I think they're well aware of how much joy they send to Christmas."

"True. I don't know. I . . . I don't know." I drop my feet and the chair stops, but my mind keeps spinning, and I bounce one knee. "It doesn't feel like they'll take anything we say seriously. Does it? They'll see any letter from me and toss it."

"You don't know that." Kris sits up from where he'd been strewn across my bed. He closes his notebook with a snap. "Plus, I'll be the one writing these letters. Don't doubt my skill."

I should smile. I can't. My stomach is a knot of strain and I can't believe I'm going to do this, to try to usurp my father's hold on these Holidays and ask them to join a collective. What we're sending them is a totally innocent request: we're inviting them to the Christmas Eve Ball. With vague mentions of a new arrangement that is more beneficial for all parties.

Nothing in the letters is incriminating, but this whole situation feels *real*. Because it is.

When they get here, we'll discuss the collective, and talk about however my dad has been coercing them, and figure out how to undo it. Iris and her dad will still be here too, obviously, and maybe Neo can be convinced that a collective is better for Easter, even if it means pissing off my dad.

So much could blow up. Fuck.

"I want this to work," I say.

Kris clicks his pen absently. "I know. I do too. And it will. Or it will as long as we can get the contact info for these other leaders. You said you had something for that?"

"Yeah." Two birds, one stone this idea—a whole section of Christmas oversees the routes Dad's magic takes him. Which means the location of every single person on earth is under our roof. I can grab the locations for all these Holiday people by accessing the route lists, while also start ingratiating myself with the head of Route Planning, maybe get some training going.

Much like I did when I set up the gift transfers in New Koah a couple years ago.

The comparison has been circling my thoughts like a beady-eyed vulture and the only reason it isn't feasting unrepentantly on the last dying heaps of my composure is thanks to my willful, vicious compartmentalization.

I'm not sending anyone gifts or willy-nilly fulfilling wishes.

It'll be fine. It isn't the same.

Nothing bad will happen.

"Okay." I scrub my face and stand. "I'll get those addresses. Meet back here in an hour?"

"You think I can handwrite all of these letters in an hour?"

"You don't have to handwrite them."

"These are our first official correspondences! I have *standards*, Coal."

"Well, I have *anxiety*, Kris, and we need to get these letters out ASAP. Type them. Print them. Done and done."

Kris shoves out of bed. "Fucking Neanderthal. Once you're Santa and we're doing this for real, there's going to be some changes around here."

I stop him halfway to the door. "I respect the hell out of your skill, I really do. And you're right, calligraphy would sell it a lot better. But we already only have a week and a half until Christmas Eve."

Holy shit. I hadn't thought of it like that. Only a week and a half left until either Kris and I pull this off, or I end up married to Iris. Which was an unbearable thing already, but now with Hex, just . . . absolutely not. I'm not content with whatever secret relationships Iris hinted at us having outside of this arrangement. We both deserve more than that.

Kris punches my shoulder. "I know, I know. Fine. Typed, *soulless* letters, coming up."

He swings the door open and we part ways, him heading to his suite, me cutting out towards the bulk of the palace.

I get halfway to where they oversee the routes when I pass an outdoor courtyard drenched in snow, frozen bushes and gray statues of reindeer making the whole area somber and icy. In it are Iris and Hex and a half dozen of our court and, of course, those damn reporters, taking a walk under a few space heaters—ah, yeah, Kris and I had been invited to that, but after yesterday's concert, where I spent the whole time two rows back from Hex *seething* over the fact that my father chose to sit right next to him, I heard Dad opted out of this event and I chose to duck out too.

Iris and Hex are making a lap of the courtyard. He's bundled up in his black peacoat but his cheeks are red with cold, most others around him in bright scarlet, gold, and green. Iris is smiling and I know she's trying to make it easy on him but my gut yanks me to a stop at the window.

I twist the skull ring on my thumb.

That should be me. Not just there, in Iris's place, but *there* at all. Hex knows I skipped this event to plan with Kris, but it's no excuse.

Would he want me out there, in Iris's place, if I could be? If the autumn collective would flip shit over the mention of a *failed* negotiation between Christmas and Halloween, what would they think about us? If there is an *us*.

It wouldn't be a huge upset for the Christmas Prince and the Halloween Prince to be together, would it? I'm not my father, and I'm actively trying to improve the very things that make the autumn Holidays dislike us. Hex wouldn't allow any of the things we've done if he thought it would endanger his Holiday.

God, I really can't shake this need to protect him.

I pull out my phone and twist it around in my hands for a few seconds.

HEX

so i gotta know. who's your stylist?

Hex looks down at his pocket and digs for his phone. His eyes go from the screen to the courtyard, scouting around, until he sees me through the door's glass.

He grins and bends away to text quickly with his fingerless gloves. He's going to lose a few appendages if he keeps wearing those.

HEX
I am. Why?

ah, okay, then you're the one i need to give a stern talking to because it is exceptionally unfair that your entire wardrobe is made up of my kryptonite

I watch him read it. Watch his grin rise again.

HEX
You're going to give me a stern talking to? If I recall, you said I was daddy.

A staff member walks past and I don't realize until he gives me a perplexed look that I made a rather pitiful chirping noise.

I try to cover it by nodding at him. "Hey, Maverick, right? From housekeeping? Excellent job with the . . . cleanliness. Really top-shelf stuff. You do the lord's work, my friend."

Maverick carries on, confusion bowing out to amusement as he leaves.

I wait until I'm sure he's gone.

Then drop away from the outside window and press my face into the wall.

And type back and delete about seven different responses until if Hex is watching the screen it'll be a constant ellipsis of my sanity-crumbling turned-on panic.

> for someone who said he doesn't have a lot of experience in this area that was a pretty big game thing to say, hallow

HEX
I don't know what you are talking about, Claus. If there is any big game play happening, it is entirely your fault, as I merely repeated facts you stated previously.

> you're wholly innocent and i'm the big bad corrupting influence, huh?

HEX
Educational influence.

And I said I was inexperienced, not innocent.

> class is in session sweetheart

HEX
I have learned quite a lot from you.

Or, rather, about you.

First, the Christmas décor kink.

Now, daddy.

> i am not going to call you that
>
> i mean i have my fair share of daddy issues
>
> but i am not going to call you that

And all he texts back, *the only thing he fucking texts back,* is:

HEX
Hm. We'll see.

This guy
Will kill me.

He only says like a handful of words at a time and somehow they're as pointed and achingly hot as everything else he does.

I pace up and down the hall because not moving will make everything inside of my body shake up like a champagne bottle.

Okay, I can't take this.

I push open the door and I'm hit with a fist of glacial wind. "Iris! Hex!" I nod back into the hall. "You guys about done?"

Hex's whole face is red now. His tone in text was suave confidence but thank god, honestly, that he's as riled up as I am because I know I'm beet red too.

Hex and Iris eye the group around them, the reporters. I have no idea how long they've been at this, but Iris smiles at the group, all geniality.

"I believe we are," she says. "Thank you for joining us. We will see you at dinner, yes?"

I bounce on the balls of my feet. *Get the fuck in here.*

She shuffles Hex away, giving me a tight eyeroll none of the court can see. Hex sees it, though, and he stifles a smile to the ground as I hold the door open for them.

They slip inside and Hex shivers, head to toe.

"Please do not take this personally," he says, "but I am very tired of this element of Christmas."

Iris moans her agreement and kisses my cheek. "My savior. I had no idea what we were supposed to be doing, honestly. A winter walk? When it's *well below freezing?* Who organized this?"

I don't care, my brain is so laser-focused on my phone in my hand, on Hex being two feet from me, on the wound-up tension trying to rip its way out of my stomach.

But the rest of their group heads for this door. And we're in a hallway in broad daylight and I *can't touch him* so I have to stand here, willing this need to fizzle out.

His lips pulse in a soft smile, his eyes holding on mine in unspoken understanding.

He looks down at his phone again, quickly types something, then stuffs it into his pocket.

Mine vibrates.

HEX
I really don't care what you call me.

As long as you say it in that way
where you moan a little.

My eyes snap shut.

I put my phone to my forehead, and breathe, deep, deep breaths, because that's all my body needs. Just air. That's all it's going to get right now so it'd better learn to be okay with it real quick.

"Coal?" Iris asks. "You all right?"

"Yeah. Yep. Definitely."

I send off one last text and holster my phone.

you play a dangerous game. just
remember: you started this

His buzzes in his pocket but he doesn't look at it. He smirks at me, that shitty grin he's skillfully suppressing, a spark in his eyes like fire, like heat.

The court disperses, and even the reporters hurry off, seemingly so cold they don't notice that Iris, Hex, and I linger. Mental note: paparazzi can be dissuaded by extreme temperatures. I might break the palace's thermostat just to fuck with them.

Then it's just us three, and I did come down this way for a reason, didn't I? What the fuck was I doing down here.

Ah, Route Planners, yeah.

Having Iris and Hex with me could be a good cover—look, I was giving them a tour of one of our great hubs, no *real* trade secrets, just friendly inter-Holiday bonding.

"You both. Come with me to the Route Planners?"

Iris and Hex give me almost identical looks of confusion.

But Hex nods. "All right. Why?"

My gaze shifts to Iris. Kris and I haven't told her what we're doing. Not yet. Even though this will eventually help Easter, I know now that it's bad enough that Hex knows as much as he does about what would more or less be me usurping my dad's plans.

"I . . . to check it out," I say, dumbly.

Her eyes narrow. "Coal."

"I swear, I'll explain everything when I can. Plausible deniability and all that."

She sighs. "Fine. To . . . the Route Planners?" She sighs again. "Christmas, always so magical."

I lead the way, cutting down another hall, and Hex shivers again.

We're alone now. Mostly. Except for Iris and anyone who might pop out of these rooms we're passing.

I can't stop myself. I loop my arm around his waist and press my body into him as we walk, scrubbing my hand up and down his side.

He leans into me with a guttural moan of relief. "Thank you."

My body sparks at that moan of his, but I shove my way past that reaction. "Oh, don't thank me yet. Like ninety percent of my brain is spiraling out over your texts and I'm trying to figure out how to get you back."

"Get me back?"

"I almost collapsed in the hall. Just full-on dropped right to my knees."

His eyes cut to mine. A quick, amused flash.

Then he says, "On your knees?" and it's so innuendo-heavy that my grin goes satanic.

"There will be another Christmas event," I promise him. "There will be another useless fucking PR stunt. And I'm going to text you something fantastically raunchy right in the middle of it so I'm the only one who knows you're coming apart in a crowd full of people."

He clears his throat.

Straightens his gloves.

Opens his mouth then shuts it and maybe we shouldn't play this game, but my god, I am utterly captivated by the way he's *flustered.*

Iris, bless her, is pretending not to hear anything we're saying. Until I catch her eyes, and she arches one brow in a suggestive leer.

I flip her off and she laughs.

We reach the Route Planners, and those looming doors inject some somberness into me. Well, somberness, and a sudden, stabbing flashback to the New Koah incident. Riots and theft and the whole damn economy crashing—

It'll be different. This will be *different.*

I shake out my hands and step away to knock. There's shuffling behind the door, a voice calling out, *"One moment."*

But that vulture of dread is looping closer and closer, so I inch back by Hex and growl, "Careful" out the side of my mouth.

His smile is suppressed. "I did nothing."

"That's the problem." I keep my voice low. "Your *doing nothing* makes me want to shirk all this newfound accountability and drag you back to your suite caveman-style."

He doesn't respond right away, and I cut a look down at him. His face is set, brows pinched.

I spin to him. "You're upset."

The doorknob twists. I have the worst timing, I truly do—

"I'm not upset," Hex assures me. "How could I be? Just—don't jeopardize your responsibilities for me."

"I know." I turn to whoever is opening the door when it's the last thing I want right now—but that's what he means, isn't it? To not choose him over Christmas. He's *telling* me not to choose him over my responsibilities, and honestly, he *has* to keep telling me that.

I have to stay focused. I *can't* fuck up again.

But a deeper part of me whispers, *Hex doesn't want you to jeopardize Christmas because he's not planning on sticking around. This isn't real to him.*

Between the sudden avalanche of insecurities and the continued pulse of *riots, theft, economic crash,* my mouth goes dry, joints feeling like they're solidifying so I can barely move my head to look up as the door opens.

A man stands there, holding a tablet in one hand, his head cocked. Behind him, I can hear the bustle of work, computers clacking, people shouting questions, something beeping.

Last time I came here, I blundered my way into an international incident.

No, *no,* it wasn't *here,* not the Route Planners; it was a different area, a different time, a different *me.*

The last time I was at the Route Planners was when Dad brought me here as a kid.

That comparison is no less unsettling.

"Um. Hi. Hello." I straighten my shoulders, digging deep for all my princely formality. "I came here to start getting a feel for how this area of Christmas operates. And you are—" I study the guy, and a smile cracks over me. "Lucas, right? Weren't you working in the stables?"

His face relaxes in a pleased grin. "That's right, Prince Nicholas. Good memory. I transferred over here a few years ago. Dare I ask if you've found anyone else to swindle sleigh wax from?"

I wince, but my smile doesn't abate. "Thankfully Kris and I grew out of that daredevil phase." To Hex—because Iris knows exactly what happened; she'd been there and flat out refused to get involved, as *the only smart one in the group*—I say, "Kris and I figured out that if you put sleigh wax on the bottom of sleds, they go a bit faster."

Hex laughs. "Only a bit?"

Lucas starts flipping through his tablet. "You know, I think I still have access to the property damage photos of the wall you smashed through—"

"*Okay.*" I surge closer to him. "Not that I don't appreciate a trip down memory lane, but—can you help me with the Route Planners? Or, us, I guess. I'd like to show the Easter Princess and Halloween Prince around as well. I figured it's about time I get down here."

Lucas's finger hovers over his tablet and he looks at me again, studiously this time, and I realize he might refuse. He'd be well within his right to. Dad hasn't authorized this; the last time I trained is infamous; it's also the highest point of the busy season.

But then Lucas smiles again in honest delight. "We'd love to have you, Prince Nicholas. Come in, please. Princess Iris. Prince Hex. All of you—right this way."

He pushes the door wide. An office space lies beyond, bigger and more open than Dad's office but still strung with the same decorations as the rest of the palace. Greenery and poinsettias, bulbs and sparkling lights. The desks vary from cluttered with photo frames and personal effects to clinically neat, and the air is buzzing with the frenetic energy of work.

That energy crashes to a halt at our entrance.

And yeah, we are out of place, Iris, Hex, and me. As I turn to meet all these gazes, most people are smiling, some are outright confused.

"Is it . . . okay that we're here?" I ask Lucas.

He's going to realize what I'm asking, *who* is asking, that Prince Coal shouldn't be trusted—

"Of course," he says. "In truth, we've been expecting you for a while."

"You have?"

"Well—yes. You're the future of this Holiday, aren't you?" Lucas pushes his grin around, eyeing people in a *get it together* way.

I scramble to figure out a logical explanation for *we've been expecting you.*

Then it hits me, and I feel like such a dumbshit.

Dad didn't let news that I was responsible for New Koah get very far. *Some* people know, of course; but he kept it under wraps as much as possible to *salvage our reputation.* So of course most of Christmas's department heads would be waiting for me to resume training. Why wouldn't they? Especially with my active steps to not be in the press since New Koah, they've all probably been wondering why I'm shaping up but not taking a larger role in things.

Which Dad would know. Wouldn't they be asking him about me?

"Now," Lucas says, "did you have some place you'd like to start specifically?"

"Anywhere," I say, because I can't very well be like, *Do you have a list of contact info for these leaders that I definitely mean nothing nefarious by asking about?*

Lucas ushers us towards the back of the room, and as we round a few more desks, a massive globe comes into view.

Dad had stood right in front of it. *"These are the people who need us. And I do mean us, Nicholas—you and me. One day, it will be your job to make the world happy."*

I rub at my chest, the spot where that ache hasn't let up.

How did I remember him so wrong? Why did I keep an image in my head of him that was so shockingly different, someone hopeful and full of wonder against someone callous and cruel?

If I hadn't stormed into his office and demanded to be a part of stuff again, would he have ever reached out? Did he hold me back because of how I've behaved, or was it something else?

Hex leans into me, lets his body rest against mine for half a beat. "Are you all right?"

Iris is close enough that I catch her corresponding concern.

"I'm not sure my dad wants me to do this," I whisper. "Take on responsibilities."

"Why?" Iris asks.

For the same reason he stages every photo op. For the same reason his one and only priority with me and Kris is *public image*: control. It's honestly easier to have a son who's getting in trouble and rebelling in stupid ways than it is to have one who questions the structures and might make changes. When Dad *did* set up training for me, it wasn't *real,* and he only ever punished me for my antics when they got problematic for Christmas.

Was he *intentionally* keeping me useless?

What exactly is my reputation among the press and our people?

But he told me about his blackmailing scheme, and he didn't have to. Or maybe he only told me as a test, like he said. He wanted to see what kind of leader I'd be—one like him, ruthless and devious, or one like . . . one like it should be.

I give Iris and Hex a forced smile. "It's nothing."

But neither of them believes me, because I'm a crap liar when people know my tells.

We reach the globe, twice my height and covered in blinking lights, and Lucas starts talking about how they track the distribution of joy across the continents as Dad—and hundreds of staff—makes deliveries. The Route Planners ensure all the people visited get a fair amount of gifts or cheer, no one gets skipped, and so on.

Iris gives me a look like she knows I'm here for a different reason. She starts talking to Lucas about this globe being similar to one in Easter, and Hex uses the distraction to twist closer to me.

"It isn't nothing," he whispers.

I sway towards him, breathing in, citrus and spice. People are watching us over their desks, so even bending into him is too much and I draw back, stomach winding.

"I don't know what they think of us. Of what we're doing and how we do it," I say.

Hex's brow bends. "Your people?"

I nod.

"They seem to love you," Hex murmurs. "I've seen the way you interact with them. You genuinely care about them, and they pick up on that."

"The staff in the palace basically have to like us. Or at least pretend to better than anyone, being directly around us all the time. I mean I don't know what *our people* think, the extended families of everyone who works for us, the community that's built up in North Pole City over the centuries of Christmas, the people Dad is always so set on manipulating. I stopped reading the tabloids a while ago, and I don't know what the general attitude is towards us."

Hex's head tips, considerate. "Your direct staff are also privy to that image and would react quite differently if opinion of you was negative. But when was the last time you spoke to someone? Outside of the palace, I mean."

I give a quick shake of my head. Never, that I remember. We used to go out into North Pole City more often when Mom was here, but even that was as a family group, for photos with people, not to *talk* to anyone.

"I need to talk to them," I say. "*Really* talk to them. Hear what they think. Preferably without drawing the focus of press or my father."

As if I have time to add more stuff to my ever-growing to-do list. But this is as necessary as inviting the winter Holidays to our ball and undoing blackmail and learning how Christmas operates—it's all interconnected, and I can't pull one thread without pulling them all. More threads keep slithering up into the bundle until I'll have a whole-ass rope of responsibility.

Hex grins. "I can help with that."

I cock my head.

Lucas is moving to another area. Iris follows, giving us a backwards glance to keep up, but I hesitate, and Hex's grin widens.

"You need to get out of the palace? Down into the city, without being seen?" He shrugs. "What, precisely, am I the prince of?"

Oh, how very dare he use that teasing tone with me, right now of all times.

"Halloween?" I guess, cheeky.

"Also known as Mischief Night." His smile is deliciously wild. "I am, when the situation calls for it, incredibly skilled at causing only the good kind of trouble."

Chapter Fifteen

I get the addresses while Iris and Hex keep Lucas distracted, and the rest of the time spent learning about Route Planning is a balanced mix of educational and alarming.

I should have been down here years ago. And not because it's my duty—I actually like this. Learning about our Holiday. Seeing the extent these people go to in order to bring joy across the world to kids who believe in Santa and parents who are struggling to make ends meet and anyone who needs a small miracle, a silly toy, a smile. I remember what Hex said, about how we give people the tools to endure whatever shit occurs in their lives, and I start to *feel* that, seeing how everyone who works here lights up when they start explaining anything to me. They're happy. Happy to be doing these jobs. Happy to be a part of this.

It's a night and day difference from when I did that staged training. Then, everyone had been tense and clinical. This is *real.*

The version of Dad I built up in my head may not be who he is, but it wasn't *wrong.*

It's our job to make the world happy.

By the time Iris, Hex, and I leave, I'm downright bouncing.

This—*that,* those people, what they do, what *we* do—is enough. Or it can be, if we stopped focusing on monopolizing and scale back to provide stuff of quality and prioritize exactly what light shines in all those people's eyes.

I'm so consumed in my own churning thoughts that I don't notice both Iris and Hex have followed me back to my suite. Kris is already inside, and I come to with no memory of having walked here.

I hold my hands out. "My head hasn't hurt this bad since I took Ethics in American Politics." Then I drop onto my bed and screw the heels of my palms into my eyes.

"Uh-oh," Kris says. "Unsuccessful?"

"Psh." I dig the paper with my notes out of my pocket and hold it up between two fingers, eyes shut. "Don't doubt *my* skill."

Someone takes it from me.

"Then what's wrong with His Moodiness?" Kris asks, and I can hear him settling at my desk, likely starting to organize where these letters are going.

The bed sinks next to me, at the edge of the mattress. It thrills me to no end that I know it's him without needing to open my eyes. I know the catch of his breath, I know the weight of his body, and I blindly sit up and drop my head into the bend of his neck. Hex leans into me, and though it's Iris and Kris, I fight for *some* decorum and hold there against him.

"I don't *know* what's wrong," Iris drones. "None of you will *tell me.*"

"You shouldn't even be in here," I say into Hex's shoulder.

"Coal."

The dip in Iris's tone is so ripe with reprimand that I pull back to look at her before I can think not to. She's glaring, and guilt surges over me.

"Mom," I shoot back.

She smacks my head. "I know you're trying to keep whatever you're doing separate from Easter, but I'm not just my Holiday. I'm your *friend.* And I want to help you with whatever this is. It's changing you, Coal, and I gotta say—I'm liking it. Plus, it *would* affect Easter, eventually, wouldn't it? So let me help now."

I point at her, half leaning into Hex, but when I say, "No," I hear how weak it sounds.

Iris drops into a chair. "That wasn't a question. I'm staying. What are we doing?"

Yeah, okay, she's right, it *does* involve her and *would* affect Easter. So . . . how bad would the fallout be if this backfires on her too? She said her court wouldn't force her dad to abdicate based on something like this, but . . .

Easter. Halloween. Christmas. Up in smoke because of me.

Really putting my degree in Global Affairs to good use here, aren't I?

The joke hurts. And I see news bulletins scrolling on a bar TV—

With a long, miserable groan, I start at the beginning and give her a quick summation of how god awful my dad has warped Christmas into being. I talk about contacting the winter Holidays, inviting them here for the Christmas Eve Ball, then confronting my dad with a united front and forcing him to make changes. I tell her about the blackmail with Halloween, but not the specifics of it—it's not mine to tell.

Iris is, unsurprisingly, slack-jawed when I'm done. She wilts in her chair, a slow head shake making her braids tumble over her shoulder. Her reaction is ripe with resignation though. The same poisonous vein that pulses through me, wanting to be surprised but no, none of this is really surprising.

"Would that work, you think?" I finally acknowledge the rush of hope that wells up behind that question. "It'd still benefit Easter, so it'd appease the assholes in your court who have it out for you, if we can convince your dad to join in. But getting *my* dad to fold first will be the biggest obstacle, and if he does, I don't see why yours wouldn't join the collective out of at least self-preservation. It'd work, wouldn't it?"

It'd get us both out of this marriage. It'd alleviate some of her stresses about Easter's own shit by giving them a safety net.

Iris reads the hope straining behind my words, in my face, and shrugs, but her posture of shock and resignation doesn't change.

"Maybe, Coal," she whispers. "I—maybe."

My racing heart stutters on a sharp inhale. "You're okay with me doing this? If you think it would fuck up shit for you . . ."

God, I have no other ideas. This is everything I've got rolled into one potentially disastrous Hail Mary, but if she thinks it'd do more harm than good, I'd *try*, fucking *try* to find something else—

Iris gives a soft smile. "Yeah. I am. Just—it's a lot to take in."

I don't know what kind of reaction I expected. Jumping up and down in relief? When the fuck has Iris ever jumped up and down in her life. This cautious exhaustion is way more understandable, and I nod at her, wrestling up a reassuring grin.

Kris spins around in my desk chair, cutting through the thick energy. "So we're good to deliver these letters? Then we wait, I guess. Terribly exciting stuff."

"How will the other leaders send their responses?" Iris shakes herself upright.

I stare blankly at her.

Kris stares blankly at her.

"You didn't tell them how they should RSVP?" she pushes. "How will you know if they're coming?"

"They'll . . . show up? Shit." I scratch my forehead. "That was dumb. But there's no good place for them to respond, is there? They can't very well send something to the *palace*. Could they use magic to drop something into my suite? Would Dad feel that?"

"Unlikely," Hex says. "We have no connection to other Holidays' uses of magic, even ones who would be linked by tithing as you are. Their magic is its own separate function."

"Though I feel like a worm asking them to use their already limited magic, limited *because of us,* on something Christmas-related. No better ideas?"

The room hangs in silence.

"Shit," I say again. "Okay. So—Kris?" I wince at the stack of sealed, ready-to-go letters behind him. "Can you add something about them sending their responses to me magically? And how we'll make it up to them."

He spins around. "We'll need to get better at this."

"What, you mean two guys who have never had to apply their foreign affairs studies to real-world situations are sucking at it right out of the gate? Who would've guessed?"

"Didn't you finish your senior capstone where you did exactly that?"

"It was a group project and the *real-world situation* was presenting a slideshow to a boardroom of government officials. It had nothing to do with espionage."

"I'm willing to bet *Dad* knew we'd suck at it. Which was part of his plan, right? That we could never do stuff like this so we'd be forced to comply with his shit."

I've been maneuvering around that realization, but hearing Kris say it, my chest aches.

Dad wants what's best for Christmas. I believe that. But I don't know how far he's willing to go to see his version of *best* through.

Hex rocks into me, a slight bump, and I feel the implication in it. *Do you still need my help?*

"When the letters are done," I say, "we can't drop them in with the normal palace mail."

"We could deliver them using magic, maybe?" Kris offers.

"Dad would know. He can sense *our* magic use, at least."

"Iris could deliver them with magic? Or Hex? Or—" Kris glances at me as he works open the envelopes. "You look like you have a plan."

I give a sly smile. "How would you like to sneak out into North Pole City?"

Kris's brows raise. "We've never done that before. Why haven't we done that before?"

"Because using magic to hop around to nightclubs across the world is more glamorous. But we should have been doing it. And, to avoid Dad finding out, I have a better mode of transport."

I grin down at Hex.

Who shoves up from my bed—unacceptable, but I'll allow it this time—and with an easy, graceful throw of his wrist, creates a *whole-ass portal* in my bedroom.

The door-size oval is shaded in black, ripples of darkness in a frame that shows an alley in North Pole City. There's the square, the ice skating rink, all under the clear afternoon sky.

Iris and Kris fly to their feet.

I follow them up and bracket Hex's hips with my hands, my smile pressing to his ear. "God, you're useful—*wait*. Wait a hot fucking second."

He glances up at me.

"Is *this* how you vanished on me at the bar?"

Hex's eyebrows bounce in a show of *duh*.

"You *imp*." I capture his hips against my body and bite his neck. He chirrups in surprise. "Fuck me, I thought I was losing my mind when you were gone."

"And I thought Coal was losing his mind too," Iris says. "I didn't see a damn thing. Impressive."

"I have my talents," Hex says, and I should be given an award for not responding to that perfect setup. "Halloween's magic thrives on joy created most by mischief. And, for as long as we are gone, provided it isn't *days,* anyone who comes searching for us will conveniently be diverted elsewhere."

"We should've made friends with someone from Halloween years ago," Kris says, lifting one hand to touch the edge of the portal. A waft of smoke uncoils, drifts around his fingers. "You didn't need a doorway? You conjured a fucking portal in midair. With a literal flick of your wrist."

"It's how we dispose of the corpses."

Kris flinches like the portal bit him. "What?"

Hex is serene. "The corpses. Once our magic wears off and the zombies stop being animated. We open a portal to a landfill and toss them through."

He lays his hand over mine where it's still on his hip and squeezes. I grin into the back of his head.

It is not even a little surprising that him fucking with people is a major turn-on.

Iris leans over to Hex and stage-whispers, "Kris doesn't know you're teasing him again."

Kris glowers at Iris, then Hex. "I know. Obviously."

"I am teasing, Kris." Hex cocks his head. "Halloween does not defile corpses."

"Uh-huh."

"I swear on my great-great-grandmother. Or I would, if we could find her. She never likes to stay in her tomb for very—"

"Okay, so, we're sneaking out into your city," Iris cuts in, saving Kris, and Hex tosses a pressed-lip smirk up at me.

I hug his hips to me one more time. "God, you're hot."

"Then we're mailing those letters," Iris continues, "and . . . ?"

I exhale, ruffling Hex's hair. "And we're going to talk to the people there. I want to find out what they think of us, *really* think of us."

"You think they'll be honest with you, Prince Nicholas?" Her eyes go up and down my body.

"Fair enough."

Kris gets back to work repackaging the envelopes and I shuffle through my closet for basic gear I don't usually wear and isn't as put together as my Wren-styled outfits. I toss some to Kris and Hex too, and Iris, who reluctantly changes out of her sleek purple coat and into a drab old gray one of mine. I grab a few pairs of sunglasses, tug a hat fully over my curls so they're less noticeable.

Hex pulls on a blue coat, his equally noticeable hair tucked up under a bright red hat. It's more the fact that he's wearing my clothes than that he's in color that has me restraining myself, again, from kissing him, and wow, yeah, this is why I opted out of the event earlier. It is way too hard to be around him and not touch him.

Iris shoves her hands into her pockets and gives me an appraising grin. "Wow, Coal. Look at you, all grown up."

I roll my eyes.

"No, I'm serious." She steps forward and points at my head. "I think I saw some gray hair, right—"

"Okay, okay." I bat her away. "Game faces. We have jobs to do."

Iris and Kris go motionless. They share a look.

"This all went from entertaining to somewhat frightening," Iris murmurs. "Who is he and what's he done with your brother?"

The square of North Pole City has the same sentiment of cheer as when we'd come ice skating, only it feels less orchestrated.

Way less orchestrated.

Wooden booths sell Christmas goods still, scenting the afternoon air with spices and cocoa and cider, and people skate and laugh. Music plays, a live band dancing to their own songs on one end of the square, with tables set up where people decorate gingerbread cookies or make wreaths or do other festive activities. Twinkly strand lights and a few bigger floodlights illuminate the area, and space heaters keep the arctic chill at bay.

Everyone, everywhere, no matter what they're doing, smiles into the frosty air. This whole square is saturated in joy, pure and unforced.

I linger at the edge of the alley. Kris, next to me, is similarly stunned.

"I forgot it could feel this way," he whispers.

It's what I was thinking. How long has it been since Christmas felt this unburdened for us?

I sniff away the severity. "We're here now—so we get to experience this joy too."

Kris doesn't say anything, but that silence is weighted enough that he doesn't need to.

I nudge him. "There. Mailbox."

He sets off, and Iris and Hex come up around me.

"Where should we—oh, cookies!" Iris grabs my hand and hauls me into the square, and I let her, because I had no real plan beyond this point.

The musicians are playing some instrumental songs, fast beats and uplifting melodies and I swear I can *feel* my stress start to peel off. I let Iris push me into a seat at a long table, and cookies are shoved in front of us, frosting and sprinkles and candy in dozens of bowls, the whole table is a disaster zone of rainbow sugary concoctions.

Hex sits next to me, Kris joins across from us, and it hits me, sinks in, that we've never done this before. Just enjoyed Christmas *anywhere*. It's always masked behind performative lead-up celebration stunts.

And here I'd thought skating with Hex would be the closest I'd get to being anything like a normal couple. I swing on him and smile and Hex leans into me, returning that smile, and for a second, for a beat, this is all that exists. No other responsibilities.

We smear frosting on cookies and pile on way too many sprinkles, and I let my mind drift out, listening to the conversations around us.

Most people are talking about their plans, what they'll be doing for Christmas and into the New Year. Someone is traveling. Someone else is having a Christmas movie marathon, and for the life of me I don't think I've ever watched more than one Christmas movie in a single *year* let alone a single *day,* but they seem excited about their binge.

There's no mention of us, and I lose focus on my cookie decorating as I realize I have no idea how to smoothly ask people what they think of their royal family without sounding like one of those aggressive reporters.

An idea springs to mind.

Oh, Iris will hate me, but she wanted to come, right?

I swing a cocky grin across the table at her. Her face sinks in that *I know you're up to something, don't you dare* glower.

"Oh my *god,*" I say, overly loud, "you look *just* like Princess Iris!"

The people around our end of the table turn from their conversations.

"She does!"

"Oh, you're lovely just like her!"

"It's uncanny!"

Iris takes a deep breath and quickly mouths *I hate you* before she turns a small smile at the nearest person. "I get that a lot. I don't mind. She's sweet, right?"

"Extremely," an older woman says. She's helping what must be her granddaughter decorate a series of gingerbread reindeer, and the ratio of frosting to cookie is irrevocably tipped in favor of frosting. "Though, I have to admit, I don't think either of them is worthy of her."

I grip my hand into a fist to keep from reaching for Hex, but I hear the sharp pull of his breath.

"Either prince?" I guess stupidly.

The woman bats my arm good-naturedly. "Don't tell me you haven't voted yet? I thought I was the only one left. It's been all the *Christmas Inquirer* has posted about for days."

"Voted?" Now my confusion is honest.

"Oh my god!" A girl leans across the table towards me. "You have to vote for the Halloween Prince! You *have* to!"

"Oh, please!" A guy next to her rolls his eyes. "He'll never catch up. Obviously our Christmas Prince will win! CHRISTMAS!"

A cheer goes down the table, a small chant, *Christmas, Christmas.*

Everyone is laughing in good fun, but the mood has thoroughly changed for me.

"You're voting on who Iris will marry?" I press.

The first woman leans towards me with a conspiratorial glint in her eyes. "It won't *really* affect the final decision, but it's fun. Maybe she'll take our opinions to heart! Who knows how they decide these things."

Okay, let's take stock of the good things I know: our people don't seem to hate us. Check.

But they don't seem to see us as people either. Voting on who Iris marries in a goddamn tabloid.

Is that any better than what Dad's doing to us?

"How do—" I catch myself, lick my lips. "What do you think of them? The . . . royals, I mean."

I could have asked that less conspicuously, but the woman is thankfully distracted by her granddaughter's cookie progress.

"They're lovely, of course—oh, honey! Enough with the chocolate sprinkles—"

"You don't think all those pictures of them are a bit . . . forced?"

The woman has turned away, but she shakes her head. The guy and girl across from me catch my question, and I wonder if maybe they're drunk, because they instantly giggle.

The girl opens up her phone and starts scrolling. "Eh, not *forced*—I mean, look, those are smiles!" She shows me her screen. It's a picture on *24-Hour Fête* from ice skating, Iris and Kris on the rink, and they are, legitimately, happy. "But yeah"—she pulls her phone back—"I miss the pics we'd get of Prince *Coal's* exploits. He's mellowed out way too much."

My gut sinks.

"Do *not* start on him again," the guy says. "It's a good thing he's not smearing Christmas's reputation."

I hate myself. "Smearing the reputation how?"

The girl flips her hair, whacking Iris in the face, and Iris full-on convulses with the shock of it. "Oh, it's—he's never been *trustworthy,* you know?" She uses a candy cane cookie as a wand as she talks. "Entertaining, sure. But what's he gonna do for Christmas? Can he keep up with what his father's done?"

"Yeah," I say. "Right. The, um, reigning Santa. He's a pretty great guy."

"Great? Ha!" She cups her hands around her mouth and shouts, "The King!"

Up and down the table, cheers bark out. Genuine cheers.

"You don't get a reaction like *that* being merely *great.* He's done things for Christmas no other Santa has!"

"Such as . . . ?"

My question seems to shake her out of her stupor for a blip. "Oh. Um—joy is up. Like, skyrocketing up."

"So if the reigning Santa, I don't know, maybe said, *'Hey, I'll get Christmas joy on a global scale, we'll have endless magic for everyone, but to have that, we're gonna overtake other Holidays,'* you'd say . . ."

This is, unsurprisingly, the moment the conversation breaks. From a friendly chat to her realizing I'm after something.

"What is wrong with you?" the girl asks. "Santa would never do that. We're *Christmas.* What's your problem?"

"Nothing, nothing. I'm . . . visiting from New Year."

I drop the other name and gauge her reaction.

Her confusion doesn't break, but she shrugs like that makes sense, like of course such an oddball person wouldn't be from here. "Well. Welcome to Christmas. *Christmas!*" She turns away to start another cheer, and yeah, she's drunk.

I can't very well base the attitude of the North Pole on this one conversation, but the fact that the whole table reacts to her cheers with the same enthusiasm sits in my stomach like iron.

This is the image my father has worked to provide. Perfection one step beyond mortal—with him as this regaled savior, me as some wild child who can't be trusted, and Kris nonexistent. He never really hated my negative image in the press, did he? On some level, he probably wanted me to keep fucking up, except when it endangered Christmas.

The only upside is that this girl seemed appalled at the idea of blackmail. So. There's that.

Iris has gone somber too. Kris whispers something to her, and she nods, pulling up that trained stoic expression.

"Christmas," I mimic the cheer, voice flat.

Hex presses into me. It yanks me out of my spiral so assuredly that I whimper in relief.

"Here," he says. "I made this for you."

He holds out a plate. On it is a gingerbread man, or what was until recently a gingerbread man, only his leg has been amputated and he's coated in green frosting, with brown chocolate sprinkles formed into eyes and a gaping mouth. There's a glob of red frosting on the missing leg, and I bust out laughing.

"You made me a gingerbread zombie."

"Christmas and Halloween." He grins.

This is the perfect opening to ask what he thinks about *us*. About *after*. Because there will be an after, all this will work out, nothing will implode. And in that after . . .

God, I want there to be an us.

But Hex threads his fingers into the gap of my jacket, misreading my strain. "You will fix this. Their opinion of you."

It sinks in, a heavy stone. Because that's what I *should be* worried about. And I am. Also. If problems were bees, I'd be a fucking hive.

I scratch the back of my neck. "I made a point to stop reading the press about us. But I guess I should start again, huh? See what my father is letting out. Or"—I inhale, sugared cookie air and Hex's own sweet, citrusy warmth—"I keep doing what I think will fix things because wasting energy on PR bullshit gives me a migraine."

"You should care what your people think of you."

"We've been manipulating them for *years*. How can I undo that? And the worst part is I was actively playing right into my dad's image of me."

"You're taking steps to undo it all now." Hex touches my chin. "You do realize how suited you are to this job, as Santa? You make people happy. You make them laugh. You bring joy. You can do this, Coal. It won't happen overnight, but you can start to change their minds now that you know the story they believe."

My eyes shift through his, back and forth, letting him center me. "How are you so sure? I don't think I've ever had half as much conviction as you put into what you said just now, and you have that much conviction about *everything*."

Hex gives another of those easy, dismissive shrugs, the ones I know are a sign that his true emotions are churning hard and fast beneath his surface.

"Would you like to know my secret?" he asks. All we've said has been low, but I lean closer, drawn into him.

"Always. Every single secret you have."

Fingers still on my chin, he twists my head and presses his lips to my ear. A shiver walks down my spine at the ghost of his breath on my skin.

"I fake it until I believe it," he whispers. "Everyone's wearing a façade, whether they are actively posing for photos or merely trying to survive their day. And so my façade is that I never let my true uncertainty show, because often the thing I am uncertain about will resolve itself once it senses no resistance in me."

I move my head, letting his lips run across my jaw. "Have I told you how incredibly hot it is when you talk?"

"When I talk? As in, all the time, or a specific—"

"All the time. Every word you say. Catastrophically hot and so damn wise I could weep."

Hex smirks, cheeks aflame. "I gave you a secret of mine," he says, pulling back. "In payment, I want a secret of yours."

I break off the gingerbread zombie's head and eat it. "Fire away. I'm an open book."

"Why do you not have conviction in yourself?"

I pause mid-chew, mouth full of cinnamon and nutmeg and vanilla frosting.

"You have an incredible amount to offer," Hex presses. "And you are not a fool—you know you are quite capable, quite smart. Yet you lack confidence in a way that makes little sense."

I fight to give one of my signature charming smiles. "Please. I exude confidence."

"You *project* confidence. But beneath that, you doubt yourself."

His hand rests on my thigh. Gentle. Not pushing me. And the way he sits in silence, I know he'd wait on me, give me space, just as I do with him.

"I'm not the pillar," I say. I stroke my fingers over his, flip his hand and trace the lines of his palm.

"The pillar?"

"The reliable one. That's Kris. And I only just realized that's the role he took on, the caretaker, and god if that didn't smack me upside the head with guilt. Because I was always the funny one. The one who made him laugh. And the one time I *tried* to be more, I fucked up. Massively." I hesitate, reluctance and shame capping me, but I grit my teeth and say to the bench, "Did you hear about the economic crash in New Koah?"

Hex is silent for a beat. "A few years back?"

"Yeah. That was me."

"That was . . . you? How?"

Breath blisters like embers in my lungs. "I arranged it so all outstanding Christmas wishes got granted in the capital city, and the entire country broke because of it."

I needed to tell him. He deserves to know exactly what type of guy he's—doing whatever it is we're doing with. But the moment the words are in the air, I realize that I'm admitting the biggest mistake I've ever made to the most self-possessed and responsible person I've ever met. The only reaction he'll have is disgust, that he ever let me touch him, and I can't stop the scalding sear of panic from burning across my face.

But Hex's expression goes serious. "That was the night we met," he guesses, brows relaxing as connection forms. "*That* was what you were talking about."

"I—yeah."

He smiles. *Smiles.* "Our conversation makes far more sense now."

My mouth drops open in an unabashed gawk. "That's all you have to say?"

"What should I say?"

"How fucked up what I did was!" My voice breaks, and I feel people look over, but I don't care, can't, so much of my being is chained to this conversation now. "How—how dangerous and irresponsible and—you're so calm. I—I don't understand."

He edges closer on the bench and squeezes my hand in both of his. "Coal. Look at me."

I'm not, though. I'm staring at the way he's holding my fingers in his, intertwined.

"Why did you do it?" he asks.

And *that* rockets my gaze up. No one, *no one,* has ever asked me that before. They all just leap to accuse me of how dumb it was or remind me of what the repercussions were.

"Does it matter?" I whisper.

Hex nods. "To me it does."

I hold. Give him another moment to realize he should be horrified by me.

Then I dig into my pocket and pull out my phone.

Hand shaking, I thumb through saved photos until I get to one. The one. An image of the letter that had been my deciding factor.

Dear Santa. Daddy left and I don't think he's coming back this time. I really want my mom to have some money for Christmas so she doesn't have to worry about him helping us, okay? All the kids at school laugh at me for still believing in you but I know you'll help us because Mom said I'm always really good. I'll trade all the toys you'll ever leave me if you'll give her some help.

I show it to Hex and watch as he reads it. His expression melts, the sinking sadness I'd felt the first time I'd read it. Hell, the sadness I still feel reading it.

"There are thousands of letters like this in our database." My voice is porcelain delicate. I don't recognize it coming out of me. "This isn't even the most heart-wrenching one, not by a long shot, and I couldn't . . . I had to do something. I *had* to."

Hex's focus eases up to my eyes. "You did not fulfill the wishes to hurt those children."

I'm halfway through putting my phone back in my pocket when I convulse at his statement. "God, no! Absolutely not—"

He holds up his hand. "I have a point, I promise. You had good intentions. And no, good intentions are not always enough. But I do not believe it was an irresponsible thing that you did. It was misguided, perhaps. Honestly, I don't know many people who could read letters like that and *not* grant whatever that child wanted. The difference lies in how you proceed now, in what you do next. If you keep doing things without considering the ramifications, or if you refuse to enact any change and surrender to complacency, then I would label you irresponsible. But, Coal—you're learning from your mistake, and you're still *trying.* That is brave and admirable, and exactly what each Holiday needs in its leader."

Brave and *admirable* pile in with *honorable* and I'm sitting here next to him unable to comprehend how he sees me like this. I almost argue with him, lay out a list of all the reasons I'm none of those things and here, this is why you shouldn't trust me, why I'm too much of a mess to possibly be *admirable,* fuck.

But he squeezes my hand again, plays with the ring on my thumb, and everything he's ever said to me has been purposeful from the start. He doesn't speak without assessing the possibilities and truth in what he says, so he wouldn't say something wrong.

He sees me as someone honorable, brave, and admirable, and in this moment, I let myself believe I really am that man.

My eyes burn. I sniff, hard, and my attention is ripped to all the people around us. Iris and Kris are talking to a group at the next table over, doing more of our duty than I currently am, but I stare at them until I can get my breathing under control, until I know I can speak without falling apart.

"If you need to make a joke," Hex whispers, "I'd be happy to give you some kind of setup."

I laugh. That laugh shatters through the tightening of emotion and I look at him in relief and raging, delirious gratitude.

Fuck everyone around us. Fuck anything that might keep me from him in this moment.

I cup his jaw in my hand and kiss him. Nothing consuming, not like I would in private. This is a conversation; this is *Thank you, you make me want to be the person you think I am.* A simple, gentle meeting of lips and tongue, the shared taste of vanilla frosting and cookie spices. It feels inadequate, but his smile when I shift back is anything but inadequate. Bright and beautiful.

Forehead to his, I look down at our hands, still entwined. "Our mom left when I was eight," I say. "Kris was seven."

I see Hex try to angle to look at me without separating our foreheads.

"And no amount of perceived perfection or joy stopped it or brought her back," I continue. "Joy is a potent magical resource, but I was so certain, for so long, that it wasn't as powerful as one person making a stupid, selfish choice."

Hex lifts my hand to his mouth and kisses my thumb, the one wearing his ring. "No. Joy wins out, every time."

I push back to see his face.

He smiles at me, soft and sad, and I know he's thinking about his sister, how she got taken from him because of one person making a stupid, selfish choice too.

"I'm starting to believe that," I whisper. "Because of you."

His smile goes a little crooked. "Because of me?"

"But you were wrong about something."

"Doubtful."

"You said—oh, hilarious. I'm serious. You said we're stewards of the things that help people endure whatever awful stuff they have to face."

He nods.

"We aren't just stewards. We deserve it too. We deserve to feel this happiness, to feel this joy, to feel this *magic*. It's ours as much as it is the world's."

"And even if we don't"—his eyes are still soft—"that's why we fight so hard for our Holidays. Because we are the lights that help people when they're at their worst. We're what remains to lift them up when everything else seems dismal."

"You really believe we have some higher purpose. That everything will work out."

"I know it will."

"Even when you were forced here as a political pawn? Even when my dad threatened Halloween? How does any of that go towards helping bring joy to the world?"

Hex's lips raise, brightening his whole face. "It did bring joy, Coal. It brought us together."

Well damn.

I kiss him again.

Because I have to. Because I can. Because he's right.

And then I drag myself away from him, a feat of incredible strength honestly, and join my brother and Iris in talking to people, because this will all work out too.

I won't let it do anything else.

Chapter Sixteen

"And what did you do today?"

Oh, the most loaded of questions to answer, particularly when one's answer involves preparing for a coup. But just, like, a minor one.

Dad sits at the head of our massive dining table, a commanding presence in crimson, me at his right, and his question makes my body freeze mid-bite.

The whole of our court and a few reporters are spread down this cumbersomely large mahogany table, Renee's best dishes strewn under flickering golden chandeliers. Utensils click on plates, voices murmur idle conversation, but only the dozen or so people on this end of the table hear Dad's question. Including Kris, nearby; Iris, next to her dad across from me; Hex, on the other side of Neo.

We'd made it back to the palace with plenty of time to change for dinner. And we'd all agreed to *come* to dinner, some overly formal affair in celebration of a lord of House Caroler's birthday, and even though Hex's magic had worked and no one had been waiting to scold us in my suite, I feel breathless.

Or is it visiting the Route Planners that Dad's talking about? Wow, I'm losing track of all the things he could berate me for. Almost like old times, really.

"Oh, um—finalized the class schedule for my last semester," I say, then realize that I do, in fact, need to finalize the class schedule for my last semester. I'm almost certain I've missed a few key deadlines.

Dad lifts one eyebrow. There's a beat where I expect him to explode on me, that he found out what I'm doing, but I hold his gaze. I hold it because for the first time in our relationship, I *know* I'm in the right, about everything.

I wanted you to be better.

Now, I'll just be better for you.

All the other people Kris and I talked to in the city felt the same as that initial couple: Christmas is superior, our king is so great he shits tinsel, why is he the best, he just IS the BEST how DARE you QUESTION IT—

It was more and more harrowing to see that Dad has, very successfully, instilled not just an unwavering loyalty to Christmas in our people, but a devotion to *him*. Though everyone I dared to mention any blackmail or seedy methods to did seem shocked by it, like it'd be more feasible to move the whole North Pole to a desert than for Christmas to do shit like that.

I try to lean on what Hex said about not changing everything overnight. This is a long game, but it has to start at the places where people are suffering most: unraveling Christmas's seizure of joy. Preventing my dad from being able to see through his blackmail threats by taking away his power. Everything else will come later. One step at a time.

Brave, admirable, honorable.

Buffeted by hope, I smile at my father.

He nods. "Very good, Nicholas. Responsible."

"It seemed the best use of my time." I turn back to my plate, glancing at Hex as I shift.

He wore another corset vest to dinner. A different one. Still black, but with vertical ribs of deep, rich orange, and the collar of his black shirt underneath is popped. The table cuts him mid-chest but I saw him walk in; I know exactly how that whole blessed contraption turned his body into an arrow pointing down, down, so tightly *down*.

I have my phone on my thighs and I inconspicuously swipe to his text thread.

HEX

you know exactly what you're doing to me, don't you?

Hex looks down at his lap.

HEX
Doing what, precisely? I do a lot.

> those corset vests. those goddamn
> motherfucking corset vests.

HEX
Wow, they certainly seem to inspire
a strong reaction from you. Is this
angry Coal I'm seeing?

> oh, no, this is a side of me you
> are well acquainted with by
> now.
>
> the side of me that wanted to
> slam you up against the
> courtyard wall earlier today and
> aggressively make out with you
> at the risk of our mouths freezing
> together
>
> or do this

I wait until he looks up at me.

Then I let a drop of gravy roll off my fork and hit my thumb. I lift that thumb, the one wearing his ring, and stick the whole thing in my mouth.

Leisurely pull it out.

His eyes bulge.

God, I'm so clumsy, how embarrassing.

Hex drops his wide eyes to the table, one hand white-knuckled around his water cup, lips flattened in a suppressed grin way too similar to mine.

Dad asks Neo something. No one is watching me so I let my gaze linger on Hex until, finally, he gives me that look of annoyed amusement and a slow head shake.

I pulse my eyebrows at him, reveling in the rose-pink flush across the tips of his cheekbones, but I'm not done yet.

now i know what you'd say to that:
but coal, you sexy beast, if just
our lips would have been at risk of
freezing together then we definitely
couldn't have done THAT outside

and to that i'd say: it's a fantasy,
hex, you sexier beast, let me paint
you a word picture

imagine the courtyard's empty,
because i don't share. imagine i
slowly strip you under one of those
very expensive space heaters until
you're shivering and begging. and
imagine i warm you up head to toe
by only putting one part of your
body in my mouth

I catch his reaction as he reads, his eyes sweeping back and forth across the screen of his phone.

His lower lip rolls between his teeth. He shifts on his seat, folding one leg over the other, and I barely restrain a crow of victory.

He doesn't look up at me, and I see him fighting not to, that bit lip getting abused viciously.

HEX
You have quite the imagination.

only when i have the proper muse

HEX
I am confused though: what,
precisely, is taking the place of the
gravy in this scenario?

the gravy is a metaphor

HEX
For?

"i licked him so he's mine"

Hex barks a laugh. A sharp crack that echoes out over the table.

My face flashes in a reckless, ecstatic smile. I haven't heard him make that sound before. Adding it to the list of noises that are now my life's purpose to bring out in him again.

Everyone at the table has gone silent as they eye Hex, see nothing funny, then gradually go back to their conversations.

Hex's cheeks are red and he takes a sip of water, mimics choking on something like that would explain what was clearly a laugh.

I have to put my hand over my mouth to hide my beaming smirk. God, I love seeing him like that, like he didn't know he was capable of this kind of happiness and it's shocking him as much as he enjoys it.

My attention tugs down the table, following the members of my court, even though every part of me wants to keep teasing him.

The moment my attention strays, though, I sit up straighter. Hex and I may be locked in secret relationship bliss, but the mood for everyone else is . . . well, it's dull, that's what it is.

I see one member of our court yawn.

There's music playing but it's like the elevator version of Christmas songs.

Iris keeps casting glances at her dad, her forehead creased with contemplative worry.

Kris is picking at his food and staring off into the middle space.

I honestly couldn't name whose birthday it's supposed to be—no one looks remotely celebratory.

It's such a stark, jarring difference from North Pole City and all that sincere joy. And it's *always* like this here; our events are strained with performative bullshit, because they're meant to be formal displays of the best that Christmas has to offer.

It's soulless as fuck.

Things are going to change, right?

They're going to *change*.

I slam my hands on the table and shove to my feet. "Let's move to the next part of the evening, shall we?"

Dad whips a frown up at me. "Nicholas?"

He wants credit so bad for how great Christmas is doing. He wants to be the one and only recipient of our people's adoration.

That's fine by me, honestly. I've never cared about our public image. So if it'll get us to where I want to go, he can have every ounce of credit.

"My father has arranged a surprise for us all," I say. "If you'll follow me."

Dad grabs my arm. "What are you doing?" His face is all calm propriety, his words all hardened steel.

"Trust me," I say down to him, hoping my voice doesn't shake, but his grip on my wrist is tightening. "New Nicholas, remember?"

For a moment, my resolve goes slippery and weak under his critical glare. Even with everyone at the table watching. Even with a few reporters lurking, as always.

He doesn't trust me and he has no reason to and that puts me in the worst position, and I already know how far he's capable of pushing things, but there's always *further.* There's always *worse.* And every single one of those possibilities hangs over me as my mind goes blank in that incapacitating way where I'm a kid again and I realized that I need to start being afraid of my father because Mom's absence changed something fundamental inside of him.

But then he says, "Yes. Let us adjourn."

He lets go of me and stands.

My chest deflates. I start for the door, and gradually, the table follows, chairs scraping back.

Somewhere behind me, I hear a half-pitiful mutter of "But what about my birthday cake?"

I wince but lead us all out the door. Dad keeps close on my heels, his eyes burning the back of my skull as I twist us through the palace—

And kick into the theater room.

Kris and I normally use it to dick around between Christmas events on various multiplayer games. But as I hold the door and step aside, I see a lot of our court give the room looks of *Wow, I had no idea this was here.*

It's not quite the size of a real movie theater, but it has tons of recliners and a massive screen at one end and a popcorn machine.

As everyone pours in, I clap for their attention. "Take your seats. The feature will begin shortly. Note your emergency exits, and—"

Dad stops in front of me. "What are we doing, Nicholas?"

We. Okay, not too bad.

I nod at the chairs. "Let me prove myself. Sit. This will be good, I promise."

He's studying me. Considering.

He walks away without a word.

Kris is on me immediately. "What's your plan?"

"Something fun." I shrug. "That dinner was killing my soul."

"How is that any different from our usual court dinners?"

"Because they're capable of feeling the joy we felt today too. And I'm fully *sick* of pretending we're *not.*"

Iris slips over, Hex in tow, but they give us space, remembering my dad's none too recent reprimanding of us all. The rest of the crowd is busy trying to figure out how to sit in recliners while basically wearing evening gowns and tuxes.

There's a door off the theater room that holds the projector equipment, a hookup to streaming services, extra popcorn and such. I back into it with pleading eyes at Iris, Hex, and Kris, and a few seconds after I slip in, they stagger in with me.

The walls are black, sound-deadening carpet, and the low light throws everything in a dreamlike haze that's hard to shake after coming out of that godawful elevator music in the dining room.

I yank off my suit jacket, unbutton my cuffs, and roll my sleeves to my elbows so when I start flipping through the streaming services, I'm all business. "Okay. Someone in the square mentioned they were doing a Christmas movie marathon and it sounds like the sort of normal-person activity to make everyone out there remember that our Holiday is supposed to bring joy to us too. So we'll need popcorn—last time I tried to run that machine, I burned it all within an inch of our lives. Someone else should take that task. And we need to bring that birthday cake here, I feel bad."

There's a pause.

I throw a glance over my shoulder to see the three of them gaping at me.

"Oh, come on, my taking charge can't be that shocking still, can it?"

Iris scrunches her nose. "Yes. It will never not be shocking. And I am not making the popcorn."

"I'll do it." Kris lifts a jar of kernels. "I can let a member of staff know about the cake too. What movie?"

I scroll through a list. "*Rudolph?*" It's the first to come up and I have a vague memory of watching it when I was younger.

"Absolutely not," Iris snaps.

"What? It's listed under *Classics*."

"And it's *classically* a misogynistic mess. One of the lines is literally '*This is men's work.*' Pass."

I flip farther down. "Like half of these are called *Santa Claus*. Oh, *It's a Wonderful Life?*"

"Isn't that one sad?" Kris asks. "He dies, right?"

"We need a few with like actual Christmas cheer. Why is *Die Hard* on this list? Wait, something called *Silent Night?* Look, there's a family on the poster."

"You have got to be kidding me."

The three of us turn to Hex. His brows are popped in a triangle of confusion.

"*Silent Night* is a horror movie," he says like he's half expecting us to laugh and say all this was a joke.

When we stare at him, he squints. "How many Christmas movies have you watched?"

"Maybe like two or three? When we were kids." I bob my head. "*Rudolph* for sure. That Charlie Brown one. And something with a career-focused dad trying to get his kid the perfect gift like that would make up for him being an absent parent the other 364 days of the year."

Hex looks, succinctly, mortified. He cups his hands over his face and gives a defeated sigh into the hollow of his palms.

"All right." He bats me away from the screen. "Step aside."

I give him maybe an inch of room so he's forced to stand right against me. He nudges me with his shoulder, then starts scrolling.

"Here." He stops on a poster for something called *A Christmas Prince*. "It's cheery and will appease everyone in that room. There are sequels, if you truly want a marathon. We can—"

He sees my wide-eyed smirk.

"What?"

"How do you know that movie?" I ask.

Hex studies my growing amusement with resignation, like he knows I'm about to tease him for whatever he's going to say but there's no helping it.

"You have to understand," he starts, tongue pressing on the side of his mouth, "that there are very few Halloween romantic comedies. I believe Easter can attest to that as well."

Iris's eyes go to slits in thought. "Oh my god. You're right. Why did Christmas commandeer *that* too? You guys suck."

"It's a sorely overlooked travesty," says Hex. "Halloween is unutterably romantic."

"I agree," I say. "So do you like to study Holidays in cinema, or . . . ?"

Hex sucks in a breath and tugs at the edge of his vest, suppressing a smile. I watch him until all he says is, "Sure. Let's go with that."

Iris is the first to giggle. "Hex is a Christmas movie fan!"

"Oh my god." Kris's grin is wide. "You're a Christmas groupie, aren't you? *That's* why you're after my brother. I knew it couldn't have been because of his personality."

"I am hardly a *groupie*," Hex counters. "I have three young brothers for whom your Holiday has, against our best attempts at reminding them of the diplomatic ramifications, *appealing* aspects, and—" He heaves a bone-cracking sigh. "There is no salvaging my dignity from this, is there?"

Even in the low light, he's blushing, and it's so damn cute I hook my thumb in the waistband of his pants.

"You like my Holiday," I say like I'm six and teasing him on a playground. "You *liiiiiike* my *Holidaaaaay*—"

"You should be more concerned by the fact that a Halloween Prince upstaged you in a fundamental tenet of modern Christmas traditions," he tries.

I consider.

Then push my face against the side of his. "You *liiiiiike* my *Holi-daaaaay.*"

He shoves against me, but it's half-hearted. "You're insufferable."

"And you're adorable."

"And I think it's time for popcorn," Iris pipes in. "I'll do it after all. Excuse me."

She snatches the jar from Kris and ducks out of the room.

A beat of strained silence falls.

"She seem upset?" Kris asks.

I haven't told him what she said to me, that she used to want the sweeping romance her parents had but doesn't believe in it anymore. It wells against my tongue. The urge to *tell him* so he can rush out there and confess his feelings to her and put us all out of our misery.

But she's my best friend, and he's my brother, and this is the weird line I always have to walk between them.

All I can settle on is to shake my head. "Yeah. Maybe. I can talk to her later." And say *what,* that hey my brother would be willing to help you rediscover your belief in love? Speaking of a Christmas rom-com.

Though I'm one to talk, aren't I?

Kris scratches the back of his neck. "All right. I'll go get that cake, then," he says and leaves.

I hit play on the projector screen. Out in the theater, the lights automatically dim, and the rolling noise of the movie kicks up in the sound system.

"So. *A Christmas Prince?*" I beam down at Hex.

"Shockingly, it is not a film about *you* or any Prince of Christmas. It's rather deceptively named."

"You've watched it before."

"We established that."

"Were you *hoping* it was a movie about me?"

He rolls his eyes. "It's remarkable your ego can fit in this projector room. I saw it before I came here."

"But after we kissed at the bar?"

His lips thin. "Possibly."

I brace his hips in my hands and press myself over him. "You were watching movies about me. You *liiiiiked* me. And my Holiday."

"Teasing me for being interested in you is hardly an effective form of mockery after everything we've done."

"No, this was before—wait, oh my god! You admit it. You had a crush on me!"

"A *crush* on you? Are we twelve? Did you have a *crush* on me?" He shakes his head. "No, you wouldn't have, would you? You didn't know who I was."

But I laugh and wobble into him and catch myself by kissing his neck. "I was, though. Interested in you. Not the Halloween Prince. Just—you."

He peels back. "You were?" His tone changes, banter to shock.

"Why is that surprising?"

He holds, eyes searching mine, uncertain, or maybe self-conscious. It makes him look so much younger, like for a flash we are back in that alley, in the dark and the hot summer air.

"I had no idea who you were," I tell him. "But all I knew, needed to know, was that you made the fuses that were burning up towards me—my responsibilities and my *irresponsibility* and my future and my mistakes—feel cut off, and in those seconds, I wasn't destined to explode. I was just *there*. With you."

He blinks quickly, rocking into me, forehead to my lips.

"You said it was hot when I talk?" he whispers. "Hardly. Can you hear yourself?"

I grin into his skin. "Come on. We're missing the movie."

The lights are so dim in the theater that if Dad was watching—and he is, I know he is—with the movie screen black, Hex and I are swathed in darkness momentarily.

I feel through the shadows and take his hand, pull him so my lips find his ear. "I want to know what other Christmas movies you like. How about you pick a few of your favorites and we watch them together?"

The movie sends a pulse of white light that floods the theater, and I pull back, but I don't step away from him. Not yet.

He looks up at me, his teasing paused, a held breath. "And when would we watch them?"

Our time is quickly becoming limited. If all goes well, the Christmas Eve deadline won't matter—I'll have the start of a collective to back me up, we can unify against any repercussions Dad threatens, and all the arranged marriage alliance bullshit can be dissolved.

But if I lose what flimsy control I have over this situation . . . what will happen?

"We have more than a week," I say and give a hopeful smile. "And then—"

Hex's eyes dip over my shoulder. "Your father is looking at us."

He steps around me and I feel like something slipped out of my hands in the last five seconds, a lifeline slithering away from me.

But I know how delicate all this is. I know what could happen if this blows up in our faces.

And then is too far off to think about yet.

Staff wheel in the cake, Iris manages to make popcorn—it's a little burned, but good—and, blissfully, the only seat left in the theater is near the back, a reclining love seat barely big enough for two people. But Iris, Kris, Hex, and I drop into it, throw it all the way in recline, and pelt each other with popcorn and gorge on Renee's chocolate cherry layer cake and settle in to watch a movie that has nothing whatsoever to do with a Prince of Christmas.

It only takes about twenty minutes into the movie before the mood of the room shifts. A few stray laughs at first. Then giddy murmurs, an overall welling of *fun*. Even the reporters relax into their chairs and end up enjoying the movie, the atmosphere.

The sequel kicks on after the first, and I expect people to take that transition as a cue to leave.

But they stay.

They stay and watch the second one.

Then the third.

And by the time that movie is over, members of my court are laughing, smiling, in ways I haven't seen . . . ever.

Everyone starts to leave as the credits on the last movie roll. I disentangle myself from Iris—and Hex, who somehow ended up right next to me, oh how did that happen; but luckily we get to our feet before any reporters can swing cameras on the dogpile all of us made—as Dad excuses himself from a conversation across the room.

A reporter from *Morning Yuletide Sun* intercepts him before he can get to me. "King Claus! Are we to expect more events of this nature? I have to say, this was unorthodox!"

Dad's eyes flare to me.

Oh, shit.

But the reporter doubles back. "In a good way! This was a refreshing change."

Dad holds his scrutiny on me. "We shall see how this progresses," he says to the reporter. He nods my way. "Good night, Nicholas."

Dad and the reporter head out of the room.

No snide reprimands. No lingering pause to yell at me for sitting next to Hex. No threat to never pull a stunt like that again.

Well, fuck me running.

Headline: *Prince Nicholas may not be a complete disappointment to his father, apocalypse possibly imminent.*

Kris punches my shoulder. "Look at you. Making good choices."

"Yeah," I say. "Maybe. How about that."

"All right, I'm going to bed." Iris shakes a popcorn kernel out of her hair. "Did I get them all?"

There's like a half dozen stuck across her head.

"Yeah. You're good."

Her glare tells me she knows I'm lying. She flicks me in the nose. "Good night, dumbass."

She pauses.

"We did good things today, Coal," she adds, gentle.

I nod. My throat is welling, or maybe I'm exhausted—today has been a *lot* and I'm not sure how I'll be able to process everything we set in motion, but I flick her nose right back.

She leaves, and Kris, Hex, and I stay to help the staff fix the disaster that this room became. Popcorn, just, *everywhere.*

By the time the room is in order, I'm fully drained, but I catch Hex's wrist as he passes me.

"Come to my suite tonight?" I ask.

"It's past midnight."

"So?"

His gaze goes molten. "So, my suite is . . . far from yours. And if I stay in your room for any amount of time, it will only get later, and later."

He can portal back to his room, but I don't mention that, because his lips unfurl in a sultry smile that yanks something deep in my gut.

The staff have left. Kris is straightening one last chair.

"Stay." My voice cracks. The plea echoes, *stay,* a request I only mean for tonight, but I can feel it tendril out, snake around Christmas Eve and get on its knees and ask him, impossibly, *stay.*

He'll leave. I know he'll leave. He was always going to *leave.*

But now that I've started thinking about our shortening time together, it's a growing, gluttonous beast arching up behind my true intent and I hate the idea of him not being under the same roof as me.

He exhales, warm breath on my collarbone. "Just one night."

No. All the nights. Every one you'll give me.

It's late enough that we don't bother trying to stagger back to my room. We walk, side by side, and don't run into anyone. Kris parts ways at my door and though he doesn't care, I wait until he's gone down the turn for his own suite.

Then I push into my room.

Hex walks in after me, almost statuesque in his movements, like he's performing again, hiding behind his façade.

The door shuts. I lock it.

And I kiss him. Claim his mouth in this dark room and he goes supple for half a second; then he grabs my neck in one hand and kisses me back like he's trying to bruise me. I let him, I want his bruises and his marks and every scar he'll leave on me, because then I'll stop thinking about how this all might end, I'll *stop thinking*.

Just stop thinking.

He makes a desperate, throaty sound, all plea and ecstasy, and maybe there's a little of that gluttonous beast in him too. He pushes me back, back, until my knees hit the bed and I drop, and before I can utter a word, he's flattening me on the comforter and climbing up my body, straddling me, fitting over the saddle of my hips.

Okay, think, a *little* at least.

"Today's been a long day," I whisper.

A column of light comes from the seam around the closed door, a soft glow emanates from a Christmas tree in the corner so we're mostly in black, some in red-green-gold. It's enough that it lets me see the way his pupils have blown wide as he leans down, the silhouette of his arching body in that corset vest, his laser focus intent, control that makes everything in me go malleable and submissive.

His lips suction to my neck. Teeth bite down.

I'm thrown fully into the cosmos, only staying in this dimension thanks to the weight of him, holding me down. His mouth, the things he can do with that *goddamn mouth*—

He takes a break from that torment to tongue the spot and I belt my arm around his torso and spin us so we're on our sides. One of his legs arches on my hip, and I run my hand up his thigh, down to his calf, his ankle. And I hold there. I *stop* there. Forehead to his cheek. Hand on his ankle. I am stone and I will not move because if I do, if I so much as *breathe* too strongly, then—then—

"Coal," he says my name like one of those hymns I imagined moaning. "Kiss me."

A shiver charges from the back of my neck down my spine, setting off a series of smaller, no less destructive quakes in my lungs, my stomach. "You're not asking for me to just kiss you."

"No," he says with Mephistophelian simplicity. "I'm not."

I rear back. "We're both exhausted. We're . . . emotional. Or at least I am. And I don't want to . . . take advantage of that."

"If anything, I'm taking advantage of you."

"That's a flat-out impossibility."

"So kiss me."

"Stop telling me to do that."

"Why?"

My hand is a vise on his ankle.

Hex takes the top of his vest in a fist that could rip apart the fabric of reality, I've seen him do that, dance magic from those fingertips. Only now he specifically undoes *my* reality, because he tugs apart the first latch.

"Hex," I growl, and I clamp my hand over his. "You don't—fuck, this vest."

He leans back in an air of such delicious, sinful defiance that I'm no longer merely on the edge, I'm plunging into the abyss. "What does this vest make you want to do to me?"

"Don't. Don't. I'm begging you—"

"And I'm begging *you*."

"You can't be. I—I'm not—hang on a second." I'm babbling. Full-on mental breakdown of all the ups and downs of emotion from today coupled with how he *is* asking me, how he *wants* this.

My eyes are shut. I don't know when I closed them.

The pillow of his thumb brushes across my eyelids. "Coal," he says again, more tender than enticing. "We don't have to do anything. I shouldn't have pushed—"

I catch his hand as it slides off my face. "That's *not* where my reaction is coming from." And I look at him, aching, how are there still raw parts of me I can show him after today? But here I am, fatalistic in the way I open his fingers, kiss the lines of his palm with my trembling lips.

Part of me will never understand how you can see something worthwhile in me. Will never understand how I got lucky enough that you not only came back to me, but want me. Is terrified that this is all some joke I'm not getting because what the fuck did I do to deserve you.

"You're nervous," he fills into my silence, a wavering, stilted guess, and I hear his own nerves in it, winding up.

My laugh is broken and frantic. Holy shit, he can read me—I don't think I've ever been *nervous* before being with someone, but yeah, that's what this is, isn't it? At the root. Nerves.

"You know what? Yes." I laugh again, that pathetic warble. "That's—yeah. Fuck. I am."

Hex presses his thumb to my chin. "Just nervous, though? Not wanting me to leave?"

"Yes. I mean, no, don't leave. Don't ever leave my bed again, in fact—unless you want to. Unless you're—"

He inches his thumb up to cover my lips. "I can work with nervous."

"Yeah," I mutter against his thumb. "Nervous is good, honestly. We should be nervous. An overabundance of cockiness in situations like this is generally—not a sign of—" He puts my hand on his vest. Uses my fingers to work off another clasp, another. "A sign of—not a sign of—" The vest falls apart and he's in my bed and he smells like popcorn and citrus and a fantasy. I splay my hand in the center of his abdomen and can feel the erratic cadence of his heart beneath his button-up, the swell of his stomach blossoming to fit my palm. "Of—shit, what the hell am I talking about?"

"Nerves." His voice is all tangled in a bated breath.

"Yes. Yeah. Nerves." My fingers have little anarchic minds of their own and pull up the hem of his shirt, and when I spread my hand on his bare stomach I careen into the sky, stars and darkness and swaths of velvet warmth.

I think, in another reality, in another version of myself, I'd be capable of making the better choice. If there is a better choice.

But the moment I look into his eyes in the shadows, there is no choice at all.

"Tell me to stop," I demand. "At any point."

He smiles. His skin is all gilded in the lighting and his black hair is half falling over his shoulder where he's bent towards me and he's unutterably, diabolically beautiful.

"I know," he whispers. He pulls at my collar. "Right now, I don't want you to stop."

I whimper, a cavalcade of falling apart, and my hand slips beneath his shirt as I scoop him up, maneuvering us so we're lying on the pillows. His hips curve into me with the pull of my hand on his lower back and I try to relax my fingers but I am all stiffness helplessly bound to disbelief, how did I get this lucky, how is this man unfurling his body for me.

"Keep talking to me," he whispers.

My mouth is dry. "I'm going to take off your shirt."

He nods. A frantic bob against the pillow.

My fingers fumble the buttons, but I work my way down, bowed over him with my thighs on either side of his. The last button slips free and he sits up, lets me guide both his vest and shirt down his arms, off. And my god, this would be enough. Just to see him half bare like this, ripples and rises of smooth, pale skin, it might need to be enough, it might be too much.

He kisses me. Rocks up against my body and his fingers work at the buttons on my shirt just as clumsily. It's a small comfort knowing he's shaking too. We're falling apart together—that word binds us, holds my vibrating pieces into one cracked whole.

I tug my shirt off and wrap my arms around him, holding him to me, skin on skin on heat on shivers. My fingers climb and descend the mountain range of his spine, his long hair tickling my cheek as I lick the contours of his shoulder, all lean, ropey muscle, collarbone protruding when he tips his head back and gives himself over to my exploration with a contented moan.

Every moment of touching him has left me rattled like I don't know what I'm doing, but no one else mattered before him, no one else could have prepared me for him. There is power, such power inherent in desire, and in this moment, I'm playing out the creation of a whole new origin story with him. It's so easy to create gods or monuments of importance or cruxes of joy, and I've done that for him now, I am his most fervent steward. But he looks at me like he's created a god of me too, and that's the clash I can feel building

up around us, isn't it? What happens when two monuments fall together. What's left behind after the impact.

"I want to taste you," I whisper into the curve of his neck.

"Where?"

Draw me that map again. Take me beyond the edges. And then,
and then, and then—

"Everywhere."

He nods, brows in a deep furrow, eyes shut, lips parted a slit to let
his shuddering breath through.

I press him back against the bed and work my lips down his collarbone, to the plane of his chest. The low prismatic light paints him
red and gold as I lick around one nipple, and he fists the comforter
with a sharp inhale. I move over, repeat the motion, and he bears
down more and I'm an earthquake in human skin.

My fingers go to the fasten of his jeans. I rest my open mouth
against his stomach, inhaling the rise and fall of his quaking breath.
Sugary citrus, spice, the musk of sweat—I pull at the button, free it.

"I'm going to take off your pants," I say, and he's looking down at
me already, black hair splayed on the pillow.

I should be saying more. Waxing on about what he's doing to me,
but all I can manage are these sharp, instructive warnings, and it
sets a mood over us of intimate focus.

He shifts up and helps me work off his boots, socks, pants, boxers,
until he's naked in my bed.

He's naked in my bed.

I dive back down over him, not giving myself a moment to come
undone. I start all over again. I have to. Collarbone, lips there, hand
on his pec, tracing lines; he shivers, I work lower. Nipple, one, then
the other, he comes off the bed with a moan. Lower, the taste of salt
and the smell of sugared oranges on his stomach. I pause at his navel
and lick and kiss until he's wriggling and he hisses something that
sounds like "Ticklish," and I smile against his skin.

Lower, hair leading in a trail down, down, leaving kisses like offerings.

I run a hand across his thigh, lift his leg so it bends, and put a kiss on the inside of his knee. He trembles, and I reel, giving myself a beat to feel his subtle reactions, controlled slips because he's still holding himself taut.

Another kiss, the inside of his thigh, skin getting progressively softer against the violent tension winding through my body, his body too, concrete and glass.

"I'm going to—" I can't find words. There aren't any. All the constant nonsense I spew, and in this moment, the only thing I have to give him is minimalism in its rawest form. Just me.

But he shudders out, "Yes," and then, "Please," and that might be better than all the whines and cries I've heard so far. *Please,* a groping word.

I take him into my mouth. Slowly, to savor it, and because finally, finally, he breaks with a swerving moan that rises from the deepest part of his chest and ends on a quake-like wail, his hands grasping up into his own hair.

His reaction is so panicked and miring that I pull away. "Has anyone ever done this for you?" I ask, throat raspy and I haven't even really gotten to work yet.

His lips are swollen like we've been kissing and his head is pressed back into the pillows so I see the underside of his chin, ligaments bundled.

He shakes his head, breathing labored, arms falling in sharp angles on either side of his body. "Given. Didn't receive. It was a mess anyway."

That has me pulling up onto my forearms. I keep one hand around him though, stroking sluggishly, and he whimpers but finally looks down at me.

"You said you were with one other person," I clarify. "You went down on them. They didn't for you? Or at least finish you off some other way?"

"Is now really the time for this conversation, Coal?" He thrusts his hips in my hand but I flatten my other palm on his thigh to hold him down.

"Absolutely," I say like I'm swearing an oath to him, and it is, an oath and fealty and acquiescent devotion. "I want to know you. All parts of you." I pause, reining in my zealotry. "What parts you'll show me, at least."

He presses his head back again, staring up at my bed's canopy. But I keep stroking him so his breath catches, so he doesn't quite topple into whatever memory is trying to creep across his face.

"It was—ah—right after Raven died," he says in breakneck succession.

I go still. Release him, come up onto my hands, and lean down over him. "What?"

His eyes slam shut and he swallows. "One of her friends—she and him had been dating before . . . and the funeral was over and we ended up alone in my room. It was stupid, Coal. It was a huge, idiotic mistake. So yes. Is that what you wanted to talk about?"

His voice grates, red color staining his chest that has nothing to do with arousal now. He's angry. But when I take his chin in my fingers and pull until he looks at me, the darkness in his eyes feels so fucking familiar, that terrified unworthiness I'd shown after I told him about the New Koah incident. Something dug up from shame and shadows.

It renders me dumbstruck. Not that he'd have something to make him sink down into that drowning pool of mortified self-deprecation; but that he was so recently a gulp of air for me in my own drowning pool, and I get to be that for him. Shared lifelines shift the perspective. Not one-sided, *me*—a delicate widening, *us*.

"You blew your sister's boyfriend after her funeral?" I ask.

Hex's laugh is throttled. "It sounds even worse without my fumbling decorum."

My turn to press a thumb over his lips. "Hex. You were grieving. He was too, I'd expect. It really wasn't surprising that you sought comfort from someone. What's fucked up is that he didn't give you any comfort *back*."

Hex's tumbled guilt and humiliation harden over. "You—you're upset that he *didn't* reciprocate. Not the manner in which we messed around."

"Reciprocation isn't the point. I'm upset he didn't take care of you," I say, and yeah, my tone goes a bit pissed, because I can see it all too clearly. Hex, so pushed to the brink of grief that he opened himself up to someone, got used for a quick one-off, then was left in his room, alone.

I plunge my fingers into his hair, unable to stop this need to lay claim to him in some way, to let touch be a reminder that he's here with *me* now, and what we make will be *good*.

All my nerves vanish, I have purpose anew, purpose and a *gift* in that purpose.

"That guy was an asshole, sweetheart. Let me show you how you should be treated." I bob my head down at where he's gone soft during this conversation. "If you think you can now."

He nods immediately. Seems incapable of saying anything verbally, but the sheer, scrambling need in his eyes is different than it was before. Stripped and whittled and that's where today has brought both of us, shucked of all our walls, all our pathetic vestiges of protection, until we have no choice but to be fully present and feel all of this.

I kiss him, letting that be the only part of us that touches until I feel his muscles give, those fluid, writhing motions that tell me he's back in his body, not his head. Then I slide down with less reverence, more hunger; I got a taste of him and I'm crazed for it, and now, now I know—this is his first. I want to ruin him for anyone else, it's only fair.

Tongue, lips, teeth, I focus on those parts of my body, because everything else is given over to nerve endings swelling under my skin. His moans start up again in a flash flood, forcing their way through his pinched lips until he's crooning to the ceiling. The easiest movements are driving him wild to the point where I almost feel cruel doing more, but I want to be cruel.

I look up at him, seeing him over the curves and planes of his body, and the sight burns into my head, becomes a fixed point: all long lines and sharp edges, laid out as a contrast on the soft bedding, hair a mess and eyes saying that mess is internal too. I remember the way he'd reacted when I pulled his hair, so I slip my mouth off him—to his garbled protest, a lusciously distressing *nuh-huh*—but pump him in my hand as I press my teeth experimentally into the soft, sensitive skin inside his thigh.

He makes a stunned noise, an intake of breath that could cut glass.

I bite at him again, soothe the spot with a kiss, my tongue. He's *shaking* now, the heels of his hands digging into his forehead. So I do it higher, the apex of his thigh; then up the length of him, gentle nips interspersed with soft kisses, sharpness and velvet.

"Coal—I'm gonna—*mmph*—" He breaks off into babbles and muttering and I think stops himself from cussing—wouldn't *that* be kind of hysterical, though—and I gulp him back down in a greedy rush.

A bright, shimmering cry accompanies his back coming fully off the bed, shoulders digging into the pillow, hips bucking into me. I have been drunk on many different types of alcohol before, but I've never had an intoxication like the one I'm getting from the barrage that is him fraying because of me. I'm so obsessed, so enthralled, that I nuzzle and lick until he flinches in an over-sensitized daze and grabs at my shoulders, my hair.

"Coal—" I cut him off by surging up to devour his mouth and he makes that cry again but it's trapped between our tongues. He digs his nails into my back, scrambling me closer, and I obey, my full weight bearing down on him, hands everywhere, his hair, the slope of his side, his thigh where it wraps around me and yanks me in.

"I want—" he rasps, and I'm already agreeing, whatever he wants, anything. "I want you inside of me."

My eyes pop halfway out of my head and I rear back, propping on my elbows.

His words hang in the air, and he looks up at me, all liquid shadows.

"We—wow, we don't have to," I say, and it comes out hoarse. "This isn't a—it doesn't have to be—"

He drags his hand out of my hair, down my cheek. "I know. I want to." He pauses, bites his lip, brows twisting in something like entreating as his chest rises and drops in jackrabbit breaths. "I assume you . . . have? Before."

"Yeah. Both ways. So if you don't want to be on the receiving end, I can—"

He smiles. He fucking *smiles* and my heart isn't in my chest anymore, it's taken flight and lapping around my head.

"I want it this way," he murmurs. "I want you."

I kiss him, I'm still in my jeans but I can feel the angles of his body pressing against mine. It hits me again, a palpitating gong—he's naked in my bed.

And then another gong, can he taste himself in my mouth? I kiss him deeper, willing him to, that awareness, that reminder.

I rest my lips on his and my nervousness erupts back over me in a brazen storm. "I meant what I said before. About wanting to make you feel good. About wanting you to want this. That's it. You don't owe me anything. That's all I—"

"Coal." He digs his nails into the small of my back, light enough to shut me up. "This is what I want. I—" He stops, suddenly, and pushes his head back into the pillow. "Is this not what you want?"

I whine and drop my forehead to his shoulder. "It's possible I'm overthinking your comfort."

He hums. "It's sweet."

"Bit of a mood killer."

"More than me telling you about my disastrous first time? No." He says it with unarguable soft confidence.

His eyes are glossy, hazed still in the afterglow, and I nod at his look, his decision.

I scramble off the bed, shaking, and dive over to the dresser on the side, wrench open the top drawer. A moment of searching reveals a handful of stuff and I present it to him like a truly pitiful worshipper bringing erotic sacrifices. A condom, lube.

Hex reaches for me, an earnest ache in his eyes. "Come here."

I step up to him, set the stuff on the bed next to him, lean in.

He grabs my neck in one hand, the other gripping the waistband of my pants and tugging intently. His forehead anchors to mine and he sets to work, unbuttoning, unzipping, I kick my shoes off and shrug out of my remaining clothes and it's warm in here, so very fucking warm in here, but goose bumps prickle up my legs, anticipation crashing headlong into reality.

I stay crouched beside the bed, bent over him, Hex sitting up, his hands blazing their own trails over my chest, stomach, hips, then—

He touches me, feather-soft fingers.

I groan, a slow-detonating bomb.

"Lie down," he tells me.

I climb over him and obey, but I can't not touch him now, and so I keep my hand on his arm as he twists, grabs the condom, the lube, and then positions himself across my hips.

My nails bear down on his thighs, fuck, this is all pain, pain on the borderland of pleasure.

His certainty wanes, chest glinting in the low lights, sweat-glossed. "I know the basics. But how should I—"

"Let me."

I take the lube and force my mind to be miles away. Eons away. To not think about the task I'm doing to him as I sit up, him propped over my lap, and snake my hand around him. He braces on my shoulders, one arm wrapping around my neck, and my mouth rests open on his stomach and I press sloppy kisses to his skin. His breathing catches, warps, cracks and reknits over and over until he's hard again between us; we're both shuddering and shaking and my skin hurts.

He holds the condom out to me. The simple function of that task, too, lets my brain have another moment to reset, which is good, desperately needed, because when I'm done with it, he puts his hand on me only it's slick now and I buck into the pillows.

God, do not fucking ruin this, do not *fucking* come *this soon*.

He's up on his knees, aligning me with him. I can feel a shake in his hand on me.

I hold still. I hold so fucking still, concrete and glass again, solid and breakable all at once, he will shatter me.

His eyes snap to mine, one hand in the center of my chest for balance. It's good my throat is nearly pinched shut, because I want to beg him, I want to sputter out all kinds of nonsense about how pretty and perfect he looks on top of me.

"Relax," is all I say. But I have to close my eyes, jaw clamped, fingers iron clawed into his legs because fuck if I can take my own advice.

He lowers down, up again, down, working in increments, but that gradualness only makes the devastation of his tightness and heat suck me in like quicksand and I beg myself now, *Open your eyes, open your eyes—*

I do. His full lips are split in a winded scowl, hair sheeted around a face set in dire concentration. Those eyes flick up to meet mine and as if he'd been waiting for that contact, that connection, he sinks all the way down.

Sparks of pleasure scattershot through my body to the point of agony, everything impacted by its barrage, veins and muscles and my hips buck up involuntarily like I can both chase and get away from the onslaught.

His sudden gasp is ruinous, and I barely have time to feel it before "Sí, otra vez," rips out of him, a rough tumble, and I don't need to use any sort of translation magic to get that meaning, because just the sensation of him switching languages has me fucking *soaring*.

I do it again, hips punching up, and I hiss at that edge coming way too close. His shivering cry tells me he's right there too, the noise so delicate and otherworldly as to be fey-like. His head dips back, and all the tension he'd been keeping at bay races on him tenfold until he's nothing but corded muscles on top of me, lines of sinew and abs sweat-painted; my lips were there, and there—

At my next thrust, he moves to meet me, hips rolling, and I hold on for dear life, half sensation, half action. My hand finds the space above where we're joined and I wrap my fingers around him again, pumping, and *fuck* it's a cataclysm now, his whole body straining and shuddering but he drags me with him as the storm builds.

"Coal—I need—" he babbles, trembling, and I feel the thrum of his words in the base of my stomach.

I sweep up, a wordless dance where my other arm braces him to me, and I hook his leg and flip us on the bed. The angle of me on top hits him deeper, so fucking deep that both of us moan.

"I got you," I promise. He locks my free hand with his, thrown overhead, gravity tangible in the space between our intertwined fingers. I'm thrusting now, entirely whittled to his need and his pleasure so that's all I am, his, and I say it again, again, "I got you, sweetheart, I got you—"

"You too," he says into my mouth, and it pitches, goes whiny and pleading, "Now, Coal, *now.*"

His body seizes up around me a moment before he cries out and then we're both falling, blurring into each other, laving tongues and heels digging into my back and dewy satin lips.

He said joy creates a foundation, and we do create that foundation, every kiss and caress sets up a reality where the sun will rise tomorrow and I'll make him tea and we'll leisurely figure out what we want to do with our day, no schedule, no events. We'll go down to North Pole City and buy ornaments and then come back and turn this bed inside out again. And in that reality, we don't worry about days passing. We don't worry about losing everything, because our everything is impenetrable, and we create and create with every shake and beg and heartbeat.

I love him.

I love him, and I can't put it into words with how big it is, so I keep talking, and showing, and creating with him.

Chapter Seventeen

I've spent most of my life trying to make the people I love smile. Stupid jokes and quippy one-liners and acts of self-sabotaging nonsense but none of it was ever enough, and I had gotten to the point where I wasn't sure what else I could do. My job, my duty, would be to bring joy to the world through Christmas, but how could I ever do that when I couldn't bring joy to my brother, to Iris, hell, even to my father?

But what I'd spent my life trying to generate wasn't joy, necessarily. Fun, sure. But not *joy*.

Because every morning now, my pillow smells like citrus and spice. I lie facing him and I watch the lights from outside rise up his body, illuminating crevices and cliffs I know by touch and taste. He wakes up next to me and I know, I know, god, I hope we have created enough joy that the reality of not having to worry is ours.

I float through these days, and it's easier and easier to find ways to spread the joy I'm generating, like I'm my own sort of Merry Measure. I don't think about it half the time now—there's another concert, and I suggest we go caroling instead, and Dad permits it. But instead of grabbing whatever pre-arranged songs are laid out, I go up to the members of House Caroler and ask what they think we should sing. What songs are in their past, our past, that don't get the stage space they should?

They confer for a few minutes, then songs are decided on, music sheets are found, and we haul ourselves through the palace, singing at the doors to the Route Planners and the Toy Factory and everywhere else. Our court belts out rather screechy renditions of songs I've never heard, but they're filled with well-wishes and cheer and laughter. The staff at the open doors stares in stunned amusement, and I see more than a few instances of our court lingering at these stops to talk to the staff working, and I don't know that I've ever *seen* our court *talk* to our staff before. Do they even know their names? I introduce them when I can, Renee and Lacie and Lucas and all the others who have been fixtures throughout my life.

And for the next event, our own cookie decorating party, it's usually stiff and formulaic. But I invite all the staff I run into on my way and tell them to spread the news and there are *dozens* of people packed into Renee's kitchen. It's a madhouse of elbows and sprinkles, and at the end, a member of House Frost asks where these cookies are going, and most of them are disastrous piles of icing at this point. But we arrange to turn them into gift boxes and ship them out, a dash of pre-Christmas magic for the people of North Pole City.

I clean up with the staff, and more than a few nobles, who linger too. I don't know what is happening but they're smiling in ways I've never seen, not the smiles of formality, but *really* smiling.

I grab Wren in passing one day and ask her why we don't have more decorations that signify *all* of our houses in our décor. The next morning, there are delicate paper bags housing softly pulsing lights lining the staircases, and Wren tells me she's working on getting woven tapestries from House Jacobs and other decorations too. Whatever that woman's paid isn't enough.

When I look at the tabloids, both those focused on Christmas and wider—okay, that does kill my soul, but I make myself do it— the photos are messier than the older ones. More candid. Smiles and genuineness. The ones that show our staff intermingled with our nobles are going *crazy*, likes and shares and effusive comments. It's hard to tell where the support is coming from, our people or any of the other Holidays who can see these tabloids, but I'll take it, wherever its source.

And then responses start appearing on my desk—the other Holidays, saying they'll come to the Christmas Eve Ball. I do what research I can on these various ruling families, trying to keep it under Dad's radar, but I won't be ignorant anymore. The responses from my invitations say they're eager to talk about the future with Christmas's heir, but *will the reigning Santa be involved in these discussions as well?*

Yes. No. He will but I'm dreading it and I have no idea what I'll say when they all show up here and I'll have to face the music, shit will hit the fan, and other such final colorful phrases.

I keep expecting Dad to flip out. For him to discover the coming guests or see the pictures in the tabloids and realize I'm changing his image of us. I keep expecting him to ban me from events or snap at me about my relationship with Hex, which I'm getting better at hiding in public but it's obvious that he's the focal point of my existence now.

But Dad doesn't intervene. He doesn't stop me. He makes eye contact with me at events and doesn't glower and I think, maybe, he's impressed? But that's impossible. Categorically. Metaphysically. I'm ruining his carefully sculpted persona of us.

Aren't I?

Maybe it's been this easy the whole time. Maybe all I needed to do was exactly what I've done and *choose* to act instead of wallowing in my own shit.

Maybe one fuckup didn't have to define the rest of my life like I let it.

I come up beside Kris at an after-dinner mixer in the courtyard and I'm at war with hating myself for taking so damn long to improve and pride that hey, this all seems to be working? Tall space heaters warm the area—and it only takes one second of thinking back on the text fantasy I'd tormented Hex with to realize that I'm probably the first person in history to be turned on by a space heater—but we're in coats still, and I've just left Iris with Hex after yet another round of *staking my claim* for the cameras. It's easier to play pretend now, knowing it'll come to an end soon.

Dad isn't here. Which isn't odd that he opted out of a low-key event, but something about his absence triggers an itch in the back of my mind.

I shrug it away, fighting to breathe through the well of anxiety.

The Christmas Eve Ball is only three days away. We're so close.

It'll be fine. It'll work.

It has to.

"I need your help," I say to Kris, but my eyes are on Hex. He's next to Iris by an ornamental pine, nodding along to something a noble says to them both.

He tugs on one of the tree's limbs. Idly. Like he's not aware he's doing it.

Then he makes me watch as he elegantly arches his middle finger and runs it all the way down the center of the branch.

My body rocks in place. I feel that finger as if he'd run it down my stomach.

He pops me a playful smile.

Is it possible to shake apart from loving someone too much? They're going to feel tremors all the way down in North Pole City and think it's an avalanche but no, it's me, combusting because of the calamitous power this one man has over me.

"Coal?" Kris snaps in front of my face.

I jump and spin on him.

He's laughing. "Good lord, dude. *You* walked over to *me,* said you needed my help, then *immediately zoned out to stare at the guy you're sleeping with.* You are the poster boy for disaster bisexuals."

"They're sending me the trophy any day now." But I shake my head, press my thumb to my forehead, and get my brain to switch tracks. "Your help. Yeah." I turn to my brother. "I need you to help me write out what to say to the winter Holidays when they get here."

Kris's face smooths from mockery to understanding. "Oh. Yeah, of course. But I kind of assumed you were going to wing it?"

"You think I'd leave this to chance?"

He gives a look I can't decipher. "What'd you have in mind?"

I shove my hands into my pockets to cover the roiling, panicky urgency in my stomach, the feeling of possession that's been growing, day by day.

"We can talk about the potential we all have together," I start. "And how much more capable we could all be if we pool our resources. And how Christmas never should've tried to stretch globally on our own because we can't be everything to everyone, but together? Together—" My mouth goes dry, and this is why I need Kris to write it out, to take these thoughts and figure out what I'm trying to say because I want to say it *all* and it needs to be *coherent*. "Together we can be the start of everything. People have a masterful capacity for creating something solid out of the smallest seed of joy, and we all contribute to giving them that. And we can—"

I stumble to a halt when I see the look Kris is giving me: surprise. Soft, startled surprise.

I'm careful to still keep my voice low. "And, uh, lots of apologizing. Obviously. Add a fair bit of groveling. And put ample redirects if and when Dad tries to cut in. Then more apologizing."

Kris's grin comes so fast it's blinding. "All right," he says. *"Santa."*

"Oh, god, I'm not ready for that."

"Too bad. You're embodying it fully. Careful, you're gonna sprout a fluffy white beard."

"Shut up."

"I hope Hex likes facial hair."

I elbow him, and he laughs.

It's late already, so it doesn't take much longer before everyone starts to trickle back into the palace and to their rooms. I make sure to position myself next to Hex as we duck inside, and I pretend the press of the crowd bumps me into him, letting my hand rest on the small of his back, my lips dangerously, achingly close to his ear.

"I can't believe you did it."

Hex intently removes his gloves, long fingers stretching in the hall's yellow lighting. "Did what?" he whispers, all innocence.

"You fondled that Christmas tree."

He tries to suppress a smile. "I have no idea what you are speaking of. I would never stoop so low to stir a reaction from you."

"Hm. Well. I must have misread that entirely."

"You certainly did."

"So you don't need me to come to your room tonight?"

"Of course not."

"And you don't need me to"—the crowd is separating, and we're pushing it already, but I lightly, quickly, drag my finger up his spine—"reenact anything you did?"

I watch his breath catch, throat bobbing emptily. He shoots me an exasperated frown.

"You always win this game of chicken," he relents, and I beam.

"Oh, sweetheart, I'll make sure you always win in the end." I wink.

He hisses, eyelids fluttering, but he's grinning.

A few last members of the court are heading up the hall. Iris, in their midst, leans on Kris to kick off her shoes then continues on barefoot, one arm looped through his.

Kris must feel my smirk. He glances back, spots me lingering with Hex, and rolls his eyes at my expression.

I wait until they're gone and the bulk of people have dispersed ahead of us before I laugh. "I'd think she was actively trying to kill him if she wasn't so oblivious."

"You have never spoken with her about it? Not even subtly?"

"Kris would kill me. It isn't my secret to tell."

Hex rests his hands in his coat pockets, pensive. He holds for a beat too long.

"Hex?"

At my questioning frown, he nods towards the hall. "You think she may not reciprocate."

Shit, he nailed that fast. "Maybe. A little." It's just been obvious that Kris likes her for so, so long. If she felt even a flicker of attraction to him, she would have noticed years ago, right?

The hall around us is empty now. Gotta love these late-night hijinks—they let me step closer to Hex in one of our too rare moments of public affection. Or, well, public in this empty hall.

"I think the larger risk will be what Easter needs." His fingers hook into the seam of my coat.

"Why would Easter's needs get in the way of her being with Kris?"

Hex goes quiet. His energy is . . . off.

I press closer, fingers fixing under his chin. "Hex? What's going on?"

He smiles. It's forced and sets me on edge. "It's not important."

"It is. What's wrong? This isn't about Iris and Kris."

"It's nothing. I have morbid tendencies, if you'll recall. Please. We can discuss it later."

"You're worried about us." The words have been pinballing around my head for the past few weeks but it doesn't make the way I say them any more confident. They come out shaky and a little desperate. "About after all this."

His smile wavers. "We only have a few days left now."

"I'm so close to fixing everything, I swear."

That sad tinge to his smile doesn't wane. "I know."

"Even if you think it's—"

Footsteps patter up the hall. The cadence is too fast, frantic, and the rhythm triggers a fight-or-flight response deep, deep in my chest.

There's a crack. Something, somewhere, in the past two seconds broke, a massive split shattering, shattering—

Iris comes tearing around the corner. Her whole demeanor sets me on edge, eyes emanating defeat. Under my hands, Hex's arms go rock solid.

I don't release him, but pivot to her. "What's wrong?"

The question sounds muted. Like I'm asking it through water.

"You need to get to your room," she says. "Now. Your father—"

I put one hand up and point at her and a hot swell of anger mixed with fear burns right through my chest.

"Don't," I tell her. "Don't say—"

"He found the letters. The responses from the winter Holidays."

He went through my room? The air sucks out of my lungs.

"Kris is trying to calm him down," she continues, and my hand drops. "He's furious."

I swing back on Hex. That feeling of being underwater is overtaking my senses and makes everything delayed until all I can do is drop my lips to his forehead.

"I'll come to your suite later," I promise.

"Do you want me to be with you?" he offers. A wince ripples across his face.

No, he can't. Not if he wants to keep his Holiday out of this.

"It'll be fine." The words are weather-beaten. *It'll be fine. It'll be fine. It'll be—*

Hex lifts his head, rests his lips against mine. "I'll be waiting," he says into my mouth.

One last kiss, and I break away, giving Iris a forced smile as I pass her. It's fine, see? I'll go to my room, and—

And explain how I'm usurping my father right to his face. No one here to back me up. Nothing at all put in motion except those letters, those damn letters.

I keep walking, and I don't look back at Hex or Iris, and my mind goes blank under the storm of everything hitting down on me at once.

Staff shut up rooms I pass with nods of good night, and then I'm at the door to my suite.

Kris is in there.

So I don't give myself the luxury of stalling.

The knob twists under my fingers and I push in to see Kris standing off to the side, arms folded, incensed, and Dad, seated at my desk, a stack of letters in his lap. The responses I'd hidden in the back of my closet.

My suite has been *tossed.*

Clothes everywhere. Cushions removed from the couch and chair. Drawers pulled out of my desk and papers rifled through and he *tore it apart.*

I'm in my coat from the after-dinner event still, and I rip it off, sweating and shaking but neither hot nor cold.

"What do you think you're doing?" I hear myself ask. "This is *my* room. You can't—"

"You are in no position to get righteous on me, Nicholas. Kristopher," Dad doesn't look at him, "you are not needed."

"Yes, I am," he shoots back.

Dad's mouth purses, but he turns away without another word. "I had begun to think you were serious in your attempts to change." He pushes up from the chair, letters in his fist. "This month, you have shown a renewed dedication to your position. I allowed your changes to our events, and while these have been unconventional celebrations, our approval ratings are increasing. Because of your choices."

His expression darkens.

The room grows cold and frost starts to crawl across the window-panes at his back. My stomach twists, but I won't show my nerves.

"But then I heard rumors," Dad says. "My contacts told me that plans are being made in other winter Holidays to travel *here*. And your change in behavior felt too . . . convenient." He holds up the letters. "Did you honestly believe you could conspire behind my back?"

"Yes." No sense denying it. No sense cowering to him.

Dad flinches. "I told you Christmas's ambitions in confidence."

"Your *ambitions* are harmful and cruel," I say, and I try to sound level.

This is it. This is my one chance to convince him, somehow, someway, that what he's doing is fucked up. That he can still be the Christmas King I believed he once was. I *have* to be calm. I can't mess this up.

Not this.

"We can't control everyone," I tell him, hoping my voice isn't shaking as much as I think it is. "We can't be the singular force at the head of something so large. Christmas, Easter, whatever Holidays you're thinking of controlling—it's too much. This isn't how it has to be. This isn't how it *should* be."

"And you, who calls himself *Coal* and has only ever made a mess of our Holiday, believe that you have a better vision than *decades* of work? You went behind my back and tried to undo all the systems I have put in place to ensure this Holiday, *your* Holiday, is secure."

"Whatever security you feel you've gotten has only come at the cost of destabilizing other Holidays. You're terrified of Christmas losing joy, of us slipping into obscurity; I get that, Dad, I *do*, but you're creating the very thing you're afraid of. Don't you see that?"

"All I have done, *everything*, has been to make sure you and your brother never have to worry about your future. To take care of the *millions* of people who depend on us."

I pity him and I'm terrified of him but this anger has grown into something bigger and wilder and it will chew me to pieces. "I care about them too. This has always been *about* them. You told me once it was our job to make the world happy. I've *always* believed that, and I always held onto the belief that *you* still felt that way. All the people in North Pole City who think we're so infallible—we should live up to their opinion of us. We should *try* to be—"

"And where would we get the resources we need to keep Christmas afloat if not for the joy gained through these Holidays? What is your plan to care for our responsibilities, to provide the services to the world that people have come to depend on, if we undo our whole structure?"

"We don't need that joy, and you know it. If we stopped focusing on spreading globally, we wouldn't *need* the extra joy. We can share success with the other winter Holidays. We can *partner* with them. If we bring the other winter Holidays into our ruling, if we work on a fair, balanced collaboration and use our magic to focus on things that foster actual joy, we can stretch so much further, *together,* not one—"

"You got these ideas," Dad interrupts, his mind working behind his narrowing eyes, "from that Halloween Prince. Didn't you?"

I've seen fury on him before.

This is new.

Pointed.

And that's where my confidence bucks. Where I can't hide the cyclone gaining ground in my lungs, ripping the breath out of my body, and I know Dad sees that little flutter of a gasp.

"Leave him out of this," I say.

He takes a step forward, and I go perfectly still, a deer in a hunter's sight. Kris, he comes closer, beside me, and I flash back to one of the first times after Mom left, one of the first times I'd actively gotten in trouble, and Kris had stood by my side and we'd both watched Dad lose his mind at me, and it hadn't felt real. This couldn't have been our father, this screaming, terrifying man.

He's real now.

Dad studies me, his rage held at bay by what he's reading on me. "Their prince has been manipulating you. I had thought inviting him here would serve to remind Halloween of the benefit in staying out of Christmas's path. What would their allies think, I wonder, if they found out that Halloween's heir was plotting to *overthrow* me? How does something like that fit into the autumn collective's ideals of fairness?"

Cold horror spiderwebs out across my body.

I stammer. "That's *not* what—"

"You were not manipulated?"

"*No,* I—this was me, this was just me—"

"Then this is your mistake only. And you will write to those leaders you summoned." He tosses the letters at me; they rebound off my chest, scatter to the trashed floor around us. "You will write and tell them that they are not to set foot in Christmas unless *I,* personally, invite them."

My lips part, I have no idea what I'll say, but Dad cuts me off.

"You have proven to be only what I most feared you would become, Nicholas: unworthy of this role. You are still nothing more than the careless, selfish person who endangered our entire Holiday with the New Koah fiasco. You are a disappointment to this family, and—"

I blink, and Kris is in front of me.

"How dare you," Kris hisses. "How *dare you* speak to Coal that way."

Dad whips his glare on Kris. "Do not think you are exempt from this, Kristopher. Nicholas has long been the negative influence holding you back, and I—"

"He's *not* a negative influence, and if you keep talking about him like that—"

"Do not interrupt me! For too long, I have allowed him to slander *our name*—"

Kris's shoulders hunch. *"Shut the fuck up!"*

Years overlap in this moment. Years of breaths held because every time I asked how much worse he could get, he'd stun me speechless, until we arrive here, the birth of all my worst fears.

Dad's arm moves. It moves and Kris screamed at him and they're *fighting*, all out *fighting*, over *me*.

I grab Kris in an agitated scramble and yank him back and hurl myself in front of him, hands up, body all fragile, breakable eggshells.

My eyes slam shut. And I hold. And go, "Please, please," because that's what I've been saying for years.

Eternity passes. Remakes itself in the air around my lifted arms, in the gasps of Kris who fell to the ground behind me, and I wait.

I reached too far. I forgot who I am, I forgot everything and tried to become someone too different, and this is my punishment, an extricating reminder that *this is what happens when I try.*

I did this. I caused this, again, and I'm falling apart.

"I'll do what you want," I say from far, far away. "I'll write to the other Holidays. I'll stop it. I'll stop everything, I swear."

I cut my eyes open.

To see Dad, his hand only stretched out into the distance, raised to make a point.

I watch him realize what I'd thought was happening. I watch the connection sizzle across him, his gaze going to his hand, to my lifted arms—my thumb, with Hex's skull ring—to Kris, on the ground.

Dad's glare goes blank.

I'm standing in front of Kris but I'm standing in front of Hex too and I'm more barricade than person.

Kris climbs to his feet. I hear him say my name, muffled, a soft plea.

Still unreadable, Dad pulls a small tablet out of a pocket on his suit coat and hits a button. "Wren."

A static crackle. Then, "Yes, sir?"

"Have the Halloween Prince begin packing. He is no longer welcome in my palace."

A beat. "Yes, sir."

Dad shoves the tablet back into his coat.

His gaze is on the wall behind my head. He speaks to it. "You will marry Iris." His voice is entirely emotionless. He, who can conjure emotion at will to appease cameras, has none to show us now. "You will shore up Easter for us. It is the least you can do to fix what you have damaged."

"Don't blame this on Hex," I say, brokenly. "I'll do it. Just . . . stop."

Dad twists to me. His eyes are bloodshot, maybe, or I just want to see something like regret in him. "Everything you've done, and that's all you have to say?"

I lower my hands. It's the only response I give.

"Send those letters rescinding your invitations, stop interfering in matters that do not concern you, and there will be no repercussions," he says.

Dad steps around Kris and me. I flinch; I can't help it, all my senses have been ripped to the surface of my skin.

He leaves, door shutting behind him.

I thought I could change things.

Me.

And I almost got Kris—

I can't think. Can't find it in me to do anything that could fix this—why can't I *fix this*—

I hear Kris texting. Then Iris is here, and she's next to me on my bed, arm around me.

Kris swings a chair close and sits in front of me. "Coal? Say something."

I sniff and shake my head, at nothing, at everything. "I have to go."

Iris tightens her grip on me. "Coal—"

"I have to *go*." I shove out of bed, but Kris rises up to meet me and doesn't step aside.

It's going to gut me, looking into his eyes. So I do.

His are strained. Downright desolate.

I was the one to drag us here, because of course I would be. Even when I try to change, I *fuck it all up*.

"I have to go," I beg him.

His jaw works. He dips his head and steps aside.

Dad is sending Hex back home. It's what Hex wants, what I want for him, what he was always meant to do.

But I tear out of my room like a madman.

Chapter Eighteen

Wren is two feet from Hex's door. Her fist already raised to knock.

"Wren!" I stumble to a halt as she turns.

Her face goes from business to sympathetic. "Prince Nicholas. Your father gave me orders."

"I know. I know. I—let me tell him. Please. Let me be the one to tell him."

Wren is one eyeroll away from making me go back to my suite, and I'm that same eyeroll away from dropping to my knees and fully begging her.

But she glances up the hall, to where a staff member is rolling a vacuum out of a guestroom.

And she nods.

I go rigid in her acceptance. "Th-thank you. *Thank you.*"

Wren steps aside, but not before she puts a hand on my shoulder. "We are quite proud of you, Nicholas."

"What?" My head snaps back. "Who—*why?*"

I am not ready to hear the word *proud,* not in the wake of all my dad's shit, and it's just as surprising to see her looking sympathetic, like she knows what happened. She just knows Hex is being sent home; why would she be looking at me like that?

"The staff, of course." She pats my shoulder. "Seeing you come into your own has been a hope many of us have shared. Whatever is happening with your father . . . it is none of my business, of course. But I am sorry."

"How much do you know?" It's probably dumb to ask that. If she knew what Dad has been doing, would she be standing here under honor and loyalty like either my dad or I is worthy of those things?

"I know the reigning Santa has . . . intentions for Christmas," she says. It'd be detached if not for the tight squeeze she gives me. "It is a mighty burden to be placed on you. You are not so alone here as you and your brother might think."

Even an hour ago, I would've done something with that hint of her being on my side.

Not now. There's nothing I can do.

Nothing, nothing, that word is sand between my fingers.

I nod absently and turn to Hex's door.

She hesitates. Then leaves with a soft hum.

I try the knob and it's unlocked and I push inside, immediately spotting him on the couch.

"Coal?" He rips to his feet. "Coal—what happened?"

He took off his coat. His hair is pulled back at the nape of his neck and he's in a black vest over a white dress shirt with a simple band collar that gives him a priest energy, but no snarky quips pop to mind because it's all too fitting, isn't it? I've thought so often about how he drives me to worship and sin and here he is, manifesting that.

I sink against the closed door. "You look stunning. I didn't get a chance to tell you earlier."

He comes around the couch. "You're scaring me."

"He found out."

He stops four feet from me. I count the spaces on the patterned carpet. *One-two-three-four.*

"What? How? Are you—"

"People reported arrangements being made in the other winter Holidays. He suspected. Trashed my room. Found the letters."

Hex closes that space, *four, three, two*—his hands go to my face, and I realize my eyes have been everywhere but on his.

"I'm sorry. I'm so sorry. Coal—"

"There were too many moving parts. He was always going to find out."

"You knew this was a possibility. But there is enough power in those united winter Holidays that they should be able to force his hand regardless. Short of barricading them at the door, there is nothing he can do to stop what you have put in motion."

A beat. And in that beat, I'm staring at the carpet. Just beside his shoulder.

"Coal." He pulls on my chin, and I do finally look into his eyes. It centers me.

"He threatened to blame all this on you if I didn't rescind my invitations," I hear myself say. "He knows you're involved. He knows I plotted with you against him. He's sending you home and if I don't stop this, he'll tell the autumn collective you tried to overthrow him. He'll *destroy* your Holiday."

Hex's face sets. Goes pale. "Coal. What did you say to him?"

His reaction is—it's not what I expected. I don't know what I expected. But he's hiding his thoughts and emotions behind that wall again, the one I thought he'd finally let me through.

"Hex." I try to close the remaining space between us.

He steps away. "What did you say to him?" he asks again.

"He was going to tell your collective that you tried to *overthrow* him. No matter how they feel about Christmas, what would they think about Halloween's heir being so malicious? And the shitty thing is—you *did* help me do this. I wasn't trying to overthrow him, but god, does it matter? Because I basically wanted that. And I got you involved, and I—"

"You agreed." His fingers go to his lips. "To rescind your invitations. To stop the winter Holidays collective."

"I'm not going to let him hurt you. I'm not going to let him ruin you or your Holiday. I'll—" *I'll find another way,* I almost tell him. But I won't. I can't, I can't risk hurting people again—I inhale but nothing goes in, nothing, sand in my lungs now, nothing.

"Protecting Halloween is *my* job," Hex tells me, his face reddening. "Your job is to protect Christmas. And you gave it up. For me."

"Damn my *job,* Hex. What should I have done? Let him make good on all his threats to hurt your Holiday? I never had a chance of doing this. I never had a chance of—"

"You did have a chance, and you gave it up, *because of me.* I told you I didn't need you to step in. *I told you not to choose me over your responsibilities.* It was the one thing I asked of you!"

He turns away, fingers on his temples, shaking his head at the carpet, at the air.

His horror slams into my gut, roils around and doesn't fit. "Hex—"

"This is all so broken," he whimpers, and I go rigid.

He shakes his head again, hands pulling back so they interlock behind his neck.

"I'm the reason your father has anything to hold over Halloween in the first place," he says to the ceiling.

"What? What are you talking about?"

He turns a little until I can see the sheen in his eyes, the tears he's trying to hold back. "My sister was the one who wanted to reach out to Christmas about an alliance. She was so—so idealistic. She saw Christmas's reach and thought with that kind of strength . . . the people we could reach too. If we pooled resources, if we helped each other, because we oversee very different aspects of the year. It was a beautiful dream, who could deny it? My parents agreed. Cautiously. But negotiations turned sour—Raven's hopes would never come to pass. I think I knew, before we tried. I knew she would be disappointed."

I don't move. I want to reach out to him but something in his posture keeps me at arm's length.

"Then she died within days of those negotiations ending." Hex licks his lips, swallows the scratch of a sob, and my heart breaks. "She *died,* and *everything* fell apart. Your father had threatened to tell our allies about our attempts at joining with Christmas, and my parents felt we could endure whatever fallout came. But me? It would have been her legacy. The last thing she did before she died, and it could have caused Halloween to be forced out of our collective. The *one thing* Raven held most dear would have been broken. I couldn't risk it. So I begged my parents to comply with whatever your father demanded. I was the one who agreed to Christmas's faux-engagement ploy. I've been the one letting all this happen from the start because she's *dead* and no one else—no one else *cared*—"

He gags, hand flattening over his mouth, and I reach for him, but he bucks backwards.

"Hex." I make his name a plea, asking to let me hold him.

I'd known his duties as Halloween's heir were tied into his grief over his sister, but I hadn't realized how much, and he's hurting and I need to *hold him.*

All Dad's blackmail. There's no way he knew how deep it went for Hex, but hearing it, I hate my father all over again. This is what he's doing; this is how he's hurting people.

"Now you're giving up your plans for your Holiday." Hex shudders, cheeks streaked red, and he droops, exhausted and resolved. "I've let this go too long. Out of fear and anguish and—I can't anymore."

He meets my eyes, finally, they're grieving and utterly wreck me.

"Do not bow to what your father wants," he whispers, shaking. "Go through with the collective, Coal. Let him make good on his threats. Let him—"

"No."

Hex flinches. "Coal. I'm telling you to do this."

"I won't let my father hurt you," I say each word purposefully. That's all I can see. Him, hurting, and everything zeroes in on it, my own grief crumbling away because this, this I can focus on. This I can stop.

"It isn't about me—"

"Now it is. For me it is. I won't let him hurt the man I love."

Hex's eyes grow wide. "The man you what?"

He has to know. This can't be a surprise. *Why is this a surprise to him.*

"I love you," I say, weak, wretched. "I'm in love with you."

But all he says in the reactive stillness is, "You can't."

"I . . . I can't?"

"You can't," Hex says again. He shakes his head, trying to negate what I've said, but it's there, and we both feel it. "You—you have to go through with this collective. I have to face whatever repercussions come. What you're doing—Raven would want that. She wouldn't want me to keep cowering. You can't base your decisions off me."

"Why not?"

"Why not?" he echoes, like the answer is obvious, and there

might be pity in the pinch of his brows. "I'm going back to Mexico regardless of what happens."

"And then?" A cliff is coming. There's a pause at the edge.

He watches me like he expects me to answer my own question, his eyes narrowing in growing aggravation. "Don't make me say it, Coal, please."

"Say *what*?" I honestly don't know, and my confusion only angers him more, lips thinning.

"You're the heir of Christmas," he says, barely contained. "I'm the heir of Halloween. How did you see this ending?"

He leaves it at that. As if it's enough explanation.

It sure as hell *is not*.

"You never saw this working between us?" The words slice my tongue.

"We are both the heirs of very different Holidays," he says, some of that anger held back behind caution. "As proven more now. We would have come to a moment of choosing between us and our duties."

"And we would have chosen our duties, no question?"

His silence is answer enough.

"So this was just a fling for you?" I muster. "This was a *dalliance*?"

I throw the word at him because he's absolutely crushing me right now, and it's a low blow, but it hits, and he closes his eyes, bracing.

"I have to think of Halloween's future," he says, "and you—"

"Are unworthy of being a part of that future. Is that it? Prince Coal, the joke, good enough to screw around with but too much of a screw-up to trust?"

His eyes fly open. "Don't twist this," he snaps like he has any right to be mad at me. "Don't you dare hide behind your insecurities. That's not what this is. You have to think—"

"*I'm* hiding behind my insecurities? What about you?"

"What about me?"

I gape at him. He's the most infuriatingly self-aware person I've ever met, and he's truly asking me that?

"Who is putting this pressure on you to choose your duties over yourself? Who put the pressure on you to bow to my dad's threats? It's *you*. You're the one choosing not to try to fight for us. You can stand here and tell me this was always going to end helplessly but I know this meant something to you, and I know you don't think for one second that I'd have let you leave here on Christmas Eve or any time and be *done* with you. Could you leave here and be done with me?"

"I need you to have something that you can be proud of." He bypasses all my questions, ignores them with a rising snarl. "I cannot leave knowing that you are stifled here when I have seen how capable you are of such resonant greatness. I need you to be *happy*."

He says it like he's accusing me of something.

My eyes shift through his. "Okay," I say slowly. "I need you to be happy too. That's what I'm—"

He rips his hand up, makes a fist, grimacing, breathless in a surge of such anger that I go silent again.

"The only thing that has mattered in my life for the past two and a half years has been Halloween. I have devoted myself to making it the best it can be for the people who need the joy we offer, because I've been consumed by how frantically needed our type of joy is. To find joy in fear and darkness, to scratch out some semblance of happiness in grief and absence. To look at something that is only terror and danger and find it *beautiful,* not in spite of the things that make it horrifying, but because of it. Since Raven's death, I have understood my Holiday on a primal level I never could before, so I committed to it. It is *everything.*

"But since coming here, all I can think about, my every waking thought consumed and clouded by, is *you*. You being happy. You having what you so deserve. *I need you to be happy,* Coal. I need to know that you're taken care of, or at least on the path to being taken care of, so I can be *whole* again. I need you to be happy so I can stop being plagued by you. I will handle whatever fallout comes from your father. It's long past time that I did—please, *please* don't give up on the winter Holidays collective."

The pieces of his logic puzzle together in my head and it's the most toxic tapestry of hope and agony.

"You don't think you could do both—be with me, and do what Halloween needs you to do?" I am being depleted of emotion. "Look into my eyes and tell me that you'd never think of me again if you knew Christmas was secure and made me happy."

He's fuming. At himself. At me, for forcing him to this, and his eyes snap to the side. "It's not that simple—"

"You love me," I tell him. "You love me and you're kidding yourself if you think everything we have would go away with you being content in my happiness over my *duties.* Because you know what, Hex? *I won't be happy without you.* Christmas could be idyllic and I'd be miserable without you."

"That." He points at me. "That is where you're wrong. We have responsibilities. Love doesn't change who we are."

"It changed who I am."

He digs his fist into his stomach, I can see the effects of this in the set of his shoulders and the clench of his lips and I know I should feel pain too, but my body has gone numb.

I step closer to him. Just enough that he has to look up.

"Say you love me," I beg him. Order him. He could change everything with those three words.

"Say you will continue with the winter Holidays," he returns.

It would destroy him. His Holiday. It would only end in disaster because that's what *happens* with me, disaster, and he thinks he can endure it now, but—but *I* can't.

We hold. Waiting for the other to break. Giving it another moment longer, one more second, please, *please—*

"You said we have responsibilities to help bring the world joy." I finally crack the tension, and Hex's eyelids pulse, a wince. "But I've never had responsibilities beyond my *own* joy, and that's why I didn't think of Christmas's future when my father was threatening everything I care about. I only thought of *my* future. I only thought of *you.* I was selfish and stupid, like I always am, like nothing's changed, because apparently nothing *has* changed."

Hex yanks in a breath that pinches into a moan, and this anger he's showing me is his façade. He's hurting behind it, keeping up this shield, and I realize that, but it does nothing to stop the hole of blackness sucking up everything in my chest.

"Coal," he tries, "this isn't how I wanted this to—this isn't—"

I pin my eyes to the wall behind him. One last shred of stoicism centers me, a lifeline thrown down into my abyss and I cling to it with all my strength. "My father is sending you home. You can leave now."

"Not like this. Coal. *Look at me*—"

He reaches for me but I put my back to him and get the *hell out of there,* slamming the door behind me.

Wren is in the hall.

I blow past her. "He's packing."

She says something. My name, maybe.

I run, shoulder crashing into walls as I take turns too quickly, staff flying out of my way with startled cries. I get back to my suite and throw myself inside and lean against the closed door, forehead to the wood.

"Coal?"

Shit, they're still here. Iris and Kris. Shit, shit—

A hand on my shoulder. My brother. He grips tight, and it's all I can take.

I slide to the ground, on my knees, and finally fall apart.

Chapter Nineteen

There's a weight on my thumb.

I grope at it, feeling the bedding shift beneath me, and my half-asleep mind thinks for a second, *I only have two days until Hex leaves* and I start to reach for him—

The weight is his ring. Still on my thumb. The pillow is fragrant with blood orange and cinnamon but it'll fade now.

Because we don't have two more days.

I grip my hand into a fist.

"You're awake," a voice says above me.

My room comes into shape around my widening awareness. White morning light. I'm in yesterday's clothes. The comforter is thrown over me and I'm knotted in it from thrashing in what restless sleep I managed, and I groggily look up at Kris, propped in bed next to me. He's in pajamas, typing away on his phone.

"What time is it?"

"Almost seven. You slept?"

I sit up, body bruised like I got pummeled last night, and I did, in a way that makes me rock forward, face in my hands. My eyes are knots of sandpaper.

"Go back to sleep," Kris says. "It's early."

"I'm fine. I need to—"

"You *need* to sleep. You didn't crash until nearly four."

"I'm *fine.*"

"You're a fucking *liar.*"

"The sooner I rescind those invitations—"

"That can wait a few more hours. Lie back down."

"Why are you here?" It comes out as a snap of anger. I immediately regret it.

"Because you don't get to be alone right now," Kris says. He doesn't react to my anger. Just patience and calm.

I stiffen and glance back at him.

His brows are up in gentle appraisal.

Guilt overtakes me. "Shit." I rock forward again, hating myself so potently that I have to sit still until my eyes stop burning.

"You shouldn't have to do this," I tell him. "I didn't want you to have to do this anymore."

"Do what?"

"Take care of me."

Kris leans off the headboard. He's silent until that silence drags me to look at him, and he holds my gaze for another quiet second with a force of presence, of heartbreak, of certainty.

"You are not a burden, Coal," he tells me.

It's like he reached down into my soul, to the foundation of my self-flagellation and anger, and grabbed onto the singular moment that started all this.

I'm not sure he realizes how enormously I needed to hear him say that. I'm not sure I did, but his words are a soft hand cupping my cheek and telling eight-year-old me that it's not my fault, it wasn't something I did.

She left.

Hex left.

Kris hasn't.

You are not a burden.

A few tears break free. "Stop it."

"Here." He hands me a glass of water that I don't take. "Iris is bringing breakfast."

"I'm not thirsty."

"Drink."

"Kris—"

He pushes the glass into my hands and he looks furious. "It's not like you went on a bender and I'm nursing you out of a hangover, dumbass. What happened yesterday flattened me too, so let me take care of you before I pin you down and waterboard you in an attempt to get you to hydrate. Now, if you're not going to sleep, *drink the fucking water.*"

I accept the glass. Take a sip. My lips crack and taste like salt.

"I love you too," I tell him. Because I don't say it enough.

He drops back against the headboard and tosses his phone onto my bedside table. I see mine there, face down, but I don't ask for it.

Kris works his tongue against his teeth, and I hold the glass to my mouth, exhaling into it, fogging it.

"You would've taken it for me," he says.

I lower the glass. Set it on the table next to my side of the bed. "Of course."

His eyes snap shut. A breath, and he looks at me, all bloodshot and angry.

"Never again," he tells me. "Never again, okay? Don't you do that again."

"Like hell. You want to take care of me? That's how I take care of you. That's how I'll *always* take care of you." My chest squeezes, a sharp stab of pain. "It's the one thing I know I can be good at. I'm on the front line, all right? You have to accept that."

Kris bites his lips together.

"Agree or I'm never drinking water from you again," I add, voice so raw but it milks a smile at the edges of his lips.

"You must not be fully decimated," he whispers, "if you're back on your bullshit."

I wilt.

There's a soft knock on the door, then it opens to Iris, a tray propped in one hand. Smells gush in immediately, bacon and savory pastries and syrup, and I should be hungry.

But I watch her come in and set the tray at the foot of the bed.

My eyes go around the suite again. Seeing it for the first time. It's all back in order. Clothes put away, desk straightened.

"Did you guys clean my suite?"

"Of course," Iris says like it's no big deal, but it *is* a big deal, every single thing they do is a big deal. "Now, what sounds good? Renee put extra cinnamon syrup in the pancakes for you."

"She . . . knows?"

Iris's face says the whole damn palace knows. But knows what? That Hex left me—no, *left*, not *me*, not just me—or that Dad threatened us or that I failed spectacularly? What story did Dad let out?

"It was announced this morning that I didn't choose Halloween," Iris says tentatively, testing each word before she adds the next to gauge my reaction. "And that's why Hex left. But . . . the staff knows you're upset. Or that it would be upsetting to you. They care about you, Coal."

At one point, I would've been appalled that the whole palace was saturated in sympathy and pity over private matters in my life. I'd have been pissed off that Dad used this intensely personal heartbreak to validate his other lies. But I honestly don't care.

Iris squishes in next to me on the bed, warm wool dress and boots and all, and arranges the comforter over us. I lean back against the pillows and she drops her head to my shoulder and throws her arm across my stomach.

"Did he sleep?" she asks Kris on my other side.

"Not enough."

"I'm right here," I say pathetically.

She hugs me. "Yes. And we are too."

I sniff. Scrub a hand over my mouth and close my eyes. "So he's really—"

"Gone." I feel her looking at me, but I can't open my eyes. "Last night."

"And I guess you and I are—"

Iris plucks at a string on my shirt. "Yeah. That was announced too," she says in a low, overcome voice.

I'd given her hope that there was a way out. That she could get something more for her life beyond duty.

I let her down too.

My arm comes up around her shoulders and I rest my chin on the top of her head.

"My, um. My phone."

"He hasn't texted you," Kris says.

I tense. Because this was supposed to happen, right? There was never any reality where he would've stayed and rushed to my room and said he loves me, because it was never going to work. He knew from the start.

The back of my throat itches and I peel away from Iris to cup my hands over my face. She locks her fingers around my forearm but I hold in my darkness for a second, just a second, using every remaining ounce of my abilities to *breathe.*

"What do I do now?" I don't mean to speak, least of all something so goddamn self-centered. Haven't I at least gotten better at that? But the question pushes up, the sole thing capable of growing in this wreckage, because it'd only been a few short weeks but he changed everything about me in a way that feels like destroying now.

I can't, *I can't,* go back to who I was before him. Aimless and useless and directionless and just, just, *less.* But the better version of me, the one I'd started to grow into, doesn't exist without him.

I don't want to exist without him.

"You eat," Iris whispers. "You sleep some more. Eventually, you get out of bed."

"I don't mean *now*—"

"I know you don't. But you can't think beyond *now.* Not yet." She sits up and nudges my hands until I let them fall.

She hands me half a croissant. "Eat."

I obey. Chew absently. Stare up at the ceiling and *my bed still smells like him.*

Now. Just think about now.

Now.

"I need to write letters rescinding the invitations," I say.

Kris settles deeper next to me, his phone back out. I see him pull up a notes app. "I'll handle it."

"Kris."

"You can't write for shit."

"I'll do it. This is my mess. I need to do it. Dad will—"

But all my thoughts trip over themselves.

I'm staring up at the ceiling, sandwiched between Iris and Kris, fighting to swallow a croissant that turns to grit in my dry mouth, and a piece connects in my brain that lets a real, deep gasp of air find its way into my starved lungs.

Dad will . . . what?

He'll blame Hex if I don't rescind my invitations to the winter Holidays. If I don't stop trying to get them to rally against him. Because together, they provide more than half of Christmas's joy—so together, they'd be enough to restructure our Holiday.

And Dad has only had to threaten them to get their compliance. He's only ever had to *threaten* anyone. All this blackmail bullshit, and there's never been any sort of scandal that came out about these Holidays. Just *threats*.

Dad *didn't* hit Kris. He didn't even try. The threat of his anger was enough.

Just the threat.

I sit up, brow furrowing, as my mind pulses and I feel half mad. Maybe I'm sleep-deprived. Grief-stricken. I am, that and more, but my heart starts racing and I think I was an idiot.

I know I was an idiot.

Because I remember the way Wren talked to me in the hall. *"You and your brother are not as alone as you might think."* And Renee and her kitchen staff, and Lucas and the Route Planners—all the pervasive, unadulterated *joy* they create.

I remember the way our people cheered for Dad because of the merriness he perpetuates, and how disgusted they'd seemed that I'd mentioned the idea of blackmail.

Dad has kept all knowledge of coercing anyone a closely guarded secret, manipulating every single story that gets out about our family—because he knows our people would be *furious* if they found out that all our joy isn't ours.

He had to create a cover for Hex being here so our people would be okay with it. He couldn't outright tell them, *We're holding someone hostage*—he had to play up that whole fake-suitor arrangement. He even silenced the Halloween envoys when they were here before they could say much more than objections to the Easter-Christmas union; he feared them spilling any details, turning his own black-mail back on him.

So does Dad think he could make good on any of his threats?

Because if he did, if he started dropping these truth bombs to the Holiday press, and it got out that all this information was coming from Christmas, then that carefully constructed façade of whole-someness he's built around our family would be eviscerated.

He can't reveal any of the shit he has.

Not without destroying the very thing he says he's fighting for.

"Oh my god." I shove off the comforter. The tray rocks; Iris makes a startled chirp; but I dive over her, I need to pace, I need to *move*.

I start walking the length of my room. Hit my desk, turn back.

"Coal?" Kris is on his feet, watching me like he thinks I'll leap out the window or start screaming or maybe both.

"He's bluffing." I whirl on Kris, relief and desperation and *stupidity*, how could I have been so *stupid*, again.

But it wasn't stupid to fear my father.

It wasn't stupid to protect my brother, to protect Hex.

I wasn't stupid.

Kris frowns. "Who?"

"Dad. He's bluffing. He won't let anything out against Hallow-een. He won't say anything against anyone. All these threats—it's a *bluff*. He's manipulating us because he knows we all fear the reper-cussions enough that the mere mention of it keeps everyone in line. But you know what? I think *he* fears the repercussions too."

I tear my hands through my hair. And I *smile*. It's deranged and pushes Iris out of the bed, fingers splayed; both she and Kris ema-nate concern.

"What are you saying?" Kris asks.

"I'm saying"—I can't breathe—"I'm saying that I'm not going to write those damn letters."

Kris's brows shoot up.

"The winter Holidays will come here. And we'll stand up to Dad.

And we'll *change things*. Because he won't release any of the blackmail he has on people. I'm calling his bluff."

"It's a big risk," Kris says. Not like he's scared. Like he's worried I'm not thinking straight.

"It is."

"It was yesterday too." He takes a small step forward.

"Yesterday, I *knew* Dad was going to hit you." My breath comes out stunted. "I *knew* he'd hurt Hex. I hadn't considered that he wouldn't follow through."

"And now?" Kris's mouth starts to lift. A smile? Encouraging, maybe, and it lets me breathe easier.

"And now, I'll dare him to. I'll be there to protect you, I'd take the hit—but I know he won't do it. I *know* he won't do it."

Kris closes the space and throws his arm around my neck. "Good," he says into my shoulder. "Good."

"Are you—" Iris's voice catches. "Are you sure, Coal?"

That reorients me in a jolting swivel, a satellite coming back on-line. Kris steps aside, and my manic fluttering grinds to a halt and I look into Iris's eyes.

"I know Dad's already made the announcement that you didn't choose Halloween," I tell her. "And everyone knows our wedding is happening now. But, fuck, Iris—I can't. We never could. Our original plan doesn't have to change: we could still try to bring Easter into the collective if we can convince your dad of it, we could still make it so you don't look at fault for anything—"

She holds up her hand. "I can honestly say," she starts, takes a quaking breath, and her eyes tear, "that for the first time in a very long time, I don't give a *shit* what my court does. I asked if you were sure, Coal, because if you are, then I am too. I'm still with you."

My face explodes in a grin but I cup one hand over my ear. "I'm sorry, I didn't quite catch that middle bit."

She flattens her gaze at me. "I said if you're sure, then—"

"Not that. One back."

Her eyes go to the ceiling. "I don't give a shit what my court does."

I glance at Kris, lips screwed up. "Did you hear that?"

He shakes his head, all feigned confusion, a stifled smile. "Hear what? Was Iris talking?"

"*I do not give a shit what my court does,*" Iris snaps, practically shouts, and she may have started to say it in exasperation, but by the time she's done, she's gasping. She scrubs quickly at her eyes and rights herself, but it's too late to cover her look of abrupt relief, a weight tipping sideways to allow her a full breath.

I sweep her into a bear hug. "Look at you, rebel princess. How'd that feel?"

"Blasphemous." She squeezes me. "But . . . freeing."

I pull away to meet her eyes again and let some of my humor slip. "What finally spurred this miraculous change?"

She hesitates. Chews the inside of her cheek.

Then answers with, "Do you want to tell Hex?"

I solidify in place.

"No." It shocks even me, but it hangs in the air, and Iris frowns.

"No? Why? This is what he wanted you to do."

I back up, turn away, trying to hold on to this agitated hope. "No, Iris. Just drop it."

"This is what he wanted you to do," she tries again.

"Iris—"

"You can't give up on your happy ending, Coal."

I don't turn. My shoulders go rigid.

"You can't give up." Her voice is small and careful. "You started to make me believe that we could change things. That the dreams I had might be alive. And now you have a way to fix what happened with him, and you're not taking it? *Why*—"

I spin on her. "Because he *broke my heart,* Iris!"

She flinches, lips snapping shut, eyes wide and inert.

The weight's still on my thumb. Hex's ring. I feel the band with my finger, and I do not think about what it means to touch it, how I kept something of his but he has something of me too, and I'm not sure he believes he has it.

"He broke my heart," I say again, feeling the words, their burden in my chest. "He didn't choose me. *I* know we're more than our roles and I don't regret choosing him, but *he didn't choose me.* Even if I told him I'm going through with the collective, that wouldn't change the fact that he was always going to break things off with me."

Iris huffs a breath. "Coal—"

"But he was right." It reopens the wounds from last night so they bleed internally all over again. "The first sign of a threat to him, and I caved to my dad without hesitating, no conviction in my position. Maybe if I'd paused for like a *second* last night, I would have realized Dad's bluff in that moment and prevented this. But I didn't, because Hex was right about me. I not only put him first, but Christmas wasn't anywhere near the top of my list. It was him and Kris and you and everyone I care about, and I lost sight of what was at stake. I haven't taken my role seriously. I've toyed with it this month, but I haven't *committed*."

Kris punches me in the arm. "You *have* committed. You've done amazing things and if he made you feel like you haven't, then fuck him."

My jaw clamps.

Kris sighs. "I'm not going to apologize for saying that. He hurt my brother."

"I hurt him too."

"Good."

"Kris!" Iris smacks his shoulder. "God, none of this is good."

He crosses his arms and mumbles, "A *little* pain for him is good."

Iris's expression is all sorrow and heartache and I want to promise her that we will get our happy endings, that there is hope for us.

But honestly?

I don't know how it'll end. I'd been so certain when I sent those gifts to New Koah that I was doing the right thing; and I'd been so certain days ago that I was doing the right thing here too. My chest twinges, dread wanting me to recoil, to take back all this and crawl into bed in defeat.

But I don't want this ending. I don't want it so much that I feel like that wanting is trying to push itself out of my skin. I don't want a reason to have been right about knowing I'd fuck it all up; I want the ending where I fixed things and it worked out exactly as I planned.

But who decides where the end is?

So I'll keep going. And going. And I'll learn and do better and sometimes I'll hate myself for not giving up and I'll rage at the shit around me but I remember what it's like to look at the world with uncomplicated hope and I can't stop until I get that back. What's the alternative?

It just takes one joyful moment. One by one by one.

I'm relying on that. I'm counting on joy to be stronger than whatever's waiting for me.

It's what a Christmas Prince would do. At least, it's what *this* Christmas Prince will do.

HEX

please don't respond to this. i
shouldn't even be texting you.
kris will kill me. i just wanted you
to know that you were right. and
i'm sorry. but i was right too. and
through whatever's going to happen
with my holiday and my dad, one
of my goals now is to fully become
who you helped me see i can be.
because i have to believe there is a
future where the heir of halloween
and the heir of christmas can be
together and you deserve the best
version of me. we made too much
joy for this to not last. and i know
you didn't say it back, but i love
you, i love you, i love—

[DELETE WITHOUT SENDING?]

[YES]

Chapter Twenty

Dad summons me the night before Christmas Eve.

It'd been too much to hope that he'd take my word for it, that I wrote the letters and was going to send them and that Iris and I are happily going along with the scramble of wedding plans. But no, of course he'd want to at least read the letters first, and while I'd hoped to milk as much time out of this as possible, stall and stall and scrape us closer to the winter Holidays coming on Christmas Eve, I finally trudge to his office before ten.

"Hey." Kris prods me. "It's going to be fine."

"It's going be a repeat of what happened in my room."

"No. It won't." Kris loops his arm around my shoulders. "You decided it won't be. Remember? *You* decided. So it'll be better."

I don't know how I'd get through this without him. This certainty that Dad's bluffing is so newly formed, and I'm clinging to it with everything I have, but so many factors are out of my control. And not just out of *my* control, but fully in my *dad's* control, and it's the most harrowing terror I've ever felt, to know that something as simple as whether the next few days will be hopeful or disastrous is based on the whims of someone else.

My lungs are permanently filled with ash at this point. Each breath is a strain.

I miss Hex.

That's the root of why this is all so deep: love. Love is the most petrifying collision I've ever experienced. Loving Hex, loving Christmas, it's destroying me and I think this is why I resisted my role in Christmas for so long, because I always knew that when I fell, I'd fall with my whole being. Not a gentle slip like falling asleep, but a hurtling, momentum-gaining plummet like a bomb whistling down out of a plane.

The palace is in absolute chaos. Decorations *everywhere*—fresh holly and ivy; garlands on every door; twinkling lights; Christmas trees all over; ornaments and bows and ribbons. There are things here from all our Houses now, Luminaria, Jacobs, Frost, Caroler and all the little bits that have come together to create them over the years, touches that weave together a subtle yet impactful display of who we are. Staff flurry around in wedding prep and I haven't seen Iris with how swarmed she is. Under other circumstances I'd be pissed, it's my wedding too, isn't it? I have no say? Antiquated bullshit.

But Kris and I get to Dad's office. The door is open.

I push in first. He's at his desk, looking through something on a tablet.

He taps an empty space in front of him without looking up. "Letters."

"I—" My throat is scabbed over. I clear it, wince. "I don't have them."

Dad slowly raises his head to look at me. "You don't have them." He leans back in his chair, arms folding over his chest. His voice is neutral the way a gray sky is neutral. "Why, exactly?"

Kris steps up beside me. "I was helping him write them."

"And—" I eye him, pleading. He can come here, support me, but *do not draw attention to yourself.* "And I've been finishing up a few last—"

Wren comes stampeding into the office behind us. "Sir! My apologies."

I'm used to her being a swirl of energy on tasks for Dad, but she seems extra out of breath now, like she'd sprinted across the palace.

She puts a stack of paper on Dad's desk. "Invoices to sign. What's this meeting about?"

My lips part. "I—"

"A matter between my son and me," Dad says. "Not your concern."

Wren touches something on her screen. "The letters to a few of the other Holidays, yes?"

Dad flips a look up at her. "Excuse me?"

Her demeanor is cool and calm, nothing changes, but my whole body has gone stiff.

What? How did she know?

Wren sees Dad's confusion and frowns. "You told me, sir. You asked me to review and send the letters Nicholas was due to write. See?" She shows him something on her tablet. "Invitations rescinded, correct? Everything was in order. They went out yesterday."

Again, *WHAT?*

Dad's eyes swing to mine in question.

And Wren gives me the briefest, fastest look of *play along.*

What the hell.

"Yeah." I shrug "Wren read them over. Sent them. Said they were fine. It's done."

Dad's suspicion sharpens, but Wren is already typing away on her tablet again.

"Wedding preparations have thrown everything into tumult. I am happy to remove any other items from your to-do list if needed?"

Dad shakes his head, and I blow out a breath at the look on his face. A look of *maybe I did ask her to read those letters.* Because if it was a simple cover of rescinding invitations, it would have been something he could have asked her to do. And, more, he trusts Wren.

"Thank you," he says, still a bit uncertain, but he clears his throat and focuses on the invoices she gave him. "Boys. You may go."

Kris grabs my wrist and has to haul me out of the office. We get maybe two yards away, enough that Dad can't see us from his desk, and we swing on each other and simultaneously mouth *WHAT THE FUCK.*

Kris points back at the open office door. *Did you talk to Wren?*

No! I mouth back. *Did you?*

Why would I have?

What the HELL was THAT then?

I DON'T KNOW.

I punch his shoulder. *DON'T YELL AT ME.*

He hits me back. *YOU YELLED FIRST.*

All of this is entirely silent until Wren slips out of Dad's office and we both shut up.

She closes the door and walks towards us, focused on her tablet. "I told you," she says to the screen. "You are not as alone as you might think."

And she flashes me a smile.

"Wha—*why?*" is all I can get out.

Wren pulls the tablet to her chest, arms folded. She seems to be contemplating something, her eyes scrunching in thought, before she drops her gaze to the side.

"Were you aware that your father arranged for a wedding invitation to be sent to your mother?" she asks.

The mention of her is a sucking absence of oxygen, a sharp, jarring yank in my soul.

With everything else going on, I hadn't thought of her being invited. This whole wedding was such a farcical thing to begin with. I didn't stop to think about *anyone* I'd actually want at my wedding because it's never *been* my wedding, it's a *lie.*

But she wouldn't come anyway. She'd rather *not* come and use it as an excuse to complain about how no one wants her to come to things, but—

It really wouldn't have occurred to me that she'd be involved in any of this.

Next to me, Kris is motionless. Barely even breathing. I glance at him, blink, and that sharp, jarring soul-yank sends a new crack up my heart.

"Kris. God, tell me you didn't know she was invited."

He whirls on me. "I haven't talked to her since that Merry Christmas text, I swear to god, Coal." There's a rawness in his tone that isn't there when he's lying, and he exhales a hurt whimper as something dawns on him. "She texted me yesterday, though."

My widening eyes are all the shocked horror I get out before he shakes his head.

"I haven't opened it. Fuck, this is what it was about though, wasn't it?" He looks at Wren, unease mangling with hope. "Is she coming?"

Wren waves her hand. "No, I'm sorry—the emphasis should have been that your father *arranged* for an invitation to be sent to her. Given the intensity of this wedding being planned covertly alongside the Christmas season, many things have slipped through the cracks and, sadly, her invitation was lost in transit."

Yeah, Wren doesn't let things *slip through the cracks,* so the saccharine apology in her voice makes *her invitation was lost in transit* sound more like *I personally shoved it into one of Renee's food processors.*

A winded laugh huffs out of me. "You're a bit maniacal, Wren."

I . . . don't know how I should feel about all this.

I should have foreseen that Mom would hear about this wedding and harass Kris over it, but he didn't mention anything, and he *did* ignore her himself. Has she texted me? I have all her messages muted and only think to check every few weeks.

I reach out and squeeze Kris's arm. His lips flicker in a forced smile but he doesn't look at me, doesn't look at Wren, just stares at the carpet in sullen thought.

"If she did text you about the wedding," Wren says, "it was only because she saw news of its announcement in the past few days. But no, she is not coming. Again, I am sorry to not have led with that. My point is that it is incredibly difficult, in a job that requires intense focus on joy, to make room for grief. But grief demands to be felt even when it is buried, and I have watched"—her eyes go to his closed office door—"your father become less and less of the leader we knew him to be as grief manifested into his need for control. I believe, on some level, he is under the impression that if he makes this Holiday fit a certain ideal, he can get her to come back."

I frown at Wren, something tight and unnamable in my stomach. "He . . . he's doing all this because of her?"

I knew he'd changed in reaction to her leaving—but I thought he just got bitter and angry, not that he's intentionally doing these things in the hope that his actions will make her come *back.*

My skin goes cold. It's such an impossibility. If she hasn't come back already, she won't.

Dad doesn't believe that?

Wren shrugs, letting that be confirmation.

"And you know *what* he's been doing?" I ask. I have to clear my throat. "To the other winter Holidays?"

"Of course. It's my job to know."

I blanch. "You never tried to talk him out of it?"

"It is *not* my job to have much influence over the reigning Santa beyond frequent insistencies that he redirect his efforts. Which, always, went unheeded. But," she straightens, "hypothetically, if someone in my position did have an opinion, it would be that this Holiday, any Holiday, has no business inflicting harm, and that what the reigning Santa might hope for has never been a vision shared by the people." She gives us a kind smile. "Now get some rest. Tomorrow will be a rather large day, for all of us."

She leaves, her finger pattering on her tablet.

Kris's chest caves so he hunches over and watches until she rounds a corner. "Should we be mad that Wren excluded Mom without asking us?"

"No. *Fuck* no," I say. "I'd be more pissed if Wren had listened to Dad and gotten her here." A pause. My stomach cramps. "I can't believe he wants her back."

Kris makes a noncommittal grunt.

That stomach cramp intensifies.

Kris can believe that Dad wants her back. Because some part of *him* wants her to come back too.

But Kris's eyes go glassy when he looks up at me, and he doesn't respond to that, not really. "Why didn't I make that connection?" he asks. "You; wedding. She'd be invited. I thought she was texting me about other bullshit, so it was easy to ignore, but it was about *this*. I didn't think for one second she'd be here."

I smile. I smile so big it can only break into a laugh, exhausted and shocked.

Neither of us thought about her being here. Neither of us worried over her or stressed about it. It didn't take up any space in our heads or our hearts.

It's a mark of healing, a goalpost of growth we've reached.

Which makes it all the more obvious now how all Dad's bullshit about solidifying Christmas, making it the best, making it *last,* stemmed from not only her leaving, but from him trying to make this Holiday fit an unreachable vision of perfection.

Love destroyed him too.

Does he know that that's what happened to him? Does he know she's part of why he's doing all this? It doesn't make anything he's done okay, not in the vaguest sense. But it explains it.

And it sets a resolve in my heart to not let my own grief swallow me up. I'd promised Kris and myself, weeks ago, that I wouldn't let the pain our mother caused continue to infect our lives. No matter what happens, I will keep that promise, and I'll add on to it that *no* grief, no matter the source, gets to make decisions for us anymore.

But I'll start by dismantling the product of my father's grief.

Kris still looks heartbroken, and I hook his neck with my arm.

"You wanna talk about it or be distracted from it?" I ask. "Wallowing in it isn't an option."

He grunts. "Jackass."

"Distracted from it, then." I haul him off, angling us back for our suites. "I will make you talk about it soon, though."

He grunts again. After a pause, he goes, "I do know one thing that'd make me feel better."

"Name it."

His face is still so pensive and emotional that when he looks up at the ceiling and whispers, "Ball tag," my brain doesn't process what he said.

Until he pops his fist down and punches me in the groin.

I plummet to my knees and Kris takes off cackling up the hall.

* * *

I have no plans to marry Iris today. But I get dressed when the stylists come calling in the early afternoon—the whole marriage sham is supposed to start before dinner so Dad can be there then slip away to oversee his Christmas Eve Santa duties. Which means he won't be present for the ball afterwards. Any fallout from the winter Holidays will only stretch until like seven, latest.

So I need to make it to seven without losing my nerve.

I can do that.

And honestly, it isn't as hard as I thought it would be to find that nerve. I'm oddly calm as the stylists help me into my, ahem, wedding outfit, and by the time they're putting the final touches on me, the fluttering panic in my gut hasn't overtaken me.

A navy blue suitcoat is trimmed in gold, with full epaulets on each shoulder, tassels too, and red pants feed into brown leather boots. The stylists slick my curls down—we'll see how long that lasts—and brush body glitter across my face and neck. And even though I look like a wind-up toy soldier come to life, it's polished and poised and I don't hate it.

It isn't until I see Kris in the hall, dressed similarly but in full navy blue head to toe, that I realize—

"Are we supposed to be nutcrackers?" I tug on the hem of my jacket.

Kris falls in step alongside me, a cavalcade of stylists and staff ushering us to the ballroom. It feels almost . . . normal. Like we could be where we were a few weeks back, ambivalently heading to the Merry Measure tree decorating.

Except I have Hex's ring on my thumb.

Kris gives a sad shrug. "That's the theme."

"*The Nutcracker?*"

"Yeah."

"The theme of my wedding to Iris is *The Nutcracker.* That's shockingly not too awful."

Kris gives me a look. "Having second thoughts?"

"Yep. The epaulets cinched it for me. I'm gonna be a married man tonight."

He rolls his eyes but smiles in mixed pity-relief that I'm back to joking again.

We reach the ballroom. It's where the guests are mingling before the ceremony, which will be held on a snow-covered lawn beyond the orchestra stage and ceiling-high windows—out there, an aisle waits, surrounded by fancy red-and-blue striped chairs and space heaters disguised in garlands. In the ballroom, the *Nutcracker* theme runs rampant, red and blue chasing each other around the décor, woven into symmetry by gold and green. The orchestra plays something soothing and light; most of the members of our Houses are talking and milling about the space. Members of the Easter aristocracy are here too, not many; but it isn't really about Easter, anyway, is it?

I spot a handful of people from a few other Holidays—Valentine's Day, sans Lily, due to Dad's insistence that she would remind people of our previous relationship. And . . . that's it. It's a testament to Christmas's place in the Holiday hierarchy: even with a wedding this monumental, yeah it came together fast, we have no allies in attendance, no actual *friends* to invite.

Reporters as always line the room. Their presence doesn't feel as oppressive and invasive as it usually does—I see them, and look away, barely registering their impact anymore.

There's a cluster of guests off to the left.

A few different groups, all together, all people I don't recognize. Members of our noble houses are talking to them, not necessarily *avoiding* them, and why would they? They don't know that Dad wanted me to uninvite these people.

When Kris and I step through the doors, I press my shoulder to his.

"Once more," he whispers.

I lean on that. On him. "Unto the breach."

We don't get two feet into that ballroom. I'm honestly shocked he let us get this far.

Dad rushes up on us in another wildly expensive red suit, but he's full-on *raging,* and he doesn't for one second try to cover it for the cameras.

"You told me you undid this," he hisses at me.

The full building swell of everything I've wanted to do crashes up on this moment, a wave slamming into a rock, and I let it wash over me, seafoam and salt and refreshing chill.

"I won't undo Christmas's future," I tell him, and it's my turn to talk while my smile is sickly sweet and performative. "If you'll excuse me, I should greet my guests."

I start to push around him.

He grabs my arm.

A few people have noticed us by now. Some in that group of winter Holiday representatives. Photographers.

"We need to speak," Dad tells me. "In private. Now."

He spins me around and hauls me out of the ballroom and I'd have to physically tear myself out of his grip to get away.

Kris is booking it to the winter reps.

Dad drags me up the hall and into a sitting room, the same one I pulled Iris into after Dad first announced our potential marriage, another fire lit, burning low, orange and heat.

I rip away from him as soon as I can. "I'm not backing down on this. We are capable of exactly what you want, ensuring Christmas lasts, but *together,* with other Holidays too. We can grow by sharing success and being a *part* of something, not the *only* thing."

He slams the door shut and starts pacing between the low stuffed chairs.

I've never seen him this furious with me.

"You're going back to Yale," he says mid-pacing. "Tomorrow. First thing."

"On Christmas Day?"

"You are stripped of all subsequent duties and appearances. You get out there, *marry that Easter Princess,* and then you are *done,* do you hear me? There is nothing left for you—"

"I'm not marrying Iris. I'm not playing this game. And, while we're at it, I'm not going to grad school. It doesn't have to be like this! Lying and fighting and manipulation. We don't have to live this way. It isn't a mark of failure to support other people, and it isn't a mark of success to stand alone."

He's pacing, pacing.

And then he stops.

Hands behind his back, facing the fire, where a steady flame crackles on sweet-smelling logs.

"You forced me to this, Nicholas," he says. "You truly are willing to risk the fallout that this would bring? I thought you cared for that Halloween Prince."

"I do care. Go ahead."

He whips a look at me. "What?"

"Go ahead. Pin all this on Halloween." My voice is level and I've never felt this swell of certainty before, no tremors, no *fear*. "See how you keep the love of your people when you start letting it slip that you've been holding all sorts of shady-ass mistakes over other Holidays. How long will you be able to keep it under wraps that you're the source of whatever information you dole out?"

His mouth drops open.

I lurch forward a step, surety soft and calm. "I am done letting you corrupt Christmas the way you have been. I am done standing idly by and letting you control every element of our lives like any amount of perfection will bring Mom back."

He full-on flinches at that. A slate-wiping shake.

"I am your son," I take another step, "and I am the heir of Christmas, and I will stand here, between you and Christmas, between you and whoever else you set yourself up against. So go ahead," I dare him. "How badly do you want this? Because I know how badly I want this. I know how far I'll go now."

Dad is half-cocked back from me, brows furrowed, face an unreadable mask of disorienting shock—he didn't expect me to stand up to him. He doesn't know what to do now.

The door opens. Kris doesn't give Dad a chance to say anything—he holds it wide.

And in come all the winter Holiday representatives.

I turn to them and spread my arms. They can likely see how my hands are shaking in the excess of emotion, and I fight to level my breathing, but it's all welling up on me.

"Welcome to Christmas," I start. "I—"

Shit, Kris had written something for me to say, and my adrenaline-soaked mind scrambles back for what I remember of it—all those pieces I'd told him about, the truths and carved bits of my soul.

A deep breath in, and I talk.

"Together, your Holidays provide Christmas with more than half of our claimed joy through the tithes my father has demanded from you. That ends now, and nothing will come from whatever threats have been made on Christmas's behalf in the past."

The group of about a dozen people gape at me for maybe half a second.

Then one man steps forward, smoothing the edges of his sharp black suit. "What has spurred this change?"

I glance at Dad. Just once.

He's staring at the fire, jaw slack.

"What's changed," I say, "is that there is a path forward for *all* of us where we instead pool resources so we can use the individual reaches of our Holidays to help each other grow. It is but one small way in which Christmas can begin making up to you for what we have done. If you will remain here for a few days, we will discuss preparations for a collective."

Hopeful, if not confused, smiles grow when my father stays silent. When he stands there, not interjecting, not countering anything I've said.

I twist so I can speak to him and the representatives, but mostly to him. To me too.

"Christmas's true origins have always been about light during winter; joy during hardship. And now, we will compensate for what has become all too lacking because of our own actions: equality. We are not a Holiday of material goods and staged charity and forced cheer. We are Christmas, and we are joy in the darkness, and we will remember that from this day forward." I keep my eyes on my dad's profile. "I swear it."

Kris, at the back of the room, cups his hands over his mouth and whoops. Someone else does too—Iris. And behind her, the door is open, the hall, what little of it I can see, packed with reporters. Wren, softly smiling. And members of our court.

A clap starts. It grows, rises to applause of agreement.

Dad, though, is oblivious to them, to the chaos of reporters pushing into the room and throwing themselves at the winter Holiday representatives. He hasn't moved at all.

Even with the winter reps waiting, with the noble House members pushing forward, set on me, I take a step closer to my father.

The part of me that used to be afraid of him just misses him now, I think. Misses what he used to be. Misses what he could have become.

Kris swims through the chaos and pulls up alongside me, Iris in tow, her pink tulle ballgown dragging the floor.

Dad finally looks at me. He's pale.

Of all the things I expect him to say, I'm not at all prepared for, "I would not have hit you or your brother."

I exhale in a rush, but he shakes his head.

"You believed I would, though," he continues. "You believed I had become someone who would do that."

"I believed—" I stop. Lungs aching. "I believed grief had changed you. And I didn't know the extent of those changes. But I also know that it doesn't have to be only negative changes. We can make something good out of this too."

Joy can come from grief. From pain. From fear.

That's what I'm choosing.

"Your original idea wasn't all bad," I say. "Every corner of the world deserves joy. Christmas can be a part of that. Just not the *only* part of that. And this way, it allows us to focus on aspects that will resonate in the people who celebrate Christmas. You said you're doing this for us, for me and Kris. This is what we want. This is our future."

Dad's eyelids flutter, attention dipping between Kris and me. He scratches at his beard, and I see a myriad of thoughts rolling through his mind, but I can't guess at any of them.

Then he walks around us and leaves the room.

Which is okay, honestly. I don't want his immediate responses. This amount of change doesn't come easily.

But we're bringing it. Even if it hurts.

Chapter Twenty-One

This sitting room is stuffed with people and conversation and no one else notices Dad's departure.

In his wake, I turn to Iris and take her hand. Mine is trembling, the aftereffects making it so my lips shake a little too when I smile.

"Iris, I love you. Will you do me the honor of not marrying me, today, or ever?"

She grins. "Coal. I love you too. And from this day forth, I promise to never marry you."

I grab her up in a hug.

Over her shoulder, I see her father at the edge of the room, looking stricken and confused.

"I'll talk to your dad with you," I say. "We'll make this work for Easter too."

She squeezes me, hard. "Later, Coal." Another hug, softer, her head resting against my temple. "But thank you."

I set her down. "How do you want to announce that the wedding is off? I'll take credit. Or blame. Whatever you think will best appease any rumors of—"

She smiles. It should be happier than it is, should be relieved; but beneath it, there's apprehension still, exhaustion that never seems to really let her go.

Iris turns to a nearby staff member and whispers quickly to them. They go momentarily stunned, then announce to the room, "The wedding is . . . off. But you are invited to partake in the Christmas Eve Ball."

Shock only seems to hit a few pockets within the room, mostly reporters who whip towards Iris and me, and I brace, angling in front of her on instinct.

My brows skyrocket at her. "Just that easy, huh?"

She shrugs. "Maybe it always was." Her voice is soft and reaching, like she's trying to convince herself that it's that easy, that nothing bad will come from making a choice for ourselves like this.

"If anyone in Easter uses this to start shit," I tell her, "they'll have Kris and me to contend with—"

But Iris cups my face in her hands and the look in her eyes shuts me up.

"Coal. I'd rather talk about those dreams we're allowed to have now."

I go rigid. Suddenly aware of Hex's ring on my thumb where I'm holding Iris's hip and I can't see her through the way my head is a struck gong of imagining what his reaction to this would have been. Would he have been proud of me? God, I hope he'd be proud of me.

Thinking about him is a tap on my emotions and I realize how taxing it is to run on pure adrenaline. I need to sleep for maybe the rest of the year.

Iris pinches my cheeks in her hands. "Coal. Did you hear me?"

She'd been talking. Shit. "Yes. Yeah. Fine."

Her eyes roll. "I *said* my only dream tonight is to dance with my best friend."

I smile. "I'm pretty exhausted. I think I'm going to crash. Dance with Kris?"

"No. You do not get out of celebrating this."

She has my cheeks fully squished between her hands now and I break away with an exasperated head shake. "You're impossible."

"We're a matched pair."

I loop my arm through hers and turn to wave over Kris—

He's gone.

"Where did—"

"Come on!" Iris tows me into the crowd. People shout for me as I pass, introductions and pleas to talk in the next few days and oh, fuck, I'm going to be in wall-to-wall meetings, aren't I? But I catch Wren's gaze in the chaos and she nods, tablet already out, and mouths, *I'll handle it.*

Again, she needs a raise. Multiple raises.

Iris drags me back into the ballroom. The orchestra has switched to faster songs and the floor is packed with people—not everyone funneled out to watch me restructure our Holiday in ten minutes while dressed as a Christmas toy.

I should want nothing more than to fling myself into dancing with Iris and Kris and shake off this stress and emotion, but the sight of the crowded ballroom only adds to my exhaustion.

I don't want to be here.

I want to be in my room, ripping off this choking suit, and lying flat out on my bed until my chest stops aching.

Today was a victory but it doesn't *feel* like a victory, and the thing that's missing is taking up so much space that I tug on Iris's hand once we're a step inside the ballroom.

"I'm going to bed," I tell her, voice raising as the music gets louder.

"Like hell you are!" She grips my hand in both of hers. "You need to dance."

"I don't. What happened to Kris? Did he get swallowed in small talk? I should go find—"

"He's over there." Iris points into the ballroom. "And you *need to dance,* Coal."

She says each word with an odd weight. A sparkle in her eyes.

I frown at her and follow her pointing to where my brother is working his way across the middle of the floor, surrounded by people who are spinning in the palpitating swell of the song, red and blue ballgowns flying and jewel-toned suitcoats lustrous—

The drain of emotion, the crash after the adrenaline, the burn of grief—my body forgets how to feel any of it. There is a sudden, splendid absence like city lights going dark to show the full vastness of a diamond-studded night sky and I am not tired, I am not lost, I am not broken, because the sight on that dance floor demands everything in my body reknit itself.

Iris presses into me. "I was going to go see him. I had a whole speech prepared and Kris wanted to come so he could tell Hex how pissed he was, but before I could leave, he was here. He showed up in my suite this morning—"

I whip my eyes to her. "He's been here *since this morning?*"

"—and asked us how he could make things right. He didn't want to get in the way once we told him what was happening, but the point is, Coal, he came back for you. He chose you."

"Iris," I gasp her name. I think I do. My voice sounds garbled.

I catch sight of Hex and lose him again as the dancers spin. He and Kris are trying to get to us, but Hex's gaze meets mine and he stops.

His black-lined eyes shift over me, even with the distance. He doesn't smile. I can see him holding his reaction for mine, that infuriating control he has over his responses, and a strand of black hair hangs out of his knot, brushing across his cheek. It flutters in an exhale.

"Go," Iris tells me, but I'm already walking, the dancers passing around me like vapor.

In and out, bodies pirouette between us, and each time I think they'll move on and he'll be gone. I'll blink, and he'll vanish, but then I reach him, and he's here, his chest rising in a sharp, shaking intake of breath.

Kris ducks away with a smile.

He's in a bright cherry-red suit, a riot of color, with a black shirt under it, the balance of Halloween and Christmas, and he has those rings on his fingers and the glint of silver piercings on his ear. He's here and we're standing in the middle of the dance floor and the orchestra drags violins in a crooning wail.

His lips part, but he says nothing, and I want to fill the silence but I know silence is an offering for him. So I just watch his eyes dip down my body again, and I feel the trip when his focus catches on my hand—on his ring still on my thumb.

A tremble shakes his parted lips.

Finally, he says over the music, "I was at that bar to see you."

I frown, head cocking.

"The bar. Where we met. I went there—" He huffs a breath, one that's fighting against a tremor. "It was the first anniversary of Raven's death. I couldn't sit at home."

My eyes widen, but before I can say anything, he looks up at me and pushes on, talking faster.

"I went because I knew you would be there, from the tabloids, and I wanted to see what kind of person you really were. I wanted you to be as bad as your father so I could point at you and say, *Look, Raven wouldn't have gotten what she wanted no matter who was in charge of Christmas.* I was so angry, and it was senseless, and I needed *someone* to be mad at. But you were—" He gasps, throat bobbing. "You were nothing like I wanted you to be. You haven't been, this whole time. You've been like *her,* and I think I—no. I know I started to fall in love with you in that alley."

"Hex," I whisper. He doesn't hear me.

"And you were right. I put those restrictions on myself, on *us,* because I could not fathom that falling for you had happened so fast. But *you,* Coal. You, with your light and laughter and joy. You, with your honor, that infecting honor, and your devotion. Somehow, I got to be the object of that honor and devotion, and it stunned me, still stuns me, that you look at me the way you do. I'm so sorry that I didn't trust myself to choose you—"

"Hex," I say, louder, and his lips snap shut, those wide eyes holding on mine. "I would never keep you from doing what you feel you need to do for Halloween. I would never ask you to choose between us and your role. I know how much it means to you, and it's one of the things I love most about you, your big heart and your bigger sense of purpose. My god, Hex, I'd sooner expect you to stop breathing than to make any concession that would jeopardize the joy Halloween brings. It's *you,* and I wouldn't change a thing about you."

He shakes his head. "That's just it. It's fine, I think, to make some concessions for myself. I am still getting my bearings with letting myself have more than Halloween, but I promise, I will learn how to fight for"—his voice catches—"for the man I love too."

My reaction surges through me and I only barely stop myself, a near painful lurch of remembering we're in a crowded ballroom and there are reporters watching.

But Hex steps closer and angles up and asks, mouthing the words, *Kiss me.*

My lungs are too thick and my heart is beating too fast. "It'll be out. You and me. What will the autumn collective think of you with the Christmas Prince?"

His eyes shift through mine. "They might hate it. Or they might see what you've done in starting your own form of equality here, and be all right with it. Either way, this isn't about them, or Halloween, or Christmas. It's about you and me, and we'll deal with whatever happens together. So now," he steps closer, imploring, "I want you to kiss me."

But he hesitates. Just a fraction, and something like uncertainty darts across his face.

"I understand, though, if you haven't forgiven me for leaving," he says, voice resolved. "I shouldn't have pushed, and if I—"

I groan, and laugh, and it all gets tangled up in *need.* "I swear to god, Hex, the two of us have officially discovered that there is such a thing as being *too* respectful of each other, and it *will* kill me."

I dive into him, like moving through a heavy liquid, melted gold, until my lips crash to his. He trills in surprise and I know nothing until his arms are thrown around my neck and I bind my hands against the curves of his hips, coming to as his lips move under mine. I brace on him in the ruckus and mayhem of his mouth back beneath me, that mouth, his beautiful goddamn mouth and this beautiful goddamn storm that has me tearing my hand into his hair and rocking back so he's lifted, so every bit of him is held up by me. He kisses me in a way that will bring me to my knees later, and I think that word like a prayer, *later.*

Cameras flash, lights out of the corner of my eyes, but they don't matter. There are no more secrets now. This is our new future, this man in my arms, the way I rock my forehead to his and breathe in his exhale and tug lightly on his hair because I need to remind my-self not to float out into incandescent space.

A new song begins. Dancers twirl around us. There are far, far too many people here, and we are far, far too exposed for all the thoughts plowing through my head.

But I rest my mouth over his. "Dance with me?"

I taste his grin. "You're going to have to set me down for that, I think."

"Under duress, let it be noted."

"Noted."

I rest his feet on the floor. I know this song, and imagine sweeping him away into the twirl of couples and the brush of motion, but I hesitate long enough to look down at him.

"I love you," I tell him. Because last time I said it, it was more sob than truth, and when I say it now, I memorize the way his pupils dilate, the ardent spark of connection as my words hit home and nestle in and he *accepts* them.

His fingers twine in the hair at the base of my neck. He's silent for one of those intensifying, emotion-brimming moments of him finding himself through his mesmerizing internal noise and I will never in my life be given a greater honor than the way he painstakingly chooses his response for me.

"I love you too," he says.

I kiss him again, a clumsy layering over of our smiles, and we're laughing and this, here, is my victory. He is my spoil of war, the most vital piece in my new-forming foundation.

Joy creates magic.

I have never believed that more than with him.

Chapter Twenty-Two

I'm really proud of the fact that I make it through two songs.

But by the end of the second one, we've given up trying to emulate a waltz—and it is *we,* not just me pushing my body closer to his. He's hanging onto me, breathing harder with every peal of music, formal dance moves deteriorating into his hips grinding against me and one of us groans, and that's it.

I grab the back of his head as a new song starts up. "Hex—"

"Yes," he answers, no, *demands.*

My breathy laugh billows his hair. "I didn't even—"

He seizes my wrist, and the next thing I know is a coil of shadow, a brush of chill—

Then we're in my suite.

I stand stricken for a moment, but Hex is in action. His teeth sink into my neck and his arms tether around my body with none of the propriety of being in public holding him back.

The sensation of having him against me, clawing at me, fogs my brain until I suck in a sharp breath and grab him by the shoulders.

"Hex." I push him back enough to look at him. "Did you portal us to my suite?"

He fumbles at the buttons on my nutcracker suit. "Mm."

"From the middle of a crowded ballroom?"

He's halfway down my chest when his eyes lift to mine. His lips are parted, fingers twisted in the open edges of my jacket, and his brows form a triangle over his pause.

He cringes. "That was probably bad form, wasn't it?"

I laugh. It turns pitchy and squeaks because this is categorically *hysterical,* but also the proof that he wants me this badly is rationality napalm. Like I honest to god should be concerned by how pliant I am for him at this moment. What does he want, anything, everything, it's his, it always was.

Need ribbons through me, chasing away any humor, anything but his lips and his body and my attention on those two things. I cup his face in my hands and kiss him, a moan rippling up from my core as I rememorize his taste, his smell, a sensory siren song of that cinnamon bourbon old-fashioned but a thousand times warmer and more intoxicating.

He moves against me, his hands still gripping my suit jacket, and he breaks the kiss when he lowers down from where he'd risen up on his toes. His eyes are shut, his breathing still hard and fast.

"Coal," he says, coarse, and it tugs at the base of my stomach. "You're very good at that."

I smile and lean in to kiss one of his shut eyelids, the skin paper-thin and so delicate. "Good at what?"

"Going—ah, going slow," he stutters. I kiss his other eyelid. "Making me feel—"

He jolts and his eyes fly open, realization shining as he looks up at me.

The realization deepens to intention. "Loved," he whispers.

My smile will never go away. I'm going to be an absolutely insufferable asshole for the foreseeable future.

Hex shakes himself and tightens his grip on my suit jacket. "But I—" He leans in and rests his forehead against my chin. "Can we go slow later?"

It takes me a beat to realize what he's telling me. *That* he's telling me something, asking me for it, and a new kind of heat sets every muscle on fire until I wonder if I'm glowing.

"What do you want?" I whisper, moving to press tiny kisses down his cheekbone.

Resolution descends over him in the way he squares his shoulders, still holding on to my coat, and he looks up at me with a level stare.

"Do not let what happens next undercut the meaning of my words," he tells me.

I frown. "Okay?"

"We can go slow later," he repeats. He licks his lips, rolls one in between his teeth. "But I believe the correct way to say this is, *Right now, I need you to fuck me.*"

Magic sizzles around him and what looks like a wad of white fabric materializes over our heads.

Without missing a beat, Hex bats it aside, and it bounces across the floor before coming to a rest by the wall.

It's some kind of ghost decoration.

A laugh gathers in my throat and is one millisecond from exploding out of me. All my thoughts go from him using his portal in the middle of the Christmas Eve Ball to now *this* when—

Holy shit.

Did he say—

I whip my gaze to him, wide-eyed.

He stares up at me like he asked me to place a food order and he's just hanging out until I fork over my credit card.

"Are you all right up there?" he asks. "Need me to say it again?"

"No. Yes, but no. Oh my god."

"Coal—"

"There's a gauze ghost on my bedroom floor because you told me to fuck you."

Hex looks caught between laughing and wincing and finally just drags his hands over his head with a self-deprecating moan. "I'm a bit off tonight. This is rather dangerous. I—"

He stops with a weighted exhale, one that trembles enough to make me step forward and touch his jaw. He looks up at me and shakes his head but there are tears at the edges of his eyes, I think I've experienced the full width of human emotion in the last forty minutes alone.

"Shit, sweetheart," I say, then he's in my arms and I couldn't be holding him closer if he was actually a part of me. He shudders and I push my face into his neck, inhaling him, and I might be shaking too.

I think about lifting him and walking us to my bed and letting us both lie together; I think about making jokes over the ghost that I am definitely going to keep.

But an energy emanates from him, an unspoken request that I consent to immediately. So I just stand there, holding him, and I think we need this simple act as much as fulfilling the desire that's sparking at the back of my mind.

He stirs, putting his face to the side of mine. "I didn't know if I'd see you again. It was only a few days, but I missed you so much, and I—*Coal*," he whines, and it ignites that desire down my spine, "what have you done to me?"

"Nothing yet," I say. It's a question. An offer. Everything all in one.

But when I go to kiss him again, he pushes me back against the closed door of my suite, his hand flat on the bare part of my chest that he uncovered.

"Let me," he whispers. His eyes flick up to mine, the lashes wet, his pupils gleaming.

I go slack against the door, compelled by his gaze on me, by his presence. It isn't until he drops to his knees that I choke out a startled noise and lean forward like I'm going to stop him.

"Hex." It rushes out, panicked, pleading.

He looks up at me, and holy fuck, the sight alone. Him reddened and disheveled from our frantic making out and all the emotion, lips puffy and eyes glistening. He reaches up and hooks his fingers in my belt. I rock back against the door and throw my eyes to the ceiling and breathe, slowly, in through my nose, out.

"Hex," I say again to the white panels above us. "I—uh, believe you told me to do something. This is not that. This is—"

"This is me realizing that, in all our time together"—he undoes my belt; it tugs my attention down and his eyes lock mine in place—"I haven't gotten to taste you." The button slides out of my pants, the zipper rattles with metallic clicks as it lowers. "This is me getting us back to a place where you can do what I told you to do." He curls his fingers in the edge of my pants and boxers and lowers both, eyes still on mine, wrenching my heart. "Because if I let you take me to bed right now, I know you would worship me, and I don't want that. Yet. I want you to ravage me first."

Holy fuck—

Then that mouth, that intentional, careful, quiet, exasperating, magical, sexy fucking *mouth* is on me, and I slam back with a heavy thud, one hand scrabbling at the door above my head as if there's something to hold on to that's capable of keeping me from going buoyant and floating away. My other hand gropes blindly, briefly grabbing his head before retreating, and he does this thing with his tongue and *hums* and I—

Hex pulls back, looks up at me, and says only, simply, "Grab my hair, please," then he's on me again.

Please. Fucking *please.*

I comply, fingers knotting in the strands until the whole tangle of it comes loose from its tie. He hums again, a needy little moan, and the laugh that ripples out of me is dark and heady.

Oh, he's good. He's very, very good. Perhaps too good because my god, if we're just getting started and he's already able to play me this succinctly?

Though, who are we kidding. He can play me with a single look. I think he just *knows* he can now, and this really is the end of me.

I tighten my grip in his hair and his moan sharpens into something desperate, enhanced by the way he sucks harder and my vision goes to starry space. I think I see a meteor, cuts of orange and glowing scarlet.

I pull again, harder, and he repeats his own form of torture until a champagne-like tingle starts in the base of my spine.

Before it rises too high, I shove him away with a gasp, a growl, and yank him to his feet. His face flashes with a smug grin that I smother in my mouth, eating at his lips and tasting myself on him as I kick off my shoes and pants then chase him backwards until we topple in a heap on my bed.

My clothes are already mostly off and the rest fall away easily; his come apart in starts and stops until I hear a jagged rip and realize I've torn his shirt off him. It thrusts me into a transitory moment where I can't remember ever *ripping someone's clothes off* before, not even at my neediest, not with anyone. But I also remember what he said once, how he was surprised when I didn't kick things off between us by having us do just this.

The memory hazes my desire, lets me pause for a breath so I see him beneath me, half naked, looking all kinds of crushingly decadent with his hair in shadowy tendrils across my pillow and his eyelashes fanned against his pale cheekbones, arms out by his sides, chest heaving and sweat-sheened already. There is an almost jarring difference between the Hex who'd told me he was surprised I took things slow, who seemed to expect me to use him and shove him out the door, and this one, who senses my pause and looks up at me with a predatory grin.

He asked me what I've done to him.

But he was always this. I just get to see it now, and he's letting me have him here, in my bed.

Fuck. He's in my bed again.

This is what he's done to me too, because he's right, I absolutely would be going slow and savoring him and edging him to the limits of both our sanities—and I will. Later. But he's the first and only person I've ever wanted this badly, this all-consumingly, and the reciprocal want I see in the goose bumps that walk up his long torso, the shiver that quakes the skin across his collarbone, gives me permission to meet him there.

His grin softens when I stay arched over him. "Coal?"

"I missed you too," I say in a rush. All that sentimental poetry he inspires in me starts to bubble up, and I think I let some of it slip out as I devour him again, kisses becoming catechisms of promises and plans and apologies. But now, now, he rises up to meet me at each one, and says some of his own to me, and it's a trade, an exchange, no secrets or worries or hesitation.

Just us.

Light turns my eyelids golden and I rise up out of sleep slowly at first, then in a jarring torrent of memory.

Hex.

Coming back to my suite last night.

God, my room is trashed again, but for a different and way superior reason. Among the discarded clothing, there are, if I remember correctly, at least two more magically generated ghosts and three rather creepy fake spiders, all courtesy of the delirious, blissed-out curse words I got out of him last night. In Spanish *and* English, because I'm an overachiever in this area.

I grin wickedly and roll over—

The bed is empty.

I flare up, feeling the sheets, eyes snapping around the room. "Hex?"

No response.

He didn't—no, not again. Just, flat-out *no,* he's here, somewhere, he has to be—

I scramble to grab my phone, drop it, pick it back up, and swipe it open to a missed text from him.

HEX

Don't worry—I did not leave. I'm in
Iris's room for breakfast. Join us
when you're awake.

The absolute *tidal wave* that is relief surging through my chest cavity flattens me back on the bed. My body actually vibrates a little.

I laugh pitifully to the empty room.

Okay. So I might have some attachment issues.

I'll work on that.

I tug on pajama pants, pocket my phone, and try not to race out of my room too desperately.

Thankfully, there are no staff in the hall just yet as I hurry, shirtless and hair gone wild, to Iris's room.

Her door is cracked open. "Iris—Iris, do you know where—"

Hex is sitting on the couch in her suite, legs folded, a cup of tea in his hands. He's wearing one of my Yale hoodies, my boxers. His eyeliner is smeared and his hair is swept over one shoulder and he looks up at me, all gleaming joy.

He lowers the cup from his lips. "You're up," he says brightly.

I cross the room, vault the back of the couch, drop to my knees on the cushions, and kiss him quite senseless.

"Coal!" Iris chirps. "You made him spill tea all over my—"

"You were gone," I say into Hex's mouth.

He pushes back, startled. "You didn't see my text? You were sleeping so deeply. I didn't—"

I drag him back and capture his mouth again. "I saw it. But you were still *gone*."

"You needed sleep."

"I need *you*."

"You have me."

"Not enough, not—"

Iris clears her throat.

Oh. Yeah. This is her suite.

I drop onto the couch next to Hex and gather him into my arms. My chest unwinds, the feel of his weight pushing down on my anxiety.

"You stole him," I accuse her.

She grabs a napkin from the tray of breakfast food and dabs at the tea spot on the carpet. "Yes. That has been my master plan all along."

Hex sets his now empty cup of tea onto the coffee table and settles back against me, head twisted so he can look at me.

A smile glides across him. The same one echoes on me, and I bump my forehead to him, burying my hand under the edge of the hoodie, palm flush against his warm stomach.

But I do, this time, remember Iris, and I pull back. "Sorry. I'll try to be less obnoxious. Maybe in a few days. Eh, months. Need to get it out of my system."

Iris tosses the napkin onto the tray and grabs her coffee cup. She's in her pajamas, purple, of course, flannel and cozy, which is *massive* for her. The only time I've ever seen her this improper is on Christmas morning.

"You guys are cute," she says. "Don't hold back because of me. I'll get my shit figured out."

I frown. "It's shit now?"

Iris's jaw works.

Her eyes go to her suite's door as Kris enters.

He looks . . . a mess, honestly. His hair is clearly unbrushed and in a frizzy bun, pajama pants and T-shirt wrinkled, deep sleepless bruises under his eyes.

I lurch forward instantly. "Are you—"

The smile he gives is forced, exhausted, but he drops onto the couch next to me and slams a gift-wrapped box into my stomach.

I cough, and he goes, "For you to give to Hex."

I hold his gaze. "Kris."

He shakes his head, and a hundred things are in that shake. *Drop it. For the love of god don't ask me now.*

Something happened. Something—

Iris won't look at me, and is *pointedly* not looking at Kris.

Oh, shit.

"Um." I fiddle with the gift box.

Kris gives me a pleading stare, a *talk about literally anything else* stare.

Weakly, I spin on Hex. "I . . . did not get you a Christmas gift."

His eyebrows go up. "I did not get you one either."

"No, you did. You came back. Slap a bow on your forehead, that's all I need."

He smiles. "Well, likewise."

"We don't get anyone gifts," Kris adds. He rests his chin in his hand, eyes drifting out.

"Well . . . yeah. But that should change too, right?" I fiddle with the edge of the wrapping paper and say to Hex, "The whole thing became as poisoned and performative as every other aspect of Christmas. Like later today, we'll open prearranged gifts the staff got for us to give to Dad and vice versa, and it'll be fake, weird stuff that'll look good for the cameras. But I should've thought ahead and planned to change that and . . . shit."

"There's always next year," Hex tries. His eyes flash between Kris and Iris too, picking up on that weird energy. But he doesn't seem surprised by it.

He knows. Whatever happened. She must have told him.

Kris elbows me. Hard. Enough that I grunt.

"Give him the gift," he says, and I relent.

"Fine, fine, upstaging me." I hand the box to Hex. "Here. Merry Christmas. Unless it's terrible, then this is all Kris's fault."

Hex takes it and begins to peel at the tape on the paper.

Both Kris and I moan in harmony. We bust up laughing, and it momentarily dispels the weirdness.

"What?" Hex holds, fingers splayed over the box.

"Rip the paper," I say.

"You don't save it?"

"It's recyclable. *Rip the paper.* It's part of the fun."

"Christmas barbarism." Hex shakes his head, but complies, working his fingers under the edge and ripping a long strip off the box. He flips open the lid, and I can't see whatever's in it, but his face breaks out in a big, cheesy grin.

He throws that grin at Kris. "Where did you get this?"

Kris is beaming. "I have connections."

"Ah, yes, the infamous Christmas black markets." Hex pulls it out of the box and twists it around for Iris and me to see.

I crack a laugh. Even Iris finally smiles up from the floor.

It's a black, long-sleeve shirt that has a stocking on it under the words *I Deserve Coal in My Stocking.*

"I am marked by Christmas yet again." Hex drapes the shirt against his chest. "Should I wear this today, or is it perhaps too tongue-in-cheek?"

I have so many comebacks to that, starting with some quip about *my* tongue being in *his* cheek and ending with *wear nothing so I really can put Coal in Your Stocking,* but I settle for rocking into him and grazing my teeth on his neck.

Kris bumps his knee against mine. "Wren set up meetings with the winter Holidays, the heads of our noble Houses, and—" He falters, gaze flicking in the general direction of Iris before refixing on me. "And King Neo. First one's with the winter Holidays in an hour, before all our Christmas Day duties." He pauses. "Dad said he'll be there."

I watch Iris. "How involved in these meetings do you want to be?"

Her eyes pop up to mine. "I haven't talked to my father yet. But I'd like to listen to what you have to say. As your friend, and as—" Her breath is level and resolved. "And as an Easter representative."

She misses my proud grin when her gaze drops to stare fixatedly into her coffee.

"Well. Good," I say slowly, eyes darting between Kris and Iris one more time.

Neither of them look at me now.

Huh.

"Good," I say again with even more hesitation. "I guess I should go get ready and let you—"

Kris leaps to his feet. Absolutely *rockets* off the couch. "Me too. I'll see you there. Merry Christmas and shit."

He rushes from the room before I can so much as get the first letter of his name out of my mouth.

I drop another look at Iris. Who is still staring down into her coffee like it'll tell her the secrets of the universe.

Oh no.

"Do you want to talk about it?" I ask.

"We can talk after all these meetings," she says. Then cuts a pointed look at my bare chest. "Preferably then you'll have clothes on."

I follow her gaze.

To see a bruise-like spot on my right pec and another almost directly above my belly button.

Heat pools low in my stomach and I fight a self-satisfied smirk.

My eyes slide to Hex, who looks up at the ceiling in unrepentant faux-innocence.

"Later," I growl at him and the corners of his lips pulse upwards.

Turning back, I shift to the edge of the couch. "Love-bites or not—"

"Ew." Iris's nose curls.

"—you can talk to me." I sober. "I know he's my brother, but you're—"

"Coal, I will egg you if you don't leave." She spreads her fingers and a decorated egg appears in her palm. Daisies on a pink shell.

I narrow my eyes at her. She has the same look on her face that Kris had, that silent, pleading *do not make me talk about it.*

I hold up my hands, surrender. "Fine. But this isn't over."

The egg vanishes.

"I swear, I'm okay." She takes a sip of her coffee and gives a forced smile. "Go. You have a lot of shit to do. You're a very important person now, Prince Nicholas."

I hold her gaze. "Not that important."

She softens. Then glares at Hex. "You've made him sappy. Gross."

"I'll do my best to turn him cynical again, but no promises." Hex winks at her and pulls me to my feet. We leave, but the moment we're in the hall and Iris's door is shut, I spin on him.

"You know what happened? Did she tell you? What did—"

He pushes up onto his toes and kisses me. "Go talk to your brother."

"What?" I grip my fingers in the neck of his hoodie. "Wait."

Back to my room to make out with Hex.

Or to my brother's room to talk about his heartache.

I grab for my phone.

KRIS

what the fuck happened

KRIS
Nothing

The kitchen's out of Nutella

That's it

I'm all torn up about it

kris

don't try to be funny, that's not
your thing

KRIS
Really, Coal. It isn't important right
now. We can talk later.

Getting tired of that deflection from people.

I grimace. "He confessed his feelings for her, didn't he?"

Hex sighs. "Possibly."

"Possibly?"

"It is not my secret to tell, as you once said."

"Ugh, my honor is infecting you."

"I like to think I possessed my own deeply set honor system before your involvement. Now," he hooks the shirt over his shoulder
and glances in the direction Kris would have gone, "go. And I don't
want you back in your room until you need to get dressed."

I sigh. "Dressed. Boo."

"I am morally opposed to the idea as well." He puts the barest tip
of one finger just next to the hickey on my pec, and as he looks at it,
the heat and hunger that intensify his expression fucking *do things to
me.*

I back up from him, shaking my head, fervidly ignoring the fact
that I'm wearing loose pajama pants and nothing else, but the hall's
still empty except for us. "You're trouble, Prince Hex. I think I've
created some kind of sex monster."

He laughs, and I can't imagine that ever not being one of my favorite sounds. "Are you complaining?"

"Fuck no. I'm ruthlessly taking credit."

"Well, then this monster is now entirely your responsibility."

Entirely mine.

The teasing dips to a steady simmer as I stare at him for a second,
watching those big eyes. "Yeah, you are," I say with a cockeyed grin.

He flushes.

I get one more step away but swing back as he's turning to my suite, and I catch his waist and spin him into me and kiss him in the hall, because I can now, because I will never, ever get tired of it.

"After Christmas wraps"—I pull up the hood of his sweatshirt—my sweatshirt—so it boxes us in—"I believe a diplomatic mission to Halloween is in order."

His nose scrunches in the most innocent, delighted smile. "I think I can arrange that."

"Good. I have a list of requirements. I'll have my people send them to your people."

"I expect nothing less. Christmas is rather demanding."

"One, I won't have—wait, we're *demanding*, huh?" I lurch in and bite his ear and he yelps.

"Go talk to your brother!" Hex shoves me away, and I let him, stumbling back with my dumb grin and my chest is flushed and god, I'm so in love I might faint.

"And then?" I ask, walking backwards up the hall.

"And then," he says. He leaves it at that, heavy with insinuation, and I spin away with an exaggerated moan of defeat.

"My boyfriend is insanely sexy!" I shout over my shoulder as I jog up the hall.

Hex's gasping laugh follows. "And my boyfriend has no sense of decency!"

I whirl to him again, and all I can manage is to let him see how deliriously happy he's made me. But he's gonna have to get used to me embarrassing the hell out of him.

We don't have to hide anymore. We don't have to lie. I can shout all kinds of romantic nonsense from the rooftops, and I will, I'll scream it to anyone within earshot, creating all the tabloid headlines myself.

Former human disaster has been thoroughly whipped by a walking contradiction of darkness and sunlight and morbidity and joy.

Eh, too wordy, but he makes me want to be poetic. Maybe:

Christmas Prince admits to having risked war crimes all because of corset vests, black eyeliner, and the things that the Halloween Prince can do with his tongue.

No, it'll have to be simple. Sometimes simplicity is all we need. Something like:

Prince Coal of Christmas is inexhaustibly in love with Prince Hex of Halloween.

Yeah. I think that fits best of all.

Turn the page
for a sneak peek at the
second **Royals and Romance** novel

———————————————

Available Winter 2025

A shamrock is found in the North Pole just as it's discovered that someone has been stealing Christmas's joy. With Coal busy restructuring Christmas, Kris volunteers to investigate St. Patrick's Day—even when their lead suspect turns out to be the nameless, infuriating student that Kris has been in a small war with at school. Prince Lochlann Patrick is loud, obstinate, and, okay, hot, and the tension Kris had with him over dumb school drama translates into every interaction; they can't get through one conversation without Kris wanting to smash Loch's face into something. But the mystery behind Christmas's stolen magic isn't as simple as an outright theft—and there's more at work behind the mystery of Prince Lochlann too. Can a spare prince even hope to unravel all this, or will Kris lose something way more valuable than his Holiday's resources—like his heart?

Lochlann throws his arm around my shoulders and spins us to face the journalists. My muscles arrest at the feel of his body pressed to mine, but I hardly get a beat to react.

"Let's buck off this formality a bit," he says to the paparazzi. He smells like that cologne again, spicy and expensive, and I keep my smile plastered to my face. "A few weeks ago, Prince Kristopher and I had a wee bit of a misunderstanding at our school. Wouldn't you say so, boyo?"

Oh, stop it with the fucking boyo. "A gross misunderstanding. Yes."

"Aye, gross indeed. Now, what's the real reason you've come to my Holiday?"

His gaze burns the side of my head.

I'm hit with a wave of panic. Did he guess that I'm here to investigate him and his family?

But when I look up at him, he's beaming down at me.

"To apologize," he says into my face.

I go even more rigid. "Well. Yes. That is the purpose of this whole—"

"Oh, no. No, hardly. The events of the next few days will be to enjoy some time together, St. Patrick's Day and Christmas. But today, this right here? Ach, the people want your apology!"

He throws a smile at the journalists, and one of them melts, blushes at his princely charade, fucking traitors. They have their cameras ready, recorders out.

My mouth goes dry and it's my turn to burn the side of Lochlann's face with my gaze. "You mean—"

"Apologize," he says. "To me. Now."

I knew it was coming. But he's *demanding* it. I haven't *offered* it. And there's a spark in his eyes that says he knows exactly what he's doing.

Apologizing is why I'm here. This is what Coal needs me to do. Eat fucking crow.

That reasoning is suddenly hard to see clearly.

Because right now, being in Lochlann's presence again, that heavy, choking wave of pretentiousness quaking off him, I'm livid.

He still has his arm around me, a pinning vise, so I throw my arm around him too, playing up this buddy-buddy bullshit.

Then, to the journalists, "What happened in the library study room involving Prince Lochlann was nothing more than a harmless prank between friends. But I am sorry, Prince Lochlann, for the negative spin it put on you."

That's the apology I wrote that Wren approved. Simple. Effective. Done—

"And?" Lochlann presses, talking out of the side of his mouth.

I fix him with my sweetest smile. "And what?" I say through my teeth.

"And that's not good enough."

All smiles. Happy, grinning, friendly smiles for the cameras. "You can't be serious."

Lochlann laughs like I said something funny. He tips his head closer to me, eyes on the journalists, and growls for only me to hear,

"You're lucky I don't make you get down on your knees and beg for my forgiveness."

My whole body goes molten so aggressively I get dizzy.

It fades, tapped by a slow drain of fury, head to toe, and with that drain goes my thinning resolve.

What am I here for?

To apologize? No.

To piss this guy off? Hell yes.

"And," I say to the journalists, "our misunderstanding in the library was entirely my fault. Prince Lochlann was merely a harmless, ignorant—"

His grip pinches on my shoulder. "All right, now."

"—witless, I mean, unwitting, victim. I am honored to spend these next few days with him to draw light to what the press should be focused on: St. Patrick's Day's magnificent grandness. Their outstanding generosity. Their kind, welcoming, marvelous spirit that I have seen reflected so beatifically in Prince Lochlann himself."

I hear a rumble in the deep of Lochlann's chest. Annoyance.

A pause for pictures. Smiling still.

"Was that the apology you had in mind?" I whisper up at him. "Or should I go on about how all the rainbows in Ireland point to the pot of gold in your asshole?"

His fingers on my shoulder are going to leave bruises.

From the corner of my eye, I watch his lips purse, smooth out, resume that forced smile, and it's only because I'm standing so close that I see the muscle tic in his jaw.

"You have na yet begun to repent," he hisses, accent thick, teeth clamped together.

"I agreed to *apologize,* not repent."

"You're in Ireland. That's what we got here, repentance and Guinness."

I angle for the cameras off to the side, smiling, and saccharinely mutter, "I will make your life a living hell these next five days."

Lochlann rocks my shoulder, stage-laughs again, then whispers,

"Now, boyo, how would that look for these nice reporters when you came here to be my wee bitch?"

My nostrils flare as journalists start asking questions about what events we'll be doing, filler crap.

I really did try to play nice.

But I'm going to get proof that he's the one stealing from my Holiday.

Then I'm gonna go Christmas nuclear all over this St. Patrick's Day fucker.

Acknowledgments

I don't know if you've noticed, but the past few years have sucked.

Somewhere between *once in a lifetime* events number seventeen and eighteen, I decided I just couldn't hack it at writing serious, heavy fantasy books anymore. Not that there's anything wrong with serious, heavy fantasy—it just didn't jive with my mental state. The world was serious and heavy and *goddamn it,* my escape couldn't be too.

I'd always wanted to write a Christmas book, and for years I'd tried to frame it as a serious, heavy fantasy (no, really; kingdoms were based on holidays and there were small anthropomorphized peppermint candies as pet-companions, but I swear, it was a Very Serious Fantasy Book, albeit an idea that just never got its sea legs). But in the midst of the aforementioned *once in a lifetime* world events, I thought: what if this Christmas book was silly instead? And not just silly, but a full-blown rom-com where I could let myself max out on puns and jokes and absurdity, and run *wild* with every little thing that makes me happy?

So, I tried it. What the hell, right; I was already writing about people with living pieces of candy as pets. It wasn't a far jump to cracking jokes about Elf on the Shelf.

And it worked.

It worked so well I fell madly, stupidly in love with a book in a way I hadn't since my debut. *The Nightmare Before Kissmas* became everything I didn't know I'd been missing in not just my career, but my escape. It let me recapture joy in a way that still feels precious, something so delightfully irreverent that I can't help but grin like a fool every time I talk about it. I poured everything I have into this book, from my sense of humor (Coal is what the inside of my head is like all. the. time.); to aspects of myself I hadn't yet shared with anyone, and had only just begun to address; to my skills as a writer. Through Coal, Kris, Iris, and Hex, I found a rare, stubborn flame of joy, and I've been sappily kindling that flame ever since, hoping like hell I get to share it with others.

I'm starting these acknowledgments on a hard mushy note to establish just how much this book and its production mean to me. So it is with utmost sincerity that I thank my agent, Amy Stapp, for bearing with me through this journey and putting up with my many varied emotional breakdowns when early versions of the manuscript amassed rejections and I went into crisis mode. You are the very definition of grace under pressure, and I know I brought the pressure with this one. Thank you for staying the course and always believing in me.

Thank you to Monique Patterson. I will never not get a little thrill of *holy fucking shit* when I see an email from you in my inbox. You are every bit the powerhouse editing force of your reputation, and more than that, you are kind and encouraging, and each interaction with you leaves me feeling over-the-moon grateful that I'm in your hands. Seriously, *holy fucking shit,* how did I get so lucky?

To Mal Frazier, who I am not yet convinced isn't actually Brennan Lee Mulligan (who else knows so many fantastically random and specific facts?). Your enthusiasm for *Kissmas* is invigorating and so, so appreciated.

Taryn Fagerness, for bringing *Kissmas* to the world like my own personal Santa Claus.

Lilith Saur, for the stunning art that graces this cover.

Caro Perny, for naming this book and championing it from the very beginning.

To all of the behind-the-scenes darlings who took this rom-com-shaped piece of my soul and brought it into being: Lani Meyer, Megan Kiddoo, Greg Collins, Jim Kapp, Melissa Frain, Katy Miller, Jordan Hanley, Caroline Perny, and Lesley Worrell.

Alison Dasho, whose excitement was both the first domino and a life raft. I will forever be in your debt.

Kristen Lippert-Martin, Lisa Maxwell, and Jaye Robin Brown—you were there for my earliest versions of this book and weren't surprised for a second when I told you it was getting published. Hashtag Vegas bitches.

Kristen Simmons (I am rich in glorious Kristens) and Beth Revis, two wondrous creatures I have had the pleasure of cowriting serious, heavy fantasy books with, both of whom put up with me juggling said books while figuring out this silly rom-com side too. I love the pieces out of you both.

Erin Bowman, agency sister (still celebrating!!) and all-around fantastic human.

Cait Jacobs, who read a very *very* early version of this book and gushed over it. I am so glad BookTok brought us together. My life is better knowing you.

To my family, who are always *so excited* for me, even though I doubt most of them will be comfortable reading a book in which I wrote, ahem, scenes that decidedly do *not* fade to black: Doug, Mary Jo, Melinda, and yes Alonna too (but Alonna, as your aunt, I must beg of you to never *ever* read my adult rom-coms, for both our psyches); Brenda and Barb; Lisa; Debbie; Dan and Annette; and last but not least in the family list, Kelson and Oliver, even though Oliver definitely will *not* read this book either, but he was so pumped that I was writing a Christmas and Halloween book, and there is nothing better than looking cool in your seven-year-old's eyes.

I haven't gotten this heart-squishy in an acknowledgments section since . . . before. Before we started measuring time in *before*. So I know I forgot people and I know it will gut me as names pop up after the fact, but I am so exceedingly grateful for each and every person who helped me get this book out in the world.

I meant what I said at the beginning:

This book is for you.

I hope it brought you even a fraction of the joy it brought me.

About the Author

SARA RAASCH grew up among the cornfields of Ohio and currently lives in the historical corridor of southeastern Virginia. She is the *New York Times* bestselling author of eight books for young adults. In her debut adult novel, Raasch offers readers all the joy, irreverent wit, and crackling sexiness of your favorite sweet-as-a-candy-cane holiday romp.